"In the chaos of postwar Europe, where names and lives are up for grabs, justice isn't often achieved. Moran knows very well all the moral—and dramatic—advantages he is putting aside. He has written love stories before, edgy ones, about loves that can't be spoken or won't work. This time, the best he can say of Anja and Walter is that they might really be 'a pair, not fit for anybody but each other. Maybe it would work.' In this new book, truth leads a quite different way."   —*The New York Times*

"Nuanced and stark."   —*Milwaukee Journal Sentinel*

"For surprises and complexity of character, we can turn to Thomas Moran's *Anja the Liar*. Moran, a onetime journalist whose fifth novel this is, seems to be saying that the war's poison, its evil, has infected both women and will never go away. We read on, wondering which of them will triumph. This is a dark, fascinating study of souls in torment."   —*The Washington Post*

"Moran expertly delves into the psyches of his fragile characters, leaving a haunting portrait of the aftermath of war."   —*Booklist*

"Moran has an impressive ability to create characters who are at once morally troubling and sympathetic. Anja, in particular, is a nuanced figure, pleading weakness but also acknowledging the pleasing sense of power her wartime actions gave her. . . . His examination of the fine distinctions between evil, weakness, and desperation is stimulating and unflinching."   —*Publishers Weekly*

"Moran views desperate lives at close range in this well-paced novel, a cautionary tale about how we are inextricably linked to our pasts. [An] affecting denouement . . . [a] searing tale."   —*Library Journal*

"Nicely nuanced, with a fine sense of place and time; good wartime fiction."   —*Kirkus Reviews*

continued...

WATER, CARRY ME

"Endearing and believable."   —*Rocky Mountain News*

"Superbly written and extraordinarily touching, Moran's novel brings an Irish world of pain and beauty to life."
—*Tampa Tribune-Times*

"One of the most remarkable characters to grace fiction's pages ... The shocking conclusion of *Water, Carry Me* will break the hardest of hearts. Una Moss's voice and story is haunting."
—*The Washington Post Book World*

"The best thing about Moran's third novel is how he so deftly manages to balance the realms of the personal and the political. The perfectly rendered frivolity of university life, with its petty feuds and callow romances, is bolstered by a subtly drawn undercurrent of sectarian violence. Irish life can often be measured by its contradictions—between beauty and brutishness, conviviality and cruelty—and Moran is wise enough to let these paradoxes resonate against one another."   —*The New York Times Book Review*

"Compelling ... This is a well-crafted, haunting tale filled with very human characters caught in a web much bigger than themselves. Highly recommended."   —*Library Journal* (starred review)

"Engrossing."   —*Booklist* (starred review)

"Vividly dramatic ... The very real strengths here are Moran's forceful characterizations of the sentient, credibly intelligent Una and the intriguing, soft-spoken Aidan."   —*Kirkus Reviews*

"With its raven-haired heroine, steely paramilitaries, and passion, *Water, Carry Me* sounds like something Edna O'Brien or Gerald Seymour might have written, and in many ways it is. ... Thomas Moran is a poetic writer."   —*New York Daily News*

THE WORLD I MADE FOR HER

"A reading experience as fresh and basic as lying down feverish on cool, clean linen with loving hands to tuck you in."   —*Time*

"Impressive . . . Thomas Moran is a connoisseur of confined spaces. [He] can immerse you utterly in whatever moment he chooses to describe. He weaves unsettling moods with playful artifice. . . . Compelling on its own terms."   —*The New York Times Book Review*

"Moran returns with a novel that is almost perfect. . . . This story rises above its grimness into a quite piercing and extraordinary elegy. For many, this will be the best book of the year."
    —*Booklist* (starred review)

"Eerily affecting . . . Takes readers inside the preternaturally fertile mind of a wrecked and nearly noncommunicative body . . . He relates the nightmarish predicament of his empathetic characters in hypnotic prose that remains compelling right up until the final scene. . . . Moran's poetic, cruel yet forgiving love story will not easily be forgotten."   —*Publishers Weekly*

"Compelling . . . a haunting, unhackneyed exploration of loneliness and its antidotes . . . Deeply affecting."   —*Kirkus Reviews*

"A heartrending love story . . . crisp, razor-sharp sentences . . . The world Moran creates is as tender as the imagined reality of his protagonist—always moving, never maudlin."   —*The Washington Post*

continued...

THE MAN IN THE BOX

ALSO BY THOMAS MORAN

The Man in the Box
The World I Made for Her
Water, Carry Me
What Harry Saw

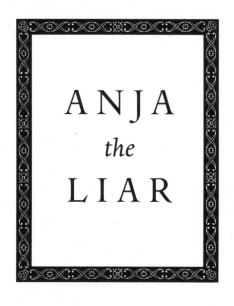

ANJA
the
LIAR

THOMAS MORAN

RIVERHEAD BOOKS

New York

Riverhead Books
Published by The Berkley Publishing Group
A division of Penguin Group (USA) Inc.
375 Hudson Street
New York, New York 10014

The author gratefully acknowledges permission to quote from
The Selected Poetry of Rainer Maria Rilke, edited and translated
by Stephen Mitchell. Copyright © 1982 by Stephen Mitchell.
Reprinted by permission of Random House, Inc.

First Riverhead hardcover edition: September 2003
First Riverhead trade paperback edition: November 2004
Riverhead trade paperback ISBN: 1-59448-037-0

The Library of Congress has catalogued the Riverhead hardcover edition as follows:

Moran, Thomas.
Anja the liar / Thomas Moran.
p. cm.
ISBN 1-57322-260-7
1. World War, 1939–1945—Italy, Northern—Fiction.
2. World War, 1939–1945—Refugees—Fiction.
3. Italy, Northern—Fiction. 4. Married people—Fiction.
5. Refugees—Fiction. I. Title.
PS3563.O7714A85 2003 2003043164
813'.54—dc21

Printed in the United States of America

10 9 8 7 6 5 4 3 2 1

for Flavia, and her father

We were born to remember. Not to forget
but to remember—that's what we're here for.

HEINRICH BÖLL

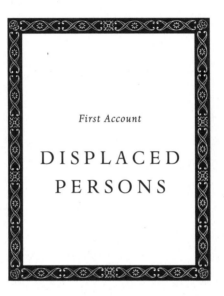

First Account

DISPLACED PERSONS

I

The girl was pale as a midwinter's moon gliding over the icy Tatra Mountains. Her hair would be called blond, but each strand was translucent as cornsilk. At night, on the blacked-out streets of crumbling cities under siege, her face must have seemed luminous.

But against the brilliant flare of this summer sun, she was nearly invisible: an empty dress, walking.

That's how she appeared to the engineer Walter Fass when he first squinted through the wire of the Displaced Persons camp near Sauerlach, a sullen gray town marring the rich ripening fields of oats and rye, the orderly orchards of southern Bavaria.

The walking dress kept well clear of the wire, which edged a more modern scar on the land, from a cut perhaps two hundred meters long, a hundred wide, into pasture and a pine plantation. Some little distance down those barbed steel strands, though, Fass observed dozens of women—lips pouty with black-market rouge, hair waved—pressing close as the wire allowed to a crowd of edgy, shuffling men in ill-fitting suits or mismatched pieces of one uniform or another. Like a Partisan formation, Fass thought.

A stream of broken German mixed with American slang, a bit of Russian, random eddies of Czech, Hungarian and Serbo-Croatian flowed rapidly between them. He listened a bit to the currents of talk: a new European pidgin, and a marriage market conducted in it.

Walter Fass understood at once. Their homes destroyed or out of reach, those they'd loved no more than shades among the ruins now, the defeated soldiers outside the wire were seeking any human connection they might make. For the women in the camp, a harder loss: their very identities. Lacking passports, birth certificates, even simple residence cards, they were nameless, stateless, shunned and unwelcome anywhere—unless they were chosen by a man with papers. A man who possessed the right to be only because his photo, his name, his nationality appeared on a properly stamped and signed official document.

So this marriage market, daily at the wire: the matchmakers hope gone absent without leave, and the brutal surprise of surviving the war only to find that the life you'd led had not.

Turning from that misery, Fass's sun-glazed eyes were drawn again to the walking dress: a flowing, flowered summer number that, he judged, would be inadequate when autumn came, in a matter of weeks. The girl would shiver, perhaps sicken. When she passed out of the bleaching light into the shadow of dun, wood-planked barracks, he was able to make out her face. A milk-white, a glacial-white, a Pomorske Cavalry–white Pole, he guessed. A girl who had journeyed a thousand kilometers only to pace this packed, almost polished ochre earth where not even the most persistent weed could sprout, where any summer shower lay for days in sheets that soaked her thinly soled shoes.

The pale one ignored the cheerless flirting of abject women with worn, woeful men. She'd not curled her hair. She'd not colored her lips. She'd not labored with needle and thread to make her poor frock more alluring. She simply paced between sun and shadow, past all caring. Who knew what she was to herself now, or who she had once been?

A common speculation, in late summer 1945. Everywhere Fass had gone, people were on the move. Or trapped in camps like this, waiting. Waiting without knowing what they were waiting for, what might come to them. It was a time of sharp suspicion. Everyone had secrets to keep from all souls—even their own. Some were more adept than others; they slept the nights through without suddenly waking rigid from dreams of death, or shivering from some cold breath of the past that had brushed them. The engineer Fass did not dream. He considered himself one of the lucky ones. Perhaps the pale girl was not.

"Hallo, little one! Come talk a while," Fass found himself calling to her in Polish as she passed not ten meters from him.

The empty dress kept moving. The girl did not look toward him or give the slightest sign she had heard his voice.

"A friendly word, little one," Fass called. "Surely you can spare that?"

The girl paced on, deaf.

"Where are you from?" Fass called, still in Polish. "Warszawa, maybe? No? Then Krakow?"

"What are you saying?" the empty dress spun and shouted at Fass in perfect German. The crowd at the wire ignored the outburst.

"I am only asking to introduce myself, and learn your name," the engineer said.

The pale one stormed straight at him with a fierceness that caused Fass to take half a step back, despite the wire between them. "I am German, you Polack idiot," she snarled. "Stop shouting at me in that filthy language."

"Surely I'm not mistaken," Fass said, stubbornly sticking to Polish when she stood furious before him, fists on her hips.

"Surely you're not actually Polish, either," she sneered. Her German, Fass noted, had the accent of Brandenburg.

"Is it that obvious? I was brought up in Stettin. I've been speaking this since I was a child."

"Gutter Polish, that's all. And even in that you're no good," she said in German.

"I am Fass, Walter. May I know your name?" the engineer asked, switching at last to the language of his birth.

"You may know nothing except that I want you to go away from here at once. Never speak to me in Polish. Do not speak to me at all."

"Czego pani sobie życzy?" Fass smiled, a friendly mischief he hoped would calm her.

"Swine! Stop whatever game you're playing and leave me alone."

"Czy pani skończył?" Fass smiled again.

"No, I have not finished. You are either a fool, or with the police. Now go away. *Odpieprz się!"*

"I'm certainly not with the police," he protested.

"Zeigen Sie mir Ihre Papiere." She was mocking him now with the precise toneless arrogance heard too often the past decade, the casual but absolute certainty of being obeyed that SD and SS men once possessed.

The engineer fumbled in the breast pocket of his suit, retrieved his identity card along with his discharge from the prisoner-of-war camp, and held them up to the wire for her. It was forbidden to pass anything through, but the American MPs seemed not to care if you did; to let your papers out of your grasp for even a moment, though, was reckless, foolish. Fass released his anyway to the girl's hostile hands. But he did not produce his most precious possession, sewn securely within the lining of his coat: a rectangle of weighty official stationery exactly as old as himself, folded and unfolded so often it was cracking a bit at the creases despite the quality of the paper.

The pale girl was blessed with eyes that were not windows to anything at all. They were as flat, blank and unfathomable as any Fass had ever seen. She studied the raggedly typed information as if she were memorizing it, held the cards up to examine the stamps front and back against the sunlight, looked from his photo to his face. She thrust the cards back through the wire.

Then she spat on the beaten ground.

"Anyone could have papers like these. Stamps are easily forged," she said. "Or used by the authorities deliberately to make a man seem what he is not. If you're not police, or a Russian agent, why were you screaming at me as if I were Polish? Why are you trying to jeopardize me?" Her fists were clenched, the muscles of her bare forearms taut.

"Jeopardize you?" Fass asked, momentarily bewildered. "How? There's no danger here. You're a refugee, in an American camp. What trouble could there be?"

"You have suffered a head wound. It has left you a little deranged, *nicht wahr?*" the girl stated quietly, her impenetrable eyes dominating his. The engineer's gaze slid swiftly away. He knew his error now.

The new rules: You never asked anyone, even obliquely, who they were, where they were from, where they had been, what they had done in wartime. You never enquired about the source of anyone's fears. You waited to be told, and you did not question what you heard. Those who became too curious were sometimes found in a ditch with their throats slit or a black-crusted bullet hole behind one of their ears. Such eliminations were frequent, easily arranged, rarely investigated.

But Fass was not afraid, only deeply embarrassed. Sometimes, weary beyond bearing, he had contemplated deliberately bringing down such a fate on himself. But he knew this girl before him could never be the instrument he'd require. A black marketeer, or a former SS camp guard trying to pass as a DP—they would do the job if he provoked them.

"Please excuse me for bothering you," he said in formal German to the girl, bowing slightly, ashamed to meet her eyes. Then he turned from the wire and walked away down a newly broadened road edged with precisely spaced pines, toward the base that an American Army armored unit had established about a kilometer from the DP camp. Near it, in a hollow beneath a careless stack of creosoted railway ties that was his home, he draped his ratty blanket over his shoulders and willed himself to forget all wounds and scars, all his mistakes and missteps. He dismissed the empty dress. He tried instead to recall how good it had felt, once, to regard each day with confidence that you deserved to live it, that you'd done no act so brutal or hideous that it made your presence on this earth an insult to human decency and natural law.

Fass felt he could never again hold that certainty about himself.

He had the sensation then that doors in his mind were slamming shut one after another, something he always felt when he attempted to imagine a world made normal again. But his heart would not shut away the remembrance of a Chetnik fighter he'd known in Yugoslavia, a young Serb physically striking in the way a falcon is: small-headed, large-eyed, sleek, with cropped auburn hair almost iridescent, like feathers. Anyone would admire that beauty, though most would fear the predatory intensity of those eyes.

Dead now, in an unmarked grave, most likely.

Yet his Serb guerrilla's face was the clearest image Walter Fass possessed, the only one that never blurred, never wavered, never left him.

He was not glad to have it so.

⊞   ⊞   ⊞

The next few afternoons Fass was at the wire, but the pale girl was not. He could not ask about her; he did not even know her name. And if he had? No one answered questions from strangers.

He sighed, lit the stub of a cigarette and leaned against one of the pocked concrete pillars that marked the camp's perimeter. A slight mistake: piercing nerve pain raced down to the fingertips of his left hand—or where that hand and those fingers should have been. He bore it, absorbed it. He watched the women at the wire, amused himself trying to decipher the odd and urgent pitches of the market.

Twice now he had seen a man allowed into the camp with an MP by his side, enter the small white building that housed the commander's office, and shortly emerge with a woman, her arm linked through his, a battered suitcase or worn rucksack in hand. Together they had walked away from this place. Toward a dubious destination, in Fass's view. A husband and wife who'd never even kissed, who likely had no shared language but the ragged pidgin? But perhaps in partnership they felt able to salvage any pieces of their past they might discover, or attempt the daunting task of building a life from nothing at all.

Walter Fass, ex–Wehrmacht captain and combat veteran, considered these couples showed more courage than he had left. Courage was not a thing that renewed itself like lost blood. He believed you are born with a certain amount, and you use it frugally or rashly. Or let it be stolen from you. Not that it mattered so much. For unless you were killed in action or suddenly cut down by accident or disease, you were almost certain to outlast your allotment, and cower toward your end.

He eased himself away from the pillar and idly examined the wire. Left over, perhaps, from Dachau. Shipped direct, possibly, from a factory in Gary, Indiana, before the war. No need to know. No need to speak of its spiky coils, its deadly electrified lines taut between posts and poles and pillars, Fass thought. For he was one of those who had made it as much a part of Europe's landscape as copses of beech and chestnut, fields of sugar beets and potatoes; as familiar as the gleaming steel tram tracks once set in weather-worn cobblestones, or the soaring swarms of pigeons only now returning to the wrecked ancient squares of every capital, every city, nearly every town.

No need, the engineer was sure, to say "Beware the wire" to anyone, ever again.

Alles klar, Fass. Except, he realized, for whatever impulse drew him day after day to the wire, full of hope for a glimpse of the pale girl so anxious to pass as German, the most hated nationality in Europe. An angry girl, who would not be pleased to see him, who would probably refuse to acknowledge his existence.

And, he thought as the doors slammed shut one after another in his mind, could it really matter if she did?

II

The pale one, who called herself Anja, was huddled in her barracks. Like a tender schoolgirl, she decided with bitter amusement, shocked to her innocent core by a man who suddenly swung his overcoat open and exposed himself on the street.

Had it been a thing so preposterous, she'd have mocked and ridiculed the pervert. For she was so far from any sort of innocence. Nearly twenty-four, she had survived six years of a bad, dark time—cruelties of every sort, coldly calculated betrayals, vicious vengeance both inflicted and endured. She had been toughened like any combat soldier. Nothing, she'd been certain, could intimidate or alarm her.

Yet she felt stripped and violated now, near terror, because of a stranger's confident assumption that she was Polish.

Cleverly evasive as a rat, she had stolen through the treacherous wreckage of Germany to escape her origins, her actions, her self. She had shed every proof of her identity along the way, so that no one would ever again recognize her as a Pole. For Poland was an execution ground for her.

Anja had believed herself safe at last when she entered this DP camp. Deloused, showered, and shown her very own cot, with a clean pillow, clean sheets and a thick olive-drab wool blanket, she'd begun to relax at once. Rough comforts, but the ultimate luxury of being finally out of harm's reach. Then this man appeared from nowhere, called to her in Polish. God damn him. Now her provisional peace lay in shards, as if it had been no more than a delicate crystal glass, swept off a table by someone's careless gesture.

Repeat your heretical catechism against guilt, your souless Hail Marys of false self-redemption, she told herself. Blame wartime for the sins that have brought you to this. Claim you were one of the victims, a girl so naive she had not even recognized her own naiveté. A girl without politics or ideology, a girl whose only structure had come from family and the Church. But even strong, loving parents and the strict Catholic schema provided no defense at all for what was to come down on Poland and the Poles. And on one vulnerable girl.

Plead that at seventeen, when the dark time began in Krakow, you had no shelter from the madness exploding all around, no matériel to build a mental bunker in which to hide. That single summer term studying philosophy before the Germans shut the University? That barest notion of Socrates, Plato, Aristotle? Worthless. You needed a strong foundation from Kierkegaard, pillars and buttresses from Kant, reinforcing steel from Wittgenstein and, especially, camouflage from Heidegger.

But you had only the ways of deception all children learn as they grow, and use until they realize the futile transparency of fantasy. So what more, Anja thought, could anyone expect of her? What more than this?

First Krakow principle: If you lie about anything—from an emotion you are ashamed you felt, to an enormous crime—with confidence and complete consistency, and repeat it over and over and over again, the lie will miraculously become the truth to you and everyone you tell it to.

Second Krakow principle: If you deny anything—no matter how despicable or revolting—with complete confidence and consistency over and over and over again, then eventually the awful thing never, ever happened.

Third Krakow principle: If you banish from consciousness and memory a ghastly act you cannot manage to deny even to yourself, in the end you never existed in that time and place. You simply were not present, and therefore could not possibly have committed the act. It had to have been someone else. Someone who looked a little like you, perhaps. Some doppelgänger.

But never you. Not you.

That childish invention had, amazingly, been good enough for the bad time. But this was so, she knew, only because she had become entirely the creature of a brilliant German master. And because of the fixed idea of her poor parents, of all those who had known her, of all her comrades in the Resistance that Anja—our little Anja, good sweet brave Anja—was utterly incapable of evil.

Yet, Anja shivered, curling into a ball on her cot, she had done the unthinkable. She had betrayed everyone who trusted and cared for her.

So many memories to banish now. She made extreme demands on her third principle. But time and distance from Krakow did not come to her aid. Now, in her fear, she saw again her ink-stained hands, the blurry purple mimeographs of patriotic, anti-German ranting she and some friends had run off and distributed for a few weeks in late autumn, 1939. How proud she'd been of those pathetic leaflets, how shocked and horrified when two SD men had snatched her off the street early one morning, roughly bundled her into a black car and taken her away.

She remembered well, against her will, the charming SD man

Richter balancing a pencil on the tips of his delicate, almost feminine fingers, heard his soft persuasions; there were no threats, no
harsh interrogation. Only a chat in his office, a room that held no
hint of his sinister profession.

A very young man, Richter. Hardly older than a student himself. He had beautiful brown hair and wore wire-rimmed glasses
in the style so many University tutors favored. He had a winning
smile, knew it and used it. There was nothing cold, no hint of ruthless cruelty, in his eyes or his manner.

Despite her anxiety, she'd admired the fashionable Berlin cut
of his charcoal-gray suit, the touch of whimsy in the violet silk
handkerchief that peeked out of his breast pocket. He held her
chair for her, seated her before his desk. Then he sat down facing
her, close to her. He offered her a cigarette, leaned forward with a
gold lighter in his manicured hand when she put it between her
lips. She'd never smoked before. "Ah, you're not used to
Gauloises," he said, a little flicker of amusement on his face, when
she coughed. "Quite strong, these French brands."

He remained leaning toward her, his elbows on his knees, his
long fingers pressed together, as if in prayer. His silver cufflinks
were set with mother-of-pearl.

"Your leaflets, I must tell you, are exceptionally good, for a
start," he said. His tone was exactly that of a young man having
coffee in a café with a girl he'd some hope of sleeping with. Anja
had heard this tone, a few times at least, in prewar days, from Polish boys. "You really should keep it up, keep refining them."

She had the humiliating wish then that she had put on a nicer
skirt and her good shoes, had taken more care with her hair before
leaving her parents' flat that morning.

"So," Richter said easily. "You'd very much like to keep up with
your pamphleteering, I imagine? Excellent. No problem. I could
even provide a bit of help, if you'll allow me. Paper, for instance.

There are bound to be difficulties obtaining mimeograph paper very shortly."

She knew at some level she was being slowly entwined in the coils of the beast. But it did not feel at all like that. No, it seemed reassuring, as if she was coming under a kind man's protection, a man who would keep her safe. He was so correct, so cordial. So attractive.

"I know what you're thinking. And you are right." Richter smiled intimately. "We would ask favors from time to time. As friends do. Nothing excessive. Merely a word or two. Small things you might hear about. Anti-German actions, plans for any sort of violence, for example. We'd very much like to avoid violence, we're at peace now, after all. A name perhaps, a place and a time. Not so very much to ask, when you think of it, is it?"

It seemed very little to her, in exchange for protection.

"And naturally," Richter went on, "everything would be handled very, very carefully. Absolute discretion. We'd never allow you to be compromised in any way. I would personally see to that."

"And if I say no?" Anja asked. God, she was actually flirting. He knew it at once.

"Please, please." Richter smiled, holding up his hands, palms facing her. "Let's not even consider anything like that. We're only just getting to know each other, Anja. We're new acquaintances. We needn't rush.

"Naturally, you've heard things, slanderous things for the most part I think. Unfortunate, the wild rumors people will spread. But a certain amount of bitterness is understandable, I suppose." Richter shook his head almost sadly. "I ask only that you keep an open mind. You'll think about what I've said? You'll consider it, at least? We're in accord, yes?"

She said nothing. Possibly she bobbed her head.

Richter beamed then.

"I'm very, very pleased, Anja. And I'm very happy we've met, had the chance to talk. I hope you'll regard me as a friend." He laughed, not at her, but pleasantly, almost shyly. "I'm already looking forward to seeing you again. I admit it! Though I know I shouldn't."

Richter rose, showed her to the door. "Write well for your leaflets, Anja. But please, do be a little more—shall we say circumspect?—about the distribution. Forgive my bluntness, but you've been very clumsy. Let me suggest, for instance, slipping batches into the bundles of newspapers when they're first dropped off at the kiosks in the mornings. Very casually, as you buy a paper. You must go carefully in these matters, you know. Subtlety, that's the key."

"Oh, a moment, please," he said, walking quickly back to his desk and returning with four packs of Gauloises. "I fear quite a few of life's little niceties will soon be hard to find in Krakow. We can thank the French and the English. It's really hard to imagine why they've declared war on us, isn't it? Anyway, a small token, Anja. We'll speak again soon, I hope."

Anja remembered walking out of the SD headquarters, which had been the House of Culture, under a lowering sky pregnant with rain. Far off, perhaps from the Jewish quarter of the city, there was the crackling of sporadic rifle fire.

She remembered the narrow, long-nosed face of Andrzej, the Resistance man Richter urged her to place herself in the way of some weeks later. She saw Andrzej's nod as she described her little group's leaflets, which of course he'd been fully informed about. Richter very delicately suggested after a while that she get closer to Andrzej, who was being given a long leash by the SD so that he might build up a large network that could be rolled up all at once, when the time came. She saw herself, embarrassed and fearful, removing her clothes in a dim attic, Andrzej watching from the mattress on the bare floorboards, the mattress on which he deflowered her.

So many other rooms, so many other men, SS Obersturmbahn-
führers and commanders of Polish Home Army units alike, German General Government functionaries and Polish bureaucrats—
anyone Richter believed might provide, if she was clever with them,
even the thinnest strand he could add to his ever spreading, ever
more intricate skein of secret information.

How tenaciously she had clung to her three principles, how
brilliantly she had learned or invented other Krakow rules. She
heard very clearly the lies she told Andrzej and her Resistance cell,
the truths of names and plans and places and times she had relayed
to Richter.

Anja would kill herself before she'd ever speak to anyone of
this.

But she wanted to scream to the world of the Polish priest, her
confessor. At a certain moment, feeling the enormity of her evil,
she had been prepared to betray Richter, no matter the consequences. She wept and tore at her hair as she told the priest everything. And he absolved her! He told her blood was not on her
hands, that God would judge the Germans.

"Damn your black soul to hell," she shrieked at the priest,
breaking the door of the confessional. "I piss on you, your God and
your unholy Church."

She ripped off the crucifix she'd worn since her First Commu-
nion, leaving a weal that took days to fade. She spit into the fountain of holy water.

She had been eighteen.

❊   ❊   ❊

And she was not yet twenty-three when the Red Army began
chewing up the Wehrmacht on Polish soil, crossing the Vistula, overrunning the ruins of Warsaw, driving deep into the heart

of the country. Richter packed his operation in, eliminating those in the SD prison. The SS was liquidating the Jewish slave-labor camp just outside the city, SS men were shooting Poles almost at random, as a sort of coda to the nocturne of terror they had played so long. So she bolted, never even saying goodbye to her parents, who had fretted and worried themselves sick for years over the risks their little Resistance fighter had been running.

She went west, of course. She hunched her shoulders against insistent freezing rains, slogged through mud which sucked at her shoes. She dodged and hid from feral packs of deserters, she gratefully jumped aboard Wehrmacht half-tracks and trucks packed with bone-tired troops whenever a vehicle slowed and one of the men beckoned her. Body jammed tightly between soldiers, breathing the stomach-turning miasma of men long unwashed, she ignored the halfhearted groping of a few dirty hands, the occasional coarse comment. The soldiers—so young, so quick with smiles and clever flirtatious words in the early years—were mostly silent, listless and depressed. Their eyes seemed blind to their immediate surroundings, but stared dolefully to the east, always to the east.

So little food anywhere. The best she got were small slices of hard sausage, often moldy, and chunks of stale rough bread the soldiers would pool for her from their own meager rations. Bad food or none at all, dirty water, lice; Anja frequently felt faint, or sick to her stomach, or near delirium with fever. She went in terror of typhus. She coughed up green phlegm so viscous she could scarely clear her mouth of it no matter how powerfully she spat. She did not sleep in a bed, or wash more than her face and hands, or change her underwear for the month or more it took to make her way.

But not once did anyone speak to her in anything but German. Until this man Fass at the wire.

Now Anja the Liar felt her defenses cracking along a fault line she had never imagined: What if one day, in a place so far from

Krakow that she finally felt able to ease her vigilance, she encountered someone who simply would not believe her?

Now, in the barracks, she felt revenge looming. She slunk to the
mess hall at dawn for breakfast, but skipped lunch and the evening
meal, for fear Fass would be among the men lingering at the wire.
She slept restlessly, or not at all. She tried frantically to reason her
apprehension away. This Fass, if that was his real name, could not
possibly know who she was, what she had done. He could not even
be certain she was a Pole. Surely no one was trying to trace her or
track her down. Surely everyone in Krakow would believe she'd
been executed by the SS, not given an SD safe-conduct pass—a
parting gift from Richter—that she carefully burned to wisps of
ash along with every other document she possessed just before
slipping into the British lines. Discovery was out of the question,
her dread absurdly irrational.

It became unendurable anyway.

III

So on the fourth day—or perhaps the fifth or sixth—Anja went to face the man who had spoken to her in Polish. Walter Fass saw her emerge into the bright sun between the barracks, sturdy legs and then a fragile face gradually materializing through the glare. When she was a meter from him, he heard a contemptuous "Why? Why are you here?"

"No place else to go just now. I didn't make it home. I tried. I couldn't get through. But I don't mean to be like them," the engineer Fass said, inclining his head toward the crowd some distance to his right.

"But you are. Exactly," the pale girl said. "Surviving isn't enough for you, apparently. It should be, but it isn't. You're after something more. You want someone, for some reason. Just like all of them."

"Do I? Would it be so wrong, if it were true?"

"Who knows? But why in God's name pick on me? I wasn't at the wire, offering myself up. That must have told you something."

"I never talked at the wire either," Walter said. "So I thought we might be a little alike."

"Such presumptions. Such egoism. Probably you're so slow-witted you haven't even asked yourself the prime question, the most difficult one."

"Which is?"

"Do you really believe, in your heart, that you deserve to go on living, after what you've done?"

Fass felt he'd been slapped, though the pale girl had not so much as raised her voice. "You have no idea what I've done," he said, switching on some instinct into Polish. "So I will tell you."

"This is no church and I'm not your confessor," Anja shot back in German. "I want you to vanish. Go off and die of remorse or loneliness or whatever afflicts you someplace else. Don't you dare burden me with it."

"I've done nothing I'm ashamed of. I was a conscripted soldier. There are millions like me, on all sides."

"But your side? Your goddamned side!"

"It was your side, too. Unless you are a little Pole," Fass said softly. Anja stiffened. "And would it have stopped the war if I'd refused to serve? If I'd gone to a camp, or been executed? Would that have saved one life?"

"More than one, no doubt. Only you know exactly how many," Anja countered, also in Polish now.

"Ask me anything you like," the engineer replied too quickly, his expression suddenly sickly, like a man who'd been kicked in the groin. Anja saw that her blind blow had hit him hard. Hard enough, she hoped, to jar her mistake out of his head.

"Question me as if you were an interrogator. Go on, do it," Fass said. "Or, if you can, as if you were getting to know someone who might become a friend. Either way, I'll answer anything you ask."

"You'd only lie," Anja said. "Everyone does. Who cares, anyway? What's it to me who you are or what you've done? There are no friends anymore. There are only two classes of people now:

those you must avoid, and those who might be useful. Which are you?"

And immediately the words left her mouth, much of her great fear of Walter Fass vanished.

❖   ❖   ❖

As she lay under her blanket that night, about to drift into what she felt was going to be the first peaceful sleep she'd had since that Fass appeared, Anja regretted that she hadn't faced him down the day after he called to her, instead of hiding and trembling like a rabbit. She knew better than to behave that way. It was dangerous. It made people think you had reason to hide. She was getting slack. She mustn't let anything like that happen again. She must be as she'd always been, since Krakow time. She must volunteer nothing. She must obey all the wartime rules, even in this new dispensation of peace. She must be Anja the Liar, always.

After six years, the lying was her natural way. She was so good at it, she thought, almost pleased with the notion.

But suddenly Anja found herself facing a blankness. What was the cost of constant deception, this eternal creation of false fronts? Lately she had begun to feel she was only a sketch, and that whoever had drawn her had put down the pencil and started to erase. Would there be anyone real left, if things kept on this way? Was there a true Anja anymore? Or was she already nothing but whatever lie she was living at the moment?

She had lost a little more of herself even here in this camp. It was laughably simple to get the Czechs and Slovaks and Southern Slavs to think of her just as she wished: a cold Prussian, snobbish and arrogant despite all misfortune. They sneered, they were pleased at her downfall, they left her alone. She was disliked by all, which was what she wanted. It was necessary.

But then a fact came to her, one so obvious Anja felt astonished she had never considered it before: She was being mourned as one of the fallen by her parents, friends and comrades in Krakow. Sweet brave Anja was, for them, among the dead. The heroic Polish dead!

So when she examined what exactly she was defending, when she recalled asking Fass if he believed he deserved to be alive, Anja wept over the utter wrongness of it. For she knew it was she who had forfeited all rights to a life.

Her weeping went unnoticed. Every night in the barracks, from one cot or another, sobs and cries arose. The women were used to this irritating noise, indifferent to the torment it signified. Night thoughts, nightmares. They meant nothing. And you had a choice: You could shrug yours off with the coming of the new day, or you could let them haunt you until they drove you mad.

❈   ❈   ❈

Anja the Liar shrugged the next morning, dismissing her anguish as if it had been nothing more than a nasty dream. That bastard Fass was still upsetting her a bit, that's all. Well, she would settle him—with an act that would leave him in her debt. If his story was true.

She'd use one of the two other women in the barracks who was as isolated as herself, an aged North German, barely coherent. The woman seldom rose from her cot, sitting there compulsively sweeping her bony, blue-veined hands through her stringy white hair, rocking her body back and forth like a disturbed child. Anja had heard the others muttering in their gross pidgin for weeks: the crone's crazy, she's broken, she'll never make it out of here.

Anja had also heard, just once, the old woman lament her home.

So the day after Fass had been at least partly neutralized, Anja knelt near the head of the old woman's cot, as if concerned. She had no compassion in her. But she did possess an inquisitiveness she deployed purposefully from time to time, if the risk seemed reasonable. For she was convinced—another Krakow lesson—that the more you knew, the more you'd have to tell if you were pressured. And beyond being good insurance, information had a greater value: It was hard currency in any Zone.

"What's troubling you? Is there anything I can do?" she asked in her kindest tone.

"Stupid child," the old one wailed. "How can't you see? All gone. Everything's gone."

"But you're alive at least," Anja said.

"In a dead world. I don't want to be," the woman said.

"What's happened to you?"

"Do you know the blue house on Friedrichstrasse? It was the house of my great-grandfather, my grandfather, my father. Helena and I were born in it, two years apart. We lived there all our lives. Never married, though she was engaged once . . . to a boy who was killed in Südwestafrika in '06. But we had nieces and nephews who loved to come to our Christmases. We'd have a fat Kashubian goose stuffed with apples. Then every year after '39, there seemed to be another empty place at the table.

"One nephew killed at Tobruk, one at Salerno, one missing at Stalingrad. Places we'd never known the names of! Where on earth are they? Why were our boys sent there?

"And the bombs on Stettin, so many nights. My niece died with her newborn daughter in her arms when the hospital was hit in '44. Houses on our street collapsed into heaps. Men worked for days to dig out the bodies but they had to give up. It began to smell awful.

"Then the Russian cannon shells started hitting. Our soldiers told us to pack one suitcase, one only. What to take but a few clothes? Everything we loved left behind in our house, all the photo albums, grandmother's Meissen tea set, the family Bible. They put us in trucks. There was gunfire. Explosions all around."

"Stettin," Anja interrupted. "Stettin, is that right?"

"Haven't you listened? Our home, just as I said."

"Yes, I just wanted to be sure I'd heard correctly."

"After that, all a blur. Trucks stuck in traffic jams, planes coming to shoot us up, a train that stopped in the middle of the night because the tracks were destroyed. We had to walk. I went to a farmhouse once to beg for some milk, a crust of bread. The farmwife—a German farmwife—slammed the door in my face! Helena couldn't go on. I didn't even know where we were. Just the side of a road, someplace. Helena was too weak to pray with me. But once she murmured, "Oh Kathrina, where shall we find a goose for Christmas?"

The woman began sobbing. Anja struggled to stop the impatient tapping of her foot. "What then?" she urged.

"I hardly know. Some soldiers in a truck, not ours, lifted us into the back. They gave us food. Helena couldn't keep anything down. They drove us here. Helena was carried straight to the infirmary. They gave me this cot.

"Every day I sat by Helena's bed for as long as they'd let me, holding her hand. Her poor hand. So cold, no strength left in it at all. And then one morning when I came, there was only an empty bed. Where is my sister? I asked everyone. They didn't understand German. Finally a man I think was a doctor said, '*Kaputt.* Sorry.' I thought, what can he mean? *Kaputt*, sorry? He looked ashamed. What is this 'sorry' they say, these *Ausländer*?" the woman was weeping again. "I don't even know where they buried her, my Helena. Together for sixty-three years."

"In Stettin, yes?"

"Stettin is gone. She can't be in Stettin."

"In Stettin, before, did you know a family Fass?"

"All gone. Everyone gone."

"Before the war. A family named Fass?

"There was always a war, wasn't there?" The woman ran her hands through her hair, her eyes directly on Anja's but unfocused, as if Anja did not exist.

"Fass. A Stettin family. You remember Stettin. Kashubian goose for your nieces and nephews every Christmas, in the blue house on Friedrichstrasse."

"Fass? There was a family Fass. They had a boy in the same class as my nephew Robert at the Benediktiner Gymnasium. Not a usual name in Stettin. From some other place, no doubt. But there were so many strange names, so many Polacks and Jews with bad names. You couldn't pronounce them. They all disappeared after our army took Poland. The Fasses were German, though. They stayed, I'm sure. My Robert is missing at Stalingrad. Do you know where that is?"

※　※　※

Fass missed the pale girl whose name he did not know at the wire that day. But the next afternoon he glimpsed the empty dress walking toward him, saw the small round face acquire features as she neared. She was not alone. She was guiding a frail, white-haired woman who blinked as if the light pained her.

"Frau Jaschke, this is Walter Fass. From Stettin," Anja said to the woman when they reached the wire. "Herr Fass, Frau Jaschke is also from Stettin."

The old lady squinted at Walter. "Your poor arm," she said. "You must be the classmate from the gymnasium my nephew Robert used to mention."

"Oh yes, good old Robert," Fass replied, flicking his eyes at Anja, then fixing on the old woman's watery ones.

"Missing at Stalingrad. My God. What can be happening to the poor boy? Was he hurt? Are the Russians starving him? It's so terrible not to know," she said. Her voice had the reedy quaver of age and exhaustion.

"Frau Jaschke, Robert is not suffering," Fass said gently. "He's at peace. He died without pain, instantly, in combat. I saw it. I saw him buried with honor in a German military cemetery there. Above his grave is a cross bearing his name."

Anja had to support the old woman, whose legs were giving way. "Oh God in Heaven, watch over his soul," she wept. "He was an innocent lamb."

"I regret being the one to tell you," Fass said.

"And I thank you, Herr Fass," the old lady said, regaining some composure. She seemed unaware her red-rimmed eyes were overflowing. "It is better to know. Better that he is not suffering."

"No suffering at all," Fass said.

"I wish I could say something of your family. But I fear I can't. You must brace yourself, Herr Fass. Stettin is gone. All gone. Everyone."

Walter nodded. Anja led Frau Jaschke back to the barracks, then came trotting over to the wire.

"So you knew her nephew? I'm so sorry, what she said about your home. It's exaggerated, I'm sure. She's not quite right in her mind," Anja said.

"What the hell was that all about?" Fass demanded. "You treat me like a dog one day, and the next you're so concerned to bring me news of my home?"

"I was feeling regretful for being so harsh with you. I thought, he probably only made an honest mistake in thinking I was Polish. When I learned she was from your home, I hoped she might be able to tell something. When I asked, she said she remembered a Fass family."

"The old thing had the wrong Fasses. I never knew any Robert Jaschke. Never heard of the family. I wasn't in Stalingrad even for a day."

"So you invented that noble tale about his death, his funeral with honor? It sounded so sincere."

"Damn you, why must you be so hard? Wartime's over," Fass said irritably. "You brought me an old woman in great pain. I lied. I hope the lie eased her a little."

"But I thought . . ."

"Christ! Did you consider the improbability of me being a friend of her nephew? Do you imagine Stettin is some tiny farm village where everyone knows one another? Think of the odds of me witnessing his death and burial even if I had known the man. But I do hope that woman will never doubt what she just heard. Even if it's false."

Anja slumped, staring down at the hard ochre earth.

"And you, whoever you are," Fass said softly but with force. "If you used that pathetic creature for some test of whether I am the man my papers say I am, I hope you rot here forever."

I V

Anja went to the wire every day after that, looking for Walter Fass. An old Krakow rule: Never avoid one who doubts you, who has turned against you. Meet him as often as you can, with the exact manner and tone you've always used. Behave as if it had never crossed your mind that you might be under suspicion. Lull your opponent, win him, gain an ally. Then, at the time and place of your choosing, use him any way you wish.

Anja knew she was very good at such maneuvers.

And the ex-captain Fass was always there, keeping his usual distance from the marriage market. He was no longer so easy, he had become touchy, even wary. Still, something about her drew him. When she discovered what it was, she would have him in her hand.

But manner and tone were difficult, since she had made two careless errors already: letting shock and fear trigger aggression, and then trying to counter it with the stupid Jaschke gambit. She could not simply open up in a friendly way, even with lies; her softening must come very gradually or it would not be credible. A sort of prickly reticence followed by small, shy hints and then perhaps a poignant detail or two about a golden childhood, a promising youth ruined by wartime? Did she ever have such a childhood and a youth? She could not remember. Not that it mattered. She could easily invent. But would this Fass find that in character just yet? Probably not. For Fass, she thought, was much more acute than she had first judged him to be. Too acute to be *Polizei* or a Red agent. A blunt singlemindedness they never managed to disguise was their calling card; Richter, with his apparent gentleness and suave manners, was a rarity in his profession.

What to speak of was almost as delicate a matter. Wartime itself? *Verboten.* In total fabrication, or even the true, total banality of the start: How amazingly quiet it had been—for all but those unfortunates, civilians and soldiers, directly in the paths of the Blitzkrieg bolts—except for the increasingly agitated voices on the radio news. No rolling drumfire, no satanic clank and grind of panzers, no Stukas screaming down the sky. Nobody shot, or blown to bits. Hard to know the Apocalypse had begun.

For three or four days Anja saw nothing and heard nothing, near the end not even Radio Warsaw. Then at last came only the mild grumble of trucks and the measured smack of bootheels, and she saw thick, swinging columns of smiling young men, rifles slung, helmets strapped to their belts: German infantry marching easily down the graceful ancient streets of Krakow. But never a shouted command, a rush to combat formations, a brief staccato of small-arms fire.

An ordinary tale. And her presence as a German in that place on that day easily explained. But what would she gain by telling it to Fass? Equally, was there any advantage in describing the descent of darkness: The morning she arrived at the University to find all one hundred forty-six professors missing, and was blandly informed by amiable German troops her own age that the professors had been arrested in the night and taken to lagers? Or, later, the look of hideous surprise on the face of an old man in a bread queue just shot in the temple by a passing SS man who happened to overhear him absently humming the Polish anthem?

No, she decided. Better to remain silent on such matters.

W alter Fass was also brooding over what he might say to this volatile girl, with the inexplicable synchronicity that sometimes occurs between people whose lives—whether or not one really believes in such things—seem destined to intersect. He was certain only that he wanted to be in her presence, wanted her to know him. But why? And how to manage this?

Talk of the war? Of Yugoslavia? Unthinkable to ever speak of how a prisoner chained to a huge burning log howls as he roasts alive. Or of the way the Chetniks revived the old Turk custom of impalement, slowly inserting a sharpened, greased pole three meters long into the anuses of captured Partisans, patiently pushing it up just under the skin along the spine all the way to the neck. Then laughing, yes, as they raised the pole to vertical and fixed it firmly in the ground, so that the impaled one—man or woman, boy or girl—hung in agony beyond comprehension. While he never intervened. While he stood there, a passive witness to barbarity.

The other face of war was also impossible. Fass could never find words to convince anyone of the most astonishing fact: its great distant beauty. The colossal fireworks displays when the artillery batteries launched barrages. The streaking tracer rounds from heavy machine guns, magical as a shower of falling stars on a warm summer night. Those Stukas, peeling off into their long dives with the graceful precision of a corps de ballet. Or the painterly effects of autumn light filtering through the dust and smoke of a panzer advance, the surprising quietude of a vast battlefield covered as far as one could see with sunflowers, when the fighting was going on somewhere beyond your vision. Only soldiers understood, and could not speak of it for fear of being thought monsters.

※　　※　　※

So difficult, conversation. So little that could be safely said. With every word, so much the shivery feeling of stepping out onto the first thin ice of early winter over very deep water.

Still, they met, and spoke—with no enthusiasm or real interest, only for the sound of each other's voices—of camp gossip, the doings at the American base. Sometimes they simply watched the marriage market together, offered a few mildly humorous observations on this woman or that man or a pair who seemed to be nearing a deal. Anja increasingly wondered about who Fass had been, before the war. He must once have been a handsome young man, but he appeared years older than the thirty-two on his papers. His hair, cropped close on the sides and back but long and wavy on top, was a sandy brown. His eyes were brown with tiny streaks of amber, his nose perfectly straight above a mouth that could, on occasion, move easily into a wide smile. He was making an effort to maintain standards; he somehow managed to shave more often than most of the men around the camp, and though his suit was rumpled and his shirt collar soiled, his fingernails were always trimmed and clean. All five of them.

Most amputees, at least the ones who'd been shot up early, had wooden arms with clever steel pincers that could hold a cigarette or pick up a piece of bread. Or at least wooden hands. Later in the war, the ones with missing limbs always pinned up the empty trouser leg or coat sleeve. Fass was the only one she had ever seen who did not bother. He stood there as if he was unaware that his left sleeve fluttered and flapped in any wind, like laundry on a line. Anja couldn't decide at first if he was ludicrous, or tremendously proud, or only one of the craven, seeking consolation and pity.

Once Anja had been intensely interested in handsome young men. Those feelings died in Krakow. Now she did not like to be touched, by anyone. She was shy of even accidental contact in the crowded communal showers of the barracks. When a slim and pretty Magyar girl had tried to slip into her cot one night shortly after she'd arrived at the camp, Anja had punched her in the face, badly bruising the girl's right cheek and eye. If it had been a man, she would have grabbed his balls and tried to rip them off.

No desire at all for Fass, then. No need or use for him in that way. So it surprised Anja how much she looked forward to their meetings, and how saddened she was when, day after day, they remained strained and difficult. What was the point or purpose? He was no threat, and not likely to be an asset, the way things were going. Why not give it up?

※　※　※

Then, on a day Anja had decided would be the last she'd come to Fass at the wire, she suddenly realized that he would accept questions, might even expect them from her, and that in this way some worthwhile connection might be made. She began at once, neutrally as she could. At first Fass's answers were clipped: Yes, he held a doctorate in engineering, from the Technical University of Berlin as a matter of fact; his thesis had been accepted in May of '39. The Wehrmacht had taken him in August; he'd served almost everywhere except Africa and Italy. Answers, Anja decided, that were not evasive or unrevealing in any calculated way. So she pressed on, and gradually he seemed to unwind into the easy, teasing manner with which he'd first approached her, though he did not ever again use Polish.

"Do you answer someone who dares to ask you how you actually spent these last years?" Anja risked inquiring one gray day.

"Certainly. I say I marched more kilometers than anyone could count, climbed more mountains than anyone could dream of, built a hundred bridges over a hundred rivers with foreign names I can't recall, and later blasted them to pieces. Everything I did, I undid. Every step I took I retraced."

A tentative smile appeared, to Anja's relief.

"Apparently none of this was of much interest to anyone. The interrogators at the POW camp certainly seemed to find me tedious. Once I caught one nodding off in the midst of what I thought was an exciting description of throwing a bridge strong enough to bear the weight of panzers, under heavy fire all the while, across a gorge. He was not impressed. That's probably why I was among the first to be released, and come to be standing before you, a free man."

"Free?" Anja laughed. She was through the worst of it now, the Jaschke fiasco forgotten, an opening made. There was no longer a need, as Fass had pointed out, to be so hard. With him at least. "You suffer from delusions as well as selective amnesia? Really, you must see a specialist about that head wound."

"Perhaps you are right. Just now, for instance, I've started hearing a strange voice in my head, ordering me about," he grinned. "I was only speaking figuratively. At least I'm no longer under anyone's direct control, or behind wire. I feel . . . unleashed, let's say. You have no idea what military life is like. Or, phew, what a POW barracks smells like."

"Mine reeks—cheap perfume, clouds of foul gossip," Anja said. "And so much tension. All the nationalities hate each other. On the other hand, there's a solid roof over my head when it rains—which it's about to, I think—clean clothes and bedding. And GI rations, as much as you can eat. I'm going to turn into a blimp. But I don't care. You know better than I that a full stomach sometimes seems the greatest gift from God anyone can receive. Assuming one retains any belief in a Supreme Being. Or the idea that He's in any mood or position to bestow what most call, with no irony at all, 'blessings.' "

"If there were any blessings passed out these past few years, they were only quick and easy deaths instead of slow, painful ones."

"How does He decide what kind we get? A sort of lottery, or something like a school report card on each of us? Never mind. We're not to talk about that, we're cheerful, never morbid," Anja said. "Look how cheerful I am. It's distressing when you start to wallow Teutonically."

"Wallow? Never!" The engineer smiled. "I live day to day, in the present tense exclusively. You're the one who dragged up this Supreme Being nonsense. Next you'll be discoursing on the difference between a state of war and a war in being. And if God is dead or simply went AWOL in '39 and is about to return because He feels guilty. A sort of beginners' philosophy class for a poor engineer obsessed with structural physics and trigonometry. You can't help it, can you? An ambitious philosophy student before wartime got in the way, that's what you were. I'm right, aren't I?"

"Now you know my dark secret. You're a good guesser. You even guessed Krakow, that day you behaved so badly, yelling at me in your pig's Polish," Anja said, obeying the cardinal rule of successful lying: Keep as close to what's true as you can without compromising the deception.

"But why Krakow?"

"Because there were good teachers, good as any except for

those philosophical God-heads at Tübingen and Heidelberg, which were too far from home for me."

"Home being?"

"Breslau. As many Poles there as in Stettin, before the war, and I'm good at languages, which is why I speak it properly and you have only Stettin pig-Polish."

"I don't like to be the one to say it, but speaking of swine . . ." Fass inclined his head toward the crowd of women who were hurriedly bidding goodbye to the men at the market and streaming toward the mess hall. "Feeding time."

"There's no hurry. The Amis always make too much. A lot gets thrown away. If the garbage dump wasn't behind the wire, every civilian in the area would be fighting over it."

"You know," Fass said, "don't you think it would be nice if at this point I was at last given the privilege of learning your name?"

"Anja," she said.

"That's it? No family name?"

"Anja will do for now. I was brought by a stork anyway. All Prussians are."

"Anja. Pretty," Fass said. Then he smiled. "But not German. It sounds distinctly . . ."

"Wolff," Anja said quickly.

"Christ! The SS general, Hitler's 'Little Wolff'? I was sure you were a Pole. Now I find you might be the niece or granddaughter or third cousin twice removed of a damned SS general?"

The slight anxious hitch Anja noticed in Fass's laugh diminished him a little in her eyes. She wished she wasn't that way, so unforgiving. Very deliberately she kept up the banter, so it wouldn't matter.

"Your Polish obsession's excessive, Walter. I'm a little Little Wolff, a former SS *Mädchen*," she said.

"Black uniform, shiny black boots, riding crop, blond hair pulled back in a bun?" Fass grinned.

"All of that, *natürlich*," Anja replied, straightfaced. "We were a stylish lot, very smart-looking as befitted our racial purity. And we wanted to be as attractive as possible, so we'd be selected for the breeding program, of course."

"Stop! Please stop." There was no hitch or hesitation in the engineer's laughter now.

"I only regret," Anja went on, playing with him, "that the esteemed General Wolff, hero of the Reich, is no blood relation. Wolff, unfortunately, is such a common name."

▨ ▨ ▨

But of course not hers, though Anja had claimed it and clung to it and wept over it before every Allied official she'd faced. Her papers had been stolen during her flight from the Red Army, she'd sworn. She was German-born, of German parents and grandparents and even great-great-grandparents. She had spent the war in an underheated factory in her home city of Breslau using an awl to sew the heavy canvas for stretchers. Her hands had been blue with cold, her fingers frequently infected from needle punctures; she hadn't known how to sew at the start, she had been a student before the war. If any birth records or school records had survived the siege of Breslau by the Red Army, they'd prove all, she'd pleaded.

But she had no papers of her own. None at all.

"Oh, dear," a baby Coldstream Guards lieutenant bravely trying to raise his first mustache had said—speaking German with a ludicrously English style—when she'd been detained after entering the British lines. As if she'd done something slightly shameful, and he was embarrassed for her. "Bit of a problem, what? No papers. You're sure? Not a stray ration booklet, not a pay chit with your name on it or anything like that lurking about? Even a letter addressed to you might help. You've checked all your things thoroughly, have you?"

It amused Anja to recall the scene. The way she wailed, the way the young lieutenant started turning flame-red the more graphic she got about her "rape" by a squad of Tatar submachine-gunners. Sobbing, she flung the meager contents of her fiberboard suitcase all over his desk: one sweater with moth holes, two pairs of cotton wool panties, a worn woolen skirt and one threadbare flowered cotton dress.

"Everything, they took everything from me," she cried and moaned. "They shot my mother before my eyes. Then they did that thing to me. The animals. I wish they had shot me. It would have been a mercy."

Her sobbing would have seemed to any rational observer completely uncontrollable.

"There now, there now," said the lieutenant, who was obviously and urgently moved to be rid, at any cost, of this extremely upsetting female. "I'll give you a refugee pass. We're setting up camps for refugees. You'll find food and shelter there. You'll be safe. Please don't cry so. Things will come right. We've won the war, after all."

From there Anja used her scrap of British paper to travel south, into the American area. She had no clear idea why. Only an inner urgency at the time to put as much distance between herself and Krakow as possible. The Amis, too, wanted papers, but got the weeping and the sobbing and the chit from the blushing English officer, who may have been all of nineteen. She clung to the story: Wolff. German-born. Parents, grandparents, even great-great-grandparents. The stretcher factory in Breslau. The squad of Tatar rapists. Wolff. German.

Krakow rules: Tell the lie until it becomes true.

When the Americans put her in this comfortable camp, she cried her first genuine tears of the last six years.

And the charming Richter, along with everyone else responsible for the black time, was at that moment, she prayed, burning in hell after being jubilantly butchered like a hog by Russians or Poles.

*   *   *

The last of the women from the market were disappearing into the mess hall.

"You'd better go," Fass said. "I've got to see about scrounging something for myself, too."

With a deft movement, Anja produced a can of Spam from the little hand-sewn linen sack she carried like a pocketbook, and passed it through the wire to Walter. Their fingers touched for an instant, but there was no pleasure in that for Anja.

"*Dziękuję,*" he said. "Thanks."

"*Bardzo proszę.*" Anja smiled, turning away. Her accent was perfect. Fass lingered at the wire, watched her pass through the door into the mess hall.

"Little Pole, you are no Wolff from Breslau," he whispered, then laughed quietly. "You must have been so easily trapped."

Then the engineer Walter Fass shuddered.

But no more easily, he admitted miserably, than me.

V

"And so. You will marry this Nazi?" asked the pretty Magyar—whose face Anja had badly bruised long ago—on an evening some weeks after Fass's first appearance at the wire. Her name was Elisabeth Battyany, called Sisi. An old Austrian custom, these cloying diminutives. The Empress Elisabeth, assassinated by a crazed Italian anarchist, was known as Sisi to all the Habsburg subjects even after her murder, when a bit more solemnity would have seemed proper, in Anja's opinion.

Ever since Anja had struck her, Sisi had skittered around making every conciliatory, friendly gesture she could contrive. Sisi was shunned and despised by the barracks women, and for that reason, as well as more practical ones, Anja accepted her friendship. Sisi was a little in love with her—though the girl knew it was hopeless, would never again try to act on it.

Useful, then. Usable.

Pleasant company, as well. Though that was of less value to Anja, who was content to keep to herself. She cared not at all that most of the women in the barracks were bovine, dull, selfish and bitchy, since she ignored their existence. But the Hungarian amused her.

Sisi, so her story went and her manner supported, was an indifferently educated but very clever girl from an old family that had its seat in the vast steppe of the Hungarian Puszta, a grand house in Budapest and a fine villa in the Fourth District of Vienna. Her family fortunes had declined when the Austro-Hungarian Empire splintered in 1918, and men redrawing the map of Europe in elegant Paris chambers created Yugoslavia, slicing off a third of the Battyany lands with a pen-stroke. The Fourth District villa had to be sold and other economies enforced, but Sisi was still sent from her Budapest home to the best—or most expensive and exclusive—boarding school in Vienna, run by the Ursuline Sisters. Where she absorbed little from her teachers but quite a bit from some older girls, intimate knowledge Sisi was delighted to pass on later to fresh new girls.

"Marry him? Don't be ridiculous," Anja said, shrugging under the thick woolen battle-dress jacket she'd shamelessly extorted from the baby Guards lieutenant, along with trousers and hobnailed combat boots. The nights were sometimes chilly now, and she was sitting on Sisi's cot, which the other women had crammed into a corner of exile, as far from the rest as possible. She tore a Lucky Strike, gave half to Sisi, who stuck the stub into her ebony cigarette holder and held a match up for Anja before lighting her own.

"A pity," Sisi said. "He carries himself like one of us, at least. I like the way he keeps aloof from that rabble at the market."

"I know nothing of his family. Don't care, either. But he claims he has a university doctorate. His POW papers show he was a captain in an engineer battalion. So perhaps it's true."

"How dull. And yet," Sisi seemed to be contemplating something slightly distasteful but inevitable, "there might eventually be work for engineers. There's a lot to rebuild."

"Unless the Russians want it all to stay a wasteland. They

might want that. They might simply plough under all the rubble and grow potatoes everywhere. Berlin, Dresden, Vienna. Even Budapest a huge vegetable plot! And they'd love to have people like you hoeing and pulling weeds for the rest of your life."

"With a kerchief on my head, wearing filthy woolen stockings and wooden clogs. Manure under my fingernails, horny-handed men with foul breath pawing at me. A Puszta peasant!" Sisi laughed. "The Americans won't let that happen."

"Why should they care? Will they fight to protect spoiled brats like you from having to work for once in their lives? Anyway, the Russians have more divisions. They want their revenge. And everything they can lay their hands on, being natural thieves."

"Slavs are like that, no better than Gypsies. We had some Croat help once, and we had to lock up everything. You never knew what would disappear next."

Sisi liked the Americans, but only in the way she'd been fond as a child of the servants in the Battyany's Vienna villa. She seemed unaware many GIs thought of Central Europeans as Hunkies or Polacks, even if they themselves were those by blood. She even harbored the odd delusion that GIs had a loyal concern for her personal welfare.

"Yes, the Amis will look after things," she said. "They've been very nice to us here. They treat us more like guests than prisoners, no?"

"I suppose they've done as well as they could, making this place comfortable. They're generous with food. And at least they de-electrified the wire, so it's no longer deadly, just ugly. Still, we are kept behind it."

"Who cares? Imagine if we were in a Russian camp. They'd be starving us, beating us, God knows what else. We'd still look like the tattered scarecrows we were when we arrived here. If we hadn't already died of typhus or something."

"Perhaps," Anja said.

"Ahhh," Sisi sighed, after she inhaled the very last of her half of the Lucky. "It could have been so much worse for us poor refugees. All I have to do is look in a mirror. No more gaunt hollows under my cheekbones. I'm almost pretty again. And look at you!"

Anja avoided the mirror; seeing her own eyes always upset her terribly. But she knew she too looked presentable. She could feel her hair had thickened and regained its cornsilk sheen, and was sure her paleness seemed natural again, ivory-like rather than the pallor of some wasting anemia.

"A beautiful Polish milkmaid, sweet and virginal," Sisi said. "That Nazi would love to have you—if he isn't a queer."

"German, Sisi. German milkmaid," Anja replied patiently. "How many times must I tell you? The only milkmaid in history to earn a degree in philosophy from the Jagiellonian University of Krakow. And I doubt the engineer was ever a Party man. He doesn't have that rancid oiliness."

"You really managed that degree before the war? Then you must be . . . let's see, it takes so many years, you'd have to have been at least twenty-four in 1939. That makes you, God, thirty! Ancient! I'd have sworn twenty-two at most, like me."

"Little liar. I'd already begun my doctoral studies when the Germans shut the University."

"Never mind. Just say you're twenty-two. They'll put that on your papers, if we ever get any. And that's the age you'll be!" Sisi looked slyly at her from under the new bangs she'd cut with scissors "borrowed" from the infirmary. Her hair had chestnut highlights and her Magyar eyes canted up slightly. "Ah, Anja."

"Yes?" Anja felt relaxed, as she did after every deception easily carried off, even if only with a gullible girl.

"Nothing."

"I know. You're fed, you're rested, you want to get out of here and on with your life. Most of all your sex life."

"I'd give anything for . . ."

"Another punch in the face?" Anja laughed. "Understand this: I do not care if I never sleep with anyone again, though I might marry a man with papers. If I have to. Which appears more and more inevitable, doesn't it? But at first I'll pretend I've been too traumatized to be touched just yet. Give me time to get used to you, I'll plead. After I've got a start with him someplace, and papers of my own, he can go to hell if he doesn't like separate beds. What could he do? Give me back to the camp commandant because I won't fuck him?"

Sisi giggled. "You're very wicked, Anja. Your Nazi will be furious."

"I have no Nazi. But you could snare someone who would take you away from this place, and do what I just said. Nothing much to worry about, I think. Those men who come around have been undernourished for years. They're exhausted, worn out, used up. An erection would be a miracle. All they want is a warm body next to them at night. Just pick the cleanest one you can find."

"I could use some warmth under the blanket even now," Sisi said wistfully. "Would you, ah, sleep in my cot? Just for the warmth?"

"You haven't been starving, Sisi. You're not exhausted." Anja laughed, shaking her head.

"You'd like my little ways. Really, you would. But I promise I won't touch you."

"No. Absolutely not. Nobody touches me. And you'd try."

"I probably would, despite my pure intentions. I'm not very good at self-restraint. Never have been. The hearts I've broken! I loved to seduce girls, and they'd love what I did for them. But soon enough I'd always find a new one prettier or sexier—or best of all, utterly innocent. Then I'd drop the old one cold."

"Magyar slut." Anja grinned.

"As if icy Prussians aren't worse. So cold and haughty, pretending great reluctance. And then practically killing the poor man with voracious sex demands."

"God, I can't even bear thinking about that. All engorged and stiff. The idea nauseates me."

"Me, too. But for a different reason, I'm sure."

"You mean you really are one of *those* women?" Anja said in mock horror, which made Sisi cackle. "Let's talk of decent things, please."

"Something pretty, yes. The good times we had, before the war."

"No memories for me. Let's leave the past where it belongs—well buried."

"I've a lot I'd like to keep fresh in mind forever. Like little Agathe, only fourteen when I . . ."

"Sisi!"

"All right. How about what's going to happen? Good things that will happen soon. What do you hope for most? What's your very best dream?"

Anja's face became a mask. She had no answer. None at all. Not even a lie.

VI

Fass's throat was raw, his nose stuffed and oozing. He'd had this cold more or less constantly all through the summer and now into autumn. A dread of pneumonia lurked in his mind, a fear of drowning in phlegm and pus that would slowly fill his lungs. He had seen weakened men go that way, knew he was weakening. As deaths went, they were easy ones. But he did not want that. He sought a harder fate. The lost arm was no more than the first payment of the debt he owed. That meant he had to go on living awhile.

Yet he needed more food than he was usually able to get. Soon he'd need better shelter, the warmth of a coal stove or a kerosene heater. His breath billowed into thin white clouds when he woke at dawn, and there was even a rime of frost on the edges of his blanket. He felt lucky to have his old army overcoat folded neatly in the bottom of his rucksack, but he'd have to attend to arranging winter quarters and better rations.

Then it occurred to him that he could no longer simply requisition a billet in some village home or farmhouse or hay-filled barn, could no longer send his men foraging for goats, chickens, cheese, flour, lard, jars of pickled vegetables and preserved fruits. It wasn't wartime anymore. He would have to move on. He would have to try to reach the one haven that might remain to him.

But his travels had sapped him badly, which was partly why he had lingered so long near the American base. He had started for Stettin from a POW camp west of Stuttgart with Sergeant Blaskowitz, a Stettin boy who had been in his company that last bad winter in Yugoslavia, had looked after him during the writhing retreat to Zell am See. Where Walter's gangrened arm had been lopped off sloppily by a weary, burnt-out surgeon, where Walter's battalion—and twenty-five thousand more Wehrmacht troops—had surrendered to Company E of the 101st Airborne Division. Wild men, those Ami paratroopers, undisciplined and disheveled and so cocky they used more energy hunting down and consuming every cache of wine and liquor in town than in seriously watching their Wehrmacht prisoners, still under arms and outnumbering them more than a hundred to one.

Fass and Blaskowitz planned to head north through the Rhineland to the boundary line between the British and U.S. armies, then more or less straight east to Berlin, and northeast toward Stettin. The verges of the autobahns, the rail lines were thronged with others on the move: ex-soldiers still in uniform but with all insignia torn off, civilians burdened with remnants of whatever they'd naively thought they could not part with, only to discard the treasures one by one the farther they trekked, leaving a pathetic trail of possessions behind them.

Fass had seen the same in Poland, the Ukraine, Bosnia, Serbia. At least fighter planes weren't strafing the staggering columns. At least it wasn't ten below freezing. But Blaskowitz, a former altar boy just turned twenty, could not get over it. "This is goddamn

Germany!" he kept muttering. "How the hell could this be happening? What shithead Nazis and shithead generals let it get to this? Let's hang all the shitheads with piano wire."

The first real shock for the soldiers, who had been so long away, came quickly: They smelt their own cities long before they could see them, still out in the fresh, unmarked green country and the pleasant leafy suburbs. A charred reek, a smoky odor tinged with the sickening, sweetish undernote of maggoty, decaying flesh. Battlefield smells. And once past the screen of the tidy outskirts around Köln, Dortmund, Düsseldorf, Essen, they saw the enormous heaps of rubble, the shells of buildings once familiar, the toppled church steeples, the gaping craters in what had been fashionable boulevards, jackstraw heaps of blackened, twisted steel girders that had once been bridges. German cities, entirely flattened. The only tall structures still standing were the plain red-brick factory chimneys, towering like cheap hurried monuments to utter destruction.

When they turned east, another shock. The roads were heavy with brisk military traffic—going the wrong way. British and American units moving west, back from territory they'd overrun in April and May. Why? Fass was shaken by the sight.

They were still ninety kilometers from Berlin, perhaps a hundred and sixty from Stettin, when they hit a roadblock manned by GIs, and he got his answer. "I'd turn right around, if I were you," said a young U.S. lieutenant in good Swabian German, not bothering to glance at the papers Walter and his sergeant proffered.

"We'll let you through, and so will they," the lieutenant went on, nodding down the road where, just a hundred meters on, a T-34 tank and several squads of Red Army infantry loitered ominously, more like a street gang than a military formation. "But farther on, we hear they're grabbing every ex-soldier they see and shipping them east to prison camps. The Russkies don't care if you've already been in one of our POW camps."

"But we're trying to get home. We've got proper papers," Fass said.

"Over there, the only thing your papers are good for is wiping your ass. Over there, there's not a hell of lot left anyway," the American said.

"We are going to Stettin. Sir," Blaskowitz said. He'd assumed the overstiff bearing that was every old soldier's way of demonstrating extreme disrespect to superiors.

"Stettin," the lieutenant said. "Probably doesn't exist. Big battles around there when the Reds drove on Berlin. Anyway, it's part of Poland now."

"That's not possible," Fass blurted. "Stettin has always been a German city, in German lands."

"Not since Harry Truman and that new Brit prime minister and Uncle Joe Stalin had a little chat in Potsdam," the American chuckled, as if some great prank had been played. "Poland's borders shifted way west. Stettin, Breslau, Danzig—a whole bunch of places now belong to the Poles. The Red Army's there to see to it. Everything past me and my men is the Russian Zone now."

"Christ!" Blaskowitz exploded.

Fass's choice was easy. Even if Stettin still stood, he'd never make it there. And he'd never learn in a Soviet prison camp what had become of his father and mother, his little sister and her two-year-old son. He'd have to remain outside the Russian Zone. He turned toward his sergeant.

But Blaskowitz was already far, far away. He had that glazed, unearthly look in his eyes Fass had observed among the natural warriors just before combat.

"I don't give a shit about those Kalmuks, or the fucking Polacks either. I'm going to Stettin, Captain Fass," he said, and reached to shake Walter's hand. "Goodbye, Captain. *Alles Gute*."

Before Fass could restrain the boy, he moved in quick-step to the Russians. Fass saw him at rigid attention while three or four different officers examined his papers in turn, and finally waved him through. Blaskowitz swung into the old route-marching rhythm and swiftly passed from Walter's life.

※   ※   ※

Fass lit the stub of a cigarette he'd found the night before near a sentry post at the American base. He shook out his blanket, rolled it tight, strapped it to his rucksack, and walked to the main entrance. A dozen men were milling there already. Fass was lucky; he was one of those picked to work—though in fact he hadn't cared much. It was one of those black days that came on him from time to time, days when every effort to survive seemed pointless, days of grief and guilt that nothing could assuage. He was set to washing clothes, then cleaning the officers' latrine with a stiff-bristled brush and a bucket of bleach: things a one-armed man could do. His pay was a lunch of baked beans and Spam, a pack of Camels, and enough Occupation scrip to buy himself some little thing to eat for dinner, if there was anything available at the ir-regular and ever-shifting black market in Sauerlach.

He tried to give a couple of cigarettes to Anja that afternoon at the wire. She pushed his hand away. "We get plenty of everything in here, you know that. Smoke those yourself. Better, trade them for some food. You need more food."

Fass thought he heard concern in her voice. Couldn't be, though. He knew she tolerated him, even seemed to enjoy their meetings, but he was sure she would lose no sleep if he simply dis-appeared one day.

Then a slim, dark-eyed girl he had never seen before sauntered over. "This is a friend of mine, Walter," Anja said.

"Hallo, Captain. I'm Sisi," the girl said in a softened, almost musical drawl.

"Viennese," the engineer said. He had always made a game of trying to place people strictly by looks or accents, the way he'd placed Anja as a Pole. He considered himself exceptionally good at it.

"By inclination and education, yes. By nationality, no. I'm Hungarian," Sisi said. "Which is why I'm here instead of in Vienna. I can't go back as long as the Russians are there. They're snatching all the Hungarians and shipping them east. The Czechs and Slovaks, too."

Sisi looked away for a moment.

"Even Galicians, Wends, Ruthenians! People no one in the world wants around. Crazy, the Russians, aren't they?" The girl laughed, as if the very real terror could be swept away by flippant irony. "Do you know a nice German boy who'd like to marry me?"

"I should think a half-dozen at least have already asked, unless you've been hiding yourself." Fass smiled.

"Sisi, destitute little rat she may be, refuses to give up her class snobbery," Anja said. "Which means she needs a boy with a von glued to his family name."

"I thought Austro-Hungarians were through with all that. The nobility nonsense was abolished after 1918," Fass said.

"By law, certainly. Symbol of the new Republic, down with monarchy, all sorts of rubbish," Sisi laughed again. "But one still has one's standards."

"Standards? You weren't even born when the Empire collapsed," Fass said.

"True. But anyway the vons and the titles returned after Anschluss. Probably now they'll be abolished all over again. Doesn't matter. It isn't the words, Captain. Only what it means about the family. And my father is very old-fashioned about class," Sisi said.

"Of course, I don't know where he or any of my family is just now," she went on, less lightly. "The last I heard from them was in '44, just before the Reds closed the ring around Budapest. And then of course I had to flee Vienna. They wouldn't know where to write, if they're safe somewhere. It's all such a mess. You post names in every missing-persons bureau the Allies have set up, and you never hear a thing."

Fass nodded in a way he hoped she'd think sympathetic. But he felt nothing for her predicament. He had registered every member of his family in every missing-persons bureau in every place he'd passed through. He tacked notes on the hoardings set up in the main squares of almost every town and city. His fluttered there, one among thousands, pallid moth's wings of loss and yearning. He scanned the thousands in each of the squares. So many people trying to find each other, so many hopes lifted for a moment and then dashed, so many feelings that had to be locked away in the deepest recesses of the heart. That's where his family resided now. He was seldom in the mood to visit.

Sisi dropped the small burlap sack she'd been holding and kicked it under the lowest strand of wire. Fass stooped and tucked it under his right arm. It was hard and heavier than he'd expected; canned rations, no doubt.

"Anja says you don't get enough to eat," Sisi said. "If I fatten you up a bit, maybe you'll have the energy to marry her and find a boy for me as well."

"You're better off where you are. You're safe. It's bad out here," he said.

"The most comfortable prison in the world is still a prison," Sisi said. "We want to be free."

"That's the worst sort of nonsense, and you well know it," Fass snapped, more sharply than he'd intended. "You're veterans. You've seen how it is. Drop the girly naiveté, for Christ's sake."

He felt tired and chilled, but he did not want to let go of the heavy bag tucked under his arm, which he'd have to do in order to get his overcoat out of his rucksack. From a place within he'd thought cauterized, shame began hemorrhaging. Looking at Sisi, he saw instead the face of his Chetnik, the forbidden one who was the object of his deepest love and deepest hate. He looked up. In all the sky there were only three high, windsmoothed clouds, very small and whiter than Anja's skin. It occurred to him that he'd not spotted a single falcon riding the wind anywhere in Germany these past months. In the farmland around the camp, the harvest had been taken in, too much of it left in the ground because there were too few hands to gather it. Here and there along the dirt lanes between the fields, lone beeches and oaks were flying little flags of red and yellow. Even as he watched, some dropped and fluttered to the ground.

"Time to go," he said softly, forgetting he had an audience.

"They've opened the mess hall," Anja said. She was already smothering the unease she felt at Fass's outburst and abrupt withdrawal into himself. Her questioning eyes went to Sisi, who briefly arched thin, carefully shaped brows.

"Tomorrow, Walter?" Anja asked.

Fass nodded.

"We'll see what we can liberate for you, Captain," Sisi said. "Until then."

Fass watched the two women walk toward their dinner. Then he headed for the stack of railway ties he called home.

That night, for the first time since her arrival at the sanctuary of the DP camp, Anja was fretful over a sense of impending loss. This bewildered her; she had long ago concluded she would never again have anything to lose. She refused to admit that over these weeks of daily meetings with the engineer she might have developed an attachment, an affinity. After all, she'd allowed Fass to befriend her only because he seemed to be someone she might employ—though she had not decided exactly how or to what end, since she'd so little sense of what she actually desired, or what she might become. But the possibility that this crippled soldier she knew so little about would leave and take both answers and aid away with him scared her.

She felt so woeful that she crept into Sisi's cot that night, whispering her fears. A few who were still awake hissed in revulsion. One—a stocky, solid woman in her thirties who wore the striped jacket of a *Konzentrationlager* inmate—marched over to Sisi's cot and declared, "I'm going for the guards, perverts."

"And I am going to the camp commandant to swear I've recognized you as an SS guard at Nordhausen," Anja said, her voice chilling. "I will say you stole that jacket from a prisoner I saw you beat to death."

"He'd never believe you," the woman said in heavily accented German.

"No? Everyone knows lots of your kind were camp guards, Ukrainian pig. And I know you've sworn you're a refugee from Galicia. Who do you think the commandant will listen to once that lie is out in the open? Who do you think he'll start investigating? They know there are hundreds like you they haven't arrested yet."

"Shut your mouth," the Ukrainian barked.

"*Papiere! Schnell!*" Anja snapped instantly, in the tone she knew so well. "Just the way you used to say it, no?"

The Ukrainian blanched, backed away. "You wouldn't dare,"

she snarled. But she did not leave the barracks. She slunk back to her cot and wrapped herself tightly in her blanket.

Sisi used a pillow to stifle her giggles. When she regained control, she stroked Anja's hair, saying over and over, "Don't worry, he'll be back. He'll be at the wire tomorrow. He's going to get you out of here."

Sisi acted as if it were an affair of the heart. Silly little girl. But Anja allowed the warmth from her clean-smelling body, the tender petting, to envelop her. Even the brushing of Sisi's soft lips against her ear as she whispered eased her, instead of repelling her. She'd been sure she had lost every emotion long ago, in that time and place she refused, as much as she could, to remember. Pale Anja had been cold as the moon so long because she knew her soul was black and brittle as coal.

But what's brittle easily breaks. Anyone can feel a sudden yearning they've long forbidden themselves to feel; everyone will one day need closeness and comfort from some other, Anja reluctantly admitted to herself.

She went pliant, tractable. She felt somehow outside herself, lighter and less burdened.

Had Sisi gently unbuttoned her flannel GI pyjamas and begun what she said she was so skilled at, Anja sensed she might almost feel real pleasure—which she'd never known with all the men in all the rooms—though she had no desire in her. Go ahead now, Sisi, she thought to herself. Be my closeness.

But Sisi was good. Sisi did not exploit the undraped fragility her instincts and experience must have recognized. She only petted Anja to sleep, and held her through the night.

VII

Walter Fass asked Anja Wolff to marry him the next afternoon. In German, not Polish.

He used the tender, romantic words a man in love would use. He tried to cloak the utter absence of love by shyly passing through the wire a bouquet of the freshest, most colorful fallen leaves he could gather. Though Anja found the gesture absurd, somehow degrading, the pleasure she felt left her agape for a moment. Then self-contempt rushed in. She was about to turn that back on the engineer, about to throw the ridiculous bouquet at his face. But Fass deliberately undercut himself.

"So much for my little performance," he said. "We both know this is really a sort of business arrangement. I have a plan and a place in mind. And, I think, the means. We would have shelter, safety and more than enough to eat. We'd have a start. Things would gradually get better. And once we are established, you'd be absolutely free to leave me anytime you wanted. I wouldn't try to prevent you, or put any obstacles in your path."

"Why should I trust you?" Anja demanded. Have to stay in character, she thought.

"Consult your instincts on that. All I can say is that I am no liar. I live up to anything I promise. And I'm promising so very little." His smile was wan.

"This place you speak of. Where is it?"

"Far to the south of here, in the Tirol. The farm of my uncle. A lovely peaceful farm. I spent all my summers there as a boy," Fass said, and in this saying the genuine hope the farm offered crystallized in his mind. Yes, that was the place where his life would make the crucial pivot, either toward a future, or toward an end he did not fear.

Anja gazed a while into his eyes, for she had sensed something more complex at work in Fass than his words revealed.

"What is it you want from me?" she asked. "It isn't love, it isn't my body, it most surely isn't my sweet temper and charming personality. You want something I don't even know if I have to trade."

"Oh, but you do." Fass lowered his head, then looked at her again. "It's difficult to say without sounding mad. It cannot be stated clearly because it isn't clear. What I need, I think, is a good strong left arm for a while."

Anja nodded. This she could understand. "Is there anything else I should know?"

"Yes." His face tightened. "I was a soldier in a place where the usual rules were ignored by both sides. Even though I commanded an engineering company, we were often in combat. I had to kill. Wartime. It wasn't my choice. But on one occasion, I committed cold-blooded murder."

"Why did you do it?"

"I won't make the excuse that I was only following orders," Fass said, his voice cracking almost imperceptably. "It's very simple, really. I was a coward. I had a choice, you see. I chose to destroy innocent people so that I could live on for one more day. I'll give you the details, if you want."

"No. You've said enough," Anja replied. He was telling the truth. The certainty she felt stunned her. He could so easily have lied.

And it was the one lie Anja knew she could never use herself, because—unlike Fass—there was one truth she could never know and then artfully hide: why she had done what she'd done, in Krakow time. She knew only that there had not been any threat of immediate death, just some sort of perverse seduction. She had allowed this, only this, to turn her.

So Anja experienced the engineer's frank confession as if he had ripped out the stitches closing an unhealed wound. She recoiled from the pain. God damn his honesty. God damn the awful blankness within her.

"Do I revolt you?" Fass said, alarmed by what he saw flicker across her face.

Anja shook her head. She did not trust herself to speak just yet.

"The farm, then? It wouldn't be so bad, at the farm." Fass smiled. "We get on fairly well, don't we? We might—though I'm not promising now—even learn how to enjoy a bit of life again."

Anja willed herself to return his smile. She could see immediately he did not detect the weakness, the falseness of it. "Well, Captain," she flirted, "you've given me something pretty to think about. Very pretty."

She held the bouquet of dead leaves under her nose, as if she were savoring the scent of good roses, and felt disgusted with herself when she saw Walter grin and bob his head.

"Think as much as you need to, Anja," he said cheerfully. "I'll come each day as usual, if that's all right. But I won't press you for an answer."

"Yes, come." She smiled, waving her dead leaves at him. She couldn't see his face clearly, because her eyes were focused on a strand of wire. It's not round like telephone or electric wire. It's octagonal, she realized with surprise. Why did they make it that way? She touched it. Much stiffer and heavier than it looked. She didn't think she could bend even a small piece with her hands. Why had she never noticed that before? How on earth did they ever string up stuff like this? What tools could they have used to do that, or to make it in the first place? She flinched when Walter touched the back of her hand with his fingertips.

"Careful of the barbs," he said. "Tomorrow, then?"

※   ※   ※

Fass was not at the wire next day, or the day after that. Her nerves abraded, Anja retreated to the comfort of Sisi's cot those nights, but her sleep was restless. Something had happened. Something bad.

She was in the usual place early on the third day. She noticed that the crowd at the market had thinned out markedly, and realized too she'd failed to note that more and more cots were standing empty in the barracks. The pace of women striking their bargains and leaving the camp with new husbands had picked up in recent weeks before her careless eyes.

Never mind. She would be safe enough here, she'd eat well, she'd be warm through the winter. Unless everyone but her and Sisi and a few others left, and the Americans decided to shut the camp and toss them out. They could do that anytime, Anja knew. It was their Zone, after all. What did they care if a few foreign women were given German nationality? What was it to them if she was Anna Wolff from Breslau or Anja Wieniewska from Krakow, a little Pole who lost her way in wartime? Everyone lost their way, lost something of themselves, in wartime. Everyone had been displaced. Even them, these Americans here.

But where on earth could she go, if the Amis did turn her out? Where but somewhere, anywhere really, with Walter Fass?

Then on the road from the armored unit's base she saw a familiar figure, his empty left sleeve flapping comically, as if the sleeve were trying to wave to her on its own. With him was a taller man she did not recognize.

"Hallo, Anja! See who's turned up out of nowhere at the Ami camp, begging for work like a vagabond," Fass called when he was still twenty meters from the wire. "An old comrade, one of those languid, frivolous Austrians. A gift for Sisi."

Fass's companion playfully bumped him on the shoulder, throwing the engineer off balance. "It depends entirely on what sort of Hungarian she is, I told you that," she heard him say to Walter. "The gypsy type won't do at all."

"You'll see, you'll see," she heard Fass reply. "She was probably welcome in Vienna salons where you'd been barred for lewd behavior, you puppy."

The taller man did look young; the war had not aged his face prematurely as it had Walter's. He was wearing a tattersall shirt and a Shetland sweater under a shaggy tweed hacking jacket; the impression was he'd just come from a dressage session with his favorite horse—until you noticed the patches roughly sewn on his faded gray-green Wehrmacht riding breeches.

"Anja Wolff, allow me to introduce ex-Lieutenant Dietmar von Scharner. Our units spent some interesting times together in Yugoslavia," Fass said. "I thought he was dead until two days ago, when he showed up at the base gates."

"I was a Jäger, which is why the Amis were more tardy in letting me go than they'd been in Walter's case," Scharner said to Anja. "Apparently the Yugos have been slandering us to the Allies. I was questioned and questioned. Very rudely, too. The details they had were startling, really. Very precise about times and places and things. But the Yugos gave them a lot of rubbish about what actually went on."

"No war talk, please," Fass said amiably. "Since you're newly free I'll let it pass this time, but we do not behave like boozy veterans before the ladies. *Alles klar*, Scharner?"

"*Jawohl, mein Kapitän*," the young man said crisply, clicking his heels. Then both of them laughed like schoolboys.

"Anja, Anja," Fass said. "I know we're being idiots. It's just been such a wonderful surprise to find a dear friend alive and well. Almost miraculous. We've drunk each other's health a bit too frequently the past forty-eight hours or so."

"Those bottles of schnapps cost me the watch the Amis didn't manage to steal when I surrendered," Scharner said. "The black-market people here, you know, are first-rate thieves. Hard to believe they're actually Germans. Of course, they're not, come to think of it. They're Bavarians. I've never cared for Bavarians."

Fass asked Anja to fetch Sisi. Anja considered Scharner a moment, smiled in assent, then trotted to the barracks. Some minutes passed. Fass and his tall friend shared a cigarette. "I'm dreading this," Scharner said. "It's going to be tremendously awkward. We'll have nothing to say to each other. You've got to take up the slack. And you are very deeply in my debt, Fass."

"Of course, of course. Now stop complaining. You need only to talk to the girl a bit. Anja will see I've made an effort. Makes no difference if you don't get on. And who knows? You may strike it lucky. You're going to have to work like hell to stay out of trouble with your father when you get home, if you don't."

"Oh, I'm dreading that much more than this," Scharner said. "I'm facing a monk's life unless I can distract him somehow."

"Well, here comes your possible somehow," Fass said, gesturing at the pair headed toward them—one dark and willowy, the other pale, small but sturdy.

"Elisabeth Battyany, this is Dietmar von Scharner," Anja said when they'd reached the wire.

"Dizzi, please," Scharner said, reaching through the wire to grasp Sisi's hand and bowing slightly as if he wished to kiss it. An enormous smile spread across his face.

"Sisi," she said. And laughter overwhelmed them.

"Dizzi and Sisi. Names for a pair of snotty brats," the Jäger lieutenant giggled. "Well, what do you expect? We Austrians are a childish people. The national symbol, after all, never really was the Habsburg double eagle but the giant Prater Ferris wheel."

"And instead of that morbid *Sorrows of Young Werther*, we have Schnitzler," Sisi said.

"Delightful Strauss waltzes instead of Wagner's awful roaring!" Dizzi cried.

"The Café Zentral, not reeking beerhalls."

"Gustav Klimt, not that depressing Otto Dix."

"No Prussian robot obsession, everyone linked at the hip by little chains."

"No Bohemian defenestration fetish. Czechs are always falling out of windows, aren't they?"

"They're fond of it."

Dizzi and Sisi went chattering on like cousins who had summered in different spas and were catching up now that they'd met back in Vienna. They found they actually had a few acquaintances in common. Presently Fass motioned to Anja to step a few paces down the wire, so they could speak privately.

"Listen, Anja, I think we may possibly have a match here, but there is perhaps a small difficulty. Dizzi's a 175," he told her, using the code number the SS had given homosexuals in the KZs. Everyone else in the camps had a colored patch: the Jews, yellow of course; hardened criminals green; politicals red. But for homosexuals, the 175. Almost nobody knew why. Some said it was the number of the article in the Third Reich's legal code making sodomy a capital crime. Perhaps the SS had adopted it with deliberate irony, since so many of them ignored that law.

"He is no fairy. He won the Iron Cross first and second class, and the close-combat badge," Fass went on. "But he likes young men, not pretty girls. He wants to take a wife home so his parents won't suspect what he really gets up to. He won't touch Sisi. Should you warn her? They seem to be getting on so well."

"You don't know how clever my Magyar is," Anja said, thinking without disappointment that Walter might be a 175 himself, and amused that the engineer had not suspected Sisi's inclinations. "And sophisticated, from living so much in Vienna. She's probably sensed everything already."

"He's very brave and very kind and not at all dissolute or debauched. There'd be absolute discretion on his part," Fass said.

"Well, Sisi's not one to live like a nun. I think she is rather experienced for her age. Naturally she would take lovers. But she is sensible enough to manage it without scandal."

"So. Shall we simply let things proceed and see what happens?"

"Very well," Anja agreed. "And Walter, could we proceed also? Shall I get the machinery underway? There's a lot of paperwork, and you have to be interviewed by the camp officers, prove who you are and everything. Tangles of red tape."

"You accept?"

"But we are clear on terms, correct? It is not to be a real marriage. I'm fond of you, of course. But there is nothing else. I will not have sex with you."

"No, I didn't suppose you would. Of course I think you're lovely—for a little Pole—but frankly I, eh . . . I'm not really wanting that sort of thing from anyone these days."

Anja smiled. "Walter, don't keep referring to me as your little Pole in that dry, sly way you think is humorous. I'm only called

Anja because my nanny and the servants were all Poles. It's Anna on my birth certificate. Allowing that I lack a birth certificate."

"So Anna it will be on your new papers. Anna Fass. But I'm going to keep calling you Anja. My tongue's got used to it. I like the way it rolls," he said. "Anyway, you do look Polish. I'm not often wrong about these things."

"Swine! You need to be de-Nazified. You're a Slavophobe."

"I've already been de-everything. Demilitarized, deloused, and now, by you, defamed, denounced and despised. Surely that's sufficient."

"You've got one more to look forward to: you'll be de-manned if you ever climb into my bed in the middle of the night."

"Neither of us need worry about that."

No, certainly no love for Walter and her. But was something else growing between them? The calm pleasure of being in sight of each other? Of being accepted, perhaps even understood a little? The faint awareness of a connection, not of blood or desire, that seemed as if it had always existed, waiting patiently for them to meet and recognize it? Anja felt almost genuine. What in the world was happening to her?

Then Anja was slapped by a corollary to her juvenile Krakow philosophy: If you dwelt on anything you very much wanted, if you allowed yourself to have too much hope—and any at all might be too much—then the thing you desired would slip out of your grasp forever. Sentiment was a luxury she could not allow herself. Today, it was as if she had been offered a gift she felt unable and unworthy to receive, but eager to have. But what about tomorrow? The day after?

"You have my word—no creeping about in the nights. Are you reassured?" Fass asked.

"I suppose so," Anja replied. "It's the strangest sensation, though. I feel I've seldom had so many questions, and so little need for answers."

"Exactly the same for me," said the engineer, taking her hand in his for the first time. A barb nicked Anja's wrist.

Fass stood there silent and smiling for a while, left sleeve stirring with each small waft of the air. One day this little Pole would unburden herself to him and he would help her through the anguish of it. Perhaps she would help him in turn. One day, all the wounds might be healed, he thought.

Or more likely, all those who inflicted and received them would die off, and everything would be forgotten.

Smile faded now, not conscious he could be heard, the engineer murmured, "It all passes. The world always turns. Our nightmares, our remorse will fade like old photographs. There's nothing we can do."

"So none of it mattered, or meant anything?" Anja was cross, and disappointed in Fass, because she did not know the thoughts behind his words. "So we are free? We've only got to look out for ourselves now, try to make a life as comfortable as we can manage? You think so? I was sure we would have to pay and pay and pay."

"Oh, we are paying," Fass said. She knew from his tone he had missed her subtle sarcasm. "It's just that one day we'll still be doing it, but not realizing it. It will be the natural way of things, so ordinary it won't give us a moment's pause."

Then came a loud laugh from Sisi and a shout.

"*Achtung!*" Dizzi called down the wire. "Dizzi and Sisi are engaged to be married. Of course Germans cannot grasp our wondrous Austrian concept of *Gemütlichkeit*, but you should have the grace to pretend. Smile! Laugh a little!"

"Blitz," the engineer said to Anja. "Combat Group Scharner has overrun Fair Hungary in ten minutes."

"I think you underestimate Fair Hungary," said Anja, her heart rising in a way that surprised her. "I think it may have been the other way around, though Scharner doesn't know it yet."

"A double wedding, I insist," Dizzi called, stretching his arms high above his head and clasping his hands. "Champagne, Herr Ober!"

Sisi stood there hugging herself, gazing not at Dizzi but at Anja, with what could only be called love.

Forever a little fool, Anja reflected, ruthlessly crushing her next thought: whom I love too.

VIII

Then Anja and Sisi were off to the mess hall; Walter and Dizzi to cram themselves into Fass's splintery den of railway ties.

"Of course we're utterly mad," Dizzi gasped as a sip of homemade schnapps burned its way down his throat to corrode his belly. "Ah, but what can we do? The world's mad. Best to keep in step with the times, I suppose. But imagine! Marrying girls we know nothing about, out of a DP camp. We're insane, my friend."

"But Dizzi, your problem is solved. Your old man will love Sisi. She is 'one of our kind,' he'll say. Your mother . . . that's problematic, if she's as you've described her. No doubt she'd prefer a demure, biddable girl from a family she's known. She'll resent Sisi's spirit, and Sisi's beauty won't help matters."

"Clashes here, clashes there, one skirmish after another! Should actually be great fun to watch. Since dear mamma doesn't matter. It's my father who has to be pleased. He has firm hold of the purse-strings after all. Spirit and beauty will certainly appeal to him. The ancient lecher may even try to steal her. So it is perfect in its way," Dizzi grinned wickedly. "A quick and easy victory.

The happy warrior returns already firmly attached to one of our kind."

"Not mine, actually. Your father's. Yours."

"Don't be so bourgeois," Dizzi said.

"Oh come on, Scharner. You know you only tolerate me. You and Sisi have probably already been mocking my burgher values. 'He's an engineer! Likes pounding rivets. Imagine!' Then laughter."

"I tolerate you because your men held the bridge over Kočevje Gorge long enough for my men to fight their way out of that Partisan ambush," Dizzi said. "And I love you like a brother for the beautiful explosion you set off as soon as we got clear. A fifteenth-century stone arch, crude but probably something those Slobos were very proud of, blasted to bits.

"Splendid! I could actually hear the Partisans calling the Great Tito's curse down on you, raging and screeching, the way they always did," Dizzi chortled. "And then there was everything else we did together. But men like us don't get sentimental, do we? Well, an Austrian might. But never a Prussian."

"As I recall, all we did together was get stinking drunk on that disgusting *rakija* and babble nonsense at each other after every action. I've managed to erase the babble from my mind, but even remembering the taste of that *rakija* makes me slightly nauseated."

"I thought it wasn't so bad," Dizzi said. "In any case, I remind myself frequently you aren't really a Prussian even when you behave like one. In birth and spirit you're as Austrian as me."

"That may be the only near-truth you've told all day—to me or to that poor little Hungarian waif."

"Waif? Do you know what the Battyany family was worth, in terms of landholdings alone? Even my father will goggle when he learns her surname."

Not much point in pondering whatever had made Dizzi one of the ardent ones. Like too many young Austrians, even more ardent than their German contemporaries. It would have certainly been a Waffen SS panzer division for him, Fass was sure, if not for his father's intervention. Old Scharner detested Himmler and everyone in the Führer's regime.

Intelligent, educated Dizzi hadn't bothered contemplating any issue larger than the pure professionalism of soldiering and the mastery of combat technique. And he never saw the war as a mistake, per se. "You know," he'd once told Fass, "I think I agree with that British boy in the Great War, Grenfell was his name, who wrote his mamma from the West Front that it was all tremendous fun. Something like, I think he called it, 'a picnic with a purpose.' Wonderful."

"Yes, and he was killed very messily not so long after," Walter answered.

"That can't be helped." Dizzi laughed. "Doesn't mean he was wrong, does it? Just unlucky."

No need to dwell on such things now. Or give any weight to the fact that Dizzi was not the least disillusioned by any of it, not even ignominious, disastrous defeat. He still gazed placidly at the ruined world in the manner of his "kind": eyes full of certainty of his place in it, and of his absolute right to behave any damn way he pleased.

The Chetniks had loved Dizzi. In the beginning, around Mihailović and a core of men from the Royal Yugoslav Army, joined by young men and women from the better, educated classes of Serbia, the Chetniks had fought the Wehrmacht occupation. But they'd backed way off when faced with the German reaction— shooting masses of innocent civilians, burning villages to the ground, executing or imprisoning their friends and relatives in Belgrade and other Serb cities. Mihailović, everyone knew, arranged local truces with the Wehrmacht commanders, and the Chetniks ended up mostly fighting Tito's Partisans, who deliberately provoked German reprisals with their tactics. It was god-awful, pitiless, remorseless, genocidal: as bad as or worse than any-thing in Russia, though on a smaller scale. Immediate execution, by both sides, of anyone captured. Hapless folk given the choice that was no choice after Partisans killed Germans in their villages: Either join us and go into the woods, or stay home and be slaugh-tered by the Germans.

It was no wonder that near the end some Chetnik units were fighting shoulder-to-shoulder with Wehrmacht formations; the Chetniks realized by then that they could expect only extermina-tion, even if they surrendered or volunteered to join the Partisans. Another choice that was no choice.

And that was the bizarre route by which he had come to be side-by-side with his Chetnik and perhaps a hundred others on the one day in his life when he truly wished he had never been born.

Dizzi, though, admired the Chetniks' wild, desperate ferocity as much as they appreciated his tireless, fantastic enthusiasm for stalking and killing Partisans.

Fass took a large swallow of raw schnapps, passed the bottle back to his friend.

"Say, Walter. Why don't you and Anya come live with us at Ischl?" Dizzi said suddenly. "The villa has, oh, just six bedrooms. Not so grand, but all the privacy you want. And you'd get on with my parents. They'd always call you Herr Doktor Fass. You know how Austrians are about any sort of title."

"And do what? Mooch about in this cheap suit, the penniless disabled veteran waiting for his meager pension? Which will never come. We don't even have a nation, just Zones. No, I've got a little plan for the immediate future, and hopes of someday practicing my profession without being shot at."

"Are you thinking of Bozen? Your uncle's place?"

"To start with. The farm seems agreeable to Anja. But I haven't dared tell her exactly where it is. Far south of here, I said, in the Tirol. And that satisfied her. I failed to mention it's in Italy."

"Why, for God's sake? Rather a silly omission, I think."

"An instinct. A fear she might balk at the idea of crossing a border. I'm not sure Anja is as anxious to get out of this shithole country as I am. Or perhaps it's the impression I've gotten that she's very leery of any official scrutiny. Which we are bound to encounter crossing the Brenner."

"My impression is that very little in this world could intimidate that one, my friend."

"You may be right. But just in case, please don't mention that my uncle's farm is across the border. I badly need to get there, and I badly need the girl to go there with me. Do you understand?"

"No. But never mind that. I won't give your little secret away," Dizzi said.

"The farm is my only prospect, that's all. My best hope for regaining at least a little peace of mind, then trying to fashion a future of sorts."

"Ischl will do for me, since I don't care about any such nonsense. It's bound to be a bit tight. I'll just have to be patient, wait for the Russians to stop squatting on Vienna and clear off the T-34s that are most likely tearing up all the fields of our place in the Steiermark.

"You know," Dizzi continued, wincing as another shot of schnapps went down, "I'd really like to sneak down there one day disguised as a farmer, hauling a cart of *Panzerfaust*s hidden under hay. I could hit a half-dozen or so before those Kalmuk savages knew what was happening. They burn so beautifully, the T-34s."

"My God, haven't you had enough of that?"

"Ah, Walter. You disapprove?" Dizzi said. "Don't deny it. I see it in your sour face."

"It's not for me to criticize anything," Fass said.

"Good," said Dizzi. "Otherwise I would have no choice but to—"

"Call me out for a duel," Fass interrupted, laughing.

"To remind you that you see beauty in the mathematical perfection of structural dynamics—such peculiar taste, but to each his own—and you took pride in figuring the load-bearing capacity of beams and trusses connected just so. I saw the way you'd look at bridges and positions you'd built. A *Künstler* of construction, extremely *künstlerisch*.

"But, and don't bother to deny it because I saw this as well, you also loved calculating the exact placement of the minimum amount of explosives required to blow a bridge or building to bits," Dizzi said, half-drunk now. "Hah! How you loved to plunge the exploder! You enjoy big booms and heaps of wreckage just as much as I."

"Perhaps," Fass said. "I'd wish otherwise, though."

"Why? Blowing things up is wonderful. Destruction is also artistic, in its unique way. I enjoyed quite a lot about combat, actually. I felt so creative, so exhilarated. There's real satisfaction in sighting in your rifle out around three hundred meters, squeezing off and dropping your man. Bam! He's down. Hell of a shot! A fine feeling."

"You're a rare one then."

"Of course I am. And after the times we had in Yugoslavia, don't go pretending it wasn't perfectly clear even to someone as dim as you that there is something essentially warped in me, according to accepted standards. And I don't mean the 175 bit."

"I thought it was just that your blood was up in battle, seeing friends killed beside you, the usual military nonsense."

"Nonsense is right! My blood was always up. I really did relish destroying things."

"People are things?"

"Certain people. Anyone shooting at me, absolutely. Anyone I don't like, frequently. I did draw the line at women and children, you know."

"Lots didn't," Fass muttered, feeling sick. He had not, and he'd never be able to atone for it.

"Now I may be a bit, shall we say, exceptional. But those bastards were sick. They should have been shot in the cradle."

Yes, Fass thought. Shot in the cradle. Failing that, shot right now.

"Where's the fun in killing helpless civilians? The thrill comes when you're up against someone as deadly as you are, someone who very badly wants to kill you first. That's why I've never gone in for hunting. Poor defenseless stags. My father thinks I'm a bit degenerate because I refuse to go slaughter stags with him."

Fass felt sicker. Dizzi did not know what he'd done with the help of a Chetnik unit during the great retreat. Dizzi's battalion had been cut off a little farther east and was trying to break out toward Maribor and the Austrian border. Walter's group was also heading for the border. He had wished to God every day of his life since that some fanatic Partisans hidden in that one pathetic village hadn't opened fire on their retreating column. Sometimes he wished the first shot had gone through his own head. Or that he'd jammed the muzzle of his Walther against his temple and pulled the trigger, rather than participate in what followed.

"Listen, my friend," Fass said seriously. "If I begged a favor, would you do it for me?"

"Certainly. Anything at all," Dizzi drawled, waving the schnapps bottle magnanimously.

"Put a bullet in my forehead, right here," Fass said, placing a forefinger exactly midway between the bridge of his nose and his hairline.

"Certainly not," Dizzi snorted. "At this range? Your brains would splatter all over me and ruin my clothes."

"Please do it, Dizzi."

"Oh come on now, Walter. Be a man. That tiny little blond thing of yours isn't that bad."

IX

In their dark barracks, snug under the drab GI blanket, sleeping Sisi warmed a wakeful Anja, one long leg draped over
hers. Anja felt she had ricocheted through the day like a
Mauser bullet fired down a narrow alley, sparks flying as each
glancing impact sent it hurtling toward the next.

Anja trembled. Sisi stirred and clasped her tighter in her sleep.

Sisi and Dizzi, Anja and Walter. A pairing of two women with
two men, once such a normal, natural process. An expected, perfectly ordinary development in ordinary lives. It was breathtaking,
really, the prodigious shift the world had made.

Was she really going to marry this Fass fellow for a set of papers? And her crazed emotions today! So unanticipated and absurd
that she wanted to laugh out loud at herself. Or weep.

Sisi had chattered delightedly through dinner and for a long
time before sleep took her. Not a single hesitant note, not a visible
twinge of regret or despair over her lost family, her lost home.
She's almost as good an actress as I am, Anja thought. But a bit too
transparent in this role.

"Dizzi was very gallant and flirtatious, but the poor man can't hide it. He only sleeps with boys, I'm sure," Sisi said, bubbles foaming over her lips as she brushed her teeth in the shower room. "He wouldn't touch a woman, he probably can't bear our smell. He'd have to rush to the shower and scrub away the pollution if he ever fucked a girl. That's perfect. Absolutely perfect!

"Do you think Walter knows about Dizzi?" Sisi asked as they slipped under the blanket together. "Men aren't very quick to catch on. Dizzi's very manly, very military. I'm sure Walter doesn't suspect. Walter probably thinks a fellow like Dizzi has screwed every women he could but keeps it to himself, being a gentleman."

"Probably," Anja said. "It is so mad, the way they are."

"Good comrade, brave man," Sisi said, attempting a hearty male baritone that made Anja giggle. "Imagine if your engineer knew Dizzi was queer? He'd probably be disgusted, or act as if Dizzi had some highly infectious disease and keep well out of contagion range."

Then she frowned. "You haven't told Walter about me, have you?"

"Of course not," Anja said. The true words had left an unfamiliar, metallic sort of taste in her mouth. "None of his business, is it? He thinks you're gorgeous. Given a choice, I'm certain he'd much rather sleep with you than with me."

"Oh Anja, that's not so. He thinks I'm as sexy as a beanpole. The way he looks at you, though! He tries to hide it, but he adores you. He's dying to see your body, nuzzle up against you, stroke your skin, kiss your breasts, all of that."

"I doubt it. Even if it were so, it's not going to happen. I'm not at all interested. That sort of frantic need is for adolescents. I can't imagine having any physical desire for anyone."

"Oh, you will again, someday. And I think Walter would be very gentle, very tender with you."

The last thing Anja wanted. The very last.

It was amusing, the way Fass accepted that she would never make love with him because there was no love. Love! She had slept with every man Richter wanted her to, every man who ever asked her, hoping each time one would recognize her for what she was and show revulsion and disgust. But her body was all they saw; they adored using it.

Perhaps she had chosen the wrong method. Perhaps it would be Fass, never distracted by her nakedness or his lust, who would finally see. Him, or some stranger who would appear one day and recoil at her rottenness.

Could Walter already sense something? Was there more than teasing in his persistence in calling her his little Pole? What did he do in Yugoslavia? It couldn't have been so bad, at least not relative to this war's scale of atrocity. Or he would never have been able to say it straight out, never have called it "murder" as he had done. No one with a sound mind was that brave.

Sound mind? What a concept. Could anyone who survived the war be sound? She was certainly twisted, perverse, unstable. Almost off her head entirely. Yet no one seemed to notice.

Anja eased herself out of Sisi's embrace and crept to the lightless latrine. In that dank place, the only private refuge available to her, she began to cry.

She could not begin to sort through her vast contradictions, find any way to handle the emotions that were making a plaything of her. No, not a plaything: a heretic before her inquisitors. She'd confess to anything to end this agony. But she did not know what to confess. What was the truth of any of it? Her idea of her past had finally become so distorted, so dislocated, that every event, every action seemed unreal. Had she actually done those things? Had there ever been a Richter, or had she made even him up?

Anja was no longer certain of anything.

She tried Krakow principles. Lie confidently and consistently.

But no one was asking her anything she needed to lie about. Deny confidently and consistently. But no one was accusing her of anything. Banish from memory . . . but she had already banished herself entirely, it seemed. Anja never existed, never was born, never walked the streets of Krakow, never lived in this camp.

So she wept. And kept on weeping until there were no more tears left in her.

She did not believe she could bear this much longer. Sooner or later she would have to kill herself. That was the only sure way to know whether she was real and alive on this earth, or long dead, and long in hell.

X

Naturally there was no champagne. Even the resourceful Dizzi couldn't organize that.

Everything else was in order. Anja and Sisi had gone through the correct channels. Two MPs fetched Dizzi and Walter from the gate, loomed over them as they filled out forms in triplicate. Two German-speaking officers scrutinized their GI-issued IDs, their old Wehrmacht paybooks, their POW discharge papers for any signs of tampering or forgery. The officers made Dizzi and Walter stand well away from their desks while they searched thick loose-leaf binders filled with the names of the wanted, of those under suspicion, searching for a match.

Then came the interrogations; the American intelligence service must have issued a handbook on these, for the questions were exactly the ones Walter and Dizzi had been asked in their POW camps: "When did you enter the Wehrmacht? Conscript or volunteer? In which units did you serve? Where? When? Were you ever stationed near a KZ? Did you ever see one? Were you personally or your unit ever attached to an SS unit? Did you ever witness an SS unit in action? Waffen SS or regular SS? Were you ever a Party member? Did you ever shoot a civilian, burn a village? Not even in Yugoslavia? That's hard to believe. Did anyone in your unit kill civilians or prisoners? No? You're sure? Did you see this done by any other units? What was its designation? Do you know the names of any members? Only that, just that one last name? Do you know his rank, where he was from? Did you ever see him in a POW camp? You believe he was killed in combat? But you aren't sure? Get out of my sight."

Another week passed. Dizzi and Walter hung around the gate most of each day. Sisi and Anja spent many hours there, talking through the wire. They had been interrogated as well. They agreed the Americans gave the appearance of being thorough, but that any reasonably clever person, even a reptilian Latvian or Ukrainian camp guard, could have slipped through their net. At the end the Amis seemed satisfied that Anna Wolff and Elisabeth Battyany were innocent victims of wartime.

Then one day the two German-speaking lieutenants came to the gate and summoned Dizzi and Walter to the commandant's office. The commandant sat behind a scarred, cluttered wooden desk, smoking a large cigar. An outsized American flag hung limply from a pole, and framed photos of Franklin Roosevelt and General Eisenhower hung on the wall. Dizzi sniffed, and made a tiny grimace; he did not approve of cheap cigars. At one side of the desk stood the American-appointed mayor of Sauerlach, a weedy little man in a black suit worn shiny in spots and fraying at the cuffs. He was constantly clearing his throat with a sort of rasping hack. Next to him, Sisi and Anja waited. Sisi had colored her lips and lightly rouged her cheeks. She even wore earrings, provenance known only to her. Anja suspected she'd "borrowed" them from someone's small hoard of possessions in a barracks. She herself stood plain in her flowered summer dress—once simply an empty dress, walking, that had made Walter laugh—goosebumps visible on her arms.

The mayor recited the civil ceremony in a rapid monotone. Fass had traded some K rations he'd earned doing laundry at the military base for a silver-plated ring, a child's ring that pinched Anja's little finger. He did not allow himself to ponder what had become of the child who'd once worn it. Dizzi had acquired a band with a garnet chip set clumsily on it, which slipped onto the proper finger of Sisi's left hand. Then Dizzi and Sisi signed three identical certificates, Walter and Anja three others. The commandant allowed half an inch of cigar ash to fall on one of Walter and Anja's certificates while he countersigned all three. Then he handed Dizzi and Walter a certificate each, along with ID cards for Sisi and Anja bearing their photos and their new names and the necessary official stamps.

"Thank you very much, sir," Fass said. He had memorized the phrase in American, just for the occasion.

The commandant leaned back in his chair. "So long, bud," he said, not looking at any of them.

There was no champagne. Dizzi and Walter smoked at the gate while they waited for Sisi and Anja to change into their traveling clothes. The October light was buttery, but there was a chill breeze from the south, where the Alps lay hidden, and Fass guessed the stubbled fields would be glittering with frost one morning soon. Time to go. Presently Sisi appeared, wrapped in a loden cape with a shearling collar which she'd somehow held on to during her flight west from Vienna and through the months in the camp. Anja was less fortunate. All she had was British battle dress, complete with ankle wraps and heavy brown boots. The smallest issue, but still swimming on her. Dizzi smothered a laugh.

"Very good, Anja," Fass called as she approached. "You'll be warm enough. We'll manage something better a little later on."

"Well," Sisi said lightly, making a Gypsy gesture against the evil eye at the commandant's office building, then at the rows of planked barracks, the bare ochre earth of the camp, and the taut strands of wire. "Let's go home, hey!"

"Absolutely," laughed Dizzi. "Forced march, the first I've ever looked forward to."

The engineer Dr. Walter Fass, ex-captain in the Wehrmacht, who rigorously made precise calculations for all his tasks, had not chosen the most direct route to his destination. That road was a lonely one, snaking through the forests and hills to the Achenpass, over it into Austria and along the Achensee, and then farther south to the valley of the Inn. Werewolf units waging guerrilla war had turned out to be just another fantastic Nazi delusion; Fass would have seen signs of it in the movements and behavior of the American troops in the area. But peril lay that way still. Fass was sure of this, from his talks with Wehrmacht men from the Italian front who had skulked through on their journeys home and had passed a night or two near Sauerlach. He believed what he had heard from more than a couple tough, experienced NCOs. There were armed men in the forests: some SS fanatics, a few Wehrmacht renegades, even small bands of mounted Cossacks who had hunted *partigiani* in Friuli for the Germans and now, long after the war's end, lived as bandits rather than surrender to the Americans. For it had quickly become known the Amis handed over all Soviet nationals who had joined the German side to the Red Army, by force if necessary. There had been at least one pitched battle between Ukranians and GIs when the Amis tried to force those POWs over into the Red lines, with more than two hundred casualties.

And, the NCOs said, there were American patrols almost as

murderous. Or, more accurately, the odds were good that any given patrol included one GI still so crazed by wartime hatred he thought nothing of shooting any German he felt in the mood to kill.

Best not to encounter such men in a lonely place, best not to meet rabid SS or desperate Cossacks in the fir forests of southern Bavaria. Best to go a longer way, along the main Allied military arteries.

So he and Anja walked south with Dizzi and Sisi to a town called Holzkirchen, just outside of which they hit the autobahn from Munich to Salzburg. They turned away from Munich—blackhearted and haunted as Nuremburg—toward the city of Mozart, trudging east beside a thin but constantly flowing stream of Allied military traffic. The fields were surprisingly green this late in a dry autumn. Far to the south, from certain vantage points, they could see the ominous black scrawl of the forests fading into higher terrain of muted browns and grays, almost no color at all really, like dust. But it was not dust, Fass knew. It was the unforgiving stone buttresses of the high Alps come down to meet the plain, streaked here and there by dark ravines filled with tenacious conifers climbing to the highest points at which they could survive.

Dizzi had traded his riding boots—custom-made by Lobb of Paris and hardly worn—at the black market for brown brogues, a pair of flannel trousers and a large baby carriage. The carriage and their packs were heavy with water bottles and whatever GI rations they'd been able to beg or liberate. They still managed to make as much as fifteen kilometers a day. Dizzi and Walter felt an easy familiarity, recalling the good early days when they marched with their men cheerfully, even peacefully, no gaps yet torn in the ranks of the fresh-faced, eager boys. A great adventure. A picnic with a purpose.

It was hard going for Sisi and Anja, whose boots were large and rough. But not too hard. For they were marching to hope, not the

cadences of memory. Walter and Dizzi were the ones who called
the early halts, exhausted, while Sisi and Anja had the energy and
will to go on. It was Walter and Dizzi who sprawled weakly on the
verge of the highway long before sunset while their new wives
walked off to beg and trade with farmwives, or those few farmers
who had returned, for bread and eggs, and a hayloft or hut in
which to pass the night. Dizzi was revealed at once to be a pro-
found snorer.

One overcast morning they passed the iron-gray Chiemsee,
which looked frigid as winter already, though swans still glided before the breezes like small, elegant sailboats tacking in and out of
the reeds near the lake's shore.

It was exactly then and there that Fass realized he had made a
great mistake. Going on to Salzburg would add a couple of hundred kilometers to their trip, and turning south now would take
Anja and him down narrow mountain defiles to a place only the
victors could visit without fear, revulsion and a ridiculously super-
stitious but still palpable awe: Berchtesgaden, the devil's own lair.
He should have turned south at Rosenheim, taken the main highway down into Austria to Kufstein, then traveled along the river
Inn to Innsbruck, and up the Wipp valley. He confessed his error.

Dizzi laughed. "My God, Walter! You're the village idiot. Or
else this is destiny, and you're to come to Ischl with us. Surely
you're not going to retrace steps to Rosenheim. That's twenty kilometers or more."

"It's how far? It's back the way we've already come?" Anja
asked.

"There's no choice," Fass said. "It's a hundred straight on to
Salzburg, and from there, round about, we'd have to head back
anyway more than a hundred to Innsbruck. This isn't flat Brandenburg. You have to follow winding valleys between the moun-

tain ranges. There's not a straight stretch of road in all of western Austria except along the Inn. It would take us weeks."

"So come to Ischl," Sisi urged.

"No, we've got to go back," Fass said.

"Back," Anja said, in a voice that would have sounded dead but for the faint sharp note of rage that edged it.

"I'm sorry. I knew all along to turn south at Rosenheim. I really just forgot our whereabouts," Fass said.

"Good thing the war is over. You've become the sort who absent-mindedly wandered into minefields his own men had just planted. Thinking deep thoughts no doubt. All of a sudden, BOOM!" Dizzi laughed.

Fass stood as if mesmerized by the passing Dodge deuce-and-a-half trucks, the jeeps, the 105-millimeter howitzers lashed to flatbed heavy-equipment haulers the GIs called prime movers. Have to wake up, have to keep sharp, can't relax, he thought. Too easy to get lost in the new Europe, too easy to blunder into the wrong place at the wrong time. Dizzi was right; officers had strolled into fresh minefields, and not because they meant to kill themselves.

But God, where was anything in Europa? It was scarcely recognizable as the continent of his father, let alone his grandfather. The art and architecture that had stood for centuries now blown to shards and dust. The best of every period—Gothic, Renaissance, Baroque—simply smashed into disorderly piles of stone and chipped brick, worse than anything the Huns did to Roman Aquileia; the Huns had no high explosives. As from a great distance, he vaguely heard Dizzi's voice: "He's not himself. I hope he's not getting ill."

All it took was two wars, and everything that seemed permanent proved as mutable as melting snow. Look anywhere on the

map, if any existed that was even close to being up-to-date. Everything familiar had vanished in a tide of migration not seen since
the collapse of Rome. The old familiar cities—now the people who
lived there, their nationality and the language they spoke, the very
names of the places had changed. To the east, Franz Josef's Lem-
berg had become Lvov, his Czernowitz was the Ukraine's Cher-
novtsy, Galatz was Galati, and Romanian. In the south, old
Austrian Agram was now Slav Zagreb, Laibach now Ljubljana.
Meran and Brixen had changed to Merano and Bressanone. To the
north, Hanseatic Danzig was Gdańsk, Stettin (or where Stettin
had been) now a Polish ruin called Szczecin. Even in the center,
Marienbad was Mariánské Lazně, and Czech. The emperor's
Pressburg changed to Slovak Bratislava, Prussian Breslau to Polish
Wrocław. The mountains alone remained untouched, and the
rivers stayed their ancient courses, but even the Moldau was now
the Vltava, the Vistula the Wisła.

And he had been there himself when the Habsburg land of the
Südtirol changed into a place called the Alto Adige, the German
street signs replaced overnight by unreadable Italian ones.

How to get and keep your bearings?

"Walter!" Anja said loudly. "What's wrong?"

"Come on, Walter. Enough daydreaming," Dizzi chided. "My
God, you'd think he was a Mann or a Mahler or someone, drifting
off on artistic inspirations. Fass, you build bridges and things.
You're practical and methodical. You're Prussian-trained. Have
the decency to do your brooding in private, please."

That brought laughter from Sisi, a frown from Anja.

"I'm sorry," Fass said, looking at them with the mild, confused
expression of a child woken from his nap. "Back it is, then."

"Back," Anja repeated. The word was bitter in her mouth.
Dizzi and Sisi would go to Salzburg, through the Salzkammergut,
and arrive at the sanctuary of the Scharner villa in Bad Ischl, the

elegant spa town where the Emperor Franz Josef and his Sisi had once held their summer court. She, instead, was going back a way she'd been relieved to put behind her.

Dizzi did not want to part. "Come with us to Ischl," he begged. "The old man's sure to've saved at least a few bottles of Krug in the cellar. The rascal probably even has hoarded tins of pâté and caviar. You'd be welcome, for as long as you'd like."

Fass was tempted. For an instant he thought they might winter there in comfort, and then move on in late spring, when the passes were free of snow. But he judged that the borders, still fairly open, would have stiffened and grown tight by then, like nearly healed wounds. And he was certain—from the unusual warmth of the summer and the mildness of the autumn so far—that the Brennerpass would be easy now, if they moved smartly. He knew his plan was sensible as any he could contrive, and he wanted to get on with it.

He put his hand on Dizzi's left shoulder, gripped it hard.

Wartime rules still, Fass thought. Obey them. Study well the faces of those you love. Remember well the exact feel of the hand clutching yours, the texture of the skin of that hand, the ache of the breaking of that touch. Record the glistening of an eye, the fleeting expression, the sweep of hair as a head bows. Note well the exact spot, the time of day, whatever scent may be in the air. Gaze long at the sky. Commit to heart the parting words, say all you have to say, holding nothing back. Embrace. Engrave every detail and sensation as deeply in your mind as you're able, for remembrance may be all that you have to sustain you later on. And never admit your desolation, but part with a jaunty wave and your brightest smile, as if nothing in the world could prevent you from being together again somewhere safe by the day after tomorrow.

Sisi, weeping, clutched Anja to her, the tall dark girl bending over the pale figure in drab battle dress.

Dizzi remembered the rules. He grinned at Walter, clapped him on the back. "Fass, you I love like a brother."

"I'll write you in Ischl as soon as we're settled. Maybe we'll train up for a visit, come spring," Walter said. He heard Sisi sob.

"I'll hunt you down if you don't," Dizzi laughed, wrapping his arms around Fass briefly, then releasing him. "You know I'm good at that, don't you, dear Walter?"

"Very, very good, my friend. One of the best I ever saw. But that's all over. Take good care of that pretty Magyar and go carefully in Ischl. Mustn't ever let your father suspect a thing."

"Oh," Dizzi laughed. "I think if I could fool those Prussian fatnecks running the army, I'll be able to keep a tiny secret from my old man. All the best, dear Walter. All the best."

He walked over to Anja and kissed her hand. Fass embraced a tearful Sisi. Then Walter and Anja stood watching awhile as the tall man and the graceful girl walked on down the highway verge, the man pushing a baby carriage, the very picture of a happy, handsome, privileged young couple out for a stroll with their first-born.

"Leni Riefenstahl," Fass said.

"What?" Anja said uneasily.

"The Führer's pet motion-picture director. Look at our friends there. She'd have loved them, loved this shot. The ideal couple in the new Germany, walking toward a brilliant future. She'd have made the most beautiful propaganda film around them—ten years ago."

"You're going mad, Fass," Anja said.

"I've been mad. I'm going sane," he said. He turned west in silence and fell into regular step. *Disziplin.* Anja was sullen beside him, ignoring the blisters the oversized British boots rubbed raw with every step. Mistrust and suspicion, flecked with anxious anger, quickened her pulse.

She understood the necessity. But going back, the very concept of it, broadened out in her mind from pure space into time, calling up an almost primal terror. One might go too far. Back to Krakow even, to the awful past and the terrible, short future she could expect there. She fought this as she always had, with lies repeated until they were truths. And she searched intently for signs that Fass harbored some sinister motive that threatened her; that this was no simple mistake.

A null. But her heart was pumping, ready for flight. She felt an almost irresistible urge to tell the engineer Fass to go to hell, and race after Dizzi and Sisi, though she had no better reason to trust them than him.

So she kept walking, now deliberately going deep into each stab of pain from her blistered feet, her right hand in her pocket, fingers locked around the identity card of Anna Fass, German citizen.

"And as for us? Where is our place, Walter?" Anja asked after some time, looking up into his eyes as if there she might see farther than this day's end.

"South," Fass said genially, pointing to where the snow-capped peaks of the Alps, just visible beyond the darkening hills, gave the horizon a jagged edge, like a saw.

"You said your uncle's farm. Not the mountains," Anja protested. "We'll freeze and die."

"Over the mountains, Anja. And into the sun," Walter smiled.

"*Dobrze,*" said Anja Wieniewska, a pale girl from Krakow slipping unaware but only for a moment into truth, into her pure Polish. "I hate snow."

XI

Anja broke on the Brenner.

The engineer Fass had taken a half-dozen labored steps through the deepening, powdery snow before he noticed his new wife was no longer beside him. He stopped instantly, and then for a moment felt the way he sometimes had in childhood dreams: He knew he must move, desperately tried to move, but remained, to his terror, completely paralyzed as whatever danger his sleep had conjured moved in on him. The snow—falling as thickly as any he'd ever seen, even in Russia—was dreamlike, too. He felt trapped in a pure-white room of unknown dimensions, grasped and enshrouded by vast, shifting sheets of gauze descending from a ceiling he could not see. "Anja!" he screamed into the smothering whiteness, but his loudest cry was so muffled it seemed to him he had merely spoken her name.

Then Fass, as if waking, found he could turn his head, twist his body, and lift his legs from the clutching snow. He forced himself to make a militarily precise about-turn, exactly one hundred eighty degrees; there was no other way to move and keep any orientation. His eyes traced each deep track he'd made, to the limit of his vision.

And there was Anja, or the ghost of Anja, an empty uniform already so coated with white he saw little more than than a few lumps of drab olive. A fallen soldier, motionless and silent, swiftly being given a temporary burial by the snow.

There was nothing dreamlike in the shift he suddenly felt in his head, the almost audible click. He saw himself, with perfect clarity, lying there like that in another snow, in other mountains, heard the hollow *whump* of mortar shells beginning their whistling arc and the crack of their bursting. He saw the snow turning deep crimson and melting all around his shredded left arm. He saw his Chetnik racing through those deadly fountains, saw the leather belt whipped off, felt it quickly wrapped around his arm just below the shoulder, felt the improvised tourniquet levered tight with a bayonet. "Leave him," he heard someone growl in Serbo-Croatian. There was the sharp snap of a Schmeisser being cocked. "He goes with us," he heard his Chetnik shout. Several pairs of hands grabbed his ankles, his belt, his right arm, lifting him from the snow. Then he was jolting down the mountain through the black forest, away from the mortar bursts, his left hand leaving a crimson streak in the snow like an artist's first brush-stroke on a freshly gessoed canvas.

Fass plunged back through his own tracks and dropped to his knees beside Anja. She was face down; he could see by the shuddering rise and fall of her back that she was breathing with difficulty. He grabbed the collar of her coat, roughly pulled and twisted her into a sitting position. No time to be gentle. Her head drooped loosely, chin touching chest. He kept tight hold of her collar, bent until his face was almost touching hers, and breathed hard, each warm exhalation blowing over her skin. Presently her eyes opened and she yawned hugely. Walter kept breathing on her face. She raised her head, her eyes seemed to focus.

"Freeze and die," she whispered.

"No," Fass said, suddenly rising but keeping his hand locked to her collar. He yanked her to her feet. "We've got to keep moving awhile, that's all."

"No, leave me," Anja moaned. "Don't want to walk anymore. Can't."

"You will walk, Anja. I'm going to help you as much as I can but you have to walk."

"Go to hell! That's where I'm going, once I sleep a little in the snow," Anja said. "Lovely soft snow."

"You hate snow, Pole," Fass growled as he carefully moved directly behind her, let go of her collar, and swiftly wrapped his arm around her chest, just below her breasts. He pulled her back to him as she began to slump. They stood swaying slightly, body pressed to body, his chin touching the top of her head.

"Move out now," he said in his command voice, the one military marvel that had impressed and stayed with him. They taught that voice in officers' training school, not just the correct words but the special way of saying them, the dispassionate yet steely tone that would compel instant obedience in young men, even move them to go forward under heavy enemy fire. Fass had mastered the voice, seen it work its magic, seen his boys rush forward, too many of them into violent collision with death. Now he was determined to send someone forward to life.

"You will put one foot in front of the other, again and again until I tell you to stop. I'm going to keep my arm around you and I will push you if you stop, yank you up if you begin to fall. You will walk. You will put one foot in front of the other. Move!"

Fass pushed against her back with his chest and Anja took a

step. He kept up the pressure, and she took another. And another and another. Each was steadier than the one before. "Bastard," she kept muttering. "Ruthless lying killer bastard."

"March!" Fass ordered. "You will march."

Into swirling snow covering everything equally: every rock, every bush, every fallen tree, every kilometer-marker stone, completely obscuring the twisting, switchback road they dared not wander off if they hoped to survive. Visibility was nearly nil. But in all Alpine passes, shortly after the end of summer, tall stakes painted bright red were driven into the ground every five meters or so just along the edges of the roads.

Fass steered Anya from stake to stake to stake. If they were lucky, they might come across a *Schutzhütte*. There'd be nothing else. They had passed through the last village near the border, Gries am Brenner, well before Anja collapsed.

"I hate you with all my heart," she spit as they marched, Fass both pushing her and keeping her upright with his arm tightly around her chest.

"Good for you. Hate me, little Pole. Curse me. You will still march," Fass said. Thank god, he thought, she's so small. And goddamn this rotten luck. No, not luck. Goddamn me.

❖ ❖ ❖

God had the right, he knew. It was, in fact, completely his fault they had come to this.

The autumn sun had warmed their faces when they'd started up the pass early that morning. The sky was cloudless, a deep lapis lazuli. White pennants were streaming north from the highest peaks where snow lay all year round. Fass had pointed them out to Anja as a rare and beautiful sight, had let the beauty of those plumes and the caress of the sun in the cold air blind him to what they portended. Storm winds from the south, spawned above the Lombardy plain and sweeping through the high Dolomites.

Within an hour an enormous mass of roiling gray clouds rolled up over the mountains like a wave and rapidly dropped, blotting out the sun. Soon the lowering sky delivered its promise: heavy rain beat down on them until their thick wool coats were sodden. Above a thousand meters the rain changed to snow, large wet flakes at first, then small crisp ones as the temperature dropped. The winds picked up as the storm funneled through the pass. Their pace slowed. Bending forward into driven snow, they trudged, blowing on their gloveless hands to keep them warm until they had no more breath to spare for anything but the climbing.

And Anja went down.

Now things were serious, not just miserably uncomfortable but dangerous. Fass made the hard admission that they might die on the pass. Go back? Gries was too far. They could only go up, hoping the storm would not worsen to the point where they could no longer see the next red stake.

But Fass did not know how much longer he could continue. He'd killed them. He began furiously barking the Wehrmacht parade marching cadence, more in rage at himself than to goad Anja, who was doggedly putting one foot in front of the other again and again. When he'd first gotten her back on her feet and moving, he counted the poles so he could estimate their progress, but lost track after two hundred twenty-three. Or was it two hundred forty-two? He couldn't remember. Say two hundred forty, five meters between them . . . that meant just over a kilometer. Not far enough. Fass shouted the cadence louder.

"Shut up! The fucking war's finished, you asshole!" a rough voice yelled from somewhere up ahead. Fass shook his head, then peered up the road. No one, nothing, just the next two or three markers. Now he was hearing things. Next he'd be seeing fairy castles made of crystal.

"And just what the hell do you think you're doing, skulking around on my pass?" the voice roared. No mistaking that. The sound of a Wehrmacht *Feldwebel* in full throat. Fass felt almost drunk with relief.

"My troops are coming to occupy the Brenner in the name of the Free Republic of the Tirol," Fass shouted madly at the falling snow in his command voice. "Lay down your weapons at once, and come forward with your hands on your heads, or we'll fire!"

"Fuck, go shoot yourself up the ass! Free Republic of my balls," the voice roared back. Proof! Ex-NCO for sure.

Now Fass quickened the pace, pressing Anja until she was almost stumbling. After they'd passed three more red poles, he saw the vague outline of a narrow, two-story stone building off to the left the road. But he could see no one through the obscuring snow.

"Machine gunners front! Bring up a *Panzerfaust*. Squads form for assault," Fass yelled at the top of his lungs. "Surrender now, and you will be treated fairly."

There was booming laughter up ahead somewhere. "Surrender what? Fuck your grandmother, you lunatic," the voice called. Then Fass saw a massive figure detach itself from the dark silhouette of the stone building and move to the middle of the road. Christ. A railway signalman. Who else would be up here? "You want my hut, come and get it. It's all yours. I'd like nothing better than to go off-duty and get my ass home, like any sane man."

As Walter and Anja slogged into clearer sight of the signalman, he exploded with mirth. "A pimp in an overcoat and some damn fool midget, walking around in this? Shouting all that army shit? Crazy assholes."

"You don't believe in the Free Republic of the Tirol?" Fass called jovially. "How will we ever occupy the Brenner if a Tiroler signalman won't even believe in us?"

"Ah, cut the crap and get into the hut before you die out here," the signalman said. "I'm Precht. And I don't want to hear any more of that military manure. Come on, come on. Get in, get warm."

The signalman shouldered open the wooden door of the rough stone hut and barged through. Fass steered Anja in, kicking the door shut behind him. All the windows were steamed over from the heat of a blazing wood stove. The signalman turned up a couple of oil lamps hanging from a ceiling beam, muttering and chuckling. "Lunatics, I get the lunatics."

Then he turned, and in the sharp yellow light from the lamps saw Anja weakly trying to shake the snow from her cornsilk hair. "Mother of God! It's a little girl," he said. "I don't know who the hell you are, mister, but you should be put against a wall and shot, dragging a little thing like that around in this weather.

"You, girl, get over here and sit," he said, grabbing a heavy wooden chair from its place at a table and easily swinging it to within a meter of the crackling stove. "I've got coffee—the real thing, not ersatz. You could use a cup, couldn't you? Poor little thing. You know this idiot? How'd you get into this fix?"

Anja collapsed into the chair, staring mutely at the broad-shouldered, thick-waisted signalman as he shrugged off his loden cape and came over to the stove. She gripped the proffered coffee cup with both hands for a while. Then she pressed it briefly against each cheek, sighed, and began to sip.

"You swine," the signalman began as he turned to Fass, bunching up his right fist.

"Not a little girl. I'm Fass and she's my wife," Walter managed. He was leaning against the door, lightheaded and wobbly-kneed.

Thin rivulets from the melting snow on his head began to meander down the sharp contours of his face. "We started off from near Steinach this morning, beautiful sunny day, and got caught in this."

"Your first Alpine holiday, is it? Storm signs all over the place and you missed them," Precht said. "And this kid's your wife? Horseshit."

"But it's true," Anja murmured. "We're married. We've got papers. We can show you."

"Don't talk like that," the signalman protested gently. Anja had the impression her words had somehow wounded him. "Do I look like an SD thug? I don't care about your papers. Here, Fass you said your name is? Sit by the fire."

Precht pushed a three-legged stool close to the stove with his foot. Then he poured another cup of coffee from the blue enameled pot and handed it to Walter.

"Now, I'm a little interested. Ex-officer—tell that by the way you shouted those orders—and your young *Frau* walking over the Brenner in a blizzard. Not something you see every day. Even officers aren't usually that dumb."

"You're right, Feldwebel," Fass grinned lamely.

"Christ, does that still show? Done my damnedest to get rid of the army stink," Precht replied. His small features were way out of scale with his body, and he had huge hands that seemed to have a life of their own: first brushing his coat, then fingering the brim of his cap, then caressing his fat chin. Finally they stuffed themselves into his pockets. He stared at Walter. "Just where did you think you were going?"

"Home," Fass said. "I'm a discharged POW taking my wife home."

"Could we take off our coats and boots, dry them a little?" Anja asked.

"Sure, lady. Sorry, should have thought of that myself. Here, give it to me." He took Anja's coat and hung it on one of a row of pegs sticking from a board nailed to the wall. Then he noticed Walter putting his cup on the floor before struggling out of his, noticed the dangling left sleeve. He snatched the overcoat and hung it next to Anja's. "Don't put the boots too close to the fire. The leather'll crack if they dry too fast. You warm enough?"

"I'm fine, thanks," Anja said. "You're very kind. You've saved us."

"Ah, what was I gonna do? Let a couple of lunatics die on my pass? Wouldn't look good." Precht chuckled. Then he turned to Walter again. "So, I'm interested. Where this home might be, I mean."

"Bozen," Fass said.

"Oh, shit," Precht said. "You might have saved yourself that stroll in the snow. Up at the border, you think they're going to let a couple of Germans, especially an ex–Wehrmacht officer, just walk into the Südtirol? 'Scuse me, the Alto Adige. Bolzano. Put an *a* or an *o* after a name that's been just fine for a couple of hundred years, and you change it from Austrian to Italian, poof!"

"One of the Duce's many brilliant ideas," Fass said. "Never mind that, oh, seventy percent of the people just go on speaking German, because their parents and grandparents and great-grandparents always did."

"He got his, that fat prick. Did you see the picture? The great Duce, strung up by the heels, his gut full of nice round bullet holes."

"It won't matter. The Italians are still Italians. Only difference now is they've got a republic and a big friend: America."

"The shits. It was the Tirol, and dammit, it still ought to be," the signalman said. "But the Italians in charge now, my friend, don't like Germans very much."

"I'm not a German," Fass said. Anja's head jerked toward him, eyes fixed on his face.

"I was born in Bozen," Fass went on. "My family always lived in Bozen. As a kid I saw the Italians take over. I was just five years old. It was exciting, all those troops in uniforms we'd never seen before, lots of cavalry clattering around the streets. You know how anything new is for kids. My father hated it. When I was older I understood why. But I'm going home anyway."

"If you're from Bozen, then why the Wehrmacht? I didn't have any choice, this side of the border, after that damned Anschluss business. You volunteer?" the signalman asked, his voice suddenly harder, suspicious. "Because I'll say it straight: No *Freiwilliger* trash stays under my roof, blizzard or no blizzard."

"Conscripted," Fass said. "I was studying in Berlin, just got my degree in May of '39. I'm an engineer. They took me right away."

"Fuck the luck—excuse me, lady," the signalman said, looking quickly at Anja. "On the other hand, if you'd been in Bozen the damned *Itaker* would have taken you. Screwed either way. You didn't serve in Italy, did you?"

"No. All over, but Yugoslavia mainly."

"That where the arm went? Worst luck in the world, you've got. I was in Italy the whole time. The first couple of years were like a big holiday, we didn't have to do shit. Then of course the Allies landed and the *Itaker* stabbed us in the back. It was rugged after '43, but at least the fighting was pretty clean with the Amis, the Brits, even that Polish division. The *Itaker* partisans were nothing much, not like I heard about the Yugos.

"You can believe almost anything you heard about that place," Fass said.

"Yeah," Precht said softly, pouring them all a little more coffee. "Tell you something really hilarious about Italy. When my unit surrendered, just over the border as a matter of fact, the Amis who took us were Japs! Imagine that! The Amis had Jap combat units. Meanwhile they're fighting a war with Japan. How in hell do you think they managed that? The Amis are a crazy bunch."

"I'd guess those troops were the sons of Japanese who had im-migrated to the U.S. before the war," Fass said. "A lot of the GIs I ran into were German, or at least their parents had been born in Germany."

"Yeah, reckon you're right. They sure looked funny, though. Little guys, they were. Their rifles and helmets all looked too big for them. You could've knocked me over with a feather, first time I saw them," the signalman said. "But hey, I'm blowing wind. Enough of this war shit. It's finished."

❊   ❊   ❊

Anja had been virtually insensible for longer than she could determine. But now, warming so rapidly her fingers were tin-gling and her face felt flushed, she was acutely aware of all that was going on around her. The coffee seemed to be racing through her veins, putting all her senses on alert.

Geography had never been one of her interests, and when Wal-ter had spoken of his plans, she'd assumed the fabled farm was in Austria. He had said the Tirol, and that was Austrian, wasn't it? An isolated place, protected by the mountains, untouched by the war, well out of the currents that had carried her so far. A perfect refuge.

Now he'd spoken of Italy. Italy was home? Anja felt a growing alarm. Suppose Walter's scheme was as aimlessly instinctive as her own continued frantic flight after she'd reached the safety of the British lines? Maybe Walter, too, was under some half-conscious compulsion to put as many kilometers between himself and his past as he could.

And now he was planning to take a risk she didn't care to run. Borders meant police, soldiers, questions. What if Walter got them embroiled with the authorities, what if their papers were called into question, what if they were sent to camps again, sent back not even to Sauerlach but somewhere deep in Germany, even the Russian Zone? Even, God, Poland itself? For their papers named Breslau and Stettin.

Once more she felt the impulse to tell the engineer to go to hell. She'd flee as fast as she could manage to Ischl, to Dizzi and Sisi. She was sure she could persuade the signalman to get her on a train going at least as far as Innsbruck, maybe even all the way to Salzburg.

"Tell you what," Precht said after a while. "You can doss down here until the pass is clear. This storm won't last, it's too early for anything really heavy. I can probably find some extra blankets, and you can sleep here by the stove. In a day or two you can take your shot at the border. Wish you luck on that, though."

"Thank you very much," Anja said quickly. "We've got some food, mostly GI rations, we can share with you."

"Oh, don't bother about that. I've got plenty stocked away here. They keep us pretty well supplied. You keep your stuff. You'll need it when you have to walk back down again."

Walk back down, Anja noted. No "if you have to." Just "when." He knows what the border is like better than Fass could. Jesus Christ.

All Anja could do now was think of the lies she'd tell to cut herself loose from Fass quickly and cleanly if it all went bad at the border. She could draw attention from herself by claiming Walter's papers were false, that he was really an SS man on the run, for instance. That she had learned this only after they'd been married, that he threatened to slit her throat while she slept if she ever revealed his secret. She could weep and wail again about the flight from Breslau, the rape by Tatars, her mother shot down before her.

But first she would have to see what Walter had up his sleeve. Then she laughed silently at herself, considering the unequal relationship the engineer had with sleeves.

For a night and a day at least, she would rest and eat and stay warm, gathering all the strength she could for what might come. Cold calculation displaced her rancor and distrust. But when she looked at Fass's worn, exhausted face, she felt only pity. That she could have such an emotion shocked her.

"Now, what do you say to something to eat? We've got some potatoes we can boil up, plenty of good cheese, and bread that was baked just yesterday," the signalman said, rising.

"No, you sit. I'll do it," Anja said. Walter, bent over on his stool with his arm across his legs acting as a pillow for his head, started snoring.

Anja woke him gently when she'd finished preparing the food and Precht had set the table. She found herself enjoying watching the big signalman almost as much as the hot meal. Precht carefully sliced a couple of potatoes into disks, which he arranged on his plate in a circular pattern. He put a piece of cheese on each disk. He sat for a moment, knife upright in one huge hand and fork upright in the other, watching the hot disks of potato melt the cheese a little. Only then did he begin to eat, and even that seemed to require a system. He started with the cheese-covered potato at the twelve-o'clock position on his plate and methodically worked his way around the circle, taking a bite of bread between each forkful. Anja and Walter simply wolfed down chunks of spuds, cheese and bread, raw hunger having precedence, as it always did, over manners or method. No one spoke. When he'd finished the orderly circumnavigation of his plate, the signalman abruptly belched, then put his huge hands over his mouth like a little boy, and muttered, " 'Scuse me."

Precht heaved himself up, collected the plates and the potato dish, rinsed them in a bucket of water near the stove and placed them in a wooden rack nailed to the stone wall. Next he disappeared into a little side room and emerged with four worn but heavy wool blankets, which he stacked tidily on his chair. He took a couple of the biggest logs from a stack near the door, opened the stove and shoved them into the mass of red coals still edged by flickering blue flames. The logs caught almost instantly, and the signalman pushed the stove door shut with his hobnailed boot.

"I'm for some sleep now," he said, stairs creaking under his weight as he climbed to the second floor. "You know, Fass, I still think you're some kind of lunatic, but that Free Republic of the Tirol is not such a bad idea. Not bad at all."

※　　※　　※

Anja woke to the aroma of coffee on the stove, and a distant clang of steel striking steel. Sunlight was refracted by the frost flowers on the windows, casting pretty patterns on the floor where she lay. She pulled on her thick socks but left her battle dress draped over the back of a chair where it had been drying all night, rose, wrapped herself in one of the blankets, and poured herself some coffee. Neither Walter nor the signalman was in the room.

Anja padded over to the window, sipping slowly. With the nail of her index finger she scraped an almost perfect circle in the frost flowers, the sun warm on her face. Across a double set of tracks, the signalman was chipping ice off the points of the siding with a sledgehammer. Walter stood to one side. She could see his mouth moving.

Why's Precht bothering? The sun would do that work. Already the long icicles hanging from the eaves of the hut were steadily dripping, each drop of water glittering like a crystal as it fell to the ground. The mountains were white, alarmingly steep and very close, but looking almost straight up she could see a deep blue sky overarching the snowy peaks. She felt cheerful in a way she'd no memory of having felt before. Even her fear of the border seemed to fade.

After lunch the three of them sat outside on a rough bench, faces raised to the sun, smoking and chatting. Precht had got a phone call from the border stop; the plows were out and the road would be passable before the end of the day. Even as they sat there one came down, its massive blade sending a cloud of snow flying off to settle in drifts that formed a waist-high wall along the road. Yesterday the snow had been malevolent. It seemed beautiful and benign now to Anja.

"It's not like this, in the north," she said.

"I've seen more days like this than I could count, ever since I was a kid," the signalman said. "The first clear day after a storm—I know I don't have the words for it, shit. It gives you a feeling in your heart. Ah, hell, you know what I mean. Sort of makes up for all the crap we go through."

"The altitude," Fass grinned. "Not enough oxygen for the brain. Causes delusions."

"Yeah, maybe that's it, though I don't know why, since I've lived at fifteen hundred meters all my life. Ought to be used to it, not like you flatlanders," the signalman laughed. "Crazy things go on in my head. I get soppy."

XII

The sun was not yet over the looming mountains when Walter and Anja said goodbye to the signalman the next morning. Precht seemed oddly shy, not at all the blustery ex-sergeant he'd been when they had appeared out of the storm. But after they rounded a switchback and were out of sight of the signalman's hut, Anja heard a very loud and very gruff "Fass, you lunatic! You'll answer to me if you don't take better care with the girl!" echoing up from below.

"*Jawohl!*" Walter shouted, not breaking stride. It was all Anja could do to keep a smile from spreading across her face. Thoughts were merely unspoken words, but she felt she lacked language subtle enough to describe the sensation this moment evoked within her. A fresh connection with the world, with that signalman? No, that seemed too banal, too vague and somehow too specific at the same time. She would have been a miserable philosopher, Anja decided.

A sort of buzzing began in her head then. She looked around and felt as if she had been dropped from space onto this spot: no road, no signalman, no storm, no camp, no Krakow behind her. No

birth, no childhood, no adolescence. No mother or father. No past
at all. And who was the one-armed man who walked beside her,
who suddenly stopped at the top of another switchback and stared
down a straight, level stretch of road? Who said, "There it is."

There is what?

Then Anja saw it, five hundred meters ahead. That wire—
spiky coils of it, lines of it taut from post to pole to pillar—blocking
the pass. Men in uniforms, rifles slung over their shoulders, stared
straight at her. She started to turn, pure reflex, but caught herself
as she saw Walter struggle out of his overcoat, take off his suit
jacket, turn it inside out, and slit the lining with his pocketknife.

Anja was baffled. But she felt perfectly clear about one thing.
"Fass," she said, her voice as remorseless as the storm that had
nearly ended them, "if there is any problem here, if I'm detained
or interned or sent back to Germany, I swear by the Holy Mother
of God I will kill you. Some day, some way I will find you again
and kill you."

▨   ▨   ▨

The border was manned by a mixed contingent of Allied
troops, Austrian *Grenzpolizei* and Italian border police. It was
not completely clear who was in charge, even to the various guards
themselves—except that it was not the Italians.

"Excellent," Fass whispered as their papers passed hand-to-
hand among the group of guards at the gate, came to rest with an
Austrian. "Pray he's a Tiroler."

Walter's POW discharge, his ID, her ID and their marriage certificate were printed in English and German. "So you've got papers," the Austrian said to Fass after reading each document.
"Fine. All is in order. But not for here. Go back to Germany. That's
where you belong."

"I'm not German. I'm Austrian. I'd like to go home," Fass replied.

"You're still in the wrong place, even if that was true. You know what this border is as well as I do. Turn around and head north," the Austrian guard said.

"I know it's a border that shouldn't exist, and on the other side is the Südtirol," Fass said.

The Austrian stiffened. Fass had counted on something like this. Even though none of the other guards appeared to understand German, a very delicate matter had been raised. Most Tirolers had never accepted the Italian annexation of the Tirol's southern region after the first war as either just or permanent.

"It's not for you or me to say anything about that," the Austrian murmured. "In any case, your papers state you are from Stettin. That would seem to make you a Prussian, not an Österreicher, let alone a Tiroler."

"See what this makes me, please," Fass said, handing the guard the paper rectangle he'd cut from the lining of his suitcoat. The Austrian slowly unfolded it. Anja saw it was very large, bore an embossed seal as well as the usual ink stamps, and was printed in the old Sütterlin script. She saw the guard's eyes widen a fraction at the sight of the black Habsburg double eagle dominating the top of the document, then narrow as he read. "Bozen," he said quietly. "You were born in Bozen on 9 October, 1913. I'd like to say welcome home to a fellow Tiroler, but this is a difficulty. I will have to get the officers."

"Naturally." Fass nodded. "I understand your position."

But Anja did not.

The Austrian turned to the American soldier. "*Moment, bitte.* Here we have problem," he said, his English obviously very newly acquired, holding up the large document. "Officers must see this."

"*Cosa c'è?*" The elegantly uniformed Italian raised his hands like a maestro acknowledging an ovation, but with a querulous expression on his face.

"*Un piccolo problema, Tenente,*" Fass said, dredging up from deep in his memory words he had stopped using when his father had taken the family from Bozen—no, it was Bolzano then—to Stettin in 1926. And inflating the man's rank by at least two grades, as was customary whenever one addressed an Italian official.

Anja grew more baffled, more agitated by the moment. They were at the Italian border. *Klar.* But Fass was claiming to be somehow Austrian and Italian at the same time, even speaking Italian. This was not clear. This was dangerous madness.

The GI strode over to the old customs house not twenty meters from the wire. The Austrian remained formal, unsmiling, but he offered Walter a cigarette, even lit it for him. Five minutes passed, perhaps ten. God, it seemed forever. Anja hated having so little idea what was happening.

"Major Schroeder," the GI called to the Austrian, gesturing back over his shoulder with his thumb. The Tiroler understood. He swung open the gate, motioned Fass and Anja to pass through, and led them to a large, high room in the customs house that was absolutely empty save for a single wooden bench, the sort found in railway stations. "Sit, please," he said. Then he disappeared behind a door at the far end of the room, taking all their papers with him.

"I warned you, Fass," Anja hissed. "What's the big paper?"

"Birth certificate," Walter whispered. "Now shut up. You can kill me later."

Eventually the Austrian reappeared and took them into a small room, where the American major named Schroeder and an Italian civilian official were sitting in cracked old leather armchairs. The Austrian guard saluted, then stood at ease. Major Schroeder looked up and studied Fass briefly, noted the empty sleeve without interest. He glanced at Anja, then turned his attention to the large document.

Finally, in good German, the major asked a single question: "Did you become a German citizen after you left Bozen for Stettin?"

"No, sir," Fass replied.

"That's all. Take them out," the major said to the Austrian, who ushered Walter and Anja through the door, closed it behind him. Sitting on the bench, the Austrian standing behind them but just beyond hearing, she began to tremble.

"My father never bothered about our family's Italian citizenship, as much as he detested the annexation, and Italy, when we moved to Stettin," Fass whispered to her. "It was something beneath his notice, just as being given it in the first place had been. By law, then, I am still Italian.

"They'll be phoning Bozen right now," he went on. "They'll be getting the birth document checked, they'll be looking for any record that my father renounced his citizenship when we went to Germany. They won't find one. But they will find that birth certificate of mine is genuine, and they'll also discover that the Fass family has lived there since at least the seventeenth century. They'll find that my uncle is a landowner, that my aunt is married to an Italian civil servant, that all the Fasses are *cittadini*."

"But you were in the Wehrmacht," Anja said.

"That cannot signify. After Italy surrendered and joined the Allies, the Wehrmacht conscripted boys all over northern Italy, some pure Italians who'd never been ten kilometers from the village where they were born, some ethnic Germans born well after the territory they lived in had been annexed. Gorizia, for instance. Trieste. Here in the Südtirol. The Wehrmacht didn't care that they were all Italian citizens. Legally, they've no way to keep me out."

"Legally?" Anja sneered. "Legally? What makes you think these people care any more about the rule of law than the Reich did?"

"If the Italians were running things, I would be worried. But I knew that the Südtirol had an Allied military governor. That American major will make the key decision."

"Suppose he hates Germans? They all hate us, don't they?"

"He's got the manner of a professional soldier. I've been around enough Americans to sense who is professional and who's a wartime temporary, I think. The professionals are as ruthless as any Wehrmacht professional. But the rulebook is God to them."

"So?"

"If he finds that my documents are genuine, he'll feel compelled to let us through, even if he'd personally rather take me behind the building and shoot me in the head with his .45. He's got his future career to worry about."

"Christ, Walter! You're counting on something as thin as that? We're nothing and nobody to them."

After a while Anja heard what seemed to be an argument break out in the office, though the sound was faint: a rapid, agitated burst of Italian followed by the slower, lower voice of the American major. Back and forth, back and forth.

They sat on the bench long after the voices in the office had subsided. Then, for Anja, things became a sort of waking dream, except for the sharpness of her fear. They were locked up for the night in holding cells in separate wings of the building, so they could not talk. Dinner was brought to her on a tin tray, food almost identical to what she was used to from the DP camp. Her cell contained nothing but a steel cot bolted to the floor, a single wooden chair and a chamber pot. As she lay on the cot, sleepless, every horrid deed she had done, every terrible consequence she could imagine came one by one and struck her, until she felt so badly beaten she could not hold on to the rage and hate for Fass she wanted so much to keep. Breakfast came, then hours more of dark apprehension. Finally the Austrian appeared, unlocked the cell door, and took her to the major's office. Walter was already there. She glowered at him, wanted to hit him. She was ready to scream, rant, weep, fall on the floor and beat her head against it; to deny all connection with Fass, to denounce him as a Nazi criminal. They were going to send her back to Germany, she was sure.

"Here's the situation, Captain Fass," she heard the major say. "In Bolzano they think the document is probably genuine. We want it checked out more. A lot more. We are giving you and your wife a temporary *permesso di soggiorno*, but we're sending you under escort to the military governor's office in Bolzano. You will register there, and report there at nine A.M. every day thereafter until the authenticity of your claim is confirmed or denied. You fail to appear even once, you will be arrested and jailed. *Klar?*"

"*Jawohl, Herr Major,*" Fass said, snapping a military salute. The major lazily returned it. Walter looked at Anja then, beginning to smile and expecting a smile back. But all he saw was a pale face that might have been a mask, and utterly empty eyes.

Anja did not seem to be present at all. Only someone who looked like her. Some doppelgänger.

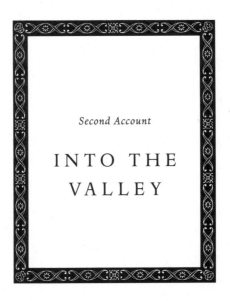

Second Account

INTO THE VALLEY

I

When the white shroud over the valley slipped away, unveiling a flourish of apple blossoms and budding vines, Anja the Liar was as pretty a milkmaid as any Sisi had pictured in her erotic fantasies. A genuine milkmaid—but Tirolerin, not Polish, not German.

Deluded little Magyar, Anja thought as she went about her tasks on the Fass farm, remembering the longing way Sisi used to look up at her from under her dark bangs in the DP barracks. Clearly Sisi had never been within ten meters of a working farm-girl in all her life, or she would never have dreamed of making love with one. Anja smiled at the notion. Pretty? Well, her bosom was enhanced by the low-cut, tight-bodiced dirndl dress hemmed just below the knee. The dress did show off a nice length of neck, and shapely calves, which unfortunately disappeared into thick woolen socks rolled above hobnailed boots not very different from her British army ones, except that these fit her properly. Add the stained canvas apron, though—not to mention the manure cling-ing to the boots and the inflamed fly bites on her forearms . . . Anja spat every time Walter passed by in the course of his own chores and insisted on calling her "fetching." Sisi could be forgiven her illusions, but Fass knew better.

She squatted for some hours each day on a one-legged stool of heavy pine, a tin bucket gripped between her knees, kneading the teats of cows that switched their tails irritably at the flies that swarmed around their anuses. She doubted she would ever get used to the creepy, repellent feel of those teats: rubbery but alive and pulsing. But it had been so much worse in the winter, when the cows were confined to the barn. She longed then for a war-surplus gas mask as she'd shoveled kilo after kilo of shit from each stall into a barrow, dumped the full barrow onto the huge pile of manure beside the barn, and then spread out fresh straw before she could even begin the milking. At least now, in the pasture, there were breezes redolent of the orchard, a warming sun on her shoulders.

And as for Sisi's romantic imaginings, what could be attractive about the aroma of manure mixed with curdled milk that seemed to cling to her skin, even after she'd scrubbed herself nearly raw in a bath as hot as she could bear?

Anja dumped her bucket of milk into the larger tin container on the sled, then walked across the sloping pasture to the last cow she had to attend to that day. The way the milk came in thin streams from those enormous udders had surprised her at first, until she considered they were designed by nature to be sucked slowly by the soft mouths of calves, not forced out by her squeezing fingers.

Now she thought of her own small breasts, swelling already, a delicate tracery of the palest blue veins just visible close beneath her white skin. By early autumn, there would be a soft mouth on her nipples, the tiny toothless mouth of an infant. She slipped frequently into reveries about the life growing inside her, placed a hand protectively over her belly whenever anyone or anything passed close to her—the instinctive, universal gesture of impending motherhood.

So far no one had noticed.

God, what a disaster. As each day grew a degree or two of arc longer, her time of grace shortened. How in the world, Anja wondered, was she going to tell Walter she was pregnant?

⊠ ⊠ ⊠

That one damn night.

As much as she wanted to blame Fass, she knew it was entirely her fault. She had seen the warning signs within a month of their arrival at the farm, as soon as they'd been rested and well fed and begun to have the lovely feeling that they were finally safe: Fass wanted her. She was not displeased. She even felt a slight attraction to him as well, or at least a curiosity, and enjoyed gently parrying his subtle advances. But—and this surprised her greatly—Fass never pressed her. He simply let her see, with some charm and grace, that he now found her pretty and desirable, that he'd be delighted if she ever chose to change the terms of their contract. That's what had beaten her. Anja cursed herself. That one time, in triumph over all probability, had created what she least wanted now. And the poor innocent infant's very existence, she feared, might take away almost everything she had gained.

It was probably what she deserved, Anja felt. She had been an insufferable brat when they first arrived in Bozen, she recalled as she finished with the cow, straining to lift the heavy pail and the splintery stool, then moving down the pasture to the sled. Withdrawn, at the beginning, then sulky, ill-tempered Anja, vexing poor Walter about it all: the hated snow, the need to abandon her deliciously warm eiderdown long before dawn on freezing mornings and face that awful stinking barn, even the unfailing kindness of his family, which felt more a burden than a gift. She could not admit how undeserving she felt, how lonely and afraid she was. She could not let go of her camp defenses, dodging all questions and too insistently repeating her old story. Walter understood. She never imagined he would be so sensitive to her inner currents. Yet how else to explain his patience with her, the clever ways he screened her tantrums from his uncle Franz, his cousin Liese and her husband Sepp, when they all lived in such close quarters?

He understood too the transparent moves she made to transform herself into a Tirolerin. She softened her North German, added local dialect words and phrases to her conversations as rapidly as she learned them. She immediately began to say *"Grüss Gott"* whenever she encountered anyone, instead of *"Guten Morgen."* She studied the conventions of the place: what the women wore, how they behaved with one another, how they acted when men were about, what could be said and what should not. She went carefully in all that she did, anxious not to become more of an object of gossip than she already was as the prodigal Walter's Prussian.

The only thing Fass missed was something much deeper, something unplanned and so contrary Anja felt she could never truly fathom it. All alone, shivering in that stinking barn with the cows well before dawn, she began to counterattack Krakow time by bringing it back as clearly as she could. The impulse seemed to come from a question Walter asked her about his own past.

It had been Advent Eve—not that it mattered to her. The most brilliant full moon lit up the snowbound valley and the mountains round about in a way that seemed more like an illustration from a beautifully imagined children's book than anything nature could contrive. She'd never seen so strange and wonderful a brightness. She stood outside the barn after the evening milking, transfixed, until Walter called her to come to dinner.

"We're going sledding," Walter announced after the meal,

bundling her like a child into a heavy loden coat, pulling woolen mittens onto her hands, wrapping a long woolen scarf round her neck, and taking her outside. He fetched a small wooden sleigh from one of the sheds, and led her through the orchard, up the vineyard slope, and finally up the steep pasture, a vast expanse of snow dominated by an enormous ancient beech with bark gray and smooth as steel, except around the base, where generations of Fasses had carved their initials, or their names and the names of their sweethearts, each inscription dated. It was so bright she could read them; she saw *Ernst + Annamarie, 1824,* maybe the first one, and dozens more, and then *W.F., 1925,* possibly the last. There was a weathered wooden bench beneath the tree, and not far away, a water trough carved from a single huge log, now covered with ice that gleamed like silver.

"Been sledding before, haven't you?" Walter asked as he turned the little sleigh to face downhill. They were at least three hundred meters above the vineyard, the brightness was dazzling, the beech cast an amazingly distinct shadow on the snow.

"No," Anja said.

"Haven't done this myself since I was twelve. You're going to love it." Walter seemed as excited as the boy he had been then. She sat on the sleigh, her legs bent up until her thighs were almost touching her chest. Walter slipped down behind her, his legs extended along the edges of the sleigh on either side of her. Then he pushed off with a great whoop of joy and they were gliding down the hill faster than Anja imagined possible, the only sound the hiss of the runners against the snow and the air rushing past her ears. It was a magical feeling, moving so swiftly and silently in that incredible unearthly light.

She told herself it was ridiculous that she thought "never before" about so many things, ever since they had made it over the Brennerpass. She ordered herself to stop exaggerating the importance of small things. It was not as if she'd been reborn, not as if she was a child again, full of wonder. It was certainly not as if she had regained any innocence.

They made the run twice more, then sat on the bench under the beech smoking and gazing out over the valley. They were silent for a long while. Anja didn't feel the cold. Then Walter started talking about his boyhood. He had lived in an apartment in the city with his mother and father, but his greatest delight was the time he spent at the farm. The seasons and the weather, fair or foul, never mattered to him at all. There was always life in the orchards, the vineyards, the pasture, the barn, always something new to see or do, and always his uncle, patiently explaining how he grafted grapevines, how to prune the apple trees properly, how the cows must be cared for. His parents let him spend every summer on the farm.

The first real sadness he ever felt in his life came on the day they left for Stettin, when he realized he might not see the farm again.

"I was in Stettin from the age of thirteen until I went to Berlin at nineteen to study. Six years. And for some mystifying reason I don't remember a single moment of that time," he said. "No matter how hard I try, no matter how much I want to, I can't recall a thing—except the street Polish I picked up. I know I must have gone to school, had classmates and friends. But I cannot name one, or see a face in my mind, or remember anything we did. I can't remember a thing my father said to me, a single family outing or occasion. I have no idea what street we lived on, what my mother liked to make for dinner, how I decorated my room. I can't even recall why I decided to study engineering. It's all a void.

"Because it was an unhappy time? Can't be that. I remember very clearly all the details of wartime, after all. But I have no sense at all whether Stettin was good or bad. It just isn't there.

"You're the philosopher, Anja, so tell me this: If we're the sum of everything we've seen, heard, said and done since childhood, what happens if a part of your life is a blank? I breathe, my heart beats, my blood carries oxygen to my brain, I think and I speak and I work. But there are six crucial years missing, years when my character must have been forming. So can I ever understand myself? Am I whole in this world?"

Anja had no answer that night. But alone in the barn the following dawn, a sort of answer came to her. Walter's lost six years were, in a way, more of a handicap than his missing arm. He was not whole in the world. And neither was she. The difference was that Walter hadn't caused either of his losses. But she had deliberately tried to amputate part of her life. She'd fought hard, still was fighting to cut off Krakow time. Yet those years were not gone. The memories could still slip past her main line of resistance and overrun her consciousness.

She was fighting, she suddenly realized, a battle that could never end, never be won. And it was draining her, keeping her from being truly alive in the present. She decided she wanted to live right now, intensely and completely. She would not let her past destroy her. She might be crippled, but she would not be obliterated.

She felt so strong at that moment. And after, though the feeling of strength waned, she willingly brought Krakow back into her mind, to face and endure the pain, and then leave it, feeling not cleansed—for she could never be—but lightened a little, the way she had felt as a girl after confession.

She started with the first, the easiest of her crimes: She'd learned, in the winter of '39, of a young Polish officer hiding as a civilian in Krakow to avoid being sent to a POW camp. She gave the details to Richter. Soon enough the young officer vanished. She had no idea whether he survived the KZ he must have been sent to. Then a thought intruded: What did it matter? If the Germans hadn't got him, he would have been shot in the Katyn Forest by the Russians anyway, like so many thousands of Polish officers. His death was not on her hands, if he was dead.

Instantly she realized Anja the Liar was not going to let go easily; she would have to be beaten down, trampled, destroyed. "I swear before God," Anja cried loudly, with only the placid, heedless cows for witnesses, "that the officer's death was my fault. I killed him. I am responsible."

That was the first punishing step. Every one thereafter was torturous. In those frigid dawns, she admitted to the cows how she gave Richter the names of three Communist organizers, who swiftly disappeared into the Germans' night and fog. How she became friendly with a railwayman, who revealed in confidence that he and a dozen others were sabotaging switches on the line from Krakow to Warsaw, and betrayed them all to Richter. It was easy enough, she told the cows. Easy enough, because she never had to witness what happened to her victims. But she crushed all the rationalizations, all the excuses. She compelled herself to confess and then mourn each of her many crimes and losses. She wept over the parents she would never see again, begged forgiveness from them and all the others she betrayed, all those who died by her words.

Bit by bit, she began to believe she was closing suppurating wounds; the scars would be ugly, she knew. But she would no longer be rotting slowly from the inside out. Maybe it wasn't too late after all.

※   ※   ※

And now, on days when the light had a certain gentle quality and the rugged mountains seemed unforbidding and the fields and orchards and vineyards almost glowed with life, days when Uncle Franz smiled on her and Liese was kind, she felt a sort of rightness she had not imagined she could feel.

She would stay tart and sassy with Walter Fass, though. She'd be damned if she would ever let him know any of this, or how her hollow heart was slowly filling with an emotion for him far greater than the one she had the best of reasons to feel: gratitude. For it had been the heavy paper rectangle that Walter slipped from his mutilated jacket on the Brennerpass that had brought her to this safe place, and his strange question under the Advent moon that started her on this hard but good path.

Then came the baby in her belly, this fiasco of a pregnancy. She might have known things were going too well to last. Anja sighed, carefully guiding the sled loaded with a heavy, sloshing container down toward the milk shed near the barn.

Bless this hideous apron, Anja thought some weeks later, on the morning when she found she could no longer fasten the bottom two buttons of her bodice. She still had not gathered the courage to tell Fass, though she knew she must. Expert as she was at deception, there was no way to hide a fact that would soon become so physically obvious. Even a dim-visioned old man like Uncle Franz would be able to see it and smile knowingly at her. Liese was probably speculating already. She must tell him. Or else disappear in the night, running away to God knew where.

Later that day Walter joined her as she rested on the bench under the giant beech, the spot that had become her favorite among all the pretty, peaceful places on the farm. Laughing, he handed her a letter scrawled on thick creamy paper with deckled edges, the sort of sumptuous stationery she hadn't seen since the war started.

Fass, you bastard, your shocking news has ruined my life. And after all I've done for you! Sisi and I had a quite delightful *rapprochement* almost at once here in Ischl. It was even more perfect than I'd hoped. Not only did the old man fall immediately head over heels for her, but, my extremely idiotic ex-friend, the little minx only goes for girls. Not a single awkward moment between us. We were like brother and sister. We loved to gossip to each other about our trysts and conquests. Then you destroy it all with a word!

Ever since Sisi learned Anja is with child, my life has been hellish. Right away she began mooning about in the oddest way. Soon she was going so far as to croon at babies she passed in the park. Then she began murmuring about how lovely it would be to have a baby of her own. The final blow came this morning, when she asked me in her sweetest, most seductive voice—the one she only uses on pretty young girls—if I wouldn't like to be a father.

I felt as if I'd been shot in the stomach!

It was your finger on the trigger, traitor Fass! I insist that you report to Ischl within the month and make the girl pregnant. Sisi probably won't enjoy the required act and neither will you—in fact it would be a great injustice if you did have any fun with her. But you are under grave obligation. Your honor as an officer is at stake. Remember, Fass, that you became responsible for putting me in this untenable position when you begged me to do you the favor of visiting that dreadful DP camp because my presence, you said, would help you ingratiate yourself with Anja.

Your duty is clear. I shall expect your arrival in Ischl presently.

Scharner

Walter was nearly quaking with mirth as Anja finished and looked up at him. She felt faint. "Why the hell are you laughing?" she demanded. "And how did you know?"

"It is fairly obvious, Anja," Walter said, gaining control with some difficulty.

"It is not. I'm not yet four months gone. I haven't even gained any weight. It doesn't show at all."

"Not like it will a few months from now, naturally," Walter said. "But there've been all sorts of subtle signs. You've been walking a bit differently, your posture's changed slightly, you make that little gesture with your hand on your belly. Your breasts are slightly larger. And you've been throwing up a lot, though you've tried very hard to hide that."

"Christ, Fass! How dare you spy on me like that! What do you do all day, just study me, stare at me? Am I a bug under a microscope? Haven't I any privacy at all? How would you know my breasts are growing? Do you peek through the keyhole when I take a bath?"

"Of course not." Walter was unable to stifle his chuckling. "But I do see you in your nightgown every evening. It hangs a little differently now. You—forgive me—looked rather like a boy before."

Anja scowled.

"As for the rest, just casual observations. None of it really registered until I connected it with hearing you retch in the mornings. The walls are only pine planks, you know. I'm sure you've heard me fart in the toilet."

Anja laughed despite herself. They were, it was true, barracks mates. They had been given a large room on the top floor of Uncle Franz's house, under the eaves. The walls were paneled in knotty pine, old and polished smooth as glass. There were two ancient armoires painted with floral designs, two plump feather beds pushed together, which was the Austrian way. Walter had shoved the beds a couple of meters apart, and created a little dressing room by hanging some sheets of thick linen from the roofbeams in one corner, so they could disrobe in privacy. It had all been fine with Anja. She knew separate rooms were out of the question; it would have seemed outlandish to Walter's family, caused all sorts of trouble.

The only trouble at all since they had come to the farm was that one night she now wanted to erase from time, but never could because of the shockingly improbable result. New Year's Eve, a crowd of neighbors and friends at the house, Uncle Franz the ebullient host urging everyone on, much too much to drink. Then Anja forgetting herself entirely, pulling her nightgown over her head, and leaping, naked and giggling, into Walter's bed. It had been, to her surprise and delight, great fun. Not transporting, not ecstatic, but the only time she had enjoyed being with a man. In Krakow she had always felt like a toy.

Despite that, the morning after had been hell. She felt shy and vulnerable in a way she was not prepared to deal with. She actually burst into tears when Walter caressed and kissed her awake. Fass was the first man she had ever slept with because she wanted to, because she cared for him. That in itself frightened her into the ludicrous posture of pretending she had been too drunk to know what had happened.

Walter humored her, and patiently remained her barracks mate. Never referring to their intimate encounter, never suggesting they repeat it. If he felt hurt or rejected, he kept it carefully hidden.

On his good days. On his good days, like this one, he was playful and flirtatious in ways designed to signal that he cared for her and wanted her still. He would be there if ever she wanted him.

But she seemed not to exist for him on those black days which had, unaccountably, swept over Fass more frequently even as life on the farm grew more settled and comfortable. No one existed for him on those days. He'd withdraw into himself so deeply that Anja was sure he did not know how sullen and ominous he seemed, like the towering thunderheads that sometimes massed in the sky over the valley, threatening a violent storm.

If you spoke to him on a black day, he would start, like a man who had been suddenly awakened, confused rather than angry. Franz and Liese and Sepp went softly around Walter on the black days. "The war," Franz murmured sadly to Anja once, seeing Walter wandering oblivious and without purpose through the orchard. As if those two words explained everything.

Yes, the war.

Fass was sunny enough before her now. He even seemed genuinely pleased by her condition. But Anja feared this pregnancy was no small matter. How could they ever maintain the equilibrium they'd established once they were parents of a child? It seemed to her far too momentous a thing not to overwhelm the barracks-mate camaraderie that had suited them quite well, so far. How would he deal with it when the darkness came on him? Could the partnership they had started with—the arrangement that had no provision for sex, let alone a child—change into a real marriage?

And already something very wrong was twisting her. Resentment toward Walter. Blame. He should have seen how drunk she was on New Year's Eve, should have thrown her out of his bed. He never should have done it to her, the bastard. How on earth could they stay together and raise the child they'd made by drunken accident?

The worst of it was the uncertainty; she simply had no answers to these questions. She felt only that a difficult complication was heading her way. It was inexcusable, blaming Fass, she knew. But she could not seem to help it. She was beginning to hate him. And that was the last thing she had the right to do.

But thank God for Walter's carefully folded, zealously guarded piece of paper, Anja thought as Fass patted her gently on the head and strolled down the pasture whistling "Für Elise," Dizzi's crazed letter fluttering in his hand. She still shivered when she thought of how close a thing it had been, on the Brenner.

III

Anja remained under the beech long after Fass was out of sight, stroking the smooth bark as if some of the majestic tree's serenity might rub off on her and ease the unease Walter left in his wake. It did not work. She plunged back into the memory of the day the American major had sent them under guard from the border to the military governor's office in Bozen, where they were registered, fingerprinted, photographed and abruptly released.

It was difficult at first to bring into sharp focus, but she recalled they had hiked three or four kilometers from the governor's office up the massif that rose northeast of Bozen. She was tired, apprehensive and a little unbelieving of where she was and what she was about to do: begin the charade of being Walter's loving wife before his family. Dusk was deepening into full night when they reached the farm. Walter rapped sharply on the massive pine door, and soon a tall, white-haired old man, taller than Walter and more heavily built, stood before them. She could not make out his features very clearly; all the light was coming from the room behind him.

"Uncle Franz?" Walter said.

"Fass, Franz. Correct," the figure in the doorway replied crisply. "But I think you are mistaken in this 'uncle' business."

"Have I changed so much? I'm Walter."

The old man took half a step back, then rushed forward, grasped Walter's shoulders and pulled him into the room so he could see him in the light.

"My God!" he cried. "Walter? Walter? This isn't possible. Twenty years, the damned war. I thought all of you were gone forever, it's been so long since I've had a letter. Oh, Walter, my God. This is too wonderful to understand."

He moved to lift Walter up, but must have felt the empty sleeve. So he hugged his nephew to him, and cried, patting Walter on the back as if it were Walter who was weeping and in need of consolation. "Liese! Liese, come quickly," he shouted. "Our Walter's home from the war."

A woman in her late twenties with blond hair done in braids came into the entranceway, accompanied by a muscular man a little shorter than herself who had a napkin tucked into his shirt collar and a fork in his hand. There were introductions: Liese, Walter's cousin, and her husband, Sepp. Uncle Franz beamed down on Anja, took both her hands in his and kissed her on both cheeks. Then they were swept into the kitchen, where two more places were quickly set at the table. Food was steaming before her, and there was a baffling rush of talk about matters she could not understand, punctuated by Uncle Franz's exuberant exclamations of "My God! This is too wonderful to be true!" every time he placed his hand on Fass's shoulder as if to reassure himself that the haggard, one-armed man seated next him was really his Walter returned at last.

There was only one somber note, when Walter asked if Franz had heard from his parents.

"Not a word for a long time," the old man replied, frowning.

"But I'm hoping it's only because there's still such confusion, and they're in the Soviet Zone. I don't guess, from what I've heard, that you can simply walk into a post office in Stettin, send a letter off to the West, and expect to have it delivered. I'd guess the Red Army has a lot on its hands, and doesn't give a damn about German civilian mail anyway."

"I sent a postcard from the hospital in Zell am See last April, but never heard back," Walter said. "When did you last hear from them?"

"January '45," Franz replied. "I've sent a letter every two weeks since. Once, in August, I got one of mine back with a Passau postmark, stamped 'Unable to Deliver.' The rest? Nothing. The letters just disappeared."

Many bottles of crisp white wine later, when Anja felt she might simply keel over from exhaustion, she and Walter were taken to the big room where they had been barracks mates ever since.

It had been more of the same at breakfast the morning after their arrival. Anja felt dazed, and must have looked it, for after they'd finished eating Walter had very gently detached them, telling his uncle he couldn't wait another moment to revisit all the haunts and hideaways of his childhood, to see his name on the beech, to show Anja the place he had told her, he lied, so much about.

The Fass lands, which had been in the family for six or seven generations, were lovely, though as a city girl Anja had no deeper feeling for what she was seeing. The farm was well above the city, not far from a tiny, tidy village called Wolfsgruben. The house was massive in the Alpine style, all dark wood with a balcony running around the second floor, the railing topped with long planters of red geraniums, and lots of fretwork along the eaves of the steeply pitched roof. It was set back a few hundred meters from the road, and the flat hectares around it were crowded with orderly rows of apple trees. Then came many hectares of stony slope, planted with grapevines. Next was pasture, rising sharply to the huge beech, then leveling out for some way until it met a fir forest. Beyond the treeline was the bare crown of a mountain Walter called the Rittner Horn.

None of the family—not Franz, nor Liese, nor Sepp—ever suggested by word or gesture that she or Walter should work, but Walter immediately pitched in, doing as much as he could with his good arm. And after some lessons from Liese, Anja took over the care of the dozen cows. The main businesses of the farm were apples and wine.

One couldn't have asked for better, despite her obligation to that stinking barn. Which made her early behavior seem all the more despicable to her now. And the difficulty she was facing almost heartbreaking.

▨   ▨   ▨

A couple of nights after Walter had revealed under the tree that he knew Anja's secret, he padded over to her bed in robe and pyjamas. She was snug under the eiderdown, reading "Tonio Kröger." She cringed when she realized he was standing right next to her, afraid that some moment of truth was imminent, and that it would be unpleasant. But he simply handed her a piece of paper, and then stepped back into his own zone a few meters away.

She read:

My dear Scharner,

If I were fit for duty, I would report to Ischl immediately, as yours of the 19th requested. I say requested because it could not have been the order it sounded, for of course I outrank you.

I regret to inform you that such a journey would be futile.

Wounds sustained in combat have left me incapable of the actions you require. Anja was and is a virgin, pure as snow. She
does remember having an almost preternaturally vivid dream
of a sexual nature, however. Based on these facts, we consider
that there has been an immaculate conception. Which is not
without precedent as you know, though it does seem to be very
rare.

I should note that we have on the farm a strapping boy of
twenty out for stud. His success rate with women of Bozen
whose husbands have purchased his services is almost a hundred percent. The fee is modest. In your woman's case, we
would of course waive the usual fee entirely. After all, friendship has no price, and old comrades should stick together.

Please advise at your convenience when we can expect Sisi
to arrive in Bozen, so that we may schedule the covering.

Yours, Fass

Anja shrieked, crushed the paper into a ball and flung it as hard
as she could at Walter, who laughed as it bounced off his groin.

"You're pigs, the both of you," she snarled. "How dare you
speak of Sisi as if she were a mare? You disgust me. This is no joke.
If she's serious about having a child, she'll have no trouble finding
someone if Scharner refuses. But what then? Suppose he won't recognize the child, or give it his name? What if he boots Sisi out?
Where will she go, what will she do? Her life is about to be ruined
and you're making jokes?"

"I've had a head wound, it's left me a little deranged," Walter
said, unperturbed. "Isn't that what you said to me a lifetime ago, in
a certain place when I was speaking a language you preferred not
to hear?"

"You go straight to hell, you supercilious bastard. Your irony
stinks."

"Ah, Anja, such a state you're in over nothing. Expectant mothers are frequently known to experience violent emotional upheavals."

"I'll show you violence," Anja said, starting to rise from her bed but stopping midway to clutch her stomach. "Oh God, it's moving. It's moving!"

"Splendid!" Walter said merrily. He was a bit too merry too many nights now, in Anja's view. Franz was generous with his wine and beer, and Walter seldom said no to one more glass of whatever was offered. "Listen to me, Anja. Scharner will either do his duty, or find someone he considers a suitable substitute. He will never risk losing Sisi. She's much too important to him. And I suspect, though he may not enjoy creating a child, he'll take great pleasure in being a father. I know I'm going to."

"What?" Anja snapped. "This is going to ruin us. Oh God, it's kicking me."

"Let me feel," Walter said.

"No!" Anja shouted, recoiling. "Don't you come any closer."

"Oh, Anja," Walter said mildly. "Nothing's going to ruin us. Does it matter there was never a grand passion? We enjoy each other, don't we?"

"Maybe," Anja allowed. Walter laughed.

"Well, I enjoy you at least. And I'm prepared to be as fine a father as I'm able. There isn't another woman I'd rather bear my child. Do you believe me?"

"No, I do not."

"We started unconventionally, certainly. But it'll be unworkable only if you make it so. I'm determined to keep our bargain. Do I need to remind you that I've been scrupulous, that I have never even tried to kiss you without your permission?"

Anja felt defeated. He was right about that, at least.

And he was offering her and the baby a life, just as Franz had offered them a home, without reservation.

"Anja," Walter went on gently, removing his robe and getting into his bed. "Nature will take its course. I will never go back on my promise. If you choose to leave, I will put no obstacle in your path.

"But Anja," he said, turning out the bedside light, "it would make me very happy if you and the baby would stay with me."

No, dammit, he's a goddamn liar, Anja thought, throwing her book to the floor and switching off her own light. He had trapped her, like Sepp trapped rabbits in a snare. She felt tears running down her cheeks but willed herself silent so Walter wouldn't know. She wanted no comforting words from him. Not when she felt on the verge of a dream that Walter Fass might be the man of her life.

IV

Every Tuesday in that first spring of peacetime, the engineer Walter Fass rose early, shaved as cleanly as he could, put on a white shirt, a blue tie and the charcoal-gray suit Uncle Franz had lent him the money to have made by an Italian tailor in Bolzano. He did not bother to pin up the left sleeve.

Then he walked down to Wolfsgruben, arrriving moments before the ancient, wheezing bus. He said *"Buon giorno"* to the driver as he dropped a coin in the fare box. The driver was always the lone Italian on the bus. As he sought a seat, Fass nodded and said *"Grüss Gott"* to anyone he recognized, Tirolers who had boarded earlier on the route along the Tafler Valley and over the shoulder of the Rittner Horn on the way to the city.

From the terminus near the Bahnhof, Fass walked across the cobbled square to a small café, settled at a table, ordered a coffee and a Faschingskrapfen. He read the morning editions of both the German- and Italian-language newspapers, ordered a second coffee, downed a glass of grappa, smoked a cigarette. He left a few coins on the table and headed out into Bolzano, searching for work.

He had started at the most obvious place: the municipal building. The first time he'd gone there, hoping to speak with the official in charge of repairing and reconstructing bomb-blasted city buildings, he hadn't gotten past a self-important young secretary who pretended to have trouble understanding his heavily accented Italian just for the mean amusement of forcing him to repeat himself. And in the end she said, *"Ma no, Signore! È impossibile,"* informing Walter that the exalted man was available to supplicants by appointment only. Fass had been able to obtain one: for five weeks from the day, so busy were the exalted in Italy. Busy going home for four-hour lunches and naps every afternoon.

Fass spent the following Tuesdays calling at private construction companies. All were Italian-owned, but not all employed snotty young women as gatekeepers. At least two of the owners, men who worked with their shirtsleeves rolled up and didn't mind mixing a little of their accented German with his creaky Italian in conversation, seemed intrigued by his claimed credentials and his experience, but threw up their hands in dismay at Walter's inability to produce proof that he was a certified engineer.

On the sixth Tuesday, Walter arrived at the *municipio* fifteen minutes before his scheduled appointment. The secretary affected not to recognize him, searching her daybook for his name, asking him twice to repeat it. *"Ah, sì,"* she said at last, inviting him to sit in the waiting room. She then behaved as if he did not exist, making a couple of personal phone calls, checking her makeup in the mirror of her compact, rummaging through her purse, then applying a layer of lipstick over layers that were still moist and thick.

No one entered or left the exalted man's office during the hour and eleven minutes that Fass waited. When Walter was at last summoned in, the exalted one looked up briefly from the single sheet of paper on his enormous oak desk. He did not invite Walter to sit, but continued studying the paper while the engineer explained his credentials.

"We have no jobs," the exalted one said when he finished. *"Addio."*

Now Fass understood Dizzi's belief that some people were only things. As he walked across the square toward the Bahnhof and the bus terminus, he felt he could shoot that man in the head as casually as he'd shoot a paper target. The Italian regime may have changed radically at the theoretical level, but the Italian attitudes that had permitted a man like the Duce to rise and rule had not.

It would be some time before the next bus back to Wolfsgruben, so Fass kept walking. Near the freightyards he watched engines shuttling cars and carriages back and forth with no apparent pattern or purpose. Workmen heaped twisted rails haphazardly across the yard; others spiked new ones onto lines of sleepers that seemed impossibly out of true with the switches they were supposed to connect. Large bomb craters, left unfilled, had turned to stagnant ponds. Italians, Fass thought. No wonder his father had sold his shoe factory and moved out of here.

Just across the street from the yard was a squat concrete building stained dark beneath the leaky joints of rain gutters no one had bothered to repair. Another *Itaker*, Fass thought, reading the small sign beside the door of the building: G. PETROCELLI, CONSTRUCTION. He pushed the door open anyway and found himself in a large room with four or five desks, a chaos of ashtrays brimming with butts, empty coffee cups, creased rolls of blueprints, tottering stacks of file folders. There was no one about except a burly, balding man who hadn't shaved in a couple of days.

"I'm Petrocelli," the man said, walking over to Fass. "What do you want?"

"Fass, Walter," the engineer replied. "I want a job."

"Sure, how'd you like to be my new managing director?" Petrocelli replied in rough, blunt German. "Just a joke. Come on, sit down and we'll talk."

Petrocelli looked steadily into Walter's eyes as the engineer told his story. Then he leaned back in his swivel chair and locked his hands behind his head.

"Listen, my friend," he said. "As you can see, all around town there is more work for engineers and builders than there are engineers and builders to do it. Jesus, even incompetent fools like Balducci—have you been to see that ass yet?—have more government contracts than they can handle. Factories, bridges, housing—the bombing was the best thing that ever happened here for business, if you don't mind my being coarse about it. I could use a couple of seasoned engineers.

"But the law is the law, even when you slip lire notes with the right number of zeroes on them into the right hands. Unless you're certified, *niente*. I could go to jail for using an uncertified engineer.

"I advise you to improve your Italian, which is pretty damn rusty, and take the certification exam. For a doctor from the Technical University of Berlin, with your practical experience . . . hell, you'd laugh your way through it. But"—he shrugged—"the exam's only in Italian, and only given once a year.

"Tell you what, though. Show me that diploma and I'll make you a site foreman on the spot. I'll put one of my wet-behind-the-ears *'dottori ingegneri'* nominally in charge. No legal problems that way. But I'd expect you to run the job. You'd have to handle the *bambino ingegnere*, though. You know how these young know-it-alls are."

"Don't I," Fass said. "I was one myself. But, being in the Wehrmacht, I got over it pretty damned quick."

Petrocelli laughed. *"Bene, bene,"* he said. "We understand each other. Let the old sergeant run the platoon for the fresh *tenente* who doesn't know shit. I've been there. Sergeant myself once."

"First war?" Fass asked. "Isonzo front? The Carso? The Piave?"

"All! Even the fucking Caporetto mess," Petrocelli smiled.

"Christ, you squareheads were a pain in the ass, excuse me. Never gave up no matter how hard we pounded you."

"Ah, but who won?"

"Never would have been us if the French and the British hadn't sent down a few divisions."

Petrocelli pulled a couple of bent cigars out of his shirt pocket, offered one to Walter, who declined, then lit up and puffed acrid clouds of blue smoke with a look of real pleasure on his face.

"You know, I came up here after the war because the government made it easy for us—they wanted to cram as many Italians into the Südtirol as they could. My father and grandfather were drillers in the marble quarries at Carrara. I didn't have a diploma in shit. But I got this business started and I got rich. To hell with pieces of paper. You come with me now to a site, tell me what you think."

"Fine," Fass said. Outside, they got into a new Fiat, sped across town and pulled up on the east bank of the Eisack River. Walter saw the wreckage of a fine old stone bridge, early eighteenth century he guessed, made temporarily fit for light traffic with a wooden truss span. Ten meters downstream, coffers stood on both banks, ready for the concrete to be poured.

"It's going to be ugly as hell," Petrocelli laughed. "But the idiots at the *municipio* got some professor to say the old stone bridge wasn't significant enough to restore, and then hired some Milanese architect to design a modern single-arch span. Modern? The guy loves concrete like the Duce did. This is the way he wants it."

"He may get it, but it'll be gone the first spring there's a really heavy snow melt and that river starts raging," Fass said.

"You claiming I'm building a bridge that's going to collapse?"

"No. It might last fifty years. If you can arrange it so the river never rises higher or flows faster than it's doing right now."

"What the hell?"

"Look at the coffers where you're going to pour the piers. Then look at where that old stone bridge starts. You're at least five meters too close to the water."

"I see it. But reinforced concrete's a lot stronger than any mortared stone."

"It is. But either one has got to be anchored solidly in the earth. High, fast water will cut the banks right out from under your piers if you leave them that close. Also, I know you've got a budget, but your man is using at least six too few reinforcing rods per square meter. Those piers will start cracking in five years even if there's no high water at all."

"Fass, you're going to cost me a bundle, goddammit," Petrocelli said. "When can you take over as sergeant on this job?"

"Day after tomorrow?" Walter said.

"*Benissimo*. I'll straighten the *ingegnere* out tomorrow and get the men started on ripping out the coffers. Then you show up and put it right. By the way, you'll see me here every day. Doesn't mean I'm looking over your shoulder. I go to all my sites every day. I like to get my hands dirty too, you know?"

They shook. Walter didn't even think to ask what he'd be paid. Whatever it was would be enough for him, for now.

"Fass, eh? Relation of that big bastard Franz Fass?" Petrocelli asked when they were back in the Fiat, heading toward the bus terminus.

"Not many people get away with calling my uncle that. To his face," Walter said stiffly.

"I did, because he wouldn't say no to me."

"There's a story here, I think," Walter said.

"*Certo*. I badly wanted to buy two hectares up at the top of his pasture where that huge tree is. Best site around for a little hunting lodge, place to get away from the wife on weekends, you understand?

"I'd bought from farmers before, and they'd start out so solemn about the family land, the heritage, the birthright, and so on and so on. Cunning pricks. So what I'd do was offer a price so ridiculously high that they'd always say yes, on the spot. Then I'd think a bit, look troubled, offer a somewhat lower price. They'd still say yes. Then I'd talk about what a strain that would be, how the bank probably wouldn't go for it, crap like that, lowering the offer each time until the man finally said no. Then I knew I'd hit the fair market price. And after some bargaining, the deal would be done.

"Well, I tried that with old Franz. Started at a quarter-million, and he said yes and kept saying yes as I went down until I knew the sum we'd reached was less than half what that land was worth. Something's wrong here, I thought. Fass is no lunatic. So I pulled out a ten-lire note from my wallet and said, this is my final offer.

"He said yes!" Petrocelli started laughing hard. "Then the clever old bastard said, 'Of course, that doesn't include a right-of-way, not even a path through my property. So you can have those two hectares. You just can't ever set foot on them. Unless you can fly.'

"It was a good joke. We wound up going down to one of his vats of new wine and getting drunk together. You tell him Petrocelli sends his best to the most devious bastard in Bozen."

Fass knocked back a couple of shots of schnapps in the café before he boarded the bus back to Wolfsgruben. A lucky day, and just the start. He would take the examination, he'd become a certified *ingegnere*, and at last he would build things—bridges, small factories, even a cinderblock shed for a farmer's wine vats—that he would not have to blow up later, that would not get bombed or shelled or fought over.

A simple desire, he thought as he settled into his seat and the bus pulled out. It was only a matter of working well and being patient. All his problems were simple now. Except one: his poor little DP. What was he to do with her?

❊   ❊   ❊

He had married Anja so that he could help her. He'd believed that helping someone—anyone—was the first of the innumerable actions he would have to take to make up for one act in Yugoslavia. He felt he had given her a chance to free herself from her past by bringing her to Bozen, and the farm.

But for whose sake, really, had he done this? Hers? Or his own? Had he been too afraid, or too war-worn and apathetic, to come back here by himself? Was he only using Anja to salve a festering wound that eventually would have killed him? Could he have been so deluded? And so ruthless?

Almost certainly, Fass decided. And it was all wrong. It was idiotic to even flirt with the notion that he could in any way balance or atone for Yugoslavia.

He forced himself to harder admissions. He hadn't a gram of altruism in him, only kilos of guilt he dreamt of unloading somehow. He had grabbed a Polish waif out of a DP camp to use her. He had inflicted an incredible cruelty on that damaged, fearful girl when he told her he couldn't think of anyone he'd rather bear his child. The truth was he would prefer it was almost any other woman. The larger truth was that he was unfit to father a child, even with a real wife, one he cherished and loved.

Fass felt loathsome, every trace of satisfaction over his luck with Petrocelli now gone. And the face of his Chetnik appeared in his mind, as clear as ever. Oh, God, he shuddered. How could anyone keep such a hold on him, even from the grave? And the worst of it was that it wasn't love or some obsessive lust; it was that the Chetnik had been the agent and witness of his great degradation, his desertion from humanity.

Yet the image of the Chetnik was so real to Fass that he felt he might reach out and touch her smooth skin. He was so much with the Chetnik in his mind that he rode right past the Wolfsgruben stop. The Italian driver didn't bother to call out to him, even though Walter was a regular on the run. *"Vielen Dank, Herr Kapitän,"* Fass growled sarcastically to the driver when he got off at the next stop. The Italian kept his eyes on the road. Walter stood in the gathering dusk for almost an hour to catch another bus back.

Everyone was already at dinner when he reached the farm-house. Sitting on his plate was a letter postmarked Berlin. Fass had written to the University some weeks before beginning his Tues-day searches for work, though he'd had little hope of any reply. Uncle Franz looked on expectantly as Walter sat down, placed one corner of the letter under his heavy plate and slit the envelope with his table knife. Walter extricated the letter and began to read. He didn't notice that Franz, Sepp, Liese and Anja had stopped eat-ing and were watching him.

"Rather amazing news, considering everything," Walter said, looking around at everyone but feeling deadened, hopeless. "It's from the registrar. Miracle number one is that the old skeleton is still alive and at his post. He says the University building is not much more than a heap of rubble. Miracle number two is that all the records were stored in a deep basement and he's hoping enough of the wreckage will be cleared that he can get down there and poke around. Apparently he's received quite a few letters from graduates like me, wanting their credentials. It may take him some months. And of course—his phrasing has a very apologetic tone—he must charge a fee, payable in advance and 'regretfully,' he says, nonrefundable should his search prove futile. Futile!" Walter threw back his head and laughed.

"I wouldn't use the word 'miracle' so lightly if I were you," old Franz beamed. "It'll be a major one, when your diploma arrives. The fee goes tomorrow."

"Well, Uncle," Walter said, helping himself to some potatoes and sausages from the platter in the center of the table, "I'll believe it when I see it." He didn't give a shit anymore if he never saw it, he thought. He helped himself to more wine.

"That's right," said Sepp, chewing vigorously. "We old soldiers know not to count the chicks before they're hatched, eh?"

"Oh, shut up, Sepp," Liese said, flushing slightly. Her husband had been in the Italian Army, it was true. But he'd been stationed in Sicily for one year before the Allies invaded in '43. And his unit had walked en masse to the landing beach, unarmed, their colonel at their head waving an enormous white flag fashioned from a bedsheet, to surrender. He had not heard a shot fired in anger.

"No, Sepp's right," Walter smiled at Liese. "But here's some real news. I've found a job, foreman at a bridge-construction site in the city. Thanks to someone who says he called you a bastard, Uncle, and got away with it. Fellow named Petrocelli."

Franz chuckled. "Yes, yes. Petrocelli. Great God. Of course he only escaped undamaged because we were drunk when he called me that. Petrocelli, hah. That's all right, Walter. He's all right."

Then Walter, now four or five glasses of wine to the good, had a sudden devilish inspiration. "And going back to Sepp's opinions on hatching and so on, here's some more news for you all," he said, clasping Anja's shoulder. "My little Prussian here has turned out to be a true Tirolerin. She'll be having a baby by the first week of September, at the latest."

"Walter!" Anja cried, shrugging his hand off her shoulder and staring at the scraps of food remaining on her plate.

"Wonderful!" Uncle Franz exclaimed, banging his beer mug on the table and then raising it to his mouth and draining it. "Was I speaking of miracles or was I not? This is one I never expected. Now I'll be a grandfather at last." His grin broadened. "In spirit at least. And with your permission of course, Anja."

Sepp was smiling at her in a way Walter took to be almost a leer. Liese smiled too, and said, "Anja, I'm so happy for you."

But Walter saw the skin of Liese's throat pinken. She'd taken a guileless, unthinking remark by her father as a slap at her, he thought. For Liese, twenty-nine and married five years, still had no child. Then Walter's war orphan, or whatever she is, gets pregnant, and Franz speaks of miracles.

Oh, shit, Fass thought, Uncle Franz has just made Liese hate Anja. And maybe me, too. It was getting to be that time again. Time to go.

V

I'm a Pole, Walter. My name is Anja Wieniewska, born in Krakow," Anja confessed at last. She was sitting with her legs spread slightly, as pregnant women do, in the shade of the beech on a radiant Sunday in early July, gazing down the valley of the Adige at the glittering ribbon of river. Fass was circling the great tree, reading and rereading the carvings in the bark. He did not reply.

"Did you hear me?" Anja asked.

"Yes," Fass said, dropping down on the bench beside her. "You're Anja Wieniewska, a Pole from Krakow, not Anna Wolff from Breslau. And your great secret is that you worked for our side, the German side I mean, in wartime."

"Now you're imagining things," Anja said, wondering why she felt no shock at his words.

"Just a guess. Like the one I made at the camp when I called to you in Polish."

"You're a little reckless with your speculations."

"Possibly. But no one runs so far from home, no one sheds their identity and fights so hard to make a new one, without a reason. So

I think, what reason could Anja have? And the only answer that comes to me is that you did something very grave in Poland."

"So you conclude I was a traitor?"

"Yes."

"Screw you, Walter."

"I didn't bring this up. You could have kept on being Anja Fass, née Wolff. I would never have asked you a thing."

"Because you didn't feel a need to. You were so cocksure you already knew it all."

"And did I?"

Anja lowered her head and began to cry. This was not the way she'd imagined it would be. She had not thought Walter would be so cold, so cruel. She'd pictured him laughing, then teasing her about being his little Pole after all. They would laugh together about it. And perhaps someday in the future she would tell him the rest.

For a moment Anja clung to the hope that Fass might still be the one person on earth to whom she could finally admit the whole truth. She wiped away her tears, searched Walter's eyes for any reassurance, but saw instead a scene she knew would change forever the way he looked at her.

It was the summer of 1940. The boy's name was Krzysztof. He was her age exactly, almost as pale and blond. They belonged to different cells, but met occasionally. Others in the Resistance said they must be brother and sister, they were so much alike. They began to see each other privately, and when Krzysztof asked to sleep with her, she said yes.

The poor boy was an inept lover on their single night together. He must have felt shamed by this, for afterward, as they shared a cigarette in his dingy little room, he began to boast. He'd read accounts of the Irish war of liberation from Britain, and found a tactic Michael Collins had put to very effective use: A small squad of young Irishmen devoted themselves exclusively to assassinating British secret-service agents.

His group acquired three Radom semiautomatic pistols. Already they had assassinated four SD men in Krakow. He himself had shot one in the head as the SD man left a bar late one night, Krzysztof proudly told her.

And she of course told Richter, who seemed elated by the information. It signified nothing to her. She knew only that Krzysztof and his friends would vanish.

They did not. A little more than a week later, on a lovely warm day very much like this one, she strolled into the square below the Wawel and saw Krzysztof. He, two other young men, and three girls were hanging by thin ropes around their necks from the arched streetlamps. Their eyes were wide open. Krzysztof and the others, swaying so freely this way and that. As if they were looking for friends who might be coming to meet them from one direction or the other.

Pinned to the corpses' chests were paper placards, the word MURDERER printed on each.

This was not the deadliest of Anja's crimes, but to her it was the most devastating, for it was the first time she had been confronted with the true consequences of her words to Richter. She ran, half-mad, straight to her priest, but came away embittered, hopeless. She wanted one of those placards pinned to her own chest. But less than a year later, hardened or numbed, she casually gave up the hiding places of Andrzej and everyone else in her group. Picturing clearly Andrzej and perhaps thirty other men and women tumbling one by one into a shallow secret grave, shot in the backs of their skulls by Richter's men. They were rotting there even now.

I pulled the trigger, Anja had said to the cows on one of those frigid dawns in the Fass barn. I placed the nooses around the necks. I was there, in that time and place. It was not someone who looked like me. I murdered them without pity or remorse.

"Well, did I know it all?" Fass asked, rising from the bench.

"No," Anja said. "No, I did not work for the German scum. And damn you for assuming so, you bastard."

"Then why did you run?"

Anja sighed, prelude to a new deception. The cows knew, and that would have to be sufficient. "Are you so ignorant? There were two kinds in the Resistance: those who supported the Polish government-in-exile in London, and the Polish Communists. What do you imagine the Communists did as soon as the Russians occupied Polish territory? They betrayed the government supporters to Red Army commissars. At best. At worst, they began to liquidate us themselves. I was not a Red. So I ran."

"I see," Fass said tonelessly.

"I doubt that you, a damned German killer, really do," Anja said. "Or ever could."

※　　※　　※

Over the past eight months, during those dawn confessions in the barn and quiet hours in the pasture, Anja felt she'd begun to understand why she had done the things she'd done, in Krakow time. Cowardice. The very thing that Fass had admitted to, the willingness to sacrifice others so that she might live on for one more day. In her case, though, the threat of extinction was never so direct and imminent as it must have been for him. Richter had behaved as if he were her best friend, even her lover. The threat was Krakow itself, or what was happening to the people of Krakow, Poles and Jews. It was the horrible liquidation of the ghetto, the stink of the slave-labor camp, the disappearance of so many into the KZs. The witnessing of arrests and shootings that had no connection to her or her work at all; she knew Richter had many creatures like her under his control. The sure knowledge that once with him, there was no quitting, no way out, except a noose or a bullet.

But there was more: Her wartime action was a game she had actually enjoyed playing. Sometimes she had gotten a thrill from it, an exciting feeling of power. She had liked it.

She would never let Fass know any of this. It was not only his cool detachment now, his ugly assumptions of her guilt. It seemed to her that his kindness and understanding had subtly diminished in direct proportion to the growth of her belly. Anja thought he was distancing himself from her and the child. One day he might even abandon them. Perhaps he would do it now, if he weren't afraid of how it would look to his uncle.

They remained silent for a while. Walter put two cigarettes in his mouth, lit them, then passed one to Anja. "Got a letter from my friend in Ischl," he said. "Care to see it?"

"Not really, Walter," Anja said. She felt like crying again, but fought it off.

"You'll like this one, I promise."

"Shit." But Anja took the letter anyway.

No salutation. Just this:

Your mission is no longer necessary, Fass. The foul deed's been done. A certain Hungarian female (who's kept busy most mornings vomiting and cursing me as if it were my fault) and I will be in Eppan in September, staying with friends who've a decrepit old castle there. It will be most uncomfortable;

they've no taste at all in wines. Sisi is of course dying to see Anja and the child. But I am looking forward with relish to watching you deal with a squalling infant. After which pleasure, I intend to deal with you as traitors and deserters have traditionally been dealt with.

Scharner

Anja started to laugh, choked it off, then let it ride right over her sadness. "So you were right after all, you smug bastard. But who's the father? Do you really think he picked some man to do it for him?"

"My guess . . ."

"You and your damned guesses. I'm so tired of them. But go ahead, let's hear this one."

"My guess, before I was so rudely interrupted by one of little faith, is that Dizzi steeled himself, drew on all his reserves of courage, and assaulted Sisi again and again until it worked. The man's too damn proud of his bloodline to let it happen any other way."

"Oh, it'll be nice to see them. I hope Sisi is here when the baby comes. I've no one else."

"You're forgetting me?"

"Well, yes actually. You haven't seemed as much a friend as you once were, lately."

"I'm ashamed to admit it, but you're right. I was full of enthusiasm at first, but the closer it gets to baby time, the more nervous I'm getting."

"Because I'm the mother? Tell the truth."

"All right. I don't really know. Maybe it's because I'm wishing I was having a child with a real wife. But probably it has nothing to do with you at all," Fass said. He had killed girls as young and pretty as Anja with infants in their arms. He felt vomit rising in his gorge, and he turned away, even though Anja was staring down at her boots.

"I think," he said when he had control of his voice again, "I am simply terrified I'll be a disaster as a father. There is so much in me that I cannot seem to come to terms with."

"How do you imagine I feel? Every day I think I'm the last person in the world who should bear a child."

"We're a pair. But feel free to say 'Screw you, Walter.'"

"Nature will take its course. Didn't I once hear that from you?" Anja felt her sadness move back a bit from the brink of desolation. Walter seemed closer again now. Tomorrow, the day after? Who knew? Maybe he wouldn't abandon them after all. Maybe Walter and she really were a pair, not fit for anybody but each other. Maybe it would work.

Anja suddenly remembered the odd dream she'd had the previous night. She saw her baby underwater, in a pool or a well or something, a tiny thing, all head and belly, swimming easily. And then the baby—she couldn't see if it was a girl or a boy—turned toward her, looked at her with enormous, alert and intelligent eyes, and smiled the only smile she could remember that had ever really warmed her heart.

"Walk with me in the orchard?" Walter asked when they'd finished their cigarettes.

Anja tried to rise, fell back, then tried again. This time Walter, already standing, took her hand and helped her, kept hold of her hand as they eased their way down the slopes to level ground, and did not let go as they strolled along the rows of apple trees, bare of flowers now. The thick-trunked trees with their low, spreading crowns of young branches looked unnatural to Anja. And of course they were, she knew, because the oldest limbs had been lopped off so that many new ones would sprout and flourish, increasing the number of apples each tree would bear.

◼ ◼ ◼

That night Anja lay awake for a long while after they'd turned off the lights, thinking of the way it had felt to have Walter hold her hand all through the orchard walk, the way it had felt when the contact was broken as they entered the house at dinnertime.

"Hey you. Fass?" she whispered at last.

"Yes, little Pole?" It surprised her that he was still awake. A part of her had hoped he wouldn't hear her. Now she had to go through with it.

"Do you think you could . . . would you mind sleeping in my bed tonight?"

She heard the rustle of his sheets and smelt his presence before she actually felt his body slip down next to hers, barely brushing her side. Then she felt lips lightly touch her forehead. Just that one brief touch. But his warmth remained so close.

"Sleep well, Anja."

VI

When Anja stirred the next morning, Walter was gone, and she wondered drowsily if she had only dreamt that he lay beside her all through the night. Dream or no, she'd slept well. She had not once jerked awake near panic, unsure of where she was and feeling utterly alone, as she had too many nights lately.

It had been months since Anja had risen before the sun to milk the cows and take them to pasture. She had been prepared to work as long as she was able to squat on the stool and hold the milking bucket between her legs. Old Franz had put an end to that when she could no longer fasten the third button at the bottom of her bodice.

"No more heavy lifting or anything of that sort for you, my dear. Liese'll take care of the cows again from now on."

She protested, but Franz was set in his mind about the capacities of pregnant women, what was good for them and what was bad. He had his reasons. His wife, Walter informed her, was over thirty when she first became pregnant, suffered two miscarriages, was unable to bear children after Liese, and died of cancer of the womb at forty-eight.

Once Anja's condition became known, Franz fussed over her, sometimes paternally and sometimes, to everyone's amusement, like a brood hen over a chick. Restricted to the lightest household chores, she had tried doing some of the cooking, which the family bravely endured—for a while. They'd been nice about putting a stop to it. Only Sepp was unable to disguise his feelings about her culinary shortcomings.

So much time on her hands. How pleasant that was. On fine days she spent hours under the beech, daydreaming and reading books she had longed to read, books forbidden or unobtainable in wartime—everything by the Mann brothers, by Döblin, by Remarque, as much Conrad in German translation as Walter could discover in Bolzano's poorly stocked shops. She wished she could get her hands on any of the works of the great Polish Romantics, Adam Mickiewicz and Julius Slowacki, whom she'd read too young to really appreciate. Or Henryk Sienkiewicz and Władysław Reymont, whom she had never gotten to.

And on rainy days, she would sit by the window in the *Stube*, her mind abroad in the fictional worlds of Schnitzler and Svevo, of Musil and Roth. But there was one group she shunned entirely: the great philosophers, the very ones she had wanted so much to study before the war. There was simply no point, after the dark years, to any of them now.

Anja shifted her body to a more comfortable position under the sheets. She knew where that early desire had sprung from. Neither of her parents had been considered an intellectual, though Anja always thought of them that way. Tadeusz Wieniewski worked as chief accountant for Krakow's municipal hospital, and Elzbieta, her mother, was in charge of one of the smaller branches of the city library. They were fanatic readers and talkers, fascinated with ideas of all sorts. Their carelessly kept little flat on Szewska Street in the Old Town was overflowing with books—sagging shelves, piles on every table, stacks against the walls. And always humming with discussion, debate, disputation. In German. Krakow was an Imperial Austrian city when Anja's parents were growing up, and the schools taught in German. Tadeusz and Elzbieta, pure Poles, decided it would be the exclusive household language so that their daughter would be fluent, in case the Austrians should one day return. Anja doubted very much that they had ever imagined it would be the Germans themselves who came. But her own schooling had been in Polish.

The sadness that weighted such remembrance lessened a little every time she allowed her mind to wander through this past. She actually had had, Anja decided in the softness of her bed, a golden childhood. There was no luxury, she was never spoiled or overindulged, but there were certainly comfort and security, and an exciting enthusiasm for knowledge in her home, as well as in her life outside. "You'll be the first Wieniewski in all the generations of Wieniewskis to be a scholar," Tadeusz said proudly on the day she received her gymnasium diploma and her letter of acceptance from the University.

And she had a circle of friends who loved to gather after school in an inexpensive little coffeehouse called, rather absurdly they all thought, the King Jan Sobieski. Or at her apartment, to talk and argue and laugh. Often they walked arm in arm in the shady Planty, or up on the heights of Wawel above the gray Vistula, their voices echoing off the majestic bell towers, the cathedral, the Royal Castle that for five centuries had been the seat of Poland's kings. Joanna and Helena and Aneta, Jaček and Kazimierz and Slawomir, a boy with hair as black as hers was blond and the softest blue eyes, the first boy she ever allowed to embrace her and kiss her and, later, one night in the Planty, slip his hand under her skirt and caress her most tender, her most covert place.

The pity of it, the sorrowful waste of it. Where were Joanna and Helena and Jaček and dear, beautiful Slawomir now? Aneta was dead, hanged from a lamppost by the SS, and Kazimierz was most probably dead, too, for he had been arrested and sent to Buna. Thank God she'd had nothing to do with their terrible fates. Thank God she had not been one of those Poles who hated the Germans but despised and feared the Jews even more, and so helped one enemy exterminate another. She had seen the terror, the disbelief, the despair of the Jews rounded up in various *Aktionen*, had seen Poles gloating as they watched. But her victims . . .

Victims. Anja shuddered as she always did whenever her thoughts reached this word, this reality. She knew she would shudder and damn herself all her life, however long it might be. Or she might go mad, a sort of Lady Macbeth, but with bloodier hands.

Maybe she already was mad. Just the other day, she had been sitting under the beech, deep in a daydream about giving birth. She felt, in her fantasy, great waves of pain and an enormous pressure building inside her, all of it quickening and intensifying until she thought she could bear it no longer, that she would die there on the delivery table. Then suddenly she felt a great release, a vast evacuation that left her limp and empty. She saw the doctor and nurses lift the baby and cut the umbilical cord. But why did they turn away from her so rapidly? Why didn't they give her the child? Finally a nurse approached, an expression of dismay and fear on her face, clutching the infant to her chest. Anja saw the perfect form and the pink, fine-grained skin of the infant's body, became lost in the wonder of the exquisitely formed little fingers, the tiny toes. Then the nurse thrust the baby into Anja's arms and she saw the horror: the creature's entire face was covered with long, coarse black hair, like a werewolf.

Anja shook that gypsy nonsense out of her head, got up and struggled into a shapeless linen smock with little edelweiss embroidered around the neckline. Walter had bought this and some similar things for her when she could no longer fit into anything else. Shortly he'd have to start buying much smaller items, infant outfits, because Anja the Wieniewski scholar had never been taught such things as sewing or knitting. She went carefully down the narrow flights of stairs to the ground floor and then into the kitchen. Standing by the window, she drank what was left of the morning coffee. The house was silent. Everyone was outside working, but within her view there was only a strip of orchard, the vineyard, and the pasture rising to the beech. She rummaged through some drawers until she found a notepad and the stub of a pencil. Then she sat and wrote a letter to Sisi.

She did not mention Walter's erratic course, his unpredictable movements between warm attention and cold, unreachable distance, his brooding and joyless drinking. She wrote that she was content, at peace. And, when she had finished, she thought that might be close to the truth. Or as close as she would ever get.

VII

My lord, Anja, you've become enormous. A regular Zeppelin!" Dizzi giggled. "But beautiful, as well. I have to say you looked rather like a plucked chicken last time I saw you."

"The Scharner charm. It's marvelous how he gets away with it, isn't it, Anja?" Sisi said, grimacing.

"Who says he's getting away with it, the great lout," Anja said.

"That's right, Scharner. You have gone too far. Those insolent letters. Now insulting my wife. It's over for you," Fass barked, snatching a Luger from a drawer of the sideboard and aiming it at Dizzi's face. They were no more than two meters apart, only the dining table between them.

"Oh, please, please," Dizzi whined abjectly, throwing his arms up in surrender. "Don't shoot, I beg you. At least not at my handsome face."

"Too late, swine." Fass swiftly cocked the pistol. They both knew by the slide's thin snap that the Luger had an empty chamber. And the two men convulsed with laughter.

"My dear Anja, I retract my statement," Dizzi said. "You do not resemble a regular Zeppelin. Not even a tiny toy Zeppelin."

Sisi looked at Anja and arched her thin, well-shaped eyebrows.

"You know what they're doing, don't you, Dizzi?" Fass said. "They're saying to each other, through their women's intuition or whatever they care to call it, that you and I are clowns, childish and absurd. They're agreeing with each other that they've married asses."

"What? They call us asses? Let it be recorded."

"So it shall be. Asses we are," Fass replied with mock solemnity. He put the Luger—which his father had carried in the first war— back in the drawer. Then he opened the bottle of Veuve Clicquot that Dizzi had brandished like a trophy when they'd arrived. A pop, four glasses brimming. Walter passed them around.

"*Prost*," he said.

"God, Fass. Will you never learn anything better than beerhall manners? The occasion demands eloquence. Which I suppose I must provide. Pay attention now," Dizzi said. "My dear friends. Raise your glass of this somewhat inferior vintage—regrettably all that's available these days—to the lovely Anja, soon to become the prettiest mother in all the Südtirol, triumphant over the great disadvantage of a somewhat inferior paternal contribution. And to the great good fortune of this child who will have Anja as a mother. I offer my congratulations, my blessings, my undying affection and my devotion to you, Anja, and to your child. And perhaps I'll even remain on speaking terms with your husband, even though he just tried to shoot me."

"Now you see what I put up with, Anja," Sisi said after they'd sipped the champagne. "I believe I'll be raising two children at once, when my baby comes."

"Ah, but the larger one, I fear, is delinquent beyond redemption, despite your good influence, Sisi," Walter smiled, immensely amused at the sight of the firm, almost perfectly round bulge in the belly of an otherwise lissome girl.

In mid-sip Walter suddenly sobered. Dizzi and Sisi were crooning and petting his little Pole as if she were an adorable child instead of a woman who would deliver one any day now. The luck has been too good, he thought. Then he ordered himself to stop. This was war psychology, combat superstition. There never were bullets with anyone's name on them. There never was an apportionment of luck or good fortune. Whatever came to anyone came impartially, or, more to the point, with blind indifference. And much of what he had now, he had earned.

First, the bridge. Petrocelli had seen clearly, once the new piers were poured, that he was right. He was going to manage to bring the project in on time, maybe even a bit under budget. He had worked like hell to do that.

And he had worked like hell with Anja. After their orchard walk, he had felt the beginnings of a closeness that might save him. He had made a very deliberate decision then to cast his lot with her, to come as near as she would allow, and to be patient when he ran up against limits she set. Anja must have sensed this new commitment, because she began to discard those limits one by one. They progressed from sharing the same bed every night to quiet but rewarding sexual satisfactions—kisses and caresses mainly, for the pregnancy made lovemaking uncomfortable for her. Fass even began to feel stirrings of the notion that Anja might be his natural mate. And the prospect of that helped him immensely through the black days that still came on him.

Then this flat, their new home. A combination of luck and work. Petrocelli owned the building, a late-nineteenth-century structure in fair condition just on the edge of the old *centro*. There were four floors, each an apartment. For forty years the ground-floor flat had been occupied by a couple, but the old man's wife had died this summer and he had gone to live with his son and daughter-in-law in Merano. Housing being in short supply because of the bombing, all sorts of people were waving lire at Petrocelli. But he'd offered it to Fass at a very fair price, the only condition being that the engineer would have to renovate it himself. So every Saturday and Sunday, while old Franz and Anja thought he was on the bridge, he had been here. Replastering, painting, rebuilding the kitchen, installing a modern bathroom, getting the old stone floors cleaned and sealed properly. A few of the men working for him on the bridge had dropped by regularly to help, accepting nothing but a few glasses of wine at the end of the day's work.

And each time he felt himself slipping over the edge into that pit he knew too well, the one in which every action, every effort, every human connection or act of kindness or even of self-preservation seemed utterly pointless, the image of Anja and their baby had pulled him back.

Now it was a fine little home. A vestibule, a dining room with a fireplace, the big new kitchen, three bedrooms, a smaller room that could be a nursery. And best of all, large wrought-iron French doors at the rear of the house opening onto a walled garden with mature wisteria vines, a decent chestnut and a small fountain, water trickling out of the mouth of a bronze Bacchus.

※　　※　　※

He had made just one mistake, but a great one: keeping the damned thing secret until August, when all the work was done. He had sprung it on Anja and his family over dinner. Their reaction dismayed him, until it came clear in his disordered mind that the announcement was more a rude shock than the pleasant surprise he'd intended.

"My God, Walter!" Franz rumbled, cross and hurt. "Why on earth have you done such a thing? This is your home here, yours and Anja's and the baby's. That's been clear from the start, hasn't it? I thought you loved it here. What have we done wrong?"

Fass scrambled then, trying to reassure the old man that he was not ungrateful, that he was not fleeing, but only establishing a place of his own.

Franz eventually leaned back in his chair then and smiled at Walter. "Yes, a man needs to make his own way. I was the lucky one, the oldest son, the one who inherited the farm and a place in the world. Your father had to make his own, and I guess you feel that, too. But Walter, I surely wish there'd been a way for you to do it right here, living with us."

"Uncle, we'll be here so often eating all your food and drinking all your wine that you'll soon wish we'd gone to the moon, not just down to Bozen," Walter said. "I know I've no right to ask a favor, but my greatest wish is that you'll do for my son, or my daughter, just what you did for me when I was growing up."

"Favor?" Old Franz frowned, wagging a thick finger at Walter. "I consider it my damn right, by God. And if you try to come between me and the child . . . I may be old, but I'll give you the worst beating of your life."

Walter grinned as Franz banged his beer mug on the table, drained it, and laughed. "So how is my grandchild to be called?" he asked.

"Sophie," Anja blurted. So now a surprise for Fass. They had never discussed names.

"Sophie Fass. Hmmm. A good name. But what if you have a boy, Anja?"

"I won't," Anja said, smiling with a certainty that unsettled Walter. "She's Sophie already."

If he'd blundered with Franz, he'd gone completely off the tracks with Anja. She seemed so calm and quiescent at the table, as if she had known all along what he was up to.

But she had nested already in their farmhouse roost, Walter realized when she exploded later that night in their room, cursing almost as fluently and inventively as that ex-*Feldwebel* Precht, up on the Brenner. He had never been raked so thoroughly in his life, not even during basic training in the Wehrmacht, when a speck of dust in a rifle barrel or the smallest imperfection in the polish of your boots brought down the wrath of Thor. And he deserved it, for the move he had committed them to without so much as a word to her. She did not want change just now, so close to her time. She was huge and waddling and growing more anxious by the day. She needed the peaceful familiarity of the farm. He was relieved that she had no weapon in reach that night except a fairly heavy ceramic ashtray, which came hurtling at him so fast that he was unable to dodge. The scar on his forehead was only now beginning to fade from bright red into pink.

But when he had shown Anja the apartment, the touches he'd taken such care over—a beautifully carved dark walnut cradle, a chest full of the finest infant's clothes he could afford—had not gone unnoticed. She loved the garden, too. She stopped sulking and cursing, smiled up at him, and kissed him full and hard on the lips with more true feeling than she had ever displayed before.

"*Dobrze,*" she whispered, holding his waist. "*Dziękuję.*"

❖   ❖   ❖

Now, just two weeks after they'd moved in—an easy job, since they possessed between them nothing more than two suitcases of clothes—came Dizzi and Sisi, motoring down from Ischl in old Scharner's immaculate 1932 Mercedes to stay with friends in Eppan, a few kilometers south of Bolzano.

It couldn't be better for Anja, Sisi being here for the birth. And Dizzi—what Fass needed most, that close friend, the one he knew he could rely on completely in any situation.

"Dizzi!" Walter called. "In the kitchen, now. These women must be fed."

"*Jawohl*," said Dizzi, pouring the last of the champagne into Sisi's and Anja's glasses.

"Oh, lord," Sisi moaned. "Army food."

"No worry about that," Walter said. "Herr von Scharner and I once learned how to do very well by ourselves with limited resources. Here the materials are rather better."

"Quite decent little setup, Walter," Dizzi said in the kitchen. "All ready to become a doting pappa, are we?"

"You'll think I'm mad, but it feels a bit like it always felt before an assault. You're never actually ready."

"Oh, horseshit, Fass. You're overdramatizing as usual. Have I told you that has always been your chief problem, my friend?"

"Frequently. But why would I listen to a fool who once babbled that war was glorious fun? Something about picnics, wasn't it?"

"Merely quoting an English twit," Dizzi laughed. "I did feel rather elated much of the time, true. But as I've grown older, settled down, well, you know how it goes. I like to think I've mellowed, like a fine port."

"Perfect. That's precisely how I'll think of you from now on, vintage 1945 gathering dust and cobwebs in some cellar for the twenty years or so it'll take to make you fit to drink."

"You have this cruel streak, Walter. You've hurt me now. And after all I've done . . ."

"For that ungrateful Fass wretch," Walter interrupted. He laid some thin slices of almost white veal on a grill, then slipped it into the oven. "You know, Scharner, it nearly kills me to admit this, but I'm very, very happy you're here."

"Gentlemen never admit such rubbish," Dizzi said. "Now get on with your chefery or whatever it's called. I'm starving. All the things in this cabinet here? Good. I'll set the table. I at least know where the knives and forks should be placed."

Presently they were lunching on grilled veal with local morels sautéed in butter and thyme, and roast potatoes and garden greens, with a couple of bottles of young white wine. Sisi had an appetite like a garrison sergeant, though vigorous eating intefered not at all with her continuous chatter to Anja, who merely picked at her food. After coffee, Walter suggested a visit to the farm, but Anja pled fatigue and Sisi stayed behind, too.

Dizzi insisted that Walter drive the Mercedes. "You won't get many chances to handle an auto like this. Just keep your hand on the steering wheel, shout 'Feuer!' every time you step on the clutch, and I'll work the gearshift for you." It was an amazing Gerät, perfectly made and in pristine condition. Delays between the cries of "Feuer!" and Dizzi's shifts caused gears to grind a few times, which made Fass wince. Dizzi just laughed.

"Can't hurt this thing. It's indestructible," he said. "The old man swears there will never be another decent Mercedes made. Ever. He claims they've ruined all their automotive prowess by wasting so many years building trucks and panzers instead of fine vehicles for people like him."

Uncle Franz and Sepp came out to meet them as the Mercedes purred up to the house. Dizzi got along at once with old Franz, hit just the right bluff and hearty note, without a trace of his usual sarcasm. Sepp was so overawed by the auto that, after a perfunctory handshake with Dizzi, he sidled off to scrutinize the machine almost centimeter by centimeter. Leaving Sepp to his examinations, old Franz took them to the wine vat out back and drew three glasses. "Any day now, yes? You'll send word the moment Sophie's born, right?"

"You're as bad as Anja. It could be a little Franz who pops out, you know. But of course, Uncle, the very instant," Walter assured him. When they'd emptied their glasses, Franz went to examine the Mercedes with Sepp while Dizzi and Walter headed up toward the beech.

"Pity all this won't come to you," Dizzi said as they climbed the pasture.

"Not really. The tradition here has always been that the entire property goes to the eldest son, so the land doesn't get broken into parcels too small to support a family. But the eldest has to pay compensation to the other children, which is where my father got the capital to start his shoe business.

"I couldn't handle it anyway, the way I am. My cousin Liese will get it, and she and Sepp will do fine. She's smart, he's not as dim as he seems and he's a demon for work. Anyway, I'm perfectly happy practicing my profession."

"Profession? I thought riveting rivets and such was a trade, actually. But I forget myself. You are, after all, Herr Doktor Fass."

"Never forget that, Scharner," Walter laughed.

They examined the carvings on the beech for a while. Dizzi found one Walter hadn't noticed before. It was small and faint and more than two meters up the trunk: R. FASS, 1785.

"Well, that puts me in my place, I suppose," Dizzi said. "The Fasses have been amongst the landed class longer than the haughty von Scharners."

"Odd you should have discovered that carving. I've been hanging around this tree for years and never noticed it before."

"You should consult an oculist, Herr Doktor."

They admired the view of Bolzano and the long, lovely valley.

The only bad patch in their sight was a complex of low factories to the east of the city, the rubble of them reminders of the Duce's efforts to industrialize the Südtirol.

"This is fine country," Dizzi said. "Real, not kitschy picture-postcard perfect like the Salzkammergut and Ischl. That place is getting on my nerves. I'd love to go to Vienna, but of course it's impossible with Sisi. You know the Russians are still kidnapping people from the Allied zones of the city? Czechs, Hungarians, Romanians. The Allies don't put up much of a fuss, I hear. Disgusting. But very exciting, I think. I'd go in a flash. Except for Sisi."

"Yes, there is Sisi. So tell me," Fass said as they walked down the pasture and through the vineyard. "How did you manage what you rather crudely described as, I think, 'the foul deed'?"

"That's very indiscreet, Walter." Dizzi huffed.

"So we've secrets from each other now?"

"Yes. No. Maybe. Oh, it's damned embarrassing. You see, it wasn't as bad as I'd anticipated. Once I realized Sisi was so determined that she'd have screwed the gardener if I kept refusing, there was no choice, of course. Couldn't let that sort of thing happen in the family. So I persuaded Sisi to lay face-down on the bed with her bottom raised up, and pretended she was a boy. Her being so slim and all helped. It was actually exciting. For me anyway. Sisi complained, *natürlich*.

"But don't take an admission of excitement to mean I've suddenly been converted and changed my preferences. Especially now that she's getting less boyish and more womanly."

Fass laughed.

"Go on, ridicule me. I'm sure it's very amusing for you. And, if it's any of your business, which you seem to think it is, she hasn't changed her preferences, either. She kicked me out of her bed the instant pregnancy was confirmed, and right away started an affair with a very young music student—a budding cellist, I think—in Salzburg."

"Bravo!" Walter cried. "You two are a true pair. I congratulate myself on bringing you together."

"And you and Anja? A pair?"

"Not exactly," Walter said. "I'm hopeful now, though."

"Here's to luck," Dizzi said, draping a strong arm round Walter's shoulders. "Just be careful not to fall in love or anything so stupid as that."

I don't know about Walter, but Scharner will be drunk when they get back, and he'll be drunker still before the evening's over," Sisi said to Anja as they strolled through the old quarter of Bolzano. There was no amused tolerance in her voice, no flippant good spirits. "He's become such a damned bore. God, look at this place. It's asleep on its feet. Do you ever have any fun here?"

"No opera, no theater, no art galleries, no university," Anja replied. "Do you ever have any fun at Ischl?"

"Used to. A bit, anyway. A few delicious affairs—when I could get away from the Scharner prison. I won't bore you with the details, but it isn't Dizzi. His problems are his own. Even when he's drunk, he behaves like a gentleman to me. He's not a wife-beater or anything."

"Then what's the trouble? You've a fine place to live, three meals a day, and no reason to fear the authorities. Isn't that more than any of us dreamed of, just after the war? Isn't that why we married strangers we met through the wire of a DP camp?"

"Yes, yes, I'm a spoiled brat," Sisi said, but without the self-mocking, ironic tone Anja remembered. She sounded petulant, nasty. "People are starving, so clean your plates, children. People are in rags, so be glad you have some nice clothes. People are dying of petty diseases, so be grateful you've the money for doctors and medicines. Of course!"

"Well?"

"Well, nothing," Sisi said, her voice suddenly familiar again, light and sassy. "I shouldn't be blathering like this, Anja. I'm sorry. You know me and my mouth. Let's have coffee and talk babies. God, I'm scared. What if I get awful stretch marks? Are you scared? No, you wouldn't be. Not you. Oh, Anja."

The girl was suddenly near tears. They sat on the terrace of a café on the main square and ordered espressos. Sisi demanded more sugar, even after the waiter explained that sugar was rationed. "Shit," Sisi said when he would not be moved.

"Have mine," Anja said, not waiting for a reply but putting the small cube that had come on her saucer quickly into Sisi's cup. "I'm not supposed to have anything sweet just now."

"Now, that's a lie," Sisi laughed. "I may be ignorant, but my doctor hasn't said anything to me about sugar."

"Oh, he'll get around to it, eventually. If you gain any weight," Anja smiled. "You don't look as if you've put on a kilo, and Scharner's right about me. I do look like a dirigible. You think there are no mirrors in my house?"

Sisi giggled, then blew on her hot espresso and took a sip. "Is this real coffee? It certainly tastes like real coffee. Am I really in Italy? I guess I must be. I seem to be breathing real air. In Ischl the air's still ersatz, I think. Like the coffee. Even if you've got the money, it's hard to find anything real there."

"Come on, Sisi. Tell me. You're in trouble, aren't you? What is it?" Anja demanded.

Sisi was staring off across the square, eyes taking in nothing much at all, a loopy smile on her face.

"You know what I wish for most, Anja darling?" she said. "I wish you and I were still cuddled together in my cot at the camp. Almost every night I wish that."

VIII

Anja went to bed that night disquieted by Sisi's emotional gyrations. Sleep was long in coming. Then, near dawn, Anja felt a strange sudden bursting inside her, and woke immediately to find the sheets sodden. She nudged Walter. "It's happening. It's started. Sophie's coming," she said.

Walter sat up abruptly, as if he had already been awake. He smiled down at her. "Excellent."

Then he swung himself out of bed, marched to his armoire, shed his pyjamas, and dressed in his one good suit, taking especial care to center his preknotted tie. He checked his appearance in the mirror, marched back to the bed, bent to kiss Anja on the forehead, and said, "I'm going to fetch a taxi. I will be back within four minutes. Do you have your bag in order? Yes? Very good."

Outside the apartment, Walter cut a sharp left and strode down the block toward the taxi stand. There was no hint in his movements that he'd collapsed into bed around two in the morning completely and incoherently drunk, after a long session with Dizzi in the kitchen. He saw three taxis in rank. He opened the rear door of the first, slid into the seat, closed the door firmly. "The hospital, please. At once."

The driver eyed Walter curiously in the rearview mirror.

"Ach!" Fass lightly tapped his forehead, realized that he had perhaps the worst headache of his life, and laughed. He gave the driver the address of his apartment. Less than four minutes had passed when he hurried back into the bedroom to find Anja sitting perfectly still on the edge of the bed, dressed and proper as a schoolgirl with her little overnight bag on the floor between her feet. She was giggling.

"Are you in pain? Should we call an ambulance?" he asked. Then he laughed and tapped his forehead once more, which produced a great involuntary groan.

"No, no. I'm fine. An ambulance for you, perhaps?" Anja smiled. "Or at least an aspirin?"

"Taxi's outside," Walter said. Then he took Anja's hand and helped her to her feet, shepherded her out the front door—which he forgot to close—and into the Fiat.

"To the hospital," he said to the driver.

"*Buon giorno, Signora.* You've chosen a lovely day for it. The hospital? *Certo, Signore.* Where else did you think I would go? A little tour of the *città*, perhaps?" the driver said, starting the engine and shifting into first gear.

Two nurses put Anja to bed, still dressed, in a room down the hall from the delivery room. Walter sat beside her, holding her hand until she asked him very calmly not to grip quite so hard. Walter dropped her hand and began instead to stroke her hair. And wait. And wait. And wait. Anja dozed a little.

Then she grimaced, eyes squeezed tight, as the first wave of pain washed over her. When it passed, she said, "That's Sophie, announcing herself." It was a while before she grimaced again, this time shifting her body slightly on the bed. "She's become a tiny bit more insistent," Anja said. "Please, Walter, stop rubbing my head."

He sat there, his good arm dangling as loosely as his empty sleeve, feeling useless, clumsy and more worried than he dared admit each time he saw Anja's pale face contort with pain. The intervals between, when her face was relaxed and she looked into his eyes and smiled broadly, began to seem shorter, although Walter had no sense of time anymore. Finally a doctor came by, felt Anja's pulse, asked her how quickly the contractions were coming. Walter couldn't follow her answer, had only the sense that her voice was composed and calm. But the doctor turned to him, smiling as if they shared some conspiracy.

"Now you must leave us, please," he said. "There's a waiting room down the hall to your left. Have patience. This may take an hour, or it may take most of the day. We'll let you know."

Dismissed as if he were a junior officer on parade whose boots were improperly polished, Walter went to the entrance of the waiting room and surveyed the place. There was no one else about. He stood very straight, held himself very carefully, for his head felt at least twice its normal size and any sudden movement made it ring like a church bell. He burst into laughter, letting the bell toll. Fass, you are an idiot, he thought. He leaned against the wall for a moment to calm himself. Another slight mistake: those sharp shocks jolted down his phantom arm. So he left the hospital, lit a cigarette, and wandered off to find a public telephone. He rang Dizzi in Eppan. Scharner and Sisi hurriedly decamped from the decrepit castle, drove into Bozen, installed themselves in the smallest of the bedrooms in Walter's apartment, and then left for the hospital. Dizzi remembered to shut the front door behind him.

They found Walter in the waiting room, sound asleep.

"Men!" Sisi sniffed. Dizzi unscrewed the top of his monogrammed silver hip flask and savored a nip of grappa.

"Well, we can't very well do it for you, after all," he said laconically. "I'll probably nap too, waiting for you. Or go out for drinks."

"You'd better not. You'd better be pacing and wringing your hands and moaning in sympathy while I'm suffering in the delivery room for your sake."

"My sake?" Dizzi said. "Now who, instead of being content with thin-thighed teenaged cellists and the like, insisted, no, threatened dire consequences to my person and reputation if I failed to get her with child? Eh? Eh?"

※　※　※

In the delivery room, Anja was grinding her teeth as the contractions came closer and closer together, each one stronger and more painful than the last. Oh, God, she had never considered this hurt. No one ever tells how much it hurts. Her mother always talked about giving birth to her as if it were nothing much at all. You simply lay down and squeezed a little. Anja clenched her jaw hard as another pain swept through her. She could feel tiny drops of sweat forming on her forehead.

In the end, it was almost as she had once imagined. There was terrible pressure, a stretching until she thought she would rip apart, but then a great evacuation and a feeling of hollowness. Afterward she went limp. She felt she lacked the strength to turn her head or move her fingers. None of this is real, she was home in bed deep in a dream, Anja thought as she saw the nurse bringing a mewling, swaddled bundle toward her. She was afraid to look at it. Suppose the face . . .

Then Sophie Fass was in her mother's arms, tiny toothless mouth open, tiny perfect fingers clenched, eyes still shut. Anja saw pale skin poreless and unblemished as the finest porcelain, saw the lovely round face, the diminutive nose. She saw on a perfect head

the wisps of hair translucent as cornsilk. Sophie opened her eyes
for the very first time. They were huge, and blue as the sky above
the Brenner that brilliant day at the signalman's hut. As Anja
began to cry, Sophie Fass closed her tiny mouth and ceased to wail,
but stared and blinked and stared again at her mother's tear-
streaked face.

※　※　※

Over the next few days Anja often felt as if she were the ring-
master of the Zirkus Sophie, newly arrived in town and
drawing great boisterous crowds of enthusiastic spectators. Uncle
Franz seemed to inflate with joy, and had to release the pressure
with uninterruptible streams of praise each time he came to the
hospital room. Sisi too, in the room every day as long as was permitted, burbled and babbled almost ceaselessly. And, she would
admit at last, mostly senselessly. Even Liese, calmer and more
serene, spoke several beats faster than usual and radiated a genuine excitement. Petrocelli barged in one morning barely visible
behind the enormous bundles of flowers he carried in both arms.
He thrust a large rough finger at Sophie, actually giggled with delight when she reflexively clutched it. Dizzi swanned in at odd
hours, usually smelling of alcohol, but always bearing gifts—once
a tiny gold cross on a gold chain for Sophie and a larger one for
Anja, another time a *Kuschelbär* for Sophie and a vial of French
perfume for Anja.

Why this tiny wailing creature should be such an attraction
eluded Anja; she felt, in private moments when she suckled the infant or simply gazed at her delicate perfection, that only she could
truly understand the real miracle: Sophie's soul-changing power.
Anja knew she would never again be the Anja she had been. She
wished Walter could know this, share it somehow. But that seemed

unlikely. He was kind, solicitous, attentive and caring, he kissed Anja on the forehead when he arrived each day and again when he departed. Yet he scarcely glanced at Sophie, as if the infant were some supernatural manifestation that would vanish if he looked too intently or tried to touch her.

Just before visiting hours ended on the fourth day after her delivery, everyone else gone home, Anja swung her legs over the edge of the bed, holding Sophie. "Here, Walter," she said, raising the child toward him. "You hold her while I go to the bathroom, please."

"I can't do that." Anja saw dismay on his face. She could not know that he felt sick to his soul. Felt his touch would pollute her, believed himself to be cursed, unfit to even look at this child.

"Do what?"

"Hold the baby. She's so tiny, and me with one arm," Walter said. "Suppose I dropped her? I'd kill myself if I dropped her." Yes, do to himself exactly what he'd done to those nameless Anjas and their Sophies in that pathetic Yugo village. He saw them now in his mind, the disbelief and terror of the mothers, the placid incomprehension on the pure, trusting, unmarked faces of their babies. Fass began to weep with the grief of it, pierced more deeply than ever before by the hopeless wish that somehow he could reel back time, undo the horror. He would accept as perfect justice the most agonizing torture and death the mind of man could contrive, if that would make whole again those he had destroyed. He went down on his knees before Anja and Sophie, sobbing.

"Walter? Walter?" Anja screened her alarm as well as she could. "You're being a bit excessive here, aren't you? Don't overdramatize so. Dizzi says you always overdramatize."

Fass shook his head.

"You can so hold her. Just don't squeeze the life out of her," Anja smiled. She had misunderstood the vector of Walter's emotions. But now came a fugitive awareness that Sophie's existence might have opened some forbidden door to his wartime. She felt he desperately needed a demonstration of trust from her.

"You've got to start sometime, so start now," Anja said gently. "You can't just never hold your own daughter, you know. Here, take her."

Fass quivered as Anja grabbed his right wrist, pulled his arm into a crook, and laid Sophie in it. He pressed the swaddled infant to his chest, considered he might be pressing too firmly, eased off, felt she might be about to slip from his grasp, pressed her to him again.

Anja stood up laughing, hands on hips, then walked off to the bathroom. When she returned a few minutes later, she sat down on the bed, gingerly swung her legs up, and lay propped against the pillows. Fass seemed not to have moved a muscle in her absence.

"God, Walter, you look comical. I mean really, you look like a comedian in a motion picture," she said gaily, anxious to pull him back from whatever abyss he had been staring into. "You should see your face. Here, you oaf, give her to me."

Fass stiffly and slowly rose so that Anja could lift Sophie from the crook of his arm. She undid the top buttons of her nightgown and exposed her left breast. She smiled as Sophie's tiny mouth found the nipple.

Fass had never seen such peace on Anja's face before.

"Can I get you anything? Some water, anything at all?" he asked, despairing that no genuine peace would ever come to him, only a series of armistices, each of uncertain duration.

"No, thanks, I just want to lie here quietly a while with Sophie. You go on home," Anja said.

"Right, then," Fass said. *"Ciao, bella."*

"But when you come tomorrow, you will hold Sophie, you will even walk around the room with her. *Klar?"* Anja said. "And you will kiss her, Walter. Our little Sophie needs to know her father loves her."

IX

The engineer Walter Fass obeyed his wife. In the execution, if not the spirit, of her orders.

And, two days later, he escorted Anja and Sophie through the doors of the hospital and down a few steps to the curb, stooping a bit so that he could support the back of his wife's waist with his arm. Waiting for them was the long black Mercedes, Dizzi holding open the rear door. He had somewhere obtained a black chauffeur's cap, which he was wearing jauntily, and he bowed as he said "Madame" and helped Anja into the seat. "Home, sir?" he said to Walter as Fass clambered in beside her.

"Correct, my man. Do use some care around the corners, though, won't you?" And the three of them began to laugh.

Sisi was standing at the open front door when they arrived at the apartment. When she saw little Anja with a bundle in her arms coming forward flanked by the two tall men, she cried and laughed at the same time. She wrapped her arms around Anja, looked tenderly at Sophie, then smothered Anja's face with butterfly kisses. "The most beautiful baby in the world," Sisi said. "The most beautiful baby that's ever been. Oh, my God, Anja. Oh, dear Anja, I love you so."

There was a small confusion at the door, Dizzi finally stepping inside first, then grasping Anja's elbow to help her across the threshold, Walter and Sisi right behind.

"There's a visitor," Sisi whispered to Walter.

"Who?"

"I don't *know* who," Sisi said. "A stranger."

"I'd like just to lie down for a while, Walter," Anja said, over her shoulder.

"Of course, dear, naturally. I'll help you to the room."

"And I'll entertain this visitor with the poor timing," Dizzi said. "Leave it to me. The Scharner charm."

But Sisi did not smile.

Walter kept his hand at the small of Anja's back as they walked down the long hall to their bedroom. Sisi had filled the place with flowers and tied a huge bow of pink silk on the cradle, which she'd made up with embroidered linens. "Here, Walter. Hold Sophie while I get into bed," Anja said. "Isn't it lovely of Sisi to've made everything so nice?"

"Are you pleased?" Walter said, crooking his arm to support the baby. Anja looked at him, and for a moment he thought her eyes had at last unshuttered, offering him a window into her being.

"In more ways than you know. In every way I can imagine," she said. Then she turned, fluffed the pillows, and lay down on top of the duvet. When she raised her arms to receive Sophie, Walter bent and kissed her. Then he brushed the child's forehead with his lips, let Anja take her from his arm.

"I'll make coffee. Would you like a cup? No? Tea, then? Or anything?" Walter asked.

"No, thanks. Not just yet."

"You're sure?"

"Yes. I only want to be here with Sophie for a bit," Anja said.

Then she thought of the phonograph that Walter had installed in their room just a few weeks before. They had a few records: Brahms's Lullaby and some lovely things by Chopin, *natürlich*, but also Dvořák, Suk, and a Hollander named van den Budenmayer whose music was darkly beautiful. "Please play the van den Budenmayer, Walter. Then go and see whoever it is that's called."

"I'll get rid of him," Walter said, gingerly lowering the phonograph needle. "Just call if you need anything at all. I'll come."

"I know," Anja said. "When Sophie falls asleep, I'll join you. I've been doing nothing but lying in bed for a week now."

"No, you've done so much more than that, darling," Walter smiled, backing toward the door. "You'll call, if you need anything?"

"Yes, Walter," Anja said. "I think I'll cook something special tonight."

"Dizzi and I already have plans for that."

"What, army food again?" Anja laughed.

"We've organized something much nicer. You'll see."

❖   ❖   ❖

Fass heard the voices as soon as he closed the bedroom door behind him—and froze, exactly as he had so many times in the Dinarics, whenever there'd been a noise in the forest that didn't seem quite natural.

"Of course I'm that Scharner," Dizzi was saying, in a particular tone Walter hadn't heard him use since the Yugoslav retreat. "And whom have I the honor of being interrogated by, if not actually being introduced to?"

"As I already told, an old comrade of Walter's." Dear sweet Christ, Fass thought, that alto voice resonating in the deepest reaches of his mind. This cannot be possible.

"Aha, a Chetnik, of course. Serb, no?" Dizzi said. "I'm acquainted with quite a few like you, although I don't believe we've had the pleasure."

"No, we have not. Anyway, names, they change with the times, *nicht wahr?*" Fass heard. "I am Mila Ćosić. Walter knows my previous one. Perhaps he chooses to tell you one day."

"Perhaps I won't care to know," Dizzi said with the easy rudeness he sometimes affected.

"Yes. It is enough for you to know I was there in the mortar barrage that cost Walter his arm. Some of us drag him down the mountain and get him to a Wehrmacht aid station. Lost my damn belt doing it. Had to use it as a tourniquet."

"How inventive," Dizzi said. "No doubt we acquired another."

"Easy. So many dead Germans lying around. But, excuse me, I come to see Walter, and you and I are so much chattering."

"Unfortunately you've arrived at an inopportune time, as you surely have noticed. I don't care to disturb him," Dizzi said.

"I think Walter himself will judge, thank you. I don't stay more than a minute or two anyway."

Fass felt outside of time, like a soldier who hadn't slept for forty-eight hours, as he entered the dining room. Sisi, backed into a corner with a hand on her belly, seemed tense as a cat treed by a dog. Dizzi was standing loose-limbed but ready for instant movement a meter from one of the chairs, blocking Walter's view of whoever was sitting there, whoever was the source of that haunting voice. A voice that should not be, since its owner was dead in an unmarked grave.

Dizzi swiveled smoothly when he heard Fass's footfall. And Walter suddenly saw the image that had never blurred, never wavered, never left him: small-headed, large-eyed, sleek, with auburn hair almost iridescent, like feathers.

"So pale, Walter! Do you think I am some ghost? Don't say you cannot believe. A smile at least, after all this time?" said his Chetnik, rising up strong and lithe and taking a step toward him.

"Old comrade, eh, Walter?" Dizzi asked. He was between them, his arms bent slightly.

But Fass's gaze was held by those falcon eyes that had fixed on him last as he lay on a stretcher while a Wehrmacht doctor frantically cut away shreds of uniform from his ripped left arm. And then had turned away from him, back to the woods, a figure in motley camouflage with the handles of stick grenades stuck in her boots, a Schmeisser machine pistol slung over her shoulder.

"Zofia? Unbelievable! I was sure you'd been killed," Fass said at last.

"They try very hard. But as you see, they fail," his Chetnik said. "And Walter, now I am Mila. Mila Ćosić, refugee from Tolmino. An Italian citizen."

"My God, I never expected . . . I've a thousand questions and I can scarcely speak."

"Then do not." Mila took another step forward, embraced Walter, and laid her cheek gently on his. It was the first time they had ever touched. The feel of her body against his was electric. Part of him wanted to wrap his arm around her like a lover. But part of him wanted to push her away, not just from the embrace but from the world of the living.

"Now you know I am real," she said. "Any doubts, ask your Jäger friend here. He has been taking me very seriously. Not the sort to talk with ghosts, is he, this Scharner?"

"Certainly not," Dizzi said, with an edge to his voice that cut through Fass's thick confusions. "Come on, Walter, who is this creature?"

"Tell him," Mila said, releasing Fass and stepping back so he could see all of her.

"Just as she said, Dizzi. Someone I fought beside for seventy-four days. Someone to whom I owe my life." My God, she's brave, coming here, he thought. Or else she's confident I have no more courage now than I had at the village.

"Zofia—Mila, I mean. How did you escape? Where have you been? How did you come to turn up here? Christ, I'm in shock."

"So it seems, my friend," Dizzi said.

"*Klar*, I think, who he speaks to, Scharner, if you do not mind," the Chetnik said.

"Dizzi, Zofia, don't."

"Nothing, Walter. No idea I had this would be such an extraordinary day for you. Or I would have waited a while to come. Your friend, he is just being protective, though of course from me there is no reason to be. Better I go now. You should be with your woman and your child."

"Yes. But wait. A drink at least. Your story."

"Too much for one day, all this. I will be in Bolzano for some little while, I think. At a better time, I come again," said the Chetnik, gathering her coat from the back of the chair. "I find my way out now."

"Where can I reach you?" Fass called as she slipped through the doorway.

"I will reach you," she said, not turning, closing the door very gently behind her.

"What on earth was that all about?" Sisi asked, coming finally out of her corner. "I was frightened for some reason the moment I opened the door and she asked for you, Walter. And I'm not so easily frightened, you know."

"Yes, a regular tigress, sweet Sisi is," Dizzi said.

"You didn't help, behaving as though you thought she was an assassin or something," Sisi said.

"And I've never known you to turn to jelly like that, Fass," Dizzi said, ignoring his wife. "What is going on here, please?"

"What you heard: an old comrade. That's the sum of it. But the jolt of having someone you were certain was dead suddenly walk right into your home," Walter said, knowing it was much, much more than that, and forever secret.

"Well, you didn't behave like this when I returned from the dead at Sauerlach," Dizzi sniffed.

"It was your clothes," Fass forced himself to grin. "They were much too ridiculous for a spectre. If I'd seen you in a tattered uniform, though, no doubt I would have panicked and run like hell."

"You looked awfully panicky to me, and she was certainly not in tatters," Sisi said. "Those clothes! The latest from Rome. They made me feel drab, like a little wren or something."

"What are you saying?" Fass asked.

"You didn't notice?" Sisi replied.

"I suppose something must have registered. I'd only ever seen her in battle dress. She looked as ragged as all the rest of us. Maybe seeing her look like a woman for the first time is part of the shock."

"But how is it a Chetnik you last saw two years ago in Yugoslavia turns up at your house, dressed to kill?" Sisi asked.

"She is a killer," Dizzi said flatly.

"And you weren't?" Fass snapped.

"Was indeed. I recognize my own kind. But I was not quite like that one."

"Oh, come on, Dizzi. You never knew her before today," Fass said, his false grin still stiffly in place.

"Do you have any rounds for that Luger, Walter?"

"What the hell are you talking about?"

"Oh, I feel a little bit like going hunting, that's all," Dizzi said, almost cheerfully. Fass recognized his "picnic with a purpose" voice.

"You're out of your degenerate mind," he said, angry now.

"No, my dear friend," Dizzi said gently. "Listen to yourself. You are going out of yours. Or soon will be. Can't stand by and let that happen, can I?"

※   ※   ※

Dizzi did not. Instead he produced, uncorked and helped Walter, with some slight assistance from Sisi, kill five bottles of champagne that evening during dinner and after, Anja looking on indulgently for a while, but returning to her room and her child before the third was dead.

Under that influence, Walter filed the Chetnik incident into a remote compartment of his mind, and, with military *Disziplin*, did not visit. He managed the same with the emotions Sophie had unbound that first day, and devoted himself to her and Anja until Anja could stand his hovering no more and sent him off with Dizzi. Which meant sending him off to drink, mainly. No harm done, except for one night, shortly before Dizzi and Sisi were due to drive back to Ischl, when the two men came home with clothes askew and Dizzi's face distinguished by a large yellowish-purple bruise. Dizzi, it seemed, had felt provoked by certain comments made about the Wehrmacht by two ex-Alpini in a bar, and invited them into the back alley to discuss the matter more fully. Walter's man, noticing the dangling sleeve, shrugged and raised his arms, palms out. The engineer took advantage of the moment to put his shoe hard into the Italian's crotch. The kick put him down on the cobbles in the foetal position, clutching his balls and moaning. Dizzi had a harder job, took a few jabs and a wild right cross to his face before doubling the ex-Alpini over with a left hook to the diaphragm, then kneeing him viciously on the chin, which snapped his head back and left him lying unconscious.

They got hell from Anja and Sisi over that. Sisi especially turned the full weight of her scorn—substantial, as it turned out—on them, which left them feeling more battered than the affair in the alley had.

Fass sometimes wondered if he had not merely had some sort of drunken hallucination that his Chetnik, her body long moldering in Yugoslav earth, had returned to the living world, come to his house, actually embraced him. Only the fact that Dizzi and Sisi asked about Mila—not too frequently or insistently but even in Anja's hearing—during the rest of their stay convinced him that Mila had been real.

But there was no corroboration from the subject herself; Mila didn't return, didn't send word. It was as if she had melted back into the woods, a Chetnik still at war.

Then, Dizzi and Sisi left, and he and Anja felt more peace of mind than they had known since '39. Their adoration of Sophie seemed to fill the house and envelop them with deeper feelings for each other as well.

Anja realized this first. The conversations over dinner became more open and more intimate as Walter drank less wine with his meals. The way they met each other's eyes grew warmer, more direct. They touched more often and more tenderly; the kisses of parting and goodnight on the cheek or forehead moved to the mouth, lingered beyond the perfunctory. When Walter was sitting up in bed reading at night, she began to nestle her head on his chest while she nursed Sophie, and she swore to herself she could actually feel every tension and upset of his working day flow out of him. He would close his book, kiss the crown of her head, and quietly watch Sophie at her breast.

The black days did not seem to come on him anymore. Or, if they did, he was able to shed whatever darkness afflicted him be-

fore he returned to their flat—more often than not bearing flowers. He had acquired, Anja knew not where, a passion for fresh
flowers in the bedroom.

Once Sophie was in her cradle, Anja found herself moving eagerly into Walter's embrace. Not quite as a lover; even after the
stitches had been removed, Anja felt too tender for a while to try
what she wanted now very much to try. She found a surprisingly
intense pleasure in the way they kissed and stroked each other before sleep. Walter, for the first time, became shy about his missing
arm. "I wish I could hold you the way you ought to be held, my
pretty little Pole," he whispered once.

"I love the way you hold me," Anja murmured back. "I want so
much now to please you as a woman. More than I did before."

"There hasn't been any before. There's just us, together now.
And Sophie. That is enough. That is far more than I'd hoped for."

The sweetest man, Anja thought. But, though she was careful
never to let it show, she could not rid herself of the anxiety that she
was too damaged ever to be the lover he needed, that what they
had now would one day be insufficient for him.

That was the only real fear left in her anymore, Anja realized
with surprise, but without delight or relief. Maybe it was actually
better to have many, she decided. Then no single one could loom so
large.

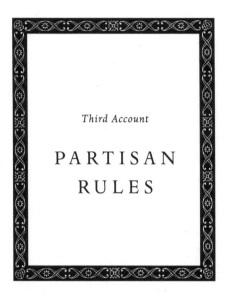

Third Account

PARTISAN
RULES

I

orgive me," Anja said, dandling Sophie on her knee, to the woman sitting near her under the wisteria vines in her garden. The November sun had been unseasonably strong, the day cloudless. Now the ancient stone walls radiated the warmth they had hoarded all day, so that even in the shade it was pleasantly mild. "It's very hard for me to picture you fighting in Yugoslavia."

"Not easy for me, either." Mila Ćosić smiled, gazing at her cashmere dress, at her legs sleek in silk stockings, at her fine calfskin pumps as if they were photos in a fashion magazine and not her own at all. "But had you seen me then! Hair never washed, clothes never washed, mud all over my face, under my nails, caked on my boots. Now I see myself in a mirror or reflected in a shop window, it's a stranger there. This is not me, I think."

Her German was serviceable. Broken here and there, with that Slav timbre and sibilance. Anja may not have been able to mark Mila as a Serb by her speech, but she'd have known instantly the woman was Slavic.

"Anja, I was so shamed. Turning up on someone's doorstep the very day she is bringing her baby home for the first time," Mila went on, sipping the coffee Anja had made when she arrived, unannounced, not ten minutes before. "Of all the days! Naturally, I had no idea. I am not even entirely sure here is the correct Fass. And, my God, poor Walter, he sees a ghost, thinking I'm dead all this time. Not my most brilliant action, excuse me. I should have written a note first."

"You did give him quite a shock. He was so confused afterward. When I asked who the visitor was, all he could do was mumble about an old comrade from Yugoslavia. It was my friend Sisi who told me the old comrade was an attractive young woman, not some burly veteran."

"Kind of her to say so. But I hope that didn't give you any incorrect impression," Mila said. "In war days, a scarecrow I looked. Another filthy Chetnik who has been too long in the woods. Out of the hundred in my formation when we link up with Walter's company, twenty at least are women. But who could know, looking at us?"

"How did you find him now?" Anja asked, wondering why Sisi and Dizzi had been so stiff and strange about this woman, why Sisi had been so frightened by her.

"Chance only. I have some business with Petrocelli. An engineer named Fass, he mentions is working for him. When I left Walter at the aid station, I am sure he would die there. His arm was—no need for details. But I ask Petrocelli for the address, and I come to see for myself. Not much hope here would be the Fass from the mountains with us. Still, you speak of Walter shocked. A big surprise for me as well! I have been embarrassed by the timing, so I wait this while to visit. Excuse me, please, if that sudden appearance spoiled your day."

"Nothing to apologize for," Anja said. She was liking this woman. "You could have been from the moon. I was in another world, one populated solely by Sophie and me. And it still feels that way, much of the time. I'm glad you finally decided to come back. I'm sure Walter will be glad, too."

"Maybe not," Mila frowned slightly. "Some people, they don't want people from the past turning up. They don't want to be reminded. The bad time, *nicht wahr?*"

"But Walter's not one of those. He handles it as well as anyone could, I think. Better than I had, certainly, until Sophie. Now it feels like I've been reborn. Recollections of those bad years never linger long."

"I very much envy you, Anja," Mila said. "Me, I am one of the haunted ones, I think. Not all the time, naturally. But once in a while, when I don't expect it, some terrible thing comes in my head. Or suddenly I see the face of a friend who was killed. I feel, how to say it, large grief?"

"I understand. For a long time I couldn't bear to think of the war at all. I did everything I could to erase those years from my mind. Of course nothing worked. But now when the sad memories come, I don't try to force them away. I just let them be, let myself cry a bit, and they fade away by themselves."

"Ah, the baby must help. A new life, in your arms."

"She's everything to me," Anja said, holding Sophie to her and murmuring the little Polish endearments that always made the baby smile. "I never thought I'd be so lucky."

God, why did she use the Polish? Bad to do that in front of a stranger, Anja thought for an instant.

But then she relaxed. For too long her fears had been almost physical, a topographic feature of her world. But the contours had smoothed, become less jagged, more like the weather-worn hills around Krakow than the thrusting young Alps. What was the worry anymore? Was this woman, whose name was not Mila Ćosić any more than hers was Anna Fass, a threat? Hardly. She would be safe forever, the legal wife of an Italian citizen, the mother of an Italian citizen.

She looked up at Mila, who was smiling at them wistfully. Damaged, this one. Burdened, and hurting. Take away the fine clothes, and Mila was only another displaced person, a woman at the wire, always on guard and tired of having to be so. She was nice-looking and intelligent and clearly more than getting by. But she was not whole in this world.

"Mila, I still can't believe you were a soldier," Anja said, shaking her head.

"But look at you, perfectly lovely with a beautiful child. Yet I think you did not stay home and do nothing during the war? You fought somewhere too, I think? You once were much like me in Yugoslavia?"

"No," Anja said, her old suspicion rising, then quickly subsiding. What could this woman know? Nothing. She was only guessing.

"No? Ah, is only that I always feel I recognize those who fought. The eyes, something in them. And I am recognized that way by others, I think. So, a lot of nonsense maybe. But it is, how to explain, like all of us who fought are wearing medals only other fighters can see."

Not medals. Hardly medals. Yet Anja suddenly felt a potent impulse to trust Walter's comrade, despite Sisi's warnings and her own past training, with at least a portion of the truth.

"I never was in combat, like you and Walter. I'm from Krakow, and I was in the Polish resistance from the start, in '39. We were on opposite sides, you and I. Enemies, I suppose."

"What's the difference?" Mila laughed. "Chetniks start out fighting the Wehrmacht. Patriots only, no ideology. Then we turn to fighting Tito and his Partisans, because Tito is a murderous pig who does not care how many innocents have to die for his ambitions. And in the end, some of us are fighting with the Germans against him, as you know. The whole world turned upside down. That old saying? 'The enemy of my enemy is my friend'?

"Ah, hell. First I kill Germans to protect Yugoslavs, then I kill Yugoslavs to protect Germans. Insanity, all of it, no? I cannot get over it. But it is surely over. A feeling came, from the way you looked at me, that you knew what people like Fass and me and so many know. The ones who did nothing will always be ignorant. They never understand."

"I wish I didn't. I wish I could have stayed out of it. But as you say, it is over," Anja replied.

"Your weapon?" Mila asked.

"What?"

"What you prefer for the shooting? For me, the German MP 40, the Schmeisser. No question. A bit heavy of course. But very good, very reliable."

"Ah," Anja said. Then she remembered Krzysztof, the boy who had been hanged. He had a gun. He shot an SD man. Or so he told her, and she told Richter. "A Radom automatic."

"Only a pistol? What caliber?"

"The usual. The seven-millimeter." Anja was improvising now.

"So little," Mila shook her head. And so wrong. She knew the Radom was a nine-millimeter, knew that Anja had no experience with guns. So what did this Pole really do in Krakow? "Only a little pistol? Ah, so stupid I am. Of course you were not in the woods. Operating secretly in a city. No battles. Naturally only a pistol. Easy to hide in your purse or something. Pull it out quick some nights, boom to a German's head. Then disappear like a ghost, correct?"

"I never shot anyone," Anja said, perhaps a beat too quickly. "My job was to gather information. The pistol was for me. In case they came to arrest me."

"Very important, this kind of work, I know. Also very danger-ous. All alone, everything secret. Me, I could not do such things.

Better to be in a combat unit, comrades all around you." And just who, Mila wondered, did this Pole gather information for? That was the thing with agents, Chetnik, Titoist, Ustaše, German. You could not know for sure. Maybe they were completely loyal, but always they could be double or even triple agents. "You are frightened, doing this work?"

"Of course. But I do not want to talk about it."

"Forgive me, Anja. It is very rude to be welcomed into someone's home and bring up awful things," Mila said, turning her face away toward the far wall of the garden in a futile effort to hide her tears. "It is hard sometimes, *nicht wahr?* Home gone, family gone, alone in a foreign place where no one even knows my name. So what, I ask? How many there are just like you, Mila? Too many to count. Enough self-pity. It is a weakness. But still the feelings come. And the talking, talking. As if that could help. Please excuse me. To burden you with any of this, I feel ashamed."

"I know how it is," Anja said. "I can't go home, either. Without Sophie and Walter and his Uncle Franz —without them? I might have hanged myself long ago. Things will turn better for you as well. You've at least two friends right here, now."

Mila tried to grin away her tears, but her mouth only contorted in a parody of a smile. Why was she moved by this Serb? Why should she care at all about someone just met, and so little known? Ah, Sophie, little sparrow. What have you done to me? Anja thought. Have you given me back a heart?

Mila rose then, dabbed at her face with a tissue she'd pulled from her purse. "No way to behave in front of you," she said. "I pray I have not upset you. A mistake to visit, I think. I must be going."

"Mila, wait. Would you lunch with us this Sunday? It's really the only time I'm sure Walter will be around, he's working so hard these days. I know he's been wanting very much to see you. Please come. You will, won't you?"

"Oh, Anja, I am not fit company, as you see. Why are you so kind?"

"Then you'll come. I'll expect you at noon. Walter will be very happy and so will I. We have so few friends here," Anja said, cradling the sleeping baby in her left arm, and taking Mila by the hand. It felt almost as strong as a man's. But unmistakably feminine, soft and shapely. So difficult to envision a knife in such a hand, or a live grenade, or a trigger squeezed by one of those fingers.

"Bless you, Anja, for your good intentions," Mila said, then turned and left the garden, went down the long corridor, and out the front door.

⬛ ⬛ ⬛

Weary almost to death of being one of the hunted, Mila Ćosić sighed heavily as she walked through the clusters of dry fallen leaves on the sidewalk. Maybe here, in this place, she might find sanctuary. So far she had not needed to use any deception or evasion, even. The little Pole was clever, in Krakow she may have been very dangerous, very good at her craft. But life had been soft with her for a while, her guard was down, she was practically tame. Already she was offering friendship. Well, she would gain a friend. If she proved useful, usable.

Two blocks ahead, Mila saw a pair of *carabinieri* strutting like peacocks, their uniforms the stuff of light opera, their intelligence the stuff of a dozen rude jokes, but a threat nonetheless. She turned down the nearest side street, highly alert but still careless of the leaves—for this was not the forest of Yugoslavia, where the snap of a twig might trigger a bullet.

Her thoughts remained concentrated on Anja Fass and her husband. They must be protected, they must prosper, even be helped to do so—oh, by a clever, trusted friend who would be kind and generous to them. Mila would be just that. She would insinuate herself so deeply into their household that Anja and Walter would come to regard her as a member of their family.

In that way, she'd find the refuge she needed.

Every day on her own was a day of risk, Mila knew. But you cannot build a fortress quickly, or by yourself. Much better to be asked to share a safe haven, a place already established, secure, the object of no one's suspicions or scrutiny.

The Fass household was beneath the notice of those who were looking for her, Mila was sure. The place did not even exist for the police. And who searched in a place that did not exist?

Mila laughed to herself even as she turned suddenly down another side street. Unless she felt the authorities closing in on her, she would make a long, slow seduction of Anja and Walter Fass. And they would become her camouflage, perhaps even the tools she'd need to make herself untouchable.

She would not hurt them. Unless circumstances left her no choice in the matter.

Anja put Sophie in her cradle, then pulled a chair into the middle of the garden, where a warming patch of sun still lingered. She closed her eyes and raised her face to the sky, basking, a thing she could never do in summer because of her fairness, but which gave her a delicious catlike feeling now. Despite the odd resonance her visitor had left behind.

What to make of Mila Ćosić? Or, more exactly, what to make of Sisi's remarkable apprehension of her? It seemed so overwrought, so uncharacteristic—especially now that Anja had met and talked with Mila. Yet Sisi had heedlessly unsettled her with extravagant descriptions of Walter's Chetnik.

***

God, the way she swept right in when I opened the door," Sisi had said, the day after Anja came home from the hospital with Sophie. "Her presence seemed somehow overpowering and sexual, but in a frightening way. Never run up against a type like that. If she was five or six years younger she could have had me on the spot. But she looked me over like she was a judge at a horse show, and then seemed to dismiss me."

Sisi admitted that had made her a little snippy, but said she hadn't gotten out more than a few choice words before Mila stopped her cold merely by staring into her eyes. There was something there Sisi didn't know how to explain, something that made her want to run like hell.

So strange. Anja had felt nothing at all like that today. Mila's eyes were attractive, almost like Walter's but a much richer, darker brown with gold flecks. They were hesitant, soft, almost vulnerable. "Intimidating" was the last thing she would call them.

Sisi claimed Scharner had also sensed something wrong as soon as he got a look at Mila, before she'd even said a word. "The short little hairs on the back of his neck stood up!" she said. "Now, that was a first. You know how self-confident Dizzi is. Overbearingly self-confident. But she'd somehow put him on guard instantly. And then of course Walter . . ."

"Oh, come on, Sisi," Anja said. "You're talking a lot of rubbish. Walter was just startled out of his shoes because he thought the woman had gotten killed in the war, and suddenly here she is. His nerves weren't too steady to begin with. I think Sophie, poor little thing, is the creature who scared him. Still does. You see the way he tiptoes around her. I think he's having trouble realizing he's a father."

"You're right, Anja," Sisi said, but the expression on her face clashed with her words.

"Well?" Anja demanded. "D'you think they were lovers, rutting away in those damned mountains in between battles with the Partisans? You think she's come to claim Walter?"

"No, nothing like that. My sense is it would take a man a lot bolder and more reckless than Walter—no offense—to wrestle that one down. And she'd have his balls as a trophy afterward, one way or the other."

Anja hooted at that.

"So says our Sisi, vastly experienced with men," she said.

"Very funny. But don't discount the way I know women. I've a sixth sense about women."

"Girls, maybe. Women? I'm not so sure. How is it, with that sixth sense, you got punched in the face for trying to molest a certain woman back in the camp?"

Sisi flushed, then started babbling nonsense about letting her hormones get the better of her judgment then, because she'd been deprived for months. "And I did eventually get that certain woman into my cot, don't forget that. Hah!"

"Just for the warmth, Sisi. Just for the warmth."

"Oh, the pity of it," Sisi moaned, then smiled that bright smile Anja so liked to see. "I'll shut up about this crazy Chetnik if you'll let me hold Sophie for a while. I need the practice, don't I?"

And Sisi held Sophie, even bared a breast and gently placed the infant's mouth against her nipple. Sophie started wailing instantly.

"Oh, dear," Sisi said. "Ssshhh, Sophie. I only wanted to see what it was like, pretty thing. Here's your mamma. Here she is. Anja, do they know their own mother by smell or something? Is that why she's crying?"

"I think she's crying because she expected to get something good to eat and was bitterly disappointed that you failed to deliver." Anja laughed.

But she found little to laugh about in other things Sisi said. Or actually refused to speak of, but revealed in her ways: the drinking, the tantrum over the lack of sugar in the café, the wild gyrations of mood. All was not well in Ischl. In fact, poor Sisi might be going through hell there. Her nerves were certainly shot.

Perhaps that explained why, on the last day, after an embrace and Sisi's normal complement of tears, her friend had whispered to her, "Please be careful if that woman ever comes back. Really, Anja. There's something very bad about her. Just be careful, please."

The sunny spot in the garden vanished, and Sophie was stirring. Be careful of what? Anja thought. It had been kind, gentle, well-meaning old Franz—not Sisi and her blather of a fearsome Chetnik or her signals of distress—who caused the worst turbulence she'd gone through after Sophie's birth: a fierce argument with Fass when she learned that Franz had arranged for the child to be christened in Wolfsgruben's church. Anja wanted no part of Catholic ritual, refused to allow the christening. When Fass asked how he could ever right this with Franz, she'd said, "Explain this marriage is loveless, nothing but a bargain we made in a bad time. And that Sophie's purely an accident."

Walter's reply stunned her. "It isn't loveless anymore, Anja," he almost whispered. "For me at least."

Anja gave in. Sophie was christened.

She lifted the baby from the cradle and walked into the house. She felt no care or worry at all. Walter would be home soon. She decided to make the Brenner meal: boiled potatoes sliced in disks and topped with cheese. She'd eat just like the signalman. And then she'd give Walter a surprise he would not forget.

III

She was here? She came here to talk to you?" Walter asked, his pleasure in the simple meal wiped out with one word from Anja: a name that was not a true name, attached to a woman whose physical existence seemed less real than the image that had lived within him. "What did she want?"

"Oh, nothing really," Anja said. "She was apologetic about showing up the day we came home from the hospital. That was her excuse for calling, anyway. I suspect the real reason was that she is very curious about your woman and your child."

"Ah, nonsense." Walter managed to smile.

"You make the mistake of thinking of her only as some hard-bitten comrade-in-arms."

"But that's all she ever was." Walter hoped his voice did not sound as false as the words felt.

"One role only," Anja said. "She was someone else before, she was more than just a soldier when she fought, and she is someone else now. Complicated. Lots of different sides to her. Like me. Like you."

"You can only know the side you've seen, isn't that so?"

"If you're insensible as an Alp, or incurably literal-minded—which engineers traditionally are, aren't they? Occupational hazard. Too much logarithmic self-abuse in their youth, probably. Didn't you have to go to confession for that when you were a student? 'Father, I've had impure thoughts and I, uh, played with my equations' or something?" Anja laughed. "But I think you've seen her more ways than one. You know as well as I she's a woman like any other. You just don't want to acknowledge that. And my guess is she had feelings for you when you were together in Yugoslavia."

Anja gave him a teasing grin. "A brief but passionate wartime romance, Walter? Yes? Come on, don't be coy. It doesn't suit you."

Fass snorted.

"The officer harrumphs! Then why does she make you so nervous, Captain Fass, sir?"

"She does not. I have nerves of steel."

"Ah, so I'm wrong. How silly of me. How girlish. A long but passionate wartime romance, then."

Was he so transparent? And where was the truth to be found? Love or hate? No chance for anything genuine in those damned mountains, that damned winter. Not even an urgent, desperate fuck. Except in his imagination. The Chetniks had the same rules as the Partisans: Any female soldier who slept with a man was subject to summary execution. Some risked it. He saw at least one, a girl of nineteen who had the bad luck to get pregnant, shot for it. And as for Mila, she would have laughed at the rule as she broke it. There was no fear in her.

But she never broke it. She seemed as icy-hearted as the most zealous mother superior in the strictest convent imaginable. Never gave the subtlest hint that she might be a woman, with a woman's desires. Not to him. Not to anyone else, either, as far as he ever saw.

And he had watched very, very closely, because he'd been half-crazed with lust, wanted those falcon eyes locked to his as their bodies joined. It was a torment that was also a blessing, for it kept the terror of the fighting at bay. Without his obsession, he knew he might have broken.

"Now you've got me," he smiled at Anja. "We went AWOL together, hid for a year in a secret cave, making love all the time. We missed the war entirely. It was a rude surprise when we heard the fighting had ended, believe me. A great disappointment. It wrecked our romance, peace did."

"I knew it, I knew it. I can see right through you, Fass."

"Then you know that I wish I could have spent the war hidden in a cave with any damned one. Even Petrocelli's wife. Or even, God, Dizzi," Walter said. "You can't imagine the conditions in those mountains. The last thing on our minds was sex, even if the Chetnik girls had been willing, which they definitely were not. All we could think of was how the hell to get out of there alive."

"She's very attractive, Walter. Very sexy," Anja went on teasing him.

"Not then. She was as tough as any trooper. It would be a transformation beyond belief, if she's become what you say."

"Well, you'll have a second chance to judge. She's coming to lunch Sunday."

"Lunch?"

"I invited her to lunch. I like her, and you were so dazed the day she was here I felt sure you'd enjoy a chance to see her again. Your old comrade. Surely you've lots to talk about." Anja laughed. "And don't you dare think of saying I ought to have asked you first. You're owed a surprise or two or three."

"True, true," Walter said, bobbing his head and smiling weakly. The blurred unease he had felt when Anja first mentioned

Mila's visit was focusing now. "So, what did you find to talk about?"

"Not all that much. Babies, men, the usual. But not you, so you can stop fretting about that. Which you are, you know. You're fidgeting in your seat. So much for nerves of steel. The war came up. She cried a bit. She said I had the look of someone who had fought, too, and would understand. A strange thing, though. I felt not only sympathy, but trust. I told her I was a Pole, in the Resistance."

"You did that? You told her?"

"Why not? You sound as suspicious as I used to, did you know that? Even if it was something to hide, which it is not, I felt safe enough with her. After all, she is the one who saved your life."

"She claimed that?"

"No, Fass! Sisi did. Mila told Dizzi and Sisi about the mortar barrage, about dragging you down the mountain to an aid post, using her belt as a tourniquet on your arm. Sisi told me. Mila never mentioned anything today about the actual circumstances you shared. From the way she wept, I think it will be a long, long time before she's able to face most of her memories."

A strong sense of trespass and intrusion came over Fass. Mila here in his home, talking like that to his wife. Talking about the war. It felt all wrong.

※　　※　　※

They ate in the garden that Sunday because the day was so bright and warm. That entire autumn had been the sunniest and mildest Walter had known here—though there was that twenty-year gap in his knowledge of Südtirol weather. He cooked his veal with morels—the single dish he had any mastery of—and as always, there were bottles of Uncle Franz's fresh, neat wine.

Yet even in that pleasantness, even though there had been

peace for more than eighteen months, the war remained a subtext of every conversation. Fass hated it. He forbade himself to ask any of the dozens of questions he needed answers to. But Anja questioned, and Mila answered as if she were relating ordinary stories, cheerful anecdotes cheerfully told.

"Did you get out of Yugoslavia with the Wehrmacht?" Anja inquired almost as soon as they began eating.

"They tried to keep us there, to die!" Mila laughed. "The bastards—excuse me, Walter—drove us away at gunpoint near the Austrian border. So tense, that moment. We were very close to firing on them. I think I would have, but there were too many. So. They go, we stay to be wiped out by the Partisans. We disband, we run, each where he would."

"How horrible," Anja said. "Abandoning you like that."

"But how German, yes?" Mila laughed again. "All Germans must be born ruthless, I think. Or they teach them this in kindergarten."

And when do Serb falcons begin their murderous training? Walter wanted to ask. And how do the falconers draw them back to the arm after every kill?

"Since Walter's a Tiroler, and I'm a Pole, feel free to say anything bad you like about the Krauts. I've no fondness for them, either."

"No, naturally. What Pole would not hate? I was fortunate, one of the few. Partisans everywhere, like flocks of crows sent by the devil, looking, looking. But they don't see one or two people careful in the mountains, people who know how to move and hide. A woman and I go very carefully across the northern Julian Alps, we move and hide, we sneak over Predil Pass to Italy, coming down south of Tarvisio. Then we go more south, towards Gorizia and Trieste, where the British and Americans are strong. The danger then was the Italian *partigiani*. If they know we are Chetniks, they shoot us. If they think we are Partisans, the same. Since by then there was a lot of fighting between the Italians and the Yugoslavs."

"But why?" Anja asked.

"The war, it is surely over everywhere else in Europe. But not on that border. Tito, he wants Trieste and Gorizia. Skirmishes and raids almost every day. Still going on, even now. All unofficial, naturally. Tito says no, my men are not fighting. A big lie, everyone knows this. But the British and Americans can't hit them with regular troops. Politics. They don't want to provoke Stalin. So they arm some people there, show them how to hunt and kill the Tito men."

"Christ, it must be a nightmare," Anja said.

"A child's game, hide-and-seek, compared to before."

"Anja, enough, please," Walter said. "Let's just agree that we're all very lucky people to have come through, that what's done is done. And poor Mila must feel like she's being interrogated, with all these questions."

"Walter, don't be too serious with her," Mila said, eyes bright. "This is the only chance I have to tell my story. It's good, among friends again, to be able to speak freely."

"So, Anja." Mila turned her attention away from the engineer. "Through some work I did, I come to know some people in Zona A, the British and American zone. I do a good job for them, the right people. You know how it goes. I get from them the papers: Mila Ćosić, born in San Floriano, a little town near Gorizia, later living in Tolmino. Like all the little places around there, Slovene for generations, even though it's Italy after 1918, Austria before. I get my Italian citizenship with it, just like all those Slovenes have. Zofia Dragović from Belgrade, who's she? Some dead Chetnik? Missing in action, never be heard from again.

"And I start my little business. I sell many kinds of valuable things belonging to Italians—who were rich before the war but poor now—to the Americans, for U.S. dollars. Then I do the black-market currency trading, pay the Italians in lire. Some dollars I keep to buy gold at a good price, which I then sell to other Italians—*pescecani*, these war profiteers—who got no faith in the lire and big trouble getting their money to Swiss banks. All they want is gold, or dollars. I gouge as much as I can out of them, no problem. Because they are dirty as hell, and their money is filthy blood money.

"I become, you could say, an angel of mercy? I relieve these dirty people of as much of their burden as I can. Good, no?"

"In every way, so it would seem. You're the best-dressed woman in the Südtirol. Here's to continued success."

"Thank you, Anja."

"But why Bolzano, of all places?" Fass asked. There was a deeper, darker side to this, he felt certain. But what he really wanted to know he could not ask. Was it pure coincidence that she had found him, or had she come looking for him? Probably coincidence. What reason could she have to trace him? It was a *senso unico* he had gone down with Mila in wartime, her uncaring and uninterested. And unaware, he hoped, of his tortured feelings.

"Out of the way, quiet, not the place anyone thinks to look for a person like me. Naturally, what I do does not please the authorities. So. A little apartment here. A safe place. I go often around Trieste and Venice, collecting the dollars and the gold. I go then to my filthy *pescecani* in Brescia, Milan, Turin. Easy train connections, reservations always in another name . . . then back to my safe place for a while. A tactical evasion, *klar?*"

"I know a little about that—evasion, I mean," Anja said.

"I suppose you must, to survive Krakow. So I do no business at all in Bolzano—except a little with Petrocelli, because he is not a *pescecane* even though he is making huge sums, and because I trust him."

"Walter's uncle, who knows him pretty well, says he is about as straight as an Italian businessman can be and still succeed."

"Ah, but there is something more," Mila said, her face mirthful. "You have seen that fat wife of his?"

"Couldn't miss her, at the opening of the bridge Walter built for him. She was grotesque. She waddles. A sort of human hippo."

"Anja," Fass sighed.

"I swear the bridge sagged when she walked across it!"

"A wonder it does not collapse!" Mila said. "A wife like that, naturally the man is a little in love with me. For me it is nothing, I'm not interested, he knows this. So he falls deeper and deeper. Mad, you know? At least two little mistresses already he's keeping, one in Eppan and the other in the city. Now he wants another? Greedy, I tell him. Your heart will fail in one of these beds. A good joke, no?"

Mila smiled neutrally at Fass. "But not a bad man. Only be sure he pays you what you are worth, Walter. He likes to moan about high costs, too much competition. Old habit, I think, from old times, when he struggled. He is making plenty now, believe me. And so should you."

"He's been generous," Walter replied, regarding her closely while Anja rose and began to clear some dishes from the table. Then the image of his Chetnik seemed to superimpose itself, more clearly defined than the face he was looking at. And they matched exactly, despite the tremendous change from ragged soldier to superbly done-up woman. Walter shook his head. Too much wine. But she was not beautiful, he realized. Not even pretty, by conventional standards. Her features were too sharp, her body too lean and hard. Perhaps it was the way she moved, her gaze. She seemed to promise something rare, unusual. And at the same time, a challenge.

Fass did not dare look at Anja for a few moments, for fear she might see his feelings in his eyes. Feelings she would not understand, because he did not.

※ ※ ※

But the Sunday lunch had not gone as badly as he had feared, when the last sip of coffee had been taken and Mila had said goodbye. There had been some pleasant moments, and Fass felt he had kept his anxiety well enough concealed.

Dizzi was right, he knew; Mila was a killer. But the Mila who sat beside him for a few easy hours? Physically she was the same woman he'd known in Yugoslavia, once he got past the almost flawless façade of lovely, expensive clothes and beautifully cut hair and the open display of powerful femininity. Yet it seemed to Fass as if a different mind, a different soul even, had now taken over that body, that face, those eyes. The predator had vanished.

But his fascination had not. She was still the forbidden Chetnik. Had she given any hint or sign that she was interested in him as a man, he would be in the deepest trouble, he realized. He would have found a way to meet her secretly in some safe place where he could finally take her as she had taken all of him. It would not be love they made. It would be an all-out assault to conquer her, to leave her whimpering and in doubt that she had ever witnessed the terrible weakness Fass had displayed in the mountains.

But Mila had shown him nothing but casual regard and little enough of that, devoting almost all her attention to Anja and Sophie.

"She's going to be a friend of mine, I'm sure," Anja said that evening, Sophie at her breast and Walter by her side in bed. "A friend to us. Won't that be nice? It's a shame she travels so often in her work. But I'm looking forward to seeing as much of her as we can."

And Walter, remembering his shy allusion to Anja just before the baby's christening that he loved her, wondered now if it had been a lie, or if he did in fact have such a feeling for his Pole, only to have it undermined now by an obsession become living woman. An obsession he was determined to be free of.

An intense sensation of being alone, of being apart from all others, came over him then. And with it a great sadness over what he had lost, and what he might be about to risk losing.

⬛   ⬛   ⬛

So. Piece of cake, as the goddamned English say, Mila Ćosić thought as she climbed the twisting stone stairway up to her apartment in the *centro*—a small space on the top floor of a sixteenth-century building, newly plastered, painted, wired and plumbed. Petrocelli had found it for her.

Inside, she kicked off her shoes and began to undress, easing out of her pullover, dropping her skirt, then hanging both in the armoire, which was neat as a rack in an exclusive shop, no item touching another. She admired the display for a moment, the harmony of the subdued solid colors she favored, the fineness of the merinos and cashmeres. She retrieved her shoes and placed them precisely in the gap in the line of other shoes on the floor of the armoire, each pair under the outfit they were meant to be worn with. Then she went into the bathroom and turned on the tub taps.

The armoire doors closed, there was little sign that the apartment was inhabited. No photos, no papers, no letters or pens on the old trestle table that served as her breakfast place and desk. No hairbrush or comb or bottles of scent or makeup on the round-mirrored chestnut vanity. The bed looked as though it had never been slept in. Not a single thing anywhere, not even a coffee cup by the sink, that could be identified as personal.

In the bathroom, Mila unfastened her brassiere, touched briefly the thick white cicatrix a Partisan bayonet slash had left on her ribs just below her right breast. She undid her garter belt and carefully rolled down her silk stockings, her fingers brushing a larger, ragged scar from grenade shrapnel high on her left thigh, and took off her panties. She folded the silk underthings carefully and placed them in a small chest of drawers reserved for them. Then she stepped into the bath and submerged herself to the chin. Closing her eyes, she let the caress of the hot water release tension from every muscle.

Blood money paid for this luxury, made me Mila and not Zofia. Time now for another way to keep what I earned.

Walter still wants me like always. That's good. And he doesn't realize how clear that is, just as he never realized what he revealed every time he looked at me when we were together in the mountains. He's suppressed the horror and disgust he felt over what I made him do, in that village with the name I've forgotten. Also good. Now, if only he keeps his head long enough, doesn't do anything rash, my way is clear.

First, Anja. Then Walter.

When he sleeps with his little Pole tonight, he will try to imagine it's my body beneath him. But he will fail. When he finally gets what he's been dreaming of ever since we met, will it be all he hoped? No. It will be too much for him. As it's been for all the others. Fragile creatures, men.

Let Fass dream on about his Chetnik. Let that Scharner, who recognized me as I recognized him, warn him again, as I'm sure he already has. It will do no good.

Anja first.

Fass?

He will come whenever I call.

IV

Deep in the darkness of a silent room in the silent city, Anja lifted Sophie from her cradle. The infant butted her face against the softness of a breast until her mouth found the nipple. Anja felt Sophie's tiny body go still, only her mouth moving, felt the flow of life between her and her daughter, and was satisfied. This was her sole virtue. If evil done could be placed on one plate of a scale and goodness on the other, she knew, there would never in her life be anything close to balance. The angle of difference would always be sharp.

So she loved these moments immoderately. She tried to imagine what Mila's nights were like at this hour: Was the Chetnik wandering the realm of sleep and dreams, or open-eyed, anxiously aware that hours are not equal, that the sleepless ones are so much longer than the rest? Or was she perhaps in the arms of a lover, her body awash in pleasure, her mind unhooked from time and memory both?

She heard Walter's regular breathing beside her. It was too measured. She sensed that he was only feigning sleep, that he had not slept at all this night, though he'd been woozy with drink when they'd gone to bed. He had worked his way through at least two bottles of wine after lunch and through the evening. Not enough, perhaps, to deaden emotions stirred by all that war talk with Mila. Not sufficient to gain a peaceful night.

Sophie, mouth still in place, drifted into sleep. Anja put the baby in her cradle, eased the embroidered coverlet Liese had made over the little creature, and slid back down in the bed. Then she felt Walter turn, felt his lips brush her eyes and nose, searching for and finding her own mouth.

Like a first kiss, Anja thought, surprised. This was sweet. She opened her lips beneath his to have more of it. She felt his hand stroking her leg from hip to knee, then sliding low on her belly, then lower still until all her senses seemed concentrated on the touch of a single finger on a single place. Very sweet. Very, very nice.

Then Walter was deep inside her in a movement so smooth Anja scarely felt the shift. But he was different this time. More insistent, harder, rougher. Almost as if there was an anger in him. She did not care. She rose to meet it, kept rising, and finally knew the transport.

"Dear Anja," Walter whispered when he finally rolled off and lay beside her, his face still close to hers. She stared straight up at the ceiling. She felt she was floating, flowing along on the slow current of a warm and gentle stream.

"Oh, Anja."

"Ssshhh," she murmured, content. "Say nothing." She wanted this flowing to go on and on. It was such a beautiful sensation, one she'd not known before.

Not as Anja the Doll, her very own creation, now perhaps left behind. Anja had never let her heart guide her actions with men—until Fass. Never went with a man because she wanted him but always for some purpose, some calculated use that had nothing to do with pleasure—until Fass. Never felt passion overrule her mind and take over her body.

So sweet, with Fass. Always it had been sweet with him. But nothing more. Anja always remained earthbound, unable to lose herself completely in an overwhelming sensual joy. She had been trying, God knew. Many nights for a month or more now, always at her initiative, she and Walter made love. The desire she felt was genuine—as far as she could tell—and Walter was a tender, attentive lover. It always started so well. But always, at a certain moment, she fell back from the peak. It became playful, it felt lovely, and she loved it when Walter lost himself in her. But it seemed that she was not fully participating, that some part of her remained detached, almost an observer. She wasn't disappointed or frustrated at the end, but sensed there was something greater that would forever elude her.

No more. Not after this time. Now, at last, she knew.

So she lay, happy. But toward dawn, when she heard Sophie begin to whimper hungrily and moved to feed her child, Anja had a revelation that first tautened her body with fury, then dropped her into despair.

Why this night, of all the nights they had slept side by side, of all the nights Walter had lain patient and passive unless she began to make love to him, had he suddenly taken her?

Why had he done what he'd never done before? In a strange yet marvelous way he never had before?

God, it was so simple. She had not been in this bed, this night, for him.

Fass had fucked his Chetnik. Not her.

▪ ▪ ▪

Anja felt, watching him rise and dress a little later, that she should hate Walter Fass. All of her history, all of her training, demanded that. But in each of his movements and accustomed touches, in every word over the morning's *caffellatte* and fresh rolls—though they said nothing of the night—she detected something that deflected her anger, turned it back on her: Fass was contrite.

There was so much irony in all of this that she almost laughed. He had finally carried her away, led her to where she'd so much wanted to go. Yet poor, pathetic Fass was guilt-ridden over his fantasy. Any anger toward him seemed absurd. Anja the Doll in Krakow, Anja allowing her body to be used in dim rooms by men she scarcely knew and did not want. Anja trying always to escape this truth by fantasizing she was making love with Slawomir, that beautiful boy who had been the first to touch her, the boy she never had the chance to sleep with, and never would. Even with Fass, she had sometimes imagined Slawomir.

And Fass was a good and decent man who cared for her more than she had any right to expect. In all their time together, he had placed her before himself, had cheerfully accepted her rules and her wishes. How could she hate him, then, for the use he had made of her body last night? It was a sort of trespass, true. But such an insignificant one, really. He had earned the right to much more.

Which she could not say of herself.

How could she ever condemn Fass for anything, least of all an ephemeral vision that had only appeared privately, in his mind? That may very well have been unwilled? He was not to blame. Neither was Mila, certainly. Any more than she and her phantom Slawomir were liable, or guilty of any true betrayal of Walter.

They had built a bond—call it love, call it whatever you cared to—and good, patient Walter nurtured it, kept to it and, God, perhaps treasured it. It was up to her, she knew, to make it clearer to Fass that she valued their connection. But how to do this?

Confession and contrition all alone in a stinking barn would not be her solution now.

Let us both go on imagining then, Anja decided, if that's what is required for now. Eventually, perhaps, if we repeat this small deception over and over and over again, we will discover satisfaction in ourselves, not in fading dreams of others.

V

"Poppy-seed cake," Mila said, cheery as always though her coat was slick with freezing rain that had lately arrived in the valley of the Adige. "And fresh coffee, from Udine, where they roast the best. Water, no problem I think." She held paper bags in each hand as she stood at Anja's door.

"Water we have, but don't stand out there in it." Anja smiled, ushering Walter's Chetnik into the vestibule.

Mila had taken to dropping by unannounced for afternoon coffee two or three times a week, ever since that Sunday lunch. The first visit after her transporting night with Fass was, for Anja, difficult in a way she hadn't anticipated. The sight of Mila raised a terrific jealousy she had to fight to suppress. But Anja decided before the end of the encounter that Mila was not only blameless, but completely indifferent to Fass as a man. Subsequent visits were cordial, relaxed. Anja looked forward to seeing her now. She even missed her when Mila was traveling.

The struggle with Fass had been of another order. But "struggle" wasn't the right word. Anja created a deliberate incitement, one she hoped would bring Walter's furtive guilt into the open and then drive it away, leaving them open to each other, without secrets. She told him about her experience with men in Krakow, about the way she had used Slawomir's image. And how, even now, this intruded into their lovemaking.

A calculated risk. But Fass's response was so earnest and disarming that Anja felt certain his Chetnik fantasy was nothing serious. "I never dreamed you'd want me at all, the way I am," he said. "I thought maybe, for some reason, you only felt obliged to do it."

Yet he did not repeat the fierceness he'd displayed, the urgency she had risen to meet on what she had come to think of as "The Mila Night." The old pattern prevailed: They made love easily, pleasantly, cozily. Not passionately. That was a disappointment, for her.

"I'm so glad to see you," Anja said, holding Sophie on her hip and fetching the coffeepot from the kitchen cabinet. "It was getting gloomy, housebound by this filthy weather. Sophie's complaining. She misses her garden."

"Brilliant, this child, I know. But complaining? In what language, please?" Mila laughed.

"Her own little one. I hear some definite crossness in her babblings. Of course, she blames me for everything."

"The burden of the mother. Imagine when she can talk. What she'll say! My mother, always she accused me of being a holy terror of a baby. But here, I have to hold her, the darling. Or you must let me make the coffee."

Anja handed the infant to Mila, who raised her up above her head, made some faces that caused the baby to chortle, and then cradled her against her chest. "You're well, little one? No? You do not like the nasty rain? You want Signor Sole to smile on your face?" But Anja saw Mila was almost as tense as a man holding such a fragile thing.

Mila was close to becoming a true friend. Already closer than anyone except dear Sisi. Mila's wartime connection with Walter was possibly a complication. But without it, she would never have met the woman. And she still had hopes of somehow using it to improve her relations with Fass.

Anja put plates, forks and cups on the table, slid the cake onto a small platter, tended to the coffee on the stove. "Ready in a minute," she said. "What have you been up to?"

"I go to Venice, in and out in a day, then Brescia and Turin. Feeding time for two of my *pescecani*. I lose track when I go like that, but it was only five days altogether."

"Five days of this miserable rain, which makes Walter more cross than Sophie, and a lot more difficult to cheer up," Anja said. "Petrocelli has him supervising some reconstruction out where all the factories are, and you can't pour concrete in the rain. So he's cooped up in his office."

"And Walter, he wants the outside, the grind and rumble of trucks and bulldozers?"

"I think. He does love the actual construction process. But he also wants an excuse to avoid studying technical Italian. He hates that. But he's got to learn it for his certification exam in February."

"An exam? For what? He's an engineer. I have seen his work. Here and elsewhere."

"His Berlin degree is just paper here. He's got to pass a test before he's legally allowed to be the engineer on site. Meanwhile, he's a glorified foreman. Petrocelli has to have little snot-nosed *ingegneri* sign off on each stage of the construction."

"*Itaker,*" Mila sighed.

"*Itaker!* Yet the longer I'm here, the more I like them. Not that I've made any friends. I just find it much more pleasant to deal with the Italian butchers, grocers and the rest than with Tiroler. They probably cheat me a little, but at least they do it with some charm. It's always *'Ahh, la bella signora Anna'* when I walk in, always 'I was hoping you would come today, for I have something very, very nice for you.' The Tiroler act is if they're doing you a favor by selling anything to you."

Mila kept Sophie on her knee when they sat down to the cake and coffee. "I get the same. From the men, anyway. The Don Giovanni act. Only an act, but amusing. The women? Eh."

"More coffee?"

"Certo, Signora. Per piacere," Mila said. "I know, my Italian is terrible. Please, don't also remind me my German is little better. Why is it you speak so beautifully?"

Anja told her a version of the Krakow story: German the household language, and so useful in her Resistance work, since her job was to get close to the occupiers. She told too about her flight from the Red Army, about the DP camp in Bavaria.

As she spoke, she studied Mila's every reaction, trying to learn the woman Fass wanted in his mind. The woman whom, she had the sudden wild idea, it might even be useful for him to have once or twice. A brief, casual affair—and she felt somehow sure that was all Mila ever indulged in—would be no real threat to her. Fass, Anja judged, would be more solicitous and protective than ever if he had a little illicit fling. And perhaps more passionate with her.

The problem was that Mila had shown no inclination toward Fass. It was her own company Mila seemed most to want.

"So, Fass marries you out of that DP camp, and here he brings you. Life becomes life again. Very good, your luck, I think," Mila said.

"Call it a partnership, more than a marriage," Anja said, in a tone she hoped Mila could recognize as confessional. "A good one, though. Over time we came to be very close, like brother and sister. Lovers only much later."

Mila raised an eyebrow, holding up Sophie.

"Oh, Walter's the father, it's true. But Sophie, God bless her, is a drunken accident," Anja laughed.

"Anja, I had the feeling at our first lunch that you suspect Walter and I, we are lovers in Yugoslavia. We never were. That's truth."

"Why would I care? Past is past. Mila, I tell you this in confidence. Sometimes I almost wish Walter had a lover here. Just for the sex. Because in bed we are like an old married couple, if you get my meaning. Suppose he gets bored with this, falls hard for some little slut? You know how men can be then."

Mila laughed. "They go crazy, it's true."

"Sometimes I think if I could give Walter a girl—just for the sex, nothing more—as a present, I would do it."

Mila stopped laughing. "This I have to doubt, Anja."

"A pretty mistress, one who'd please and satisfy him in the one way I do not? It would make our partnership stronger, don't you see? You know Walter is too upright, too honorable to go off and find himself a lover. I've been hoping some woman—a safe one, of course, maybe a married one—will find him."

"I still don't believe you." Anja saw just a trace of suspicion in the Chetnik's eyes, a predatory flash behind them. And she saw, with Krakow reflexes, how Mila instantly screened it.

"Never mind." Anja grinned. But instinctively she backed away from the idea of Fass having Mila, wished she had never begun this conversation.

"I have never met a Pole before. But deviousness, this is the word I think, must be native to you. As it is to the English."

"Should I be insulted or flattered?"

"For you, a compliment, because of your motive. If you are speaking true. For the English, a curse worse than any insult. I hate them to the heart."

"May I ask why?"

"Another time, I tell you how they betray, always betray. But just at this moment, I think my *bella* Sophie needs a change of diapers."

"*Scusa!* She hasn't stained your dress, I hope? You should have given her back to me."

"No, no problem, please," Mila said, handing Anja the baby. "I felt only a dampness to the hand."

Mila followed Anja to the bedroom, watched her remove the soft cotton diaper, wipe the baby and apply a bit of cream. "It is so strange. She's a woman in miniature already. Ah, I must sound ridiculous. I have not been much around babies."

"From the moment they're born. By the time she's eleven or twelve, she'll start to have hair there, and not so long after to bleed like we do," Anja said. "Baby boys, they're so funny, tiny pricks no bigger than the tip of your little finger. Amazing to think what they'll become."

"Anja, you are mad! Maybe it is you who needs the lover, not Walter."

"You may just have hit the perfect solution without even knowing it," Anja said. But the lie grated in a way few lies had before. "Do I shock you?"

"More than a little, I think. I had formed a different sort of opinion of you. But, I begin to believe that you and I are very much alike. Very good, the idea of a stable home with a man—one always needs a safe refuge. But no man have I found I could live with. So I take my pleasure with whoever I please, as men do. A partnership, you called it? Yes. Perhaps that's the best. Though not so easy to arrange, *nicht wahr?*"

"No, not so easy unless one is very clever or very lucky." Anja knew she'd become much too reckless, but was unable to find a plausible way of retreating. "Once you have the partner, though, then how much different is what we're speaking of from, say, old Petrocelli and his two mistresses?"

"You are correct. But he is a man, it's expected. For a woman? Some risk there, I think."

"I do think we are more clever than any Petrocelli."

"And I do think you are right in this. Perhaps we are sisters, as they say, under the skin?"

"*Certo,*" Anja said. "We must practice our Italian. For I think we will find what we seek among those men, not the Tiroler."

"Again I say, you are mad. Like me. But you already have your Walter. The problem for me will be to find such a partner. The lovers? They are everywhere. One has her pick. This I can show you, anytime you want."

"Ah, I talk a lot but I'm not quite ready for that. Too timid still, I think. Perhaps later, when Sophie is older and everything is more stable," Anja said smoothly, at last easing herself out of what she had gotten herself into. "Lunch this Sunday? Walter's veal probably, since that's all he knows. But we'll have a good time."

"Delighted." Mila smiled and kissed Anja on both cheeks.

Lunch was fine that Sunday, and again the following week, though as she was leaving then, Mila said it was feeding time again for some of her *pescecani*. She would not be in Bolzano for a while.

"But when I am back, a day out for us, Anja? Women's amusements, me and you?"

"That would be very nice."

"Then we do it, for sure. Say Thursday after next?"

VI

Mila sent a note, and the engineer Walter Fass came.

He came loping through the snow like a mountain wolf on a scent, and afterward Mila sent him home to his little Pole, obedient as a house pet. He was her creature now. Anja could keep him for her until she wanted him again.

There had been a danger, Mila knew. Whenever a man finally possesses an object of obsession, disillusionment can follow. The reality does not live up to what the mind has made.

So she made it unreal. She made it as overwhelming as she could, far beyond anything he had likely known.

Anja had given her all the knowledge she needed. The bland sex, Fass's unwillingness to take a lover, the long nights next to a desirable body that he could not fully enjoy—for Anja was very much more desirable than she knew, but without daring, without great passion. Fass, Mila concluded, was a man on the verge of explosion.

She detonated him.

First in the bath, hot and scented, with her mouth alone. And later in the bed, Walter beneath her while she took him to the brink, paused for as long as she dared, then violently drove him over.

"When I see you at the door tonight, snow all over your coat and hat, I think of the mountains, Walter. What we could not have there, what I wanted so bad," she said afterward. "I thought my heart would crack, when I leave you at the aid post."

"Why didn't you give me a sign? We'd have found a way."

"On a pine bough in the snow? Dirty, lice-ridden? Only the flies of our pants open? I wanted much more than that, or nothing at all," she said. "What we had now, yes. Long and slow. You see all of me, touch all of me. That was my desire. No time, no place for this in the mountains, *nicht wahr?* And then you were dead, after the mortars."

"And you were killed somewhere up there in the woods, but you stayed with me every day. In the hospital, in the POW camp, here in Bozen."

"Did you look for me? Did you try to find me?"

"No. I was so sure you were in a grave, one I could never go to. There were times, after I left the POW camp, that I wanted to die, too. I even had the means in mind."

"Thank God you did not do that. Then all my search . . . useless. Such a search, all on the little hope that by God's grace you had not bled to death."

"How could you have known where to look?"

"A long story. A bad time."

"Tell me."

So she told him, stretching languorously in her bed. She told the truth. No, only facts. Not the meaning, or the purpose.

"When I come out of Yugoslavia, I am a target for every side. But remember what I say in your house about the fighting around Gorizia and Trieste? Yes? So I went to the damn English and, how would you say, offered my services? The treacherous bastards are glad to have me, they need fighters of experience for what they call the Divisione Gorizia. A good lot. Italian ex-soldiers from the area, some who'd fought with the Germans in Russia, some who'd fought in Africa or Greece. Arditi only. Local Slovenes who had been *partigiani* against the Fascists but hated Tito and his Reds worse. Even some Austrians, once Waffen SS. And Serbs and a few Croats who'd been Chetniks. All hating the Tito swine.

"The British arm us, Stens, Brens, GI Thompsons, the best they got. We slaughter Yugo raiders, we raid across the border to butcher Yugos. We blow up trains, bridges. I make a beautiful ambush, one entire company of Tito swine wiped out in ten minutes! The British and Americans are so happy.

"I fight for a year. Then, bad luck, a grenade." Mila guided his fingers along the jagged scar on her thigh. "And the bloody British surprise me. They don't abandon me, which I expect, they give me a reward for my work. This identity of Mila Ćosić, this Italian citizenship."

"Christ," Fass said.

"I was lucky. The woman I come to Italy with, she's captured during a raid. I don't have to say what happens to her."

"Your wound heals, you're given papers, you're free to go as you please. But that tells me nothing of how you found me."

"We know, being among the English and the Americans, what happens in Germany. So I think: If Fass doesn't die, he cannot go back to Stettin because of the Russians. So. Where does he go? Then I remember, on certain nights in the mountains when we'd all drunk much *rakija*, you used to talk about boyhood in Bozen. So first chance I get, I look in Bozen."

"I thought you came to deal with Petrocelli."

"For sure. In my business, clients who are happy direct you to their friends. A *pescecane* in Verona sends me to his *amico* Petrocelli. And from him, I get the way to you. So there I am, in your flat. A miracle to see you alive, but to find you married, with a baby? I almost left Bolzano for good the day after."

"But you stayed."

"Stupid hopes. But now maybe not so stupid. Even if we only have this one time, I am happy I found you again."

"We'll have more than tonight," Fass said. "We'll be together now."

"We will not, Walter. I care too much for Anja and Sophie. With me you cannot be. Already I have betrayed Anja, who has been a friend to me, the only friend I've found." Mila made herself weep. It would cause Fass to believe she had a heart like his. It would make him move the world to keep her and still honor his commitment to Anja and Sophie.

A thing that could be done, Mila thought. If the man had courage and kindness and honor. Fass was such a one, though a bit light in the courage. She had seen his soul on the day of the village. He could be made to do what must be done. He could be given the courage.

And Anja would help, without even knowing she was doing so.

◼ ◼ ◼

Anja was in bed, reading, when she heard Walter's key click in the front-door lock, heard the rustle of his overcoat being hung in the foyer, and his measured footsteps in the corridor.

"Petrocelli kept you working so late, in this weather?"

"Not working. A cigar and a grappa. He did all the talking, as usual. I don't think he likes going home to his wife very much," Fass said. "Then an hour or so with a damned little *Itaker*. Petrocelli found me a tutor, a young man who teaches science at the high school. Young, yes. But what a *professore* already! A natural pedant."

"Poor Walter." Anja looked at the bedside alarm clock. It wasn't so late, just past ten. "There are dumplings and a bit of chicken in the kitchen, if you're hungry."

"Thanks, but I'm too tired. I'll just wash up and come to bed, I think."

His face in the bathroom mirror was not the face he normally saw there. Fass spat at it, watched the spittle slide down from just beneath the eye to the lips. "Fucking coward," he hissed.

He sniffed his hand, then washed it thoroughly before he undressed, hanging his shirt and suit on a hook and dumping his underpants in the hamper. He soaked a washcloth, soaped it up, and scrubbed his chest, his belly, his genitals and his legs. He rinsed the cloth, then wiped away the soap, all the while standing before the sink, staring at the mirror. Finally he washed his face, ran his wet, soapy hand through his hair several times, and toweled himself dry. Pyjamas on, he walked into the bedroom and slipped into bed beside Anja, who did not look up from her book. He kissed her on the cheek.

"*Buona notte, Signore,*" she murmured, turning a page.

"And what has you so absorbed?" he asked, settling flat on his back under the blankets.

"*The Emperor's Tomb,*" Anja said absently. "Beautiful writing."

"Ah," Walter said, sitting up. "And how's my beauty? Good Sophie or bad Sophie today? I've got to see."

"Mostly bad Sophie. A lot of wailing. But when she's good . . . don't wake her, Walter."

The engineer padded softly around the bed and peered down into the cradle, gazing at the small round face and cornsilk hair of his daughter. There was nothing of him in her at all, he thought. She was Anja in miniature, all Anja. Liese said she had his mouth and something of his nose, but he could not see it. And that was probably for the best.

His heart lurched with the absolute love of the helpless creature in the cradle, the strength of the affection he felt for her mother. Yet it seemed to him that he had abandoned them both.

He believed he had been on a mission, to dominate and subdue a soul he despised as he took a body he'd long wanted. To erase the debasement and degradation she had once inflicted on him. But that Chetnik bitch had beaten him again.

How was it possible that he was able to stand here now, gazing at his wife and child, feeling for them what he was feeling? He had no right to feel. He wasn't a man. The face he had seen in the mirror was not the face he had lived behind all his life.

"Anja," he murmured, getting back into bed.

"Ssshhh," she said, glancing at him with a smile. "I'm in the midst of a wonderful passage."

He closed his eyes. And inside his head he saw his Chetnik straddling him, felt her warmth. He was disgusted with himself. Yet he stroked Anja's hip.

"Please, Walter," she whispered. "Don't."

His mind suddenly stopped its mad revolutions. His Chetnik faded, then vanished. All he could see were the random flashes of light one always sees against one's eyelids: red fields, vanishing circles of blue, clouds of black sweeping from one side to the other, starbursts of white and yellow. He knew it was Anja beside him, her sweet familiar scent. He knew he was in his own bed, in his own home, on sheets he had slept on a hundred times. And he wished to God it had been Anja astride him earlier, right here, her head thrown back in pleasure.

❖   ❖   ❖

Fass answered the front bell early the next morning to see a tall woman in a loden cape, a thick scarf and a fur hat of Russian style, smiling at him.

"Mila?"

"*Morgen*, Walter," she said, brushing past him and walking

back to the kitchen, where she sat as if it were her usual place at the table and began to sip the coffee Anja placed before her.

"We are going to have some fun today, yes?"

"Oh, lots. I know just where to go, and where we can have a nice lunch, also," Mila said. "An exceptional day, bright sun, blue sky, a bit of snow sparkling everywhere. Not so drab, Bolzano, on this type of day."

"I'm looking forward to this."

"To what?" Fass asked. He felt shaken by Mila's presence, her cool composure. How in hell, he wondered, could she be so brazen?

"Women things, Walter," Mila said easily.

"She means shopping."

"And my *pescecani*, unknown to them, are going to give Anja a nice outfit or two, and shoes to match."

"Ah, now, Mila. None of that," Anja said.

"They never will miss it. It is gone from them already, in fact. And you will need, forgive me please, one or two good things for Ischl. Didn't you say you must go there, when it is Sisi's time?"

"Yes, but that's not for a while yet."

"No matter. All the nicest things will be gone if we wait," Mila said. "No work today, Walter?"

"Naturally, yes. I've got to be going."

"You feeling all right? You look peaked," Mila said.

"I'm fine," Fass said. No, he was as far as one could be from fine. He would never be fine.

"He slept like a stone last night. I was up fussing at four in the morning with a wailing baby, and Walter snored through it all," Anja said.

"Men!"

"You sound exactly like Sisi," Anja said.

"Who does not like me much, this I know. I think I made her, would you say, a little timid? When she was here?"

"That was just a mad sort of day. When she gets to know you, it'll be all right," Anja said, sitting down with Sophie and sipping her own coffee. "Walter? Still here? Won't you be late?"

"Ah, better hurry. *Ciao*, Mila. See you tonight, darling."

Anja only glanced at him.

"Darling? I think he's trying to sweeten me up, Mila. He never calls me that," she said, then turned back to Fass. "Don't worry, Walter. I won't spend all our money."

"*Ciao*, then," Fass said. When Mila and Anja heard the front door close behind him, they smiled at each other.

"He is very funny today. Like a boy?"

"Boyish," Anja agreed. "He gets that way whenever he's confused. A little awkward, a little dazed. I think he is very surprised you and I have become friends. He doesn't know what to make of it. I'm sure he expected we'd clash. Male vanity."

"You mean, he imagined there would be tension, jealousy, some things like this? He does flatter himself, I think."

"Don't they all?"

"Yes. So, forget them all. We have our plan. First, we take you to the little man who does my hair."

"Wait a moment. We didn't speak of this." Anja had not cut her hair in years. Since she was a girl, she had simply pulled it back into a single braid, one which now brushed her waist. And she was not at all sure she wanted it any other way.

"Anja, this braid, fine for a farm. Perfect for dirndls. Also fine for a student. But without style, *nicht wahr?* Beautiful hair you have. This man will give it just the right cut to suit your face. Not some fussy thing, rollers every night and so on. Just a good cut. You must trust me. You will look more beautiful than you have in your life."

Did she care about that, Anja wondered? Beautiful? Nothing could make her that. And what would be the point? She looked well enough for Walter. If she wanted anyone, it was only him. "Couldn't we just see some clothes?"

"But the hair must be right first, to judge the clothes? Please, I know this."

"Mila, you exasperate me," Anja sighed.

"Only because you know I am correct. You have a new life for a while now, Anja. So a new look, why not that, too? I've found it is very pleasant, the feeling this can give." Mila smiled.

VII

Anja allowed herself to be led along twisty, narrow streets of the old town she had never bothered to explore. Mila ushered her into a small salon she would have strolled right past, on her own. Mila must have been known there; everyone greeted her cheerfully.

Soon a young woman was washing Anja's hair, gently massaging her scalp and working the shampoo down the long unbraided mass. She rinsed it for a long time with pleasantly warm water, then wrapped Anja's head in a terry towel and guided her to a slickly upholstered chair.

Anja was draped with a soft linen sheet, facing a mirror. Behind her, Mila gently rolled Sophie's carriage back and forth, chattering with a thin, black-haired man who held scissors in one hand and a large comb in the other. They smiled at her. "Carlo, begin," Mila said, and the man in the mirror bobbed his head.

Anja stiffened, squeezed her eyes shut. Beneath the flowery shampoos and dressings, she noticed a tart undernote of dyes and bleaches. She cringed a little when she felt him cut a great arc of her unloosed braid.

Snipping and combing and snipping. It seemed an extraordinarily long time before she felt the sheet whipped from around her shoulders and heard the hairdresser say, *"Ecco, Signora! I più bei capelli in tutto Bolzano."*

She did not recognize the image in the mirror. Her face seemed less round, attractively angular, and her thick hair, parted on the right, swept down just to her shoulders in two graceful waves.

"The American film star, Veronica Lake!" Mila cried. "You will be mistaken for her, I think. People will ask for your autograph. My God, I wish for hair so beautiful as yours. You are stunning me, Anja. You are making me very jealous, with this hair."

Tentatively at first, then with more vigor, Anja tried tossing her head, and each time her hair glided smoothly back into those face-framing waves.

"Carlo is a genius, *nicht wahr?* Carlo, you belong in Rome, not in this Bolzano. You are brilliant."

"Grazie mille, Signora. To cut your hair, and the hair of so lovely a *signora* as your friend, is an honor for me."

"Ah, Carlo, you are a genius, but you have never made me look so perfect."

"La signora Mila is only teasing me now."

Anja couldn't help stealing glances at herself in the mirrors as they left the salon, or in the shop windows as Mila, pushing Sophie's carriage, led her deeper into the *centro* along unfamiliar streets.

"Now, Anja. Two dresses to be made. One for the day, one for the night," Mila said, stopping in front of a window that displayed only cascades of fine, flowing fabrics, and the name "Luciana Lucino" in discreet gold leaf on the glass. Inside, Mila was greeted by an impeccably dressed woman flanked by two girls in blue smocks. While Anja lifted Sophie from the carriage and cradled her, Mila and the older woman moved arm-in-arm among the vast array of fabrics, Mila doing all the talking, the older woman nodding from time to time and pointing to bundles of cloth, each of which Mila fingered and scrutinized. At last Mila pointed to one bolt and then another, which the two assistants removed from the shelves, placed on a glass-topped table in the center of the shop, and unrolled a meter or two.

"Come, Anja, give me my pretty little one, and see," Mila said, reaching out and taking Sophie in her arms.

"Here, for the night, in a sort of sheath," Mila nodded at the first bolt, which Anja saw was watered silk of gray so deep it was almost black, but with hints of mauve in its waves. "And for day, this, with a fuller skirt but yet close enough to the body," Mila said of the other, a fine light wool herringbone in russet and chocolate.

"Beautiful," Anja said. But impossible, she thought. She moved closer to Mila and whispered in her ear, "We can't afford this." The older woman had gone to the rear of the shop, where a small pedestal stood surrounded on three sides by tall mirrors. She was removing a tape measure, a box of pins, a pair of scissors, and some sheets of paper as thin as tissue from various drawers and cubbyholes.

"It is no problem. Luciana, she is practically giving it away," Mila whispered back. "Dollars, understand? It will be nothing."

"You're sure?" She'd never had any really nice clothes. It would be lovely, she thought. But the expense! It was Walter's money. She couldn't do this.

"Anja, do not worry. The cost is probably less than one of your Sunday lunches, the fabric is superb, here the workmanship is the best. I have my things made here. Really, you cannot afford to pass this by. For years these dresses will last. *Stile classico*, yes?"

Sophie was quiet as a mouse in Mila's arms, Anja soon stood stripped to her slip on the pedestal, bewildered but excited. One of the assistants used the tape to measure every part of her, calling out the numbers to the other, who wrote them down in a little notebook. The older woman circled Anja, studying her as if she were a statue. When the measuring was finished, the older woman began to cut pieces of thin paper and pin them to Anja's slip. I'm a doll, even Mila's treating me as if I'm a doll, Anja thought for a moment. But it was only a moment, and then the dressmaker said, *"Bene, Signora,"* as she unpinned all the paper and carefully laid the pieces on a table. "Two fittings, one next week and one the week after. I think you will be pleased. Your friend Signora Mila has chosen very well."

Then on to another shop, this time for pullovers and skirts. Anja was drawn to fawns and pastels. "No, no. You are too fair, in those colors you will vanish," Mila said, selecting instead a merino twin set in deep blue. She stood behind Anja, facing a mirror, and held the sweater against Anja's body. "See how striking, with your hair and face? Heads will turn!" They left the shop with the twin set, a black cashmere pullover, and two woolen skirts, one charcoal, one a blue only a shade lighter than the twin set. Then another shop for shoes: a pair of black kid pumps with medium heels, and a pair of cordovan flats.

"Enough! You've ruined me. Walter will have my head because we won't be able to pay next month's rent," Anja said once they were back on the street. She was laden with bags; Mila insisted on pushing Sophie's carriage. "Give me the bad news all at once. How much do I owe for all of it?"

"A little lunch?" Mila grinned. "Just for taking you around. My *pescecani* have taken care of everything else."

"No, I won't have that," Anja said, the awful feeling of being only a doll coming over her again, threatening to destroy all the pleasure she had been feeling. A new pleasure, one she had never enjoyed before. The luxury of all these things. But she had to pay.

"Anja, please. Everything was so cheap. The dollars, you understand? Extra I squeeze from the *pescecani*. They must be spent, it is risky with the finance police for me to have them around. And I liked very much the shopping," Mila said softly. "It will hurt me if you do not accept such a small thing. Anja, please. Only take me to lunch. For friendship."

They went to a trattoria Mila knew, ate gnocchi with porcini, had a glass of wine each. Anja retreated to the ladies' room to feed Sophie before the coffee came. She felt very self-conscious, a part of her rebelling at the way Mila had taken control, and another part grateful for what she had given her: a great treat she would never have given herself. But now this sense of obligation . . . she stopped herself. A friend had given her a gift. She ought to accept it gracefully.

The smile on Anja's face when she returned to the table was genuine. She was excited about wearing her pretty new things, loved the way her hair felt, the way it swayed as she walked. But there was one thing she must clear up. One question to be asked.

"May I hold Sophie for a bit?"

"Of course," Anja said, handing the baby across the table to her friend.

"She stares at me as if she could see my soul," Mila said, looking down into the baby's eyes. "Stupid Serb superstition. But I hope not. She will be frightened, and hate me."

"I worried very much over that, at first," Anja said. "Then I realized how silly it was. She sees nothing, really. No one does, least of all an infant. She only senses whether the arms holding her are loving or not. She smiles and stares when she feels secure. She cries when she doesn't. So she feels secure with you. Otherwise, the whole place would hear her protesting."

"Ah, I'm an idiot. I have done unspeakable things that no one would ever suspect. I know no one can see into me, that my past is blank to everyone, except those I choose to tell. But somehow the look of this innocent . . . madness, but there is the feeling she can see."

"Choose to tell me one thing?"

"Ask, then."

"How is it that a woman who spent almost all her adult life at war knows so much about hair and fine clothes?"

Mila burst into laughter. "Oh, Anja, I am dreading for a moment you are going to ask about something awful. My God! Well, the answer, so simple. I was brought up to it."

"Brought up to it?"

"My father was a surgeon. My mother, a professor of literature at the university in Belgrade. Both from families of culture. Very serious about that, and their professions. But they did love their style. My father, he is what the English call a dandy? His suits have to be just so, his shoes custom-made, you understand? And my mother, an addict of fashion. She gets all the Paris magazines, has her dressmaker copy from them.

"So. As a child, she dresses me well. Then when I am old enough to have my own taste—around thirteen or fourteen, when I also begin to have a taste for boys, my God—she encourages me, guides me, steers me away from mistakes.

"I was a sight at university, I think now. A bit too much concerned with how I looked, whether my shoes were just right, nonsense like that. I am twenty-one when the Germans invaded. Poof. Farewell to all my pretty frocks, my lovely shoes, my hairdresser. Into the woods, battle dress and combat boots, hair cropped like a boy's."

"A soldier's."

"Yes, that's what I became. But as soon as that is *kaputt,* and I earn a bit of money, I revert instantly. As you no doubt see. Very frivolous, very flighty, almost a sacrilege when you think of the wartime. But what are we to do? Go about in rags, something like this? We survived. We are alive. So. We should live, *nicht wahr?* I feel I have earned any luxury I enjoy, and I will have all I can afford for as long as I can."

Anja grinned. "I think you have a more healthy attitude than I. With me there is a guilt about even surviving when so many close to me did not. So, I have a hard time accepting, as you saw today, anything nice. I feel I ought to be plain, have only the most basic things in my life: a roof over my head, enough food so that I stay healthy for Sophie, only the simplest, necessary clothes."

"This I understand. But there is another thing to think of. When will be the next war? The Americans and the English using Europe as a battlefield against the Russians? Who can say? So I tell myself, Mila, live now as well as you can, live quickly. Because it may all disappear in a moment, with no warning. Just as it did once before."

"As I said, a more realistic attitude than mine. Perhaps if I was making my own way . . ."

"Listen to me, Anja. You have been given nothing. You have worked for all. Fass, I think, might still be wandering Germany like a vagabond, slowly starving like most everyone there, if he had not found you. So this marriage thing is not what we all dreamed of when we were girls? Bah! Your partnership, I think, draws Walter back to life, to the idea a new one could be made. And it has— Walter with his profession, you with Sophie."

"I wish I had your clarity."

"And I wish for this solid base, as you have. At the moment I am a dirty gypsy, more than a little outside the law. This I cannot keep up too long. I must find a safer way to make my living. And," Mila said, "a safer home."

Walter moved like a sleepwalker through his day. Even the most familiar, ordinary things were not what they seemed, he felt. Strangest of all was the absolute sense, when Mila had breezed bright and relaxed into his house that morning, that those hours with her the previous night had been hours spent alone with only some part of his mind for company. Then he realized what it really was: the numbness that followed defeat in combat. He knew that well enough. All soldiers did.

"Fight with the wife?" he heard Petrocelli say as the man sat heavily in the chair next to Walter's desk and lit a cigar. "Can't let 'em get you down, these damn women. They secretly hate us, I'm convinced. They love to torment us. Mine does, anyway."

"No trouble," Walter said. "Just a strange night."

"War dreams, eh? They come to me from time to time, even after almost thirty years."

"Not dreams, exactly. I was awake, I think," Walter said. "You know Mila Ćosić, don't you?"

Petrocelli laughed. "Well, Walter, I've done a little business with her, some financial things. But I wouldn't say I know her. She's not an easy one to know." He blew an enormous smoke ring. "Maybe dangerous to know."

"I don't know how to explain it, but she's a concentrated dose of wartime to me."

"Seems a reasonable reaction, her fighting beside you when you were wounded. Or so she mentioned to me," Petrocelli said, taking a long draw on his cigar, then examining the thing from coal to tip. "She's what upset you?"

"Not directly. I see her quite a lot. She's become great friends with my wife, they're always having coffee together. She comes to lunch most Sundays. And we keep the war talk out of it."

"Well, then?"

"You'll think I've gone *pazzo*."

"Nah, we're all crazy, one way or the other."

"Mila is wartime, Anja is peacetime. I thought I had the two in separate compartments. Now they're all mixed up. When the two of them are together, I don't know which time it is."

"It'd confuse the hell out of me, too, if I were in your place," Petrocelli said. "But I'll tell you something, make of it what you want. For a long time after the first one, I tried locking away the war someplace deep. Can't be done. It always escapes, dreams or whatnot. Best thing is not to try. Just live your life as if it were one straight progression with a really nasty bit somewhere in the middle, but you've moved on past that. Hell, that must be the way Mila manages. Never seen a haunted look on her face, or any sign of what she went through.

"I think," he added, "I'd be damned glad about Mila and Anja being friends. Might free you up from some ghosts, once you get used to it."

✦ ✦ ✦

It was no ghost that, for a moment, unmoored Fass entirely when he walked into his kitchen that night. He simply did not recognize the pretty blond woman who turned from the stove to greet him.

"Oh, Jesus," she said. "Is it that bad? The look on your face is making me very nervous, Walter."

"No, no," Fass said. "I'm amazed, that's all. You look so incredible I didn't know you for a second. Thought I'd wandered into the wrong house."

"Was I so plain and drab before?" Anja laughed.

"No, and you know it very well. I've always thought you were pretty. But I never imagined what a haircut could do. You are absolutely stunning!"

"Good. Much better. I was about to start crying there for a second, seeing the look on your face. And I was thinking of killing Mila, who made me do it."

✖   ✖   ✖

Mila sent a second note a few days later. And the engineer Fass went into the assault once more, but without much hope of winning.

VIII

A chilling shriek of steel skidding heavily against steel. A jolting stop. Hollow shouts in Italian, American, German. An acrid reek of scorched oil, hot metal. Anja cleared a small circle on the fogged window of her second-class carriage with the cuff of her coat and peered out at the station platform. It was noon, yet the light seemed fugitive as dusk. Fat wet flakes of snow sank slowly into billows of white vapor from the engine, the figures on the platform only phantoms in fog.

The Brennerpass.

They'll come now, Anja thought, a vein at the base of her throat throbbing. And presently two Italian border policemen slid open the door of her compartment, glanced at the passport and ticket she proffered, smiled at the baby sleeping undisturbed on the grubby upholstery of the seat bench, and passed down the corridor. Then two other guards in grayish-green uniforms she had hoped never to see again, accompanied by a lone American in battle dress the color of mud, blocked the door. *"Zeigen Sie mir Ihre Papiere, bitte,"* one of the green-uniformed guards said.

Words she had hoped never to hear again.

But here was something new, she realized as she handed over her passport and ticket. *Bitte*. Please. A word never before attached to that ominous demand. The American said nothing, only gazed at her without expression while the two Austrians examined her papers. They were slower, more careful than the Italians had been. Too deliberate, Anja thought, wisps of panic gathering, closing on her. Why? Her papers were as genuine and correct as their own! But then they handed back the passport and the tickets. They touched the brims of their caps in unison, and one said, *"Danke, Frau Fass."* Then they closed the door of the compartment. She slumped in her seat, heart slowing. *Bitte* and *Danke*. All right. Quite right.

At the sight of those uniforms, the sound of the words, Anja had wished for an instant that Fass was beside her. But the engineer was in Bolzano getting ready for his certification exam. He had asked her to wait for him, but she'd refused, confident she could face alone a journey into the dark lands. The Allies were occupying Austria, there was no reason at all for any fear. Yet she'd had an apprehension, she'd hesitated on the steps up to the carriage just before the train pulled out from Bolzano that morning. Suddenly a forgotten Krakow rule came to her: Face those who might doubt you, face them naturally and casually.

Which she'd just done, the pleasure of it bringing a smile to her face. She smoothed the little plaid blanket covering Sophie, stared at her child's round, pale face, her slightly parted lips, her eyelashes as delicate as spider silk. Then she looked again through the circle she'd rubbed on the window, which was already beginning to fog over again. The engine vapors had wafted away. The figures on the platform, mainly men in uniforms, were clearer now, and benign.

The Brenner. A dangerous barrier between her and sanctuary, when she and Walter had first approached it from the north more than a year ago. A place where her future would be decided. But this time merely a station stop along the passage through the Alps. She started humming a Polish lullaby. Sophie did not stir in her slumber.

There was a slighter jolt, a milder screech of steel on steel, an almost playful whistle as the train moved into Austria. She had hours and hours yet before Salzburg, and Dizzi and Sisi. From her bag she removed a sandwich and the thermos of coffee Walter had made for her, but kept her face to the window as she ate and drank, hoping for a sight of the stone hut where the signalman Precht had sheltered her and Walter from the storm that almost killed them. The train passed two huts, and she was not sure which had been Precht's. Some day she and Walter would come up and find him, at his hut or at home in Gries am Brenner, and show him Sophie, and thank him.

And what of her laughing, lively Hungarian, her lovely Sisi? Due to give birth within a week or so, Sisi wrote in the letter that had drawn Anja out of her comfortable home and aboard this train. Sisi's letters of the last few months had made Anja very uneasy. Nothing explicit, no proximate cause for worry, but hints that such existed. Was it only normal anxiety, the sort she had felt before Sophie came? Or something deeper, more serious; something gone wrong in Sisi's arrangement with Dizzi?

Probably it was only vain Sisi fretting about losing some of her beauty, Anja thought as the train swayed along the descent to Innsbruck. Or frightened a little by the mysteries of handling her newborn. She hoped it was only that. Because in those matters she could help.

But a problem with Scharner . . . Such a strange man. Such an unnatural, devilish mix. His carefree love of life and his close— God, almost affectionate—relationship with killing. She doubted she could ever sleep easily beside someone like that. But of course

Sisi did not share Dizzi's bed. Sisi also had reserves. To look at her and hear her, most would think Sisi flighty, foolish and reckless. But there was a toughness in her, a resilience. Sisi would be all right. Sisi would face down anyone or anything.

And then Anja laughed. They wouldn't recognize her! She had let Carlo work his wonder with her hair again, Mila close beside to supervise, just a few days ago. She studied her indistinct reflection in the fogged window, shook her head, and admired the fall and sweep of her hair. She was wearing the deep blue twin set Mila had picked for her, one of the nice woolen skirts and her cordovan flats. In her suitcase were only the other nice things she had acquired with Mila.

No one from before would recognize her. She could walk the streets of Krakow and even men she had slept with—if any still lived—would wonder who the attractive stranger was. When she turned up at her parents' flat—if they were alive and still there—they would surely think a woman they didn't know had knocked at the wrong door. They would not step back in fear from the ghost of their dead daughter.

Dead daughter. All lightness left Anja's heart. She'd allowed—no, she had made herself forget that Anja Wieniewski was no longer of this earth to those who had loved her most. She had liquidated herself. It hadn't been the Germans, the ones her dear mother and father would always blame and hate for murdering their daughter. Oh, God.

Anja brushed her eyes roughly with the back of her hand. Damn Krakow time! But then something else towered over her grief and anger. Would such pain be her destiny, too? Would her Sophie one day be taken from her by whatever malignant forces interfere, at their pleasure, with the course of our lives? Anja searched in her mind for some power she could beg to spare Sophie from all harm, all damage. And all knowledge of what her mother had been: one of the evil ones who had inexplicably been granted a second chance. "Let Sophie, on my soul, not be the price I'll have to pay for that chance," she prayed to a god she could not find. "When the reckoning comes, let it fall on me alone."

※　　※　　※

Only Dizzi, tall Dizzi in a charcoal suit and a camel-hair overcoat, was at the Salzburg Bahnhof to meet her. And he missed her. He walked within a meter of Anja, glanced at her without a flicker of recognition, and walked on another ten paces down the platform, scanning the faces emerging from the cars, before he slowly turned, cocked his head and stared at her. Anja had a brief but startling glimpse of a cold, pitiless man. Until Dizzi's familiar broad, half-mocking but loving smile appeared. He pulled off his fedora and covered those ten paces in three long strides that were almost leaps, until he was within inches of her.

"My God, Anja!" he cried. "Quick! Take my arm. I'm going to faint." Then he burst into a booming laugh that quickly descended into the sort of giggle one would never expect from a man so imposing.

"Zeppelin-gazing, Scharner?" She smiled.

"I've my own: The Fürstin Sisi—yes, she now believes she's a princess, or at least the Virgin Mary. Unfortunately grounded, though fully inflated. She refuses to leave the house," Dizzi said, snatching Anja's suitcase in one hand and Sophie in the other, at the same time bending to plant a kiss on each of Anja's cheeks and a short one full on her lips. "There, there Sophie. I've rescued you from this mysteriously lovely kidnapper. You're safe now, and soon I'll return you to your rightful parents. Don't stare at me so! I feel I'm being judged."

"And in a moment the verdict will be rendered. Wails if you're guilty, a smile to break your heart if you're not."

"Ahh," Dizzi said. "Now then, Sophie, what's it to be? Do you approve of your uncle Dizzi? Is it a smile I see? Yes? Then I'm going to give you a ride in very large car. We'll take your kidnapper with us and hand her over to the police."

"Not even in jest," Anja said, as Dizzi wheeled and led her through the station—bomb damage still only partly repaired—to the street outside, where his father's black Mercedes was parked.

"Anja, this transformation is amazing," he tossed back over his shoulder. "You're going to make the Fürstin very, very envious. She moans and groans all day long about how fat, frumpy and dumpy I've made her. I! Everything is my fault, naturally."

"Naturally. You are the culprit, no?"

"Under extreme duress. Blackmailed, really," Dizzi said, dumping the suitcase in the trunk, assisting Anja into the seat, and handing the baby back to her. "Actually, that you look so lovely may not depress Sisi at all. I should think it might give her hope. She's convinced herself she's become terminally repulsive.

"So tell me all," he rattled on, threading the big auto through the narrow streets of Salzburg. "Clearly motherhood agrees with you. You glow, you shimmer. And that dull engineer of yours? Not moping too much, not mumbling equations in his sleep, or brooding over his concrete?"

"He's fine, you'll see for yourself in a few days when he arrives," Anja said. But part of her mind was completely captive to the beauty of Salzburg, the baroque buildings, the river and the castles on the high hills around the city. So much like Krakow in atmosphere. So unlike dreary Bolzano. And for a moment she was strolling under the great trees of the park around old Krakow, talking with Slawomir and Aneta and Kazimierz and Joanna and Helena and Jaček, the Wawel and its towers above them, the old beauty promising a stable and beautiful future. Broken promises. All broken.

Very quickly they left the city behind and were tooling along an undulating road past lovely lakes edged by mountains, a landscape that looked almost designed, the artistic creation of some eighteenth-century genius.

"To the left there, that's Schloss Fuschl," Dizzi said as they passed a Schönbrunn-yellow palace sited carefully on a little rise of meadow and embraced by copses of trees that sloped gently down to an iced-over lake. "And the Fuschlsee. Up ahead, that pretty little village is Saint Gilgin, the lake is the Wolfgangsee. Beautiful here in the spring and fall. Rains like hell in the summer, especially August. Which is when the Germans come here for holidays. Or used to. Gloom and rain, the German idea of a fine holiday."

Dizzi spoke as rapidly as he drove. In less than an hour they were turning between large stone columns supporting a black wrought-iron gate, skidding along a curving drive through parkland blanketed by snow. Anja saw a low villa, in that typically Austrian yellow stucco, its great center door of dark wood flanked by French windows at least three meters high. The two floors above were windowed identically, but on a much smaller scale. As Dizzi braked to a stop before the entrance, a tottering old man made his way down the broad low stone steps, opened the door for Anja and helped her out. Dizzi dashed around the car and linked his arm with hers. Three steps up and they were in a compact but very grand entrance hall.

"Well, here is the Camp Scharner at Ischl," Dizzi said. "Your room is ready, old Alois will have your bags there in a moment. Would you like to rest or bathe or anything, or do you feel up to seeing the Fürstin at once? My parents are out back in the orangerie, drinking tea of all things. Imagine! Every day at precisely the same time, they must be in the orangerie drinking that vile concoction. Except during hunting season, when the old man spends his days perched in a tree up one of the mountains, guzzling pear brandy as he waits for a deer to walk into the sights of his rifle. Never moves his rifle from its rest, mind you. Insists the deer come to him. Some sort of perverted *droit de seigneur*, I think."

"Dizzi, Dizzi! A little slower, please. You've not given me even a chance to say how good it is to see you," Anja said. "So now I shall: Scharner, you great thug, it is good to see you."

Dizzi laughed and kissed her hand. "Off to Sisi, then. Prepare yourself for a shock," he said, bounding up a broad stairway to the second floor, Anja trailing much more slowly behind, taking in only a fraction of the details—the family portraits on the walls, the Meissen vases on the windowsills, the Persian carpets—but absorbing a sense of luxury she had never encountered in any private house.

Then she was in Sisi's room, light streaming through the tall windows onto a high bed of ancient dark wood. And there, under a thin damask coverlet, lay Sisi, dozing. "Looks like a garden snake who's swallowed a huge toad, doesn't she?" Dizzi said. It was true; Sisi seemed as thin as ever, except for her enormous belly. Her eyes snapped open and fixed on Dizzi. "Get out of here, Scharner. Oh, Anja! Throw that brute out and come kiss me. God, you look fantastic. I'm ashamed. Quick, come kiss me, darling."

"Well!" Dizzi said. "I have a sense, call it intuitive, that my presence is not required or desired at the moment. Ladies, *au revoir*." He bowed formally, then left the room.

Anja laid the sleeping Sophie on a brocade settee and sat on the bed. Sisi pulled her close with her long, slender arms and planted kisses all over her face. "God, it's only been a few months but it seems like a lifetime. I can't believe you're here. Now I can relax. I was afraid you wouldn't come, that I'd be left all alone in this lunatic asylum," Sisi said, her cheek pressed against Anja's. "And that's what it is. You think Dizzi's a bit eccentric? Well, you'll soon see. They're all mad here, he and his parents and even the servants. Oh, Anja, thank you for coming. Now let me look at you."

Anja sat up straight, Sisi's hands still grasping her waist. "So is this what happens when I turn my back for a moment? You transform into a beauty? Who's done this to you? Will it happen to me after the baby comes?"

"Nothing but a haircut and some new clothes, little sparrow," Anja said. "On the advice of a friend. Anyway, it's you who looks beautiful, the same lovely Sisi. You've not changed a bit."

Sisi grimaced. "I'm disgusting. My skin's all dry, my hair's limp, I ache in all my joints. I've even got a wrinkle now at the corner of each eye. Look! See them? How horrible."

"You look like an adolescent, much too young to have that belly."

"Oh, Anja, after the baby comes, let's you and I run off and live together, just the two of us and our children. To hell with these men. We'll get a place in Salzburg, just us. We'll be so happy. But who is this 'friend'? Don't tell me you've changed your mind about women. You'll break my heart."

"No, nothing like that. A true friend. You'll laugh. It's Walter's Chetnik, Mila."

"Anja!" Sisi's face turned serious in an instant. "How could you? How could you dare?"

"I know she frightened you, but really you got the wrong impression. She's been wonderful. She's not some Balkan peasant. She's very sophisticated, from a good family in Belgrade. Not that I'd care very much if she were a peasant. The important thing is that she's kind, she understands things."

"I wonder," Sisi said, "why she's adopted you? What's she really up to?"

"Not a thing. She's lost and lonely. She's like us: No way to go home. She needs a friend as badly as I do, given that you're up here in all your splendor. Dizzi calls you the Fürstin."

"He would, the useless wretch. Oh, it all looks very luxe, but he and his people are out of their minds. And not because of the war or anything. I think they've always been mad. It happens in these old families."

"Old families? Well, I suppose that answers all the questions I've had about you. Do decadence and depravity go along with the madness?"

Sisi laughed. "I've been a very good girl. Only a few discreet affairs. Certainly no more than a dozen since the camp."

"A dozen? Why, Sisi! You're cruel. Leading me on with that pretty idea of us living together, knowing I could never count on you to be faithful."

"And don't you flirt with me, darling. You'll get all my hopes up and then you'll just dash them. It's very unfair. Just look at me. No one will ever want me again. I'm miserable."

"Surely it's not that bad."

"Worse than you can imagine. You'll see," Sisi said. "Now show me Sophie. And after I've had a good look, please help me up so I can get dressed. We'll be expected for dinner. Oh, you'll see then. Something you've never seen before, I think. The happy warrior as whipped hound."

❖ ❖ ❖

Propped on one elbow, Mila stared down on Fass's sleeping face, assessing not his features but what lay behind them. His character was all that interested her. And she felt now it had not changed since wartime.

Such fantastic good luck to have found this Fass alive. She knew he hated her. But not enough! He could never match her bloodless nihilism. For the engineer Fass was a man with a moral center, an essentially good heart, not an abyss. Yet he did not know it. He considered himself almost as evil as Mila knew herself to be, only less resolute. A perfect pliability, then, in Fass. Like those reeds that can be twisted and turned and woven into sturdy baskets without splitting or breaking.

Mila kept him supple by giving him just enough to make him desire more, which bent him ever further from self-awareness. She limited their encounters strictly, not only for that reason but to ensure the affair remained secret—for a while longer anyway. It was necessary Anja and Fass remain together, while she eased between them. This was essential, if Mila were to achieve her ends.

So far her tactics had worked perfectly.

Even though Anja was in Ischl, Mila would not let Fass stay the night. He would want to, she knew. But she would send him home presently, order him to keep studying for his exam. For he must be certified as an engineer.

Perhaps once or twice a week after Ischl, whenever she was in town, a note would arrive at Fass's office and he would come, just as he had for months now. But more often she would be with Anja and Sophie. Mila was determined to be the best friend Anja could wish for, even as she fucked her man behind her back. Then, at the decisive moment, Anja would support her, perhaps even recognize and make all on her own certain moves Mila required. Fass might waver a bit, but he would go along meekly.

Only patience was required now, Mila thought. She'd made her deployments shrewdly, just as she'd done in the mountains along certain trails she knew would be used. Everyone in their proper place, waiting. Sooner or later, the Partisans would simply walk into intersecting fields of fire that left them no way back, no way forward. No way out.

Mila blew softly on Walter's ear. He stirred slightly. She could afford some patience. If she moved carefully, she had perhaps six safe months left in this "business" of hers. Not all the police were stupid, not all were corrupt. They knew what was going on in the black market. They had caught quite a few of the less disciplined or less clever ones. They knew nothing of her yet, she believed. But in time one of them would hear something, learn a name, scoop up someone who would give them another name, someone who would point toward Mila Ćosić. Then the police would wait a bit, for some of them had patience as well as intelligence, until she walked into the ambush they set.

But they would wait forever. She laughed softly. For it would not be Mila Ćosić coming up the trail. Mila would be on some other path, one they never considered. An honest, legal one.

She blew again on Walter's ear, whispered his name. His eyes opened, he turned his face to hers, and reached up to draw her close. She allowed his lips to brush one of her breasts, but then slid out of bed, walked across the room and slipped into her robe. Then she returned and sat next to him. "Time you went home, Walter," she said, allowing the scrim to slip from her eyes for just an instant, the instant required to remind him of the falcon. He groaned. "Must I?"

"Even now. Anyway, I leave tomorrow for Venice. Very early, the train. A week's trip, there and other places. You will take your examination, then go to Anja and Sophie and that Scharner. We'll meet when you come back from Ischl."

Then Mila kissed the engineer deeply, broke it with a gentle bite on his lower lip, and walked into the bathroom, closing the door. She did not open it until she heard the lock catch on the front door and Walter's heavy steps going down the stairs.

❖ ❖ ❖

The shriek of steel sliding heavily against steel, the shuddering jolt, the shouts, the reek of scorched oil, the blue uniformed Italians and the gray-green Austrians asking for his papers at the Brennerpass: random impressions evoking nothing special for Walter Fass, who was much too far along on another journey to be called back so easily.

The examination had been laughable, even with his imperfect Italian. He had gone up to the farm afterward to get drunk with Uncle Franz. In celebration. But also because he'd arrived at a very hazardous junction—not that he could explain it directly to anyone, especially Franz.

Walter Fass knew he had lost his secret, second war.

Despite the first drubbing, he'd gone back to Mila the next time and every time after that determined to defeat her. He outflanked her attempts to take control as she had in their first encounter, then dominated her into performing acts that every other woman he had known would have found humiliating.

Still, he was beaten. Mila met his aggression with only sham submission. The more perverse his orders, the more eager she seemed to obey them. She deflected his anger into her own pleasure, making Walter feel he was the deviant one. He could not pretend anymore that he was inflicting punishment on her for Yugoslavia, making her as abject before him now as he'd been before her there. Nothing he devised made her abject. He felt soiled after each encounter. Each time, he swore to himself that he was finished with her.

Yet, a day or three or five later, when a note in her handwriting turned up on his desk, his pulse quickened and he hurried to her apartment as soon as he could.

It was the Chetnik's eyes. Beautiful yet horrible eyes, full of horrible truths about him. He went to her because he feared her so. And, to his disgust, that fear overrode every decent instinct and emotion he possessed. Including his love for Sophie and Anja.

What he wanted at the farm that night was some sense of how strong his family ties really were. He'd given up on his parents and sister, though Franz had not. Uncle Franz methodically posted a letter to Heinrich Fass at the old Stettin address every second Wednesday of the month. With no response, no sign that his letters had not simply vanished in the Soviet Zone.

So there were only Franz and Liese. And he got what amounted to a declaration from Franz, after the first glass of wine. "Want to show you something, Walter," Franz said, urging him outside, coatless in the cold, puffing up through the vineyard and the snow-mantled meadow to the great beech. It was a clear night with a crescent moon low in the west. Franz shone his flashlight on the tree's trunk, and Walter saw fresh yellow wood where steel-gray bark had been carved away: *Walter & Anja Fass, returned 27–10–1945*, and beneath that, in larger letters, *Sophie Fass, born 17–9–1946*.

"Cut it in just today, while you were taking your exam," Franz said. "Felt like an idiot for not having done it sooner. Liese came up to watch me. She was all for it, Walter."

So Fass mumbled something to make the old man feel good, and then they went back to the house and polished off a couple of bottles, Franz's mind seeming to drift farther back in time with each glass until he was telling tales of what Walter used to do around the place when he was a boy. How he once, at seven or eight, kidnapped three-year-old Liese from her bed on a fine summer night and half-dragged the little thing up to the tree, where they camped under the bench until well after dawn.

"You gave Heinrich and me quite a fright, you rascal," Franz laughed at his own recollection. Walter had no memory of it at all. "When we found both your beds empty that morning, my God! We searched everywhere before Heinrich figured it out. He said, 'I know exactly where they are,' led me up to the tree at a trot, which we could both manage pretty handily in those days, for we were younger than you are now. And sure enough, there you were. He paddled your ass on the spot, remember? I expect you do!"

Walter did not remember that, either.

But the carving was as clear in intent as any army order he'd ever received. Anja and Sophie were Fasses, now and forever. Should Walter ever abandon them for another woman, he would be shunned and reviled as a man of no honor, no decency. Blood ties would be severed. Franz would hate Mila and him. Obstinately, forever unforgiving. Tiroler, no matter how bighearted, had that capacity. Franz would cast his lot with Anja and Sophie.

Fass scarcely noticed the lurch and acceleration as the train pulled out and began the descent toward Innsbruck and Salzburg. He didn't think to look for the signalman's hut. An idea flashed across his mind: If something happened to Anja and Sophie, then he would be free. The sickness within that could produce such a notion made him shudder. Pain raced down his empty sleeve and curled his phantom fingers spasmodically. Sophie's absence from his life was unthinkable; he was sure he could never absorb such a loss and remain sane.

Yet that cursed Chetnik bitch drew him irresistibly. He knew he had brought this disaster down on himself. What if he had ignored Mila's first note? He might have remained haunted by her for a long time, but surely that would have faded. Especially since his heart had been captured by his own beautiful child. And by Anja. They'd had such a good chance at making a life together. Such a good chance.

But Mila had not died in the mountains, she had come to Bolzano, and he had been fool enough, twisted and perverse enough, to respond when she beckoned. In his saner moments, he knew what he desired most was a quiet, satisfying life with Anja and the joy of raising Sophie. But he was too weak to resist Mila. He had always been too fucking weak.

Figure this one out on your goddamned slide rule, Fass, he ordered himself. Devise a logarithmic curve in which everyone gets what they want, and no one loses a thing.

IX

It's a lunatic asylum. Sisi warned me the instant I saw her. And she's right!" Anja whispered urgently to Walter in bed the night of his arrival.

Very late to bed, a platoon of drained wine bottles left standing in disorderly rows on the fireplace hearth. Dizzi and his father reeling up the stairway in step, trailing Dizzi's mother to protect her from damage should her body decide to make a sudden retrograde movement under a surprise assault by gravity. All three humming the Radetzky March.

The engineer Fass, in only marginally better condition, seemed disinclined to agree with his wife. Or unable to form an opinion. Saying anything sensible was beyond his powers. "Can't be like this every night," he slurred. "Special occasion, that's all."

"Then every night's special in this place," Anja said. "And every night starts with lunch, continues bottle by bottle through the afternoon, and ends just as you saw."

She may as well have been in conversation with her pillow. Walter was snoring, emitting vinous fumes that made Anja slightly nauseated.

Poor Sisi.

Anja had thought it was just nerves. She'd thought her Magyar was exaggerating. She'd thought Sisi was being Sisi. Until they had gone down to dinner that first night—just an ordinary dinner, just the four of them plus Anja. You'll see, Sisi said. And Anja had.

Dizzi seemed another man entirely when he introduced her to his father and mother. Nervous, even submissive in a way Anja had never imagined possible. His mother was very tall, vine-thin, her hair that dead shade of blond gone more than half gray. Her face was the sort you could never remember as a face entire; only a slack mouth and unsteady eyes and the skin of her neck crêpey, with unwholesome liverish spots.

Old Scharner had a face one would want to forget, but probably could not. Taut as a death mask. A death mask of Dizzi, so identical were their features—except for two creases like sabre slashes that ran from the old man's nostrils to his jawbone on either side of his thin, white-lipped mouth. And lines almost incised—they were that sharp and deep—that radiated from the corners of his eyes, which were cold as a lizard's. When he spoke, even when he laughed, his mouth scarcely opened and his eyes took no part in the proceedings. Oh, but he was full to bursting with words and what he seemed to think was laughter.

He began immediately after they sat down to table and a maid served the soup course.

"So, here is Anja the Prussian among us, the good friend of our Hungarian filly—or should I say mare, now, Sisi?" he said, with what must have passed in this family for humor. "An unnatural alliance, Prussians and Hungarians. Something off in that mix."

"More unnatural than German Austrians with, say, Slovenes and Croats and Ruthenians?" Anja said flippantly, already disliking the man.

"Oh, don't leave out those Bukowina Jews with the red fox hats the Emperor was so fond of. And the Slovaks and the Wends and all the rest," old Scharner riposted. "But naturally, Anja, they were people of conquest. One didn't mix with them."

"Didn't we once have a Czech count to dinner, in Vienna?" Dizzi's mother asked in a tone that made Anja wonder whether she was already drunk, or slightly senile. "I'm sure we did. And others, too, with extraordinarily odd names, from very strange places."

"Of course, dear. Certainly. People of our sort. Even Magyars. It was, after all, the Austro-Hungarian Empire," old Scharner said patiently, as if she were an idiot.

"Father, must we?" Dizzi ventured.

"Must we what?" Old Scharner stared at his son. "Come on, boy, speak up. Out with it. Or keep your peace and let me make my point. My point, Anja, is very simple. All these nationalities with their pretensions to a true culture, which really only consisted of peculiar folk costume worn by the peasants, ruined Austria. The Hungarians stabbed us in the back, forcing that Dual Monarchy nonsense. Where would these people be without our Austrian culture? The Magyars are simply puffed-up barbarians from God knows where, Mongolia probably. Now, the thing I admire about the Prussians is that they had the good sense to simply get rid of the rabble in their lands. East Prussia, for example. Once full of heathen Lithuanians. The Teutonic Knights simply cleared 'em all out, drove 'em away. The Habsburgs, unfortunately, were too soft."

He was utterly mad.

"Take our Sisi here. Descended from steppe nomads, if you go back far enough," he said.

"And take the Scharners here. Descended from Ostrogoths and Avars, if you go back far enough," Sisi said.

"Now, Sisi, I think what I am speaking of here is a little beyond your reach, so you may as well quietly finish your soup," old Scharner said, with his almost invisible but somehow threatening smile. "So Anja, your people were landowners? Lost it all to the damned Soviets, eh?"

"No," Anja said. "Intellectuals."

"Intellectuals? Intellectuals? How curious. I suppose they didn't hunt? Too busy in the library and so forth?"

"Something like that."

"No hunting. What a shame," old Scharner said, as if it truly was a pity.

"It's difficult to call the shooting you do 'hunting,' " Dizzi said.

"Oh, you lack the stomach for it, Dietmar. I do wish you'd bred true to the Scharner line. Too much like your mother's people. Something soft there."

"Oh, we always hunted in Steiermark," Dizzi's mother said. "Lots and lots. Great parties. Horns all over the walls of the lodge."

"I think most of the horns were hung on the men of your family," old Scharner said. And the satyr actually winked at Anja.

"No, the walls, I'm sure," Dizzi's mother said. "It was never a custom to walk around with your latest set of stag or chamois or ibex horns. Not even at costume parties. My father shot the last ibex in the province, you know. The very last. He was quite proud of it."

"I'm sure he was, dear. And what do you Magyars do with horns, Sisi?"

"Generally, hang them on Austrians," Sisi snapped. The girl was tense as a coiled spring.

"Ho ho! Some spirit in the young mare still," Dizzi's father laughed.

"Why would they do that? Is it a custom, Sisi?" Frau von Scharner asked.

"You could call it a custom. Our men have been doing it for generations."

"How odd. And do the Austrians enjoy it? Is it a sort of honor?"

"Your husband would know better than I."

"Hah! Hah! Dietmar, are you sure you haven't let a cuckoo get into our nest, eh?" old Scharner said, draining what Anja estimated to be his fourth or fifth glass of wine.

"Now, Karl, you're getting awfully silly. Mixing up birds and horns and God knows what else. What do birds have to do with hunting trophies on the walls?" Dizzi's mother said. Dizzi was silently matching his father glass for glass, not daring to meet his eyes.

"Never mind, dear. Dizzi and I are having a little father-son exchange."

"That's nice," the old woman smiled.

So it had gone on and on through the courses, the different wines with each course. At the end of the evening, old Scharner—"But you must call me Karl now, Anja," he said—insisted on showing her up to her room. On the third-floor landing, he cornered her and practically drooled seductive flatteries he imperfectly remembered from his younger years. Anja'd had to dodge very quickly when he lunged to kiss her.

And the next afternoon he caught her alone in the orangerie with Sophie in her arms and turned vicious, actually kneaded her buttocks. She slapped him smartly, first a blow with her right palm to his left cheek and then a backhand to his right. She may as well have hit a marble statue. He did take his damned hands off her bottom. But his face remained dead, except for a reddening where she had struck him. Absolutely expressionless, except for his lizard eyes, which seemed to lick her from head to toe. "You make me want to vomit," Anja said. "Touch me again and I'll take your eyes out with my fingernails." And that lecher had the nerve to say, "Yes, yes. Let's go into my gun room. There's a leather couch there. You can claw me like a cat."

Anja fled the orangerie and would have left the house, if not for Sisi. She had to stay for Sisi's sake.

Disgusting man, among the worst she had ever encountered. Sisi at least tried to bite back. Surely she did. But Dizzi? That shit. Anja doubted he would have intervened even if he caught his father groping Sisi, or groping her. He was *worse* than a whipped hound. Much worse.

Old Scharner might be the true face of the defunct European ruling class, Anja thought. Because she had been well-dressed and well-spoken—and because she was known as the especial friend of a Battyany—the Scharner ménage had assumed she was one of their kind, and had not bothered to put up the front they showed to the lower orders. A front that artfully mixed gravitas with arrogance to produce a sort of condescension they imagined plain people expected from their betters. And perhaps the plain people they had contact with—the grocers, the bank managers, the tenants on their estates, the gunsmiths, the butchers, the wine merchants— expected just that. How else to explain the little bows, the almost inaudible heel-clicking of the banker, the local mayor and the wine man she saw call on old Scharner in the days after her arrival?

Poor Sisi, caught in this nightmare of cruelty. It must have been a horrifying surprise for her, the first time she saw strong, confident Dizzi turn to mush in the presence of his father. And now she was trapped in the toils of a rotting family who squabbled about money even as they squandered it, who preferred to witness their own decline in a state of more or less constant drunkenness, who tortured each other for amusement.

No wonder Sisi was frightened.

Sisi told her, near tears, that there was no income from the Scharner estates in the east because the Russians were there. Old Scharner was drawing down his Liechtenstein bank accounts faster and faster. And the villa had been mortgaged to the hilt. In two or three years they might not even have a roof over their heads. And they weren't doing anything about it. Not one god-damn thing. Dizzi would have one hell of a shock when the last schilling was gone and he'd have to find work if he wanted to eat!

Anja looked at the man snoring beside her, and felt sure that she and Sophie would never lack a home or food, thanks to this Fass. Dizzi was charming, Dizzi was a loving and loyal friend. But he was feckless and reckless and the worst kind of coward. Sisi could not rely on him. She would have nowhere to turn when the Scharners crashed. There was still not a word from her family in Budapest. She was, she confessed, almost at the point of accepting that they were all dead.

Sophie began calling for her in her mild way. Anja slipped from the bed and went to the cradle that the Scharners had dredged up from their vast store of furniture and placed in her room. Sophie only cried lowly when she was hungry, was other-wise placid and patient. Anja often thought—though she knew it was ridiculous—that she glimpsed a wisdom in the baby's stare, a sort of tolerance for the lapses and failures of her parents when it came to her needs. A common delusion of motherhood, no doubt. Anja sat in an overstuffed chair near the window, wrapped in a thick loden shawl, and fed Sophie. It must have been about four in the morning. Outside, the light of a cold moon cast dark gray twins of the ancient black trees down on the brilliant snow.

God, what an odd pass her life had come to. One that—even tipsy and dreamy up on the Wawel with her friends before the war—she would never, ever have imagined. Her world then, for all the books and the talks with her parents, all the shared aspirations of her friends, had been narrow as a single line of longitude, inter-secting exactly the point where she stood: The start of a life as a

scholar, a life entire in Krakow, a life mainly of the mind but perhaps one day broadening a bit to include a man—a husband—
who also stood where she stood.

And now? Sophie, an unexpected gift who had seemed like a
curse when she was only a foetal mass of multiplying cells in Anja's
womb. A comfortable life, though lacking any intellectual compo-
nent beyond her reading, lived among strangers, with a man she
could not seem to physically adore despite her love for him.

Mila was a godsend, a friend she felt she might depend on.
There was Sisi, of course, but Sisi had gotten herself into a fix,
insisting on having a child when she must have seen how difficult, how ill-omened that would be among the Scharners. Dizzi
would do anything for Walter if Walter needed help; probably
he would do anything for Sisi as well. The problem was that Dizzi
would never go up against old Scharner—a rough customer, but
very far from the roughest Dizzi must have encountered in the
war. His failure of nerve baffled her, and what Sisi had slipped into
with him was pure looming disaster.

If it all blew up, Sisi and her child would come to live with
them in Bolzano, Anja decided. Walter surely would be certified as
an *ingegnere*, and if what he could make of that was not enough—
though she felt confidence in his ability—then she herself would
find work, any sort of work, once Sophie was weaned and could be
left safely through the days with Sisi and her child.

And then of course there was Mila, so clever and strong. Mila
would help them all find their way through any labyrinth they
encountered.

It would work out, Anja was sure. They had, all of them, survived harder, harsher times.

Fass, you bastard," Dizzi said. "You got me into this. Get me out."

"Done that already once. The bridge over that gorge in Yugoland? Eh? You're not so drenched in alcohol that your memory's as bad as your liver must be, are you?" Walter grinned.

"No, though I try my best. It's very painful to recall how exciting life used to be. I'm bored to death, the old folks drive me insane, the Fürstin over there with your Anja has been insufferable for months on end. As soon as she started getting rejected by the little skirts she was always chasing . . . Christ, the sulking and sullenness. No more delicious gossip about our peccadilloes. Nothing but endless whining about getting out of here. God, the shit I've had to listen to. What choice do I have besides drinking myself nearly insensible? And I do wish you'd wipe that infuriating grin off your face. This is no joke."

"Ah, Dizzi. It could be so much worse. We could still be targets for Partisans."

"Wish the hell we were. That was some sport. That gave life a little frisson each day. A reason to wake up in the morning, anyway."

"You're depressed because no one shoots at you anymore? Haven't we had this ridiculous conversation before?"

"Very likely. Shit on it all. Have another drink." He snapped his fingers to attract one of the waiters circulating with silver trays arrayed with flutes of champagne.

They had parked themselves in a corner of the villa's small ballroom. The party in progress was to mark the christening of Dizzi and Sisi's child. And it was completely depressing, Walter thought. There were a couple of dozen old men and women, friends and relations of Karl von Scharner and his pathetic wife, perhaps twenty or so boys and girls, all Scharner relations, too young to have fought in the war; and scarcely anyone from Dizzi and Sisi's generation—except for Anja and him, a couple of young widows whose brittle merriment was patently false, and a former Luftwaffe pilot who wore a black silk mask to cover the melted mass of scar tissue that had been a face before his Focke Wulff went down in flames over Normandy.

Through the swirl of celebrants, Walter glimpsed Sisi seated in a chair so large she looked like a little girl—a little girl holding an infant wrapped and draped in a christening gown with a silken train that bunched on the floor around her feet. Anja was beside her. Sisi's smile was forced. And she held the child as if it were an inconvenient bundle she wished a servant would relieve her of.

She had her reasons. A hard birth, for one, almost twelve hours in labor. And then, because her hips were so narrow and the baby inside her surprisingly large, an emergency cesarean. The child was perfect, a delightful little girl who looked—everyone said so, though Fass found newborns indistinguishable—exactly like Dizzi, without a trace of Sisi's Magyar blood to be seen. Ah, but that might manifest itself later, in the temperament.

Anja hit it right, Fass thought. This place was a lunatic asylum. But that did not explain what troubled him most. Madness wasn't contagious. So what on earth had happened to his friend? The Dizzi beside him now was scarcely recognizable as the bold, cheerful Jäger Fass had known so well. Driven mad by his father? Hard to credit.

But who was he to judge? He was mad as well. No one with a normal mind lost it over a coldhearted killer, no matter that she was a desirable woman. He was a masochist. Dizzi must be one, too.

"Drink up, you *verräterisch* Tiroler," Dizzi said, draining his own glass and snapping his fingers again for a waiter. He was beginning to sprawl in his chair, his long legs a tripwire for anyone unwary enough to pass within a meter of him.

"*Achtung*, you superannuated Jäger." Fass forced himself to laugh. "You want fun, excitement, travel, that little frisson you mentioned? Well, you can have it if you like."

"Don't even mention it. The Légion Étrangère in Indochina? God preserve me. Can you think of a worse combination than Frog officers commanding a lot of renegade ex—Wehrmacht men in the goddamn jungles against the Viet Minh? A royal fuck-up. Anyway, I don't like heat and humidity."

"Unplug your ears for a moment, ass," Fass said. Then he told Dizzi as much as he knew about the dirty war over the Trieste region.

"Now that sounds at least a little interesting. I never did consider that I'd killed quite enough Partisans. Felt I'd fallen short, you understand? Hadn't met my quota, as our Red friends would say. But how good is your information?"

"Frontline report from a professional."

"Oh, Christ," Dizzi said, suddenly sharper than a man who had drunk as much as Scharner had any right to be. "That Chetnik bitch? She was down there, was she? Of course she was. That's the only way you'd know."

"Perhaps."

"And the only way she'd tell you is if you'd taken up with her. Goddammit, Walter! You've done it, haven't you?"

Fass ignored the question, knocking back another glass of champagne. "I imagine the fighting's cooled down a bit. But some sniping across the border? An occasional raid? All of a sudden it could get very hot. Then full support from the English and the Amis."

"I'll make my own judgments about that, if I take a little excursion down there, Herr Bridge-Builder. But you're evading my question. Have you disregarded my advice? Have you or have you not got mixed up with that crazy Chetnik?"

"That's a private matter," Fass said.

"Private? Private? You dare say that to me?"

"Well, she and Anja became friends. I hardly knew it was happening."

"But you certainly knew what was happening when she invited you to start fucking her, didn't you? You didn't need to pinch yourself awake or anything. You were of perfectly clear mind about that?"

"Dizzi, you are coming very close to insulting me in a way it will be difficult for me to forgive."

"I'll risk it, Herr Bridge-Builder. You're thinking, I know, 'Scharner has made such a mess of his own life that he has no right to comment on mine.' *Klar*. There is a certain amount of truth to that," Dizzi said, leaning very close to Walter. "But my friend, that woman means you no good. What in hell do you see in her, anyway? You could find a much better mistress with ease. This cunt'll smash you up without a thought. She'll wreck you."

"Maybe you underestimate me, Scharner," Walter said, achingly aware of how false the claim was. "And in fact you know nothing of her beyond your inexplicably hostile encounter in my home the day Anja brought Sophie back from the hospital."

"I felt what I felt. If my instincts about people were not excellent, do you think I would have survived the war, fighting the way I fought it? I'd have been killed in the mountains long before you and I hooked up during the retreat."

"Maybe, maybe not. There is this little matter of destiny, you know. We are not entirely in control of our own lives."

"Bah! I'm not in control now because I am a piece of shit. But you? And what of Anja and your daughter? Do they count for nothing?"

"Judging from the way you quail before your old man, judging from the abuse you accept . . . more, I think, than Sisi and your child count for you."

Dizzi laughed then, but with a deep bitterness that seemed to slide too easily into regions of hopelessness and despair. He should never have said such a thing to this man, this comrade, Fass thought.

"Please forgive me, Dizzi. That remark was uncalled for."

But Dizzi only laughed again, wildly and wild-eyed. "Forgive? When you are so goddamned right? I should have beaten him to death long ago. Or at least cursed him to hell and taken Sisi away. But instead I stood here like some stupid calf and let him cut off my balls."

❊ ❊ ❊

Look at the pair of them," Sisi said to Anja, nodding toward Walter and Dizzi. "Goddamn men, thinking it's all a lark. They've no idea what we go through. And if they did, I doubt they'd care."

"Sisi, Sisi," Anja said, placing her arm around her friend's shoulders. "They're drunk, they're celebrating. Forget them."

"Celebrating what?" Sisi said. She was near tears.

"What you should, darling. Look at your lovely daughter, look at the perfect little Lilo Battyany von Scharner. She's part of you."

"Poor little Lilo, then," Sisi choked. "Part of nothing. And I don't feel part of her. I don't want her. Oh, God, Anja. I'm the worst bitch in the world. All I want is to run from her and Scharner and this place as fast and far as I can."

X

The longest day of the year, Anja thought cheerfully that morning, making coffee while Walter dressed for work. Sophie rapped a tiny silver spoon—one of Mila's many presents—against the tray of her high chair in a rhythm only Sophie knew. The summer solstice—was it the twenty-second or twenty-third of June? Anja had lost track. Her units of time had little to do with calendars anymore.

"I'll probably be late today," Walter called from the bedroom. "We're a bit behind on that new building."

"Very late, probably," she called back. "Your men will have enough light to work until at least—oh, I don't know. Maybe nine-thirty or ten?"

"As late as that? God, the way they'll sulk. And the overtime cost. Petrocelli hates to pay overtime." Walter came into the kitchen and drank his coffee standing. He had passed the exam and become Petrocelli's fully certified chief engineer. And although Petrocelli had doubled Walter's salary, he'd come close to doing the same to his workload, gleefully dismissing most of the little Milanese snots as soon as Fass could legally direct a site.

"And he hated all that rain this spring, when nobody could work and the project fell behind schedule," Anja said. "He hates to pay, he hates the rain, he hates everything. You'd think he would just give it all up. Give it to you, perhaps."

"Ah, he does hate it all, now that he doesn't need any more money. But there is one thing he loves: complaining. He lives for it. I think he needs a certain level of grievance, real or imagined, to feel normal. He complains to me about the work even when it goes perfectly. I think that's why he has his mistresses. He can complain to them about his awful wife. And if she were a saint, he'd complain about that instead."

"And who do you complain to about your saintly wife?"

"Oh, strangers on the tram. Passing pairs of *carabinieri*. The teller at the bank. The welders. Though I try to avoid the welders. I don't know what it is with welders. They always get so serious, shut down their torches, lift off their helmets, offer their own experiences and suggestions. Slows down the work."

"Poor Walter. Poor Dottor Ingegnere."

"The welders are sympathetic, too." Walter grinned. "Whenever I describe some of your bad behavior, they always nod thoughtfully, and then say, '*Dio*, Signor Ingegnere. *Una cattiva* you have. But this is nothing. My wife . . .' I'm treated to fantastic descriptions of their own domestic burdens and how they deal with them."

"And how do they deal with them?"

"They generally say—now, I don't know if they actually do this, but they claim so—that they spank their wives regularly, whether they've been provoked or not, as a preventive measure. Backfired on one fellow, or so he laments. 'Now, she likes so much to be spanked, Ingegnere, that whenever I do she drags me to the bed and I have to make love to her, *subito*.'"

"*Subito!*" Anja laughed so hard she spilled her coffee. "He wishes it were so. Now you. Get out and go earn some money, Herr Doktor Ingenieur. And stop gossiping with welders."

And stop the drinking and the brooding you have begun to do too much again, Herr Ingenieur, she thought to herself. Probably it was only the war, as Franz used to say. An episode that would pass. Day to day, they were more affectionate with each other than most married couples she had observed, certainly kinder and more considerate toward each other. And Walter was absolutely mad for Sophie. A finer father she could not imagine. A good, sound partnership, she concluded.

"*Jawohl.*" Walter smiled as he moved to leave, not neglecting to swing Sophie out of her chair and kiss her.

After she fed Sophie and cleaned her up, Anja considered the day. It was lovely: a breeze funneling down the valley from up toward Merano moderating the blaze of the sun, a few cumulus fluffy as unsheared sheep moving placidly along the southern horizon. A nice day to go to the farm. Sophie loved to crawl around in the long grass, every so often trying to stand but always tumbling back down into the lush green mass of it. Franz would happily tote her around and put her hand against the soft wet noses of the cows, which always made her squeal with delight. Liese would give her a cookie and fresh milk and coo at her. Perhaps the farm, then.

But she decided to write to Sisi first. She sat in the garden— this year she had been active there, planting all sorts of lovely annuals in huge old terra-cotta pots Walter'd salvaged—in the shade of the wisteria, Sophie crawling and rolling happily in the little playpen old Franz had made for her. But after "Dearest Sisi," no words would come.

What to say to a friend who was only enduring the life she led? No, that was going too far. Sisi's letters immediately after Anja and

Walter had left Ischl had been progressively more cheering. Acerbic, ridiculing the Scharner ménage with that gay, amusing, optimistic air Sisi had always possessed and seemed to have lost to some sort of depression just before Lilo was born. Anja had been frightened for her, worried at how low she was just after the birth, too. Even the nursing had started badly. "It's repulsive," she said. "Makes my skin crawl. I didn't ever think it would feel so creepy, when I watched you with Sophie." But after a few days Sisi seemed to enjoy it. "Rather peaceful, almost comforting somehow," she said.

Then yet another turn. Every day they had gone to Ischl, just the two of them and their babies, and spent some hours in a quiet *Konditorei*, drinking coffee with *Schlag* and eating more pastries than they should have. They gossiped and laughed, even flirted with each other.

Away from the Scharners, Sisi was still Sisi. The problem was that Sisi could not get away enough. She was so isolated in that mad villa, in that pathetic town where everyone seemed to be doing their best—and a more stupid effort could hardly be imagined—to pretend that Old Austria still lived, that two wars hadn't turned their world upside down, destroying forever whatever they thought was so appealing about the Franz Josef days. Some Anja had met were actually nostalgic over nostalgia itself. For only dinosaurs like the senior Scharner had actually lived in the days of Empire, dead now these thirty years. Those of Dizzi and Sisi's generation who had survived the second war had nothing but the nonsense their elders spouted to go on. Certainly, for them, life had been easier, or at least more luxurious, in Imperial times. But who knew how it felt to live each day? Was luxury happiness? Was it contentment? Was it peace of mind?

So there was Sisi, young and full of energy. And lacking even a single sympathetic friend.

Dizzi had let Sisi down with a thud.

Oh, perhaps she was too hard on the lot of them. It was easy for her to criticize, with the great good luck she'd had. But they were slowly draining Sisi's spirit. And Anja did not know how to help. If only she had her own resources, like Mila did.

But possibly Sisi would not leave even if she had a place to go. On the train home with Walter, Anja had broached the idea of offering her a refuge. Fass agreed that the situation at Ischl was bad, he was heart-sore over Dizzi's debauched boredom, his utter failure to adjust to a life without the excitement of combat. But he said it was his sense that Sisi was bold enough to leave anytime she wanted to. Anja shuddered at that observation. Perhaps Sisi was in her natural element. Certainly she was amongst her own class. She might sneer at Anja's little life in Bolzano. Maybe her heart's true desire was just an improved version of the Scharner household— one with old Scharner safely in his grave.

Or maybe all Sisi really wanted was to be an unencumbered young woman who slept with whomever she could seduce, went to grand parties, had nice clothes and a fine house. But surely she must realize that the money had to come from somewhere, and it would never again come from her father, still lost in the rubble of Budapest. That Puszta estate? Probably a collective farm on the Soviet model by now, ten or twelve peasant families crammed into the main house, burning eighteenth-century furniture to simmer their goulash.

Well, maybe Sisi was making the necessary adjustments. Her letters seemed to indicate that. She had taken to calling old Scharner "Old Hard-On," referring to his wife as "Dearest Mamma," which, she'd written, was what "The Capon"—her new name for Dizzi—actually called that crêpey-skinned idiot when he thought no one could overhear. "Dearest Mamma"—from Dizzi! The thought of it had made Anja laugh out loud.

Too damn many maybes, though. Anja felt depressed then in her lovely garden, realizing how little she truly knew of Sisi. She began to wish Mila would drop by for coffee in the afternoon. But you never knew with Mila. She came and went without a word, a little business here and a little there, and then she would be in Bolzano and dropping by almost every other day, full of entertaining tales if Anja was quiet, or listening intently on those days when Anja wanted to pour out previously hidden parts of her own story. It occurred to her that she did not even know Mila's address, where exactly in the city the woman lived. What a strange thing, after all this time. Mila had more secrets than an owl. It was probably smart, perhaps a deliberate protection of her; if the authorities ever came around asking about Mila, Anja would not have to lie. She could truly say she did not know anything of the whereabouts or activities of Mila Ćosić.

And she felt relieved by that, for Anja the Liar was no longer much with her. She had told Mila almost every intimate detail of her life—except for Richter and the betrayals. True words no longer left the peculiar, coppery taste in her mouth they once had. She had almost abandoned her three Krakow principles, and all the Krakow rules, with Mila and Walter at least. And Sisi too now knew—a confession in that Ischl *Konditorei*—that Anja was no Prussian from Breslau, but a Pole from Krakow, too young to have had the chance to earn that degree in philosophy she had claimed in the DP camp. When Sisi heard that, she had laughed as if Anja had just revealed some enormous practical joke.

Anja never noticed the passage of the hours. There were one or two diaper changes, Sophie fed and put down for a nap, time enough under the wisteria to read two or three of Conrad's short stories, her favorite being "Freya of the Island." She had not finished her letter, but no matter; when the doorbell rang, she hoped very much that it would be Mila.

It was not. Opening the door, she saw instead a pimply boy in a shoddy blue uniform. Who handed her a telegram, gawked at her wild tears as she read it, and yet lingered on the front step expecting a tip.

❈   ❈   ❈

S isi is dead."
       Fass heard the words, and he did not. The words were only vagrant wafts of air rustling leaves he could not see. The garden air was blue. It had assumed that twilight hue even as everything with true color and solidity dimmed and grayed. Night did not fall here. It rose up from the valley, driving the light remorselessly toward the vertical north, until only the highest peaks—snow there permanent as the rock it covered—still gleamed like old gold. This you had to accept: That the darkness would come first among the living. You could not live on the peaks, you could not escape the night even there. For the gold beacons above were a hollow promise. An hour after electric lights flicked on in windows everywhere and the streetlamps of the town cast their meager lucency on cobbles and concrete, the darkness would overwhelm the peaks, too.

"She is dead."

Fass heard a rushing in the darkness. The sound you hear when it is very quiet and you are very afraid, the one he had heard so many times in the mountains, the loud rush of his own blood in his ears.

"No!" Walter heard the word. It was his. Yet it seemed to come from quite far away, beyond the stone bastions of the garden. No way to tell in the obscuring air. Anja moved toward him, a little slip of paper fluttering in her hand. "Dizzi sent this two days ago. The day before the funeral. The wretched *Itaker* got around to delivering it three or four hours ago.

"Sisi, all alone. So alone."

The flat, dull words were coming from Anja's mouth. Her face glowed like a wraith's—the only clearly visible thing in the dark garden.

"Why?" It was not a word. It was not a question. He understood that.

▩　　▩　　▩

Old Scharner, not Dizzi, responded to Fass's note of condolence. A long letter, scrawled on heavy embossed stationery. Anja watched her husband sit stiffly at the kitchen table, reading the thing. As he scanned the first page, she saw his jaws clench, the edges of his nostrils go white, his hand tighten on the remaining sheets. She watched him roughly fold the letter and stuff it into his pants pocket, then reach out and pour himself another glass of wine, which he downed in one gulp.

"Show me," she demanded.

"Better not," Fass said, his voice a hoarse combination of grief and rage she had never heard before. "You don't want to see what he's written."

"I do. Sisi was my friend as much as Dizzi is yours, and Lilo is my goddaughter. I have the right to know."

"I'll tell you."

"I don't want your version. I want Scharner's. Are you forgetting who you are talking to? Give me the damned letter."

"Christ, Anja. Sisi committed suicide. Isn't that enough to know? We've lost a friend. Isn't that grief enough to try to bear?"

"Enough that you cannot simply say suicide and expect that's sufficient explanation. Because it was all over your face as you read, and it's in every word you've said since, that monster Scharner told a lot more. I want to see it. I have to see it. Now give me the goddamn letter, you prick," Anja shouted.

Fass, head bowed and tears in his eyes, pulled the unevenly creased sheets from his pocket and slowly slid them facedown across the table. Then he grabbed the bottle of wine, swallowed several great gulps, and left the house, slamming the front door.

The first page was hypocritical, self-absorbed shit. Exactly what she expected from a beast like Scharner: "Grateful for your kind words and prayers," "a tremendous loss that has stricken us all," "Dietmar is devastated." Then the second sheet:

As Dizzi's former comrade-in-arms, and as his closest friend, you have the right to know the facts of this tragedy. It is my painful duty to report them. Elisabeth Battyany was the cause of much trouble here. She viciously badgered my son to take her away. Dizzi was naturally reluctant to leave his home and family at the whim of this unreliable, unstable girl. She redoubled her efforts, going so far as to ridicule my son as a coward at social gatherings, and slanderously implying that he was a sexual deviant. My son behaved as a gentleman despite these embarrassing abuses. Then she began to ignore her own daughter, neglecting the child so badly that we had to hire a nursemaid.

Failing to gain her end through these tactics, the Battyany took the ultimate step to blacken our name. She abruptly left the table during a large dinner party. She went to her room, locked the door, turned on the water taps of her bath. Then she entered the bath and slit her wrists with a razor.

This creature left the taps running—deliberately, I feel certain. The result being that very shortly, blood-tinged water from the overflowing tub began to seep through the ceiling directly above the dinner table. My son raced upstairs, kicked open the locked door, and found her body.

My son was sorely grieved, for he forgave all her transgres-

sions and her obstinate ingratitude for the home we had provided for her and her child. Only his pleas had prevented me
from expelling her from our household months ago. I accept
responsibility for the disgrace this weakness of mine has
brought down upon our family.

I must further report that Dizzi's state of mind deteriorated
rapidly after the funeral. In his grief, he began to consume
large amounts of alcohol. He has since suffered a complete nervous collapse. He is being treated in a private medical facility
specializing in such cases here in Bad Ischl. We are hopeful
that he will make a rapid and complete recovery.

The infant Lilo has been sent to a foundling home run by
the Ursuline Sisters near Bregenz, where she will receive the
finest care. When she is old enough, she will be moved to one
of the boarding schools run by the Sisters . . .

Anja ripped the letter in half, ripped the halves in half, and repeated this until all that was left was a pile of thin shreds of
Scharner stationery. These she took out to the garden, placed on a
flagstone, and burned to ash.

Then, swinging a hoe with all the strength she possessed, she
smashed into shards each of the twelve old terra-cotta urns she had
so lovingly planted that spring.

🔳   🔳   🔳

Anja was curled on their bed, rigid as a corpse in rigor mortis
with a cold fury she had not felt even during the worst of
Krakow time, when she heard footsteps in the corridor and a scrab-
bling at the locked and bolted door. "Anja," she heard Fass say
softly, "it's me. Please open up."

The voice disgusted her. She did not move.

"Anja, please. Please open up." The voice was louder now. He must think her asleep. As if she could sleep.

Fass tapped lightly, twisted the doorknob, called to her again. She rose slowly, moved toward the sound, and placed her lips almost against that thin space between the door and its frame.

"You will never enter this room again," she hissed. "You are one of her murderers."

"Anja, are you drunk? I've been drinking, too. It hasn't helped. I feel broken inside."

"God damn how you feel."

"What are you saying? This is mad."

"You should have stopped it. You could have stopped it. You saw your brave, bold friend throwing Sisi to his beast of a father. And you did nothing. I hold you responsible for the murder of Sisi. And I am glad—glad, you hear?—that your favorite 175 has gone insane. May they keep him in a padded room forever."

"Anja, Anja. That's crazy talk. You're drunk."

"I have not had even a sip of wine. I have never been more clear about anything in my life. You saw Dizzi was a coward and you saw old Scharner was a monster and you saw they were destroying poor Sisi. And all you did was get drunk with your spineless queer."

"What could I have done. Anja? What could I have done?"

"You could have asked Sisi to bring Lilo and come live with us. You could have convinced Dizzi to take her away from Ischl. You could have killed old Scharner, smothered him in his drunken sleep with a pillow. If you were any sort of man at all, you would go to Ischl tomorrow and kill that evil son of a bitch."

"Suppose I had asked Sisi to come with us. Do you really think she would have?"

"We'll never know now, will we? Because you did not. She would have, I know it. She respected you, God knows why. She would have listened to you."

"You could have asked her, Anja."

"How? Is this my house? Is it my work that supports us? How could I have brought her here?"

"It is your home as much as mine. You could have asked."

"Easy to say now. I wonder what your reaction would have been if I had?"

"We'll never know, will we? Because you did not."

The rightness of Fass's words nearly drove Anja out of her mind, drove rage to levels she could not control at all. She began to scream at him in Polish.

"It was murder, a girl murdered because you wouldn't inter-fere. You stinking cocksucker, you filthy bastard. You will never share a bed with me again. If you so much as try to enter this room, I will take Sophie and we'll run and you'll never see either of us again. Probably you'll be glad of it."

Fass couldn't understand even half of what she was saying. But Anja could not bear to think or speak in that hateful German, the language that was his and the coward Dizzi's and the monstrous Richter's and that satanic Scharner's.

"It was lies, all lies, what he wrote about Sisi. Old Scharner must die the most painful death that anyone ever died. Long and agonizing beyond belief," she shouted. Sophie was wailing in her crib but even that could not divert Anja now.

"Did you say lies?" Walter called back. "Of course I know that. Do you think I excuse Dizzi? Do you imagine I don't despise him? Do you imagine I don't hate his damned father as much as you do? Do you think I believe a single word he said about Sisi? I was there. I saw it."

"And you didn't stop it, Fass. It was in your power to stop it and you did not."

"Anja, nothing was in my power. If you really believed that, why didn't you insist while we were in Ischl that I do something? I would have done whatever you asked."

"Filthy liar. You wouldn't let yourself admit that Dizzi was a worthless coward who cared more for his comfort and his little playmates than for Sisi and Lilo!"

But again Fass was right, Anja realized. She could not stand him being right. Because it meant it was her fault. Oh, dear God! Sophie was screaming now.

"Go away, Walter. Go sleep in the other room. I have to tend to Sophie," Anja said in German. "Only now leave us. For the love of God, leave me be."

XI

The sun had just edged above the horizon, washing the stars from the sky but unable yet to drive night from the valley, when Anja rose from the bed in which she had lain sleepless. She carefully folded her few clothes—the nice things Mila had bought her, the well-worn everyday things she had gotten with Fass's money—and put them in her suitcase. Then she packed all Sophie's clothes, and her *Kuschelbär* and the silver rattle that had been the first of Mila's gifts, in a smaller bag. She pinned her money, the lire she had saved bit by bit from the housekeeping funds Walter gave her each week, inside the waistband of her skirt. She changed and dressed the baby, fed her.

Then she slipped out of the house, locked the door behind her and placed the key in a crack of the stone steps that was just wide enough, just deep enough to hide it. The two suitcases in her right hand, Sophie securely cradled in her left arm, Anja walked down the silent street, avoiding the small circles of light cast every fifty meters or so by the streetlamps.

The first bus to Wolfsgruben was idling, waiting for the minute-hand of the big clock on the terminus wall to signal the

start of its working day. She boarded. The driver was standing at
the little kiosk next to the ticket windows, smoking, sipping an
espresso, gossiping with the woman in a pale-blue smock who ran
the place. There were no other passengers. Anja settled in the rear
seat, suitcases at her feet.

"We're running away, little sparrow," Anja murmured to Sophie. "Your mamma is very, very cross with your pappa. She's very,
very unhappy. Poor mamma has no *Kuschelbär*. Will you be my
Kuschelbär? No? Then what can mamma cling to when mamma is
scared and unhappy, the way you cling to your little bear?"

Sophie gurgled and stared up at Anja, her tiny fingers gently
rubbing the soft, furry head of her teddy.

Running away. Christ! The traitor of Krakow who had calmly
put her life on the line every day for six years, now reduced to this,
Anja thought, hating herself. Running away? A few kilometers to
old Franz. Where had her courage gone? Where had she lost it?
Where had Sisi lost hers? Sisi had plenty, once. Where did Dizzi
and Walter lose theirs? Or did they have only the phantom bravery
of men so terrified of disgracing themselves in front of their comrades that they would face the bullets and the grenades as a lesser
terror?

Dizzi the warrior! Anja almost spat on the floor of the bus in
disgust. Two Iron Crosses, the close-combat badge, citations for
bravery under fire. What a farce, what a sham. Another of God's
great practical jokes. The war hero scared to death—a living death
in a madhouse—by Sisi's suicide.

Selbstmord. No "suicide" in German. Their word is "self-
murder." So correct. So precise. So pitiless. So very, very Germanic.

There were only two truly irrevocable decisions one could take
in life, Anja thought. Every decision could be reversed, renegoti-
ated, backed out of somehow. Except two: having a child, and com-

mitting suicide. And the second is dubious, when you really consider it. Thousands of people try to kill themselves in ways they know will never succeed, ways in which they'll be discovered and rescued before they actually die. Clever little faux suicides. Young girls are good at that, young men sometimes too clumsy, sometimes failing in their plan.

Imagine their horror when they realize they've botched it, they've blown the timing; that no one will appear to snatch them from death!

Anja laughed bitterly.

Serves the bastards right, that extra bit of horror before the final annihilation, she thought. And instantly felt sickened: Had Sisi really meant to die? Had she only been attempting a grand, dramatic gesture of protest, one that might at last have stirred Dizzi into action, into getting her out of that rats' nest? Dear God, she hoped Sisi had been truly determined to die. And yet how terrible to hope for such a thing.

And God damn Dizzi for lacking the courage to at least save Lilo. He must have known she would have taken her, raised her with Sophie, modestly but decently and lovingly. But the worthless bastard collapsed, allowed old Scharner to condemn that innocent to a living purgatory in the cold, loveless hands of nuns.

A wail from Sophie jerked Anja off the tightening spiral her mind had been traveling. The bus was grinding up the curves toward Wolfsgruben. Anja had not noticed that other passengers had boarded, hadn't noticed the driver starting off. Above the dark city now, the sun was slanting across the land, slanting through the windows of the bus, glaring in Sophie's eyes. Anja held a hand above the child's face to shade it.

The most useless word in any language is "why," she thought. It's a question with no answer, never any answer, its only purpose to make us crazed. She was crazed now, she knew, because she could not stop asking it. Why Sisi? Why Lilo and Dizzi? Why any of it?

"I swear on my soul I will never utter that word again," Anja murmured in Polish. "I will never think it. I will never allow it to appear in my mind in German or Polish or Italian or even in that wordless form that ideas sometimes assume. The dead are dead. Full stop. No questions. We go on, into life, Sophie and me."

That was the sum of it, the only viable response. Though she knew very well her vow would be impossible to keep.

▨ ▨ ▨

Anja, my dear, you're as wrong as wrong can be. Absolutely wrong," said Franz. They were under the great beech, she leaning into him and weeping, his big arm around her narrow, heaving shoulders. Her stern comforter. But her only comfort just now.

"Wrong, you understand?" His voice was full of stiff conviction, yet as merciful as any she had heard. "I know you think I'm simply an old farmer, no education, no claim to knowing much beyond this land of mine, this valley and these mountains. You're right. But I am clear about a few other things, I think. First, none of us can choose our feelings. They come on us, they're stronger than we are, we're stuck with them. Nothing we can do about it.

"But we do have a choice in how we act on the damned things. And I've always found it better if I don't act at all for a while. Just let those feelings be, until they settle down. Like letting the sediment in new wine settle. Then it gets clear. And then I can think properly, and act in what I decide is the proper way. You moved too soon."

"But Walter should have . . ."

"If I was sure Walter could have saved that poor girl and just didn't try, I'd go find him this very day and beat him to a pulp," Franz said. "Your feeling is he could have done something. It's a right enough feeling. Is it true? Maybe, maybe not. For what you've told me is more feelings than facts. Facts take time to emerge."

"It was me, too, I know. I'm to blame as much as Walter, though it's damned hard to admit that."

"Maybe even more to blame, Anja, if you're set on following that line. But I'm thinking you are confused. About assigning blame. Is there any? Sisi did what she did. Who could have known? Great God, Anja, there are things in this life that aren't ours to know."

"What should I do, Uncle?"

"Weep. Grieve. Pray for her soul if you're inclined to believe that would do her any good. Or do it even if that sort of thing helps only you. Curse Walter if that's your need. Or curse the damned world. You and Sophie can stay right here with me while you're about it. In peace. I'll make sure Walter doesn't come around. For as long as you want."

Anja the Liar would have laughed at this old man, scorned him as a fool. But she was not present. Sometimes Anja wondered if the Liar hadn't gone as finally as poor Sisi. But that was probably too much to hope for. The Liar was in retreat, in hiding. Now there was only Anja, mother of Sophie and a wife of sorts to Walter Fass, here in the comforting arms of a decent, good man.

They sat silently for a while, Anja feeling herself in almost perfect harmony with Franz Fass. His patience seemed boundless, his affection and care deep and genuine. He was a blessing she surely did not deserve, had not earned.

After a time, Anja rose and they went down to the house, where Liese had been minding Sophie. The child was hungry, butting gently against the bosom of Anja's blouse as soon as she picked her up. She stepped outside to nurse her, watching the cows move ponderously through the pasture, the big bells on their necks clanging mildly. When she stepped back into the kitchen, she saw that Liese had set out lunch for her and Franz. They spoke very little. But Anja felt a sort of silent love, and wonder. These people had taken her into their family without any hesitation or reservation. Why? No, she reminded herself. She was never to ask why.

After lunch Franz and Sophie had a good roll in the long rich grass of the orchard. Then the old man bundled her like a small feed-sack under his arm and took her to the pasture to touch the cows. Anja watched them from the rear stoop, Liese standing behind her.

"I wish you'd come more often," Liese said. "Just look at my father! He adores the girl. He misses her terribly when he doesn't see her for a few days."

"How about every day?" Anja said. "Could I come up and milk the cows? I still remember how."

"And do you still remember how you wanted a gas mask to wear when you mucked out the stalls that first winter? You're not a farmer, Anja."

"That's certain. But it's summer, no mucking stalls. And I think it's good for Sophie to be in the clean air. She seems to glow after she's been up here. And I'd like to do some work. I've got to do something to get my mind off this thing."

"No need to ask," Liese said. "You know you're welcome anytime. You can milk all you want, you can help with the haying, all sorts of other chores. My father and Sepp would be pleased to teach you about the vines and the trees, if you cared to learn. My father'd be thrilled. He still wishes you and Walter and Sophie were living here. And I'd be very glad of the company."

"We'll see if you still feel that way after a few months of having this city girl under your feet."

Anja and Sophie took the three-o'clock bus back to Bolzano.

⬛ ⬛ ⬛

Mila Ćosić, wearing a sleeveless dress of black linen and black leather sandals, was leaning against the door of the house, smoking and staring up at the sky. Anja got close enough to see a dozen butts ground out on the pavement. She slowed her pace, pleased to see Mila but dreading having to break the news about Sisi. Not that Mila would care very much. But Anja did not want to relive it through the telling. Could she say nothing? No, not with her friend.

The only one she had, now. No more Sisi. No more letters. Never another visit, never an embrace, never the pleasure of laughing together, talking of whatever entered their heads. All gone. Wasn't that what the old woman from Stettin kept saying in the camp? All gone. All gone.

She saw Mila take a last, hard drag on her cigarette, send the smoke skyward and the butt to the pavement. Then she swiveled her head up and down the street, and glimpsed Anja. Her eyes were wet, Anja noticed with surprise, and then she felt Mila's arms wrapped around her, heard Mila's voice: "Anja, Anja, it is so terrible. My God, a tragedy. What can I do for you? Tell me, please, how to help?"

"Ah, Mila," Anja said, dazed. "There is nothing to do. You know it better than I. But I'm glad you've come, glad to see you. You've been waiting here a long time?"

"Some hours. It's nothing. But why are you carrying suitcases? Have you been away?"

"Only in my mind. It's a complicated story. Let's not stand here, though. Come, let's go inside."

Mila took the suitcases while Anja fished the key out of its hiding place and opened the door. "Go on into the kitchen, Mila. I've got to put Sophie down for her nap."

When Anja had finished tucking the baby into her cradle, she found Mila had set the table, put slices of cake on the two plates, and filled two glasses with a honey-colored liquid Anja presumed was wine.

"Picolit, from the Collio near Gorizia. A little special, not much of it around. We drink to your friend, okay? The full bottle, just us to her."

Anja sipped the wine, found it only very slightly sweet, with a delicious subtle flavor that seemed to increase and grow more distinct after she swallowed.

"*Gut, nicht wahr?* It will go to our heads softly, you will not feel it until we've drunk it all. Then you will feel very, very nice.

"To those who have gone!" Mila cried, draining her glass in one gulp.

"Yes," Anja said, following her example. Mila immediately refilled their glasses from the deep-green bottle that bore no label. That was Mila all over, Anja thought. She knew the world, knew how to move through it getting what she wanted, knew which things were worth having and which were not. Anja doubted she would ever know how to move in the world.

"Now we sip the wine, eat the cake. We celebrate that we are alive," Mila said. "Ah, I see on your face. The wrong words from me again. I will never get this German correct. It is not a language for emotion."

"No, I understand you very well," Anja lied. Celebrate? What can there be to celebrate?

"If you knew Serbo-Croatian . . . the thing we mean is only we hope the ones who have gone have gone to a good place, and those left behind . . . we have a duty to them. After the weeping and the tearing of the hair, we have the duty to live the best, the good life. Not good like priests or nuns. Good like, how would you say . . . full? completely? Ah, I make a mess of this, Anja. We have to live the life they cannot."

"I understand."

"A genius, you must be then. I know I have not said what my heart has inside. You must think I am some barbarian. Everyone thinks we of the Balkans—the Serbs, the rest—have no culture. Not like the great cultures of Poland, France, Italy. This is true, we have no Chopins, no Caravaggios, no Renoirs. But, anciently, we have our great poets, our great writers at least. They knew the heart, how to tell it.

"Ah, my nonsense again. One does not know what to say to you, about your loss. In war it's different. You walk away, knowing that's just the way of it. We never say a thing. We just walk away and live."

"Perhaps that's the best way," Anja said, draining her glass. Mila refilled it.

Last night Anja had felt entirely alone. That God-cursed letter from that God-cursed man. It was as if Scharner had murdered Sisi all over again, as if he'd not been satisfied with killing her once, but had to kill her twice. That was his Austrian barbarism. That was the moral equivalent of executing someone, then cutting the dead body into quarters and displaying the pieces on pikes above the castle gate.

But then Franz, and now Mila. She wasn't alone after all. She was heartbroken and grieved, but she had strong friends on either side of her, supporting her.

What about Fass, though? Where did Fass stand now? Did he

feel any real grief? No, that wasn't fair. He had not wanted her to see the letter. He had wanted to spare her from it, bear the burden of it himself. And she had offered him no comfort, when surely this affair pained him almost as much as it pained her. His best friend was not dead, but he was destroyed. She had been no true friend to Fass, but viciously heaped blame on him. And surely he must need someone.

"You asked about those suitcases? I was running away from here. Or thought I was," Anja said. Then she explained how she had locked Walter out of their room, lain sleepless all last night, slunk away like a fugitive in the dawn. She told how she had gotten no farther than Franz's farm, had not had the courage to board a train for Munich or Milan or anywhere.

"Anja, you are too hard on yourself. Where could you have gone? What good would come, to run far away? With a little baby, only a little money I think?" Mila said. "How would you live? I am traveling very much, as you know. Only last night I return to Bolzano from a trip. And I tell you, it is hard everywhere. Some few are getting rich, living very well, but most? It's almost worse than the wartime. Most don't get enough to eat, cannot find work, I see little children with swollen bellies and crooked little legs. They are starving!"

"But I had to do something, anything."

"This I know. The rage. When you have the rage, you must act in some way. This terrible letter. I myself would have wanted very much to go kill this scum Scharner."

"That's what I wanted, but I couldn't do anything but go to old Franz and weep in his arms," Anja said, emptying her fourth glass of the Picolit. The wine had blurred things slightly, eased her tension.

"Anja, listen to me a moment," Mila said, dropping her voice almost to a whisper even though there was no one anywhere who might overhear. "This old Scharner, he should die, we agree? This I can do. With my own hands, or else by people I know. I must have a little plan so that the police will never trace it back here. But it will be so simple. It can be done so the police say, *'Aha, Selbstmord!'* The grief, too much for him. He shoots himself. No need to investigate. You understand?"

My God, she's serious, Anja thought, amazed not only at that but by how little she was shocked. She felt she must be quite drunk, maybe even hearing things. Mila, smiling coolly, was staring at her, and Anja fancied she could see a gleam in her own eyes reflected back at her from the Chetnik's. No, her friend's, Anja corrected herself. Why did she still think of her sometimes as "the Chetnik"? Because Mila knew things she would never know? Because Mila had done with her own hands what she had done only by proxy?

"Revenge," Anja muttered.

"Normal," Mila said. "That fight when Walter lost his arm? No ordinary ambush. It was revenge."

"What do you mean?"

"They trail us and track us and hunt us down, then hit with every mortar and machine gun they have," Mila said. "Walter, he never told you?"

"We don't like to speak much about the war."

"Then it is not for me to tell why we were hunted down."

"Yes, it is. I want to know. Walter volunteered once long ago that he murdered innocents in Yugoslavia, and offered details. I told him I didn't want to know. But now I do."

"He never murdered *innocents*," Mila said brusquely. "We did what we had to do in a Partisan village after an ambush. It was war only."

"No, something happened there. It's the one thing that seems to haunt him."

"It was something necessary. Wartime. We did to them what they do to us. But then all the Partisan units in the area hunt us down. Walter lost his arm. I lost more than half my comrades."

Anja looked into Mila's rich brown eyes for some sign of sadness, or regret, or remorse. All she saw was cold anger. And she finally understood what Sisi had meant. For, at that moment Mila was terrifying. Yet even as Anja stared at her, Mila's eyes changed back, as though a softening scrim had dropped over them.

"Ah, God, Anja," Mila said. "God damn Tito, the bastard destroyed all the rules. We have to fight like the Partisans fight. No choice. I have to believe they left us no choice, or I go crazy."

Anja could find no heart in her words. The lines sounded memorized, flat as those spoken by an actress grown bored after a hundred performances.

But then how did she sound, when she spoke of Krakow?

"Anja, a favor," Mila said. "Forget what I say about that old Scharner. I cannot do this thing. No more can I do this type of work. Please forget."

Then Fass was standing there, left sleeve dangling, an expression between shock and relief flickering across his face.

"Oh, Christ, Anja. I've been worried all day. Where did you go? Why did you take all your things? Where's Sophie?" he said, than darted out of the kitchen and into the bedroom. Anja heard Sophie wail once, and then silence. He'd picked her up, awakened her.

"Better I go now," Mila said, rising from her chair. "You and Walter, there are things to say to each other. I will come back soon."

"*Bis später*, Walter. Must leave," Mila said, sliding by him as he walked into the kitchen with Sophie cradled in his right arm.

But they did not have much to say to each other. Their eyes would not meet. Anja kept her head slightly bowed, so that her face was partly hidden behind a wing of her cornsilk hair. She told him that she had gone to the farm, had talked with Franz, and then had come home. She managed, with difficulty, to say she was sorry for blaming him, for raging at him. But she found it easier to say that she needed privacy for a while, that she hoped he would not mind moving into the middle bedroom.

"As you wish," Fass said calmly. "I ask only that if ever you decide to leave, tell me first. Don't sneak away. Don't take my daughter from me as if I have no right to hold her and kiss her goodbye. I love Sophie too much to bear that."

It was only some hours later—Sophie fed and washed and asleep again on the crisp linens of her cradle—that Anja jerked upright in bed, her mind more focused than it had been all day.

Mila said she only returned to Bolzano last night. How could she have known about Scharner's letter? Christ, how could she even have heard of Sisi's death?

Walter. He had gone to her last night, when he left the house.

And how was it then that Fass knew the way to Mila? How was it Fass knew, when after all this time, all the intimate confidences shared with Mila, she did not?

Then, from deep within herself, she heard a hollow, ghostly laughter, and the nearly forgotten voice of Anja the Liar of Krakow. Why ask such things, when you understand everything about deception? Why wonder, when it is perfectly clear your husband has gone to your friend, and your friend's bed, on many nights before?

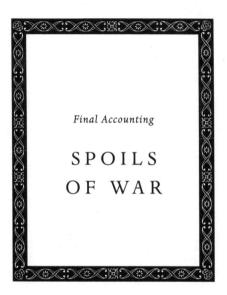

Final Accounting

SPOILS
OF WAR

I

Anja instantly went on war alert.

She did it subtly but decisively, with the cold calculation of the professional she had once been. Her mind centered. She attended to the strategics bloodlessly, mechanically. And she sealed her heart, with only Sophie in it, in the deepest bunker she could construct.

But this cost her almost everything. She felt it as a sort of death. For, here with Fass, she had briefly known a free, peaceful life in the light.

Now there was simply no choice but to return to wartime ways. Sophie and she were at the gravest risk. In ruined Europe, the most basic things—a safe room, enough coal or wood to keep from freezing in the winter, sufficient food and untainted water, clothes and a pair of serviceable shoes—remained treasures sought and fought for. All these, and so much more, she'd had with Fass. These she would do anything to keep.

Alles klar. She could never again depend on or trust Walter Fass. Or Mila Ćosić. They had betrayed her.

So it was Krakow rules once more, Krakow principles from now on. She must move very cautiously, very deliberately. And keep every motive disguised, every design secret, every human and humane feeling suppressed.

At the start, then, Anja's new war was invisible to everyone around her. It appeared, in fact, as if she were making peace.

Through the drowsy, heat-hazed summer, she and Sophie were out of the house and on the bus to Wolfsgruben most mornings before Fass had even finished dressing. Anja took to wearing dirndls and boots again as a practical measure, and she did her chores with Sophie always near in a little wooden wheelbarrow lined with quilted cotton. She began to wean the child; she nursed her only once, early, when she awoke. For the rest, there was milk still warm from the cows Anja tended, vegetables boiled and mushed with a well-used wooden potato-masher.

She needed the work. The milking, the weeding in the vegetable garden, engaged just enough of her attention to keep a crippling regret from her consciousness. So when she rode back down to Bolzano each afternoon, returned to the front line, she was clearheaded and calm, able to face any crisis that might suddenly confront her in the dangerously strained atmosphere of the apartment.

It was no good there anymore. Always there was Ischl, an almost palpable thing that seemed to lurk in the shadowy places, in the words that were never said. Always—and much more menacing—there was Fass's faithlessness, the one thing she had never expected, the thing that had taken her completely by surprise. She and Walter continued to sleep in separate rooms, and for a while they slipped uneasily around each other, touchy and tense. They spoke only of the necessary things—Sophie's needs, an electric bill past due, getting a plumber to fix one of the taps in the bath.

Of the past, of the future: nothing.

But that would not do, Anja decided within a few weeks, under the new dispensation. It was undisciplined, tactically unwise. So she forced herself to gradually behave again with Fass as she had before. He brightened instantly when she began to speak to him once more in the tones he had been used to, at her first tentative displays of the old affection. But she noticed at once that he could not cloak a wariness of her that bordered, she felt, on true fear. He did not want to lose Sophie and her. That was to the good. A weakness she could exploit.

Just as Anja went to the farm, the engineer Fass reported for duty each day promptly, carried out his tasks with precision and efficiency, and, although summer was his busiest season, almost never failed to report home in time to play a bit with Sophie before dinner. He insisted on putting the child to bed himself, and then returned to Anja in the kitchen. He responded eagerly whenever Anja chose to talk to him of any little thing. If she was quiet, he seemed content to sit silently in her presence, drinking his nightly bottle of wine.

It was only the farm that gave her the strength to manage the false truce with Fass, Anja considered early one September evening, waiting in her garden for the man she had once thought of as hers. As well as the courage to continue a false friendship with Mila: The coffees in her kitchen or at a café, the occasional shopping excursion, the joint sessions at Carlo's.

All this a good Krakow subterfuge. Never let those you suspect know they are under suspicion.

And these seemingly normal relations with Fass and the Chetnik also helped mute her rage. The uncontrolled fury toward Fass over Sisi's death and his affair with Mila had been a risky lapse. She had violated an important lesson from Krakow time: Never let anger, hatred or desire for revenge inform your planning, your actions.

She'd thought at first, when wrath unmoored her, that Mila had made a stupid mistake by letting her knowledge of Scharner's letter slip out and carelessly unveiling her stealthy relationship with Fass. But Anja felt certain now that Mila was much too smart to err that way. The Chetnik had deliberately chosen to reveal the affair obliquely. Mila had been testing her, putting strain on the bond between Anja and her man to gauge its strength. Anja the Liar, now resurrected, admired her enemy's skill; the manuever had been made suddenly but perceptively, exactly at the moment of Anja's maximum vulnerability.

Anja understood that the Chetnik had been intriguing from the very beginning to use Fass and her for her own purposes. Time now to unmask Mila's motive and goal. Time to assess the threat, deploy countermeasures to deflect it, destroy it completely, or best of all, turn it to her own advantage.

Meanwhile, Fass was welcome to fuck Mila—and any shopgirl, young widow, or prostitute in all the Adige—if he cared to. Most likely he would not dare. But if he did she would tolerate it so long as he remained what Krakow rules specified:

Useful. Usable.

And Anja still doubted that Mila wanted Fass as a lover. The Chetnik had merely used sex as a tool to manipulate him. Very much the way she had employed close attention and demonstrations of affection to turn her own head. Well, Anja's head at least would never again be turned.

In her garden, the fountain plashing softly, Anja watched dusk spread over the valley and begin its climb toward the peaks. Sophie was already fed and put to bed. Anja wondered briefly what had delayed Walter, when he would come home. But she was not concerned.

Poor Fass, with his notions of right and honor. Poor Fass, she knew, was twisted and torn in the worst way. He might even have convinced himself that Mila was in love with him, that eventually he would have to choose between his Chetnik and his family. No doubt he had tortured himself. No doubt he was in torment. Too bad. It was nothing to her. Not anymore.

Ah, but it would mean a great deal to Mila. Mila had surely factored into her calculus of deceit the possibility that Fass might lose his head and wreck whatever scheme she'd set in motion. But that Anja might seize the initiative? She did not believe Mila had allowed for that contingency. Because the Chetnik had only ever seen the mild, meek Anja of Bolzano.

A potentially mortal mistake. Mila obviously needed her friendship, for she had kept cultivating it so prettily and generously. Why would she bother, if all she wanted was to take Fass for herself? Why would Mila have tried, with her artfully shadowed disclosure, to parse her possessiveness? Because, Anja concluded, Mila wanted to be sure there would be no accidental explosion that might blow the connection between the three of them to bits.

Mila needed both her and Fass. This was certain. Mila was only waiting now for her to react.

Let the Chetnik wait. Anja would approach this as she'd approached every mission Richter had assigned her. She would bide her time until she was certain of her opponent's stance and plans, and confident she had means to circumvent them. Perhaps she would make Mila come to her.

※　※　※

At that moment, across the city, in the stained concrete building near the freightyards, Mila Ćosić carefully emptied a small suede sack onto a square of black velvet she had placed on Petrocelli's desk. He leaned forward in his chair, carelessly dropping his cigar into the engine piston that served as his ashtray. Blue smoke spiraled up into the air as he gazed at the dozen or so diamonds of various sizes that refracted brilliantly the dim light of his office.

"Not bad, Mila," he said, keeping his eyes on the jewels, rolling one or two over on the velvet with a thick forefinger.

"You old fraud." Mila laughed. "Not bad? The best you have ever seen in your miserable life. Do not, how is it you like to say, be breaking my balls."

Petrocelli, his eyes still on the diamonds, searched around the blackened edges of the piston with his left hand until he found his cigar. He stuck it between his lips and sucked until the coal glowed bright red.

"Ah, you do not know even how to smoke a cigar properly," Mila taunted him. "Too much to expect, that you know what is glittering at you. But you must have them, no? You want them more than your little whores, I think. Getting old, for sure."

"Old, you think? I'll wager this one," Petrocelli said, slipping a dirty fingernail under one of the diamonds, "that if you spend one night with me, you will never be the same."

Mila chortled. "And I, I wager that one and this canary one that you are right. Because you will be dead in the first five minutes. Poof! Heart stopped. Then I have a big, fat body in my bed to explain to the *carabinieri*! And they put me in jail for murder. So we have this little experiment in your house, your bed. Then your wife can deal with the dead body and the *carabinieri, capito?*"

Petrocelli leaned back in his scarred wooden swivel-chair and roared with laughter. "*Tu sei pazza*, Chetnik. Okay? Petrocelli does not go up against the mad ones, especially the beautiful mad ones. Since my heart would not go poof, you would stab me to win. I don't like to see my own blood. Not even for you."

"My money, I would like to see, though," Mila said, swiftly gathering the diamonds back into the suede sack and tucking it deep in her cleavage. "Then the bag comes out."

"Mila, I love you." He opened the lowest drawer of the desk, produced a key from his pocket. Mila heard metal entering metal, two sharp clicks. Then Petrocelli withdrew a wad of worn lire thick as a dictionary, some of the bills the size of a magazine page.

"This is not our deal. None of the big ones. They draw too much suspicion. I said small ones only. These"—she patted the center of her bosom where the suede sack nestled—"stay with me."

"*Senti*, Mila. This is not reasonable. For so many small ones we'd need a truck," Petrocelli said, puffing until his cigar glowed too red again.

"Only a shopping bag, I think, bandit," Mila said. The fool, she thought, lets himself get stuck with these huge notes the government made just so they could trace them, and thinks he can stick them on me. "And I have my own. So you fold these newspapers you are trying to cheat me with and bring out the useful bills. Maybe I let you reach for the little bag yourself, then."

"*Dio, sei difficile.*" He opened another drawer, unlocked another steel box, and pulled out some stacks of lire notes much thicker than a dictionary, but much smaller. "You are robbing me again. I only let you rob me because you are so beautiful."

"No, because I am not beautiful, as anyone sees. You only do what I say because you know with me there is no danger from the finance police," Mila said, rapidly counting the notes with her long, strong fingers. "This is seeming okay. This is seeming all right. But I count again."

"And then I get to retrieve the bag?"

"In another life, maybe," Mila said, withdrawing the suede sack with one hand while still counting lire with her other. "As we agreed," she said when she'd finished, tossing the bag of diamonds into his lap.

"Ah, Mila, why didn't I meet you twenty years ago?" he said as he locked the bag in one of the steel boxes.

"Pig!" She laughed. "A six-year-old girl? Still, the size would have been about right for you, *nicht wahr*?"

Petrocelli grinned, produced a bottle of grappa, poured two glasses. "*Salute, cattiva!*"

They downed the glasses in single swallows and Petrocelli re-filled them. Not a bad man to do business with, Mila thought. His little tricks were only a game he enjoyed, nothing serious. He was not scum, like most of them. She liked him. Him, she could deal with. Him, she would drink with.

"Ahhh." He let out a huge, weary sigh, leaning back in his chair. "You know, Mila, I'm getting damned tired of this shit. Petrocelli, I ask myself, why are you still breaking your ass in this fucking business? You got more than you can ever spend. I think, why not relax? Why not take the youngest one, the one in Eppan, and go live in Forte dei Marmi? Hell, Capri! And when she gets to be thirty, trade her in for two younger ones, eh? Life is short."

"Shorter and shorter for you, I think. So sell out, run off with your little *puttana*, let her make you happy every day. If you don't live longer, better at least."

"Exactly, Mila. But one small problem. Who will buy? I'd never sell to those other bastards, the ones who've tried to wreck me every chance they got. They'd love that too much. No more Petro-celli, taking the cream of the business. I want somebody to keep busting their balls when I'm gone."

"Fass," Mila said. Holy Mother, here was the opportunity that might appear once for the briefest moment in a life, then vanish forever if it was not seized. She had planned all along, of course, to use Walter and his little Pole in some way. But this chance? Beyond her best hopes. Unique. So very, very big.

"Walter? A good man, true. But no money."

"What would you take?"

Petrocelli blew a smoke ring, watched it expand as it floated through the still air, and pulled a figure out of it.

"Then you work here until you die," Mila said. "Insane, what you say. Nobody will pay that for, what, this shack, a couple of trucks, a couple of earthmovers and cranes, and a couple of contracts? Not even your biggest competitor. He laugh in your face."

"Negotiable. A little. Maybe I throw in that building where Walter lives, one or two others I own?"

"Think a minute, if your head is not so thick. Even if you come down fifty percent, some fool pays it just to be rid of you. Then you got to pay most of it to the government, for the tax. And you got no more money coming in. Very clever, Petrocelli."

"So, you have some brilliant idea to tell me?"

"Take something reasonable—half clean and legal, half in cash, gold, diamonds. But also a contract that you get a percentage of the profits every year. For the government, the company books say the profit is small, your percentage is small, you don't pay tax worth thinking of. Just like you run things now. But the profits are big, only hidden. Your real percentage comes in cash, long as you live. No tax. Easy for the new owner to arrange. No risk for you. *Perfetto, no?*" Mila said.

She could see the greed that had driven him all these years growing in Petrocelli's eyes. He was shrewd, but not so cunning as she. She had bested him in every deal they'd done, and he'd never known it. And the fool really did want to run off with his tart and live like a prince in the sun. It was all over his face. This idea she'd just planted, it would not leave him in peace.

"Ah, I don't know. It sounds too good. Anyway, who could I trust not to screw me?"

"Me. For sure."

"For sure, yes!" Petrocelli laughed. "But I'm talking about the business."

"You think I am talking about anything else? You think I make a joke?"

"You buy the business?" Petrocelli laughed louder. "I see you now, out in the mud in your beautiful clothes, directing the workers. This is a picture I see so clearly."

"I don't build, *cretino*. Fass builds. I handle the contracts, the money."

Petrocelli abruptly sobered. "Now this I know you could do—the contracts, the bribes, the books. Ah, Mila. Maybe you're tired of your business too? Maybe you want something a little less risky? Yes, you would. But I don't think you have the money either. And it won't work without Fass."

"The money, we'll see. Maybe I get a partner, financial only," Mila said. "Fass, I have."

"Anytime you want, I think. Now a lot is getting very clear to me. *Certo*. Fass you probably do have. Old comrades! Hah-hah. Close friends with the wife, that little Anja. And her husband in your pocket. Mila, you are a devil. I drink to you."

"Write down your real price on a little piece of paper. Fold it in half, and give it to me. I'll be back soon and we will see then how you think."

"*Va bene*," Petrocelli said smiling. He ripped a corner off a manila envelope, thought for a moment or two, then scribbled some numbers. He handed the folded tan square to Mila.

"*Ciao*, you bandit." Mila stood, slipping the square into her purse and picking up a shopping bag from her favorite shoe store, now filled with boxes of lire notes. "You think a little on this. I will be back. Who knows? Maybe I make you more filthy rich than you already are."

"*Per piacere*, Mila. *My* pleasure."

※ ※ ※

A few days later, Anja was prising potatoes out of the farm garden's rich black soil and putting them into slatted bushel baskets when a shadow fell on her from behind, then passed over her. She saw fine leather shoes and long shapely calves straddling the row she was working along. She looked up. There was Mila, impossibly tall at this angle, her auburn hair shining, her eyes shining, too.

"So, my little one, see how you are ruining your hands. Gloves at least should be worn, *nicht wahr?*"

Anja glanced down at her hands, saw the broken fingernails, the dark earth pressed into the whorls of her fingertips.

"Carlo will go into hysterics, I am telling you. He'll fuss and flutter like a hen. He will feel offended, as an artiste, that you take so little care with your beauty." Mila laughed.

Anja rose, roughly scrubbing her hands together to remove the looser dirt, then running them back through her pale hair.

"Sacrilege!" Mila cried. "To touch such hair with those hands. Carlo would die on the spot if he saw. But that dirndl, those boots. These he would find amusing. On you, he would say, they achieve a certain style."

"Ah, you're mad. You become madder all the time," Anja said. "But what a surprise to see you here."

"I have been here for a certain time already, but I was delayed by Franz, who must have me taste a wine or two from the casks. A 'No' he would not accept. With a bear like that, you must humor him, yes? So where is *la bellissima* Sophie?"

"Over in the shade." Anja pointed toward a shed about fifty meters away. "She naps for quite a while, after lunch."

"In that wheelbarrow thing? Anja, Anja! I know you have liked this farm-visiting all these months, but my picture was something different. A stroll in the orchards, reclining on a nice blanket in long grass under a tree. Not a laborer."

"It's the work that I like. You should join me," Anja said. "It's very good for the mind."

"So you've said. Still, I thought more of the orchard walk, the reclining. Not kneeling in the dirt, ruining your hands. Like me in wartime, rooting like a badger for a little shelter. Never again, thank you."

"So I invite you to stroll, then," Anja said, linking her arm through Mila's and leading her out of the garden, through vines sagging under the weight of great clumps of fat grapes and up the pasture toward the beech. She kept a gentle hold on Mila's arm as they sat on the bench beneath the tree. A Richter trick.

"Ah, now this," Mila said, sweeping her hand across the view of farms, the city, and the river running down the valley below. "This is good. Splendid, I think."

"But you didn't come all the way up here to admire a vista."

"No," Mila said. "Nor to spy on you. News. I have some to tell." And she spoke about her conversation with Petrocelli.

"But this is very important. Suppose Petrocelli sells out? Walter could lose his job. You should tell him," Anja said. Yet she was not alarmed. She sensed Mila was at last about to give away her purpose. Anja felt ready.

"Not before you. I have some idea to make an amazing thing of this for all of us, that you must hear first," Mila said. Then she explained the deal she had proposed to the man. "Good, do you think? If yes, we should go to Walter together, because it depends on him, the engineer."

"Oh, very good. In theory, anyway. But there is something else you should tell me first," Anja said, still gripping Mila's arm but turning away from the view and meeting her eyes.

"Yes?"

"You should say that you and Walter have been lovers for quite a long time now."

"You don't mind?" It was not really a question. There was no hesitation, not a bit of surprise in the Chetnik's voice.

"You let me know yourself, remember?" Anja said.

"Naturally. But I was not sure you understood. You stay calm, friendly, just the same as always with me. I expect at least some anger, maybe a fight. Then, this is honest, I would have broken off with Fass, and tried hard to keep your friendship. But you were so good, I could not know if you caught my hint."

Anja simply looked at her, eyes as blank and unreadable as they had once been to Fass through the wire of a DP camp. Her Krakow eyes. Windows to nothing, certainly not to her thoughts or emotions, let alone her soul. She could feel Mila lose her balance a little.

"It was never love," she said.

Anja gazed unblinking at her.

"You must believe. Some sort of obsession, Fass had. Since Yugoslavia. I knew it then, knew it was still with him when I see him again here."

"And?" Anja asked, in just the tone she remembered Richter using when he required more information.

"It is *kaputt*. A big joke on Mila, you could say. And laugh like anything at me. Two weeks, maybe a little more after that disgusting letter from old Scharner, Walter comes to my place one night, very stiff. He says straight off, all over with you, Mila. Finished."

Anja nodded, never taking her eyes from the Chetnik's. She would get the truth out of Fass, later.

"So, very bad? Oh, Anja, I was lonely. I know it is wrong, but I invite him in my bed. My heart, it's too cold for love. But the body needs comfort sometimes, *nicht wahr?*"

Anja remained silent until she felt the muscles of Mila's arm tensing. "The lovers are everywhere. This I could show you," she said then, mimicking a thing Mila had once said to her.

"It was very bad," Mila admitted. "I am bad. But how to say to a woman you care for that I want to borrow your man for my bed, okay with you? Too much a coward, I was. I just let it happen. Do you hate me?"

"Mila, don't you think it's a little late to ask that?" Anja laughed. "After you've been sleeping with my husband for months?"

Mila blushed. It was the first time Anja had ever seen her do that. And she noticed tears in Mila's eyes. But not genuine, she was sure.

"Do you hate? Because if you do, I will go away from this place. Disappear. You and Walter won't see me again."

She was lying outrageously now. Mila would never go away, not when this Petrocelli deal could provide her with exactly what Anja sought for Sophie and herself: security, safety. And that, Anja realized, had been the Chetnik's main objective all along. She mustn't push Mila too hard just yet. She must go very carefully with Mila. The situation had turned almost full-circle. Both Mila and Fass together were necessary to make the Petrocelli thing work for her and her child.

But God, her heart ached for what she knew beyond doubt was irretrievably lost. A few times lately she'd had the impulse to tap on a door late at night and whisper, "Hey you. Fass?" He would have come to her, she was sure. But she had not done it. The impulse was a weakness she could not afford, until she had won the secret war she was waging. Now it was clear she never could tap and whisper, even in victory.

"No need for you to go. Under the right circumstances, and if it is finished," Anja said as coolly as she was able, dominating the sorrow that had come near to overwhelming her for a moment.

"You are sure?" Mila asked. There was worry in her voice that even this devious Chetnik could not screen from someone whose senses were as finely tuned as Anja's. "Life is very strange, yes? And you, you are like no one I ever know before. I have more love for you than for Walter."

"Don't speak to me like that. Lies aren't needed anymore. You know what we are really talking of is securing our own futures."

"But it is true anyway, Anja. In my soul, it is true. And one thinks of old ways. What we were taught, what we imagined when we were girls about marriage. A new way shocks everyone, *nicht wahr?* Me, right now I am in shock a little."

"You will be over it before you're out of my sight. I'm thinking the only one who will truly be shocked is poor Fass," Anja said. "The question that counts is this: Can you really bring off this deal with Petrocelli?"

"My God, yes, with you and Walter with me." Mila managed a small smile. "Old Petrocelli, I have in my palm, I think. I squeeze him a little, we get what we want. Not for nothing, naturally. Walter will have to find some of the money. It will be hard for a year or two. After that . . ."

"And Fass. He will have trouble believing in this scheme."

"Walter, you have in your hands. You and Sophie. This I have always known," Mila said.

But you never completely realized the implications, Anja thought scornfully. And even now you would do anything to regain control of Fass—perhaps murder—if his little Pole balks, you Chetnik bitch.

"Owning our own business, owning our own home. Security." Anja's mind was calculating rapidly. Certainly worth the attempt.

And if Mila failed to deliver, Anja decided she would simply elim-
inate the Chetnik. Permanently. A few words in the right ears, police ears—she had done that easily enough before.

"Ah, Anja. I embrace you," Mila said, kissing her on each cheek
twice. Anja bore it without flinching, though she would have preferred to spit in the Chetnik's face. All of it—the friendship, fucking Walter—had been ruthless treachery. But Mila did not fully
understand that she'd been figured out. Or was at least uncertain if
her true designs were truly known. Anja would keep the Chetnik
this way. A bit off-balance, but useful. Usable. Krakow all over,
Mila caught in her coils.

"Invite me to dinner tomorrow night," Mila said. "Then we
tell Walter everything."

"Not everything. I think it wisest that he not be told I know
about you and him," Anja said. "Come early, before Walter gets
home from work. We'll talk a little about the best way to go. Then,
at dinner, the engineer Fass will learn what we are going to make
of his life."

Mila nodded, looked at her with a complicity that disgusted
Anja.

Then Anja watched the lean, graceful woman lope down the
pasture and disappear among the vines.

Unaware she is trailing invisible strings I've attached to her,
Anja said to herself. Unaware that I can add Mila's name to the
long list of those I have destroyed, anytime I choose to do so.

Anja smiled then. But only because it helped keep her from
weeping.

11

Mila slowly slid the rim of her wineglass back and forth along her lower lip, watching the little Pole and her engineer. They had finished eating, the plates had been cleared away and now it was time for business. Fass and Anja were studying the paper she had handed them. It was not the small manila square with Petrocelli's scrawled price. It was a sheet of good stationery on which she had written another figure, and all that was linked to it, including Petrocelli's off-the-books percentage of the profits.

Fass would say it was impossible, Mila thought, sipping the wine, lightly stroking her lip with the glass again. So much money! Fass's brow was furrowed already. Best to start this way. Then when she got to the real terms, he would feel relieved, the numbers would seem smaller than they actually were.

Good idea that Anja forbade any mention of the other thing. Because a part of Fass's consternation now came from his great guilt. Yes, he had ended the affair, exactly as she'd told Anja. But he must be very anxious anyway that this deal would bring them too close together. Mila his ex-lover, Mila his business partner. He was confused, he was having difficulty holding the two ideas in mind at the same time.

Excellent. It was easier to strike a bargain with a man who was not fully concentrated on the business at hand. Always, Mila knew, it helped to encourage her *pescecane* to start dreaming there might be something more between them than a simple exchange of gold or diamonds for currency. This was even better, since Walter had been in her bed so much. The effect was more intense.

"Mila, this kind of money . . ." Anja began. They had discussed the approach they'd use with Fass earlier, they had agreed on it. Mila smiled at her, sipped her wine.

Self-satisfied cunt, Anja thought. Mila had no idea how precarious her position was. She believed she had won, when the decisive battle was only now beginning.

"Impossible," Fass burst out. "I haven't even a hundredth of this saved up. It's hopeless. It'll be years before I could even dream of striking out on my own."

"Not on your own, Walter," Mila said. "Us. The three of us. Partners, *nicht wahr?* Partners, Anja, yes?"

"Seems a sound plan."

"But neither of you is answering how we could raise so much money," Fass said. "I've almost nothing, Anja's got nothing at all. Banks? They would only laugh at us."

"And report us to the financial police. A little irregular, this financing. So no, no banks, Walter," Mila said. "First thing, Petrocelli will come down on the cash payment by twenty percent. This is for sure."

"Why should he do that?" Fass asked.

"He gives a little, we give a little. The way business goes, no? I say to him, 'Petrocelli, you bandit, so-and-so is all we can pay. But we increase your percentage from eight to twelve.' And he thinks, 'not a bad bet. I don't need so much right away.' And he thinks,

'Fass can build anything, that Chetnik hustler can handle the bribes and bid-faking and all the rest of it. The two of them will make a fortune. I just sit here in Capri with my *puttana* and they send me twelve percent of the fortune for life. A fantastic return on capital. Not a bad bet at all.' This is what he thinks."

"We do not have the money, even if he does come down," Fass said.

"Pretty well I have been doing with my little ventures," Mila said. "I have right now at least fifty-five, maybe sixty percent of what we need."

"Which leaves something that does not exist. Where could I get that? Mila, this is impossible," Fass said.

Poor man, his face was so easy to read, the Chetnik thought. In business, he would be eaten up. But he was beginning to want this very much. Good, very good. Because what he will have to do will be hard for him.

"Your uncle the bear. He will invest in you," Mila said.

"I can't ask my uncle for money."

"I can," Anja said. "It's not a gift we're asking for. It's a simple loan. Mila and I will show him all the figures, all the contracts, give him a schedule of repayment with interest."

"Expenses we will have to cut for a while," Mila said. "But the deal includes this building and one other. The rents from those apartments are enough to pay old Franz each month. That he will see at once. And I do this. Money from Franz or anywhere else you get it, that is your percentage of ownership. I give up any claim on the buildings and rents. I put up fifty-five percent of the cash, I get fifty-five percent of the construction business only."

"That's better than fair, Walter," Anja said.

"Jesus, how can I go to Franz? How could I risk what he's worked for all his life?"

"What is this risk? No risk. There are contracts that take us through at least the next eighteen months. More I will get before they are finished, for sure," Mila said. "Franz gets his money from the very first month, no matter what. The apartment rents, *klar?* He will be so happy, Walter having his own business."

"If you won't go to Franz, Walter, I will. And Mila and I will own Petrocelli Construction," Anja said. "If you want a job, there will be one for you, at your current salary."

"Jesus Christ! You damn well can't do that!"

Mila only stroked her lip with her wineglass. Anja laughed. "Oh, but we can, Walter. We will. The only thing Franz will think strange is that you don't want to be part of this, that you're afraid to speak with him about it."

"Great God," Walter said.

"You sound like him," Mila said. "And like we have just been ambushed by the Partisans is how you look, Walter. Pale. So pale. Okay, big surprise for you. But this is all very sensible. You think Anja and I are not sensible?"

"This is incredible." Fass's voice was strained, barely under control. But he wouldn't go all stiff and angry, Mila thought. He only needed some moments to consider his position.

"The two of you, behind my back . . ." Fass started, then stopped dead. Correct, Walter. You cannot speak of behind the back. All those months in my bed, never telling Anja.

"Listen to me, Walter," Anja said. "This is our chance, it won't come round again. What can you say against it, logically? Nothing. Which means you are just too cowardly to act."

"But something is just not right about this," Fass managed, shaken by Anja's accusation.

"Was it more right to marry without love because you wanted a good left arm for a while?" Anja pressed him mercilessly. "Was it right for you to be secretly sleeping with Mila—yes, Walter, I know about that—when you had a wife and a daughter at home?

Don't speak of right, Walter. You are on very thin ice, speaking of right."

Good for you, Anja, Mila thought, surprised that she had brought that matter into play. With the perfect tone, perfect timing.

The engineer Walter Fass looked at the little Pole he had first seen as a walking dress in a DP camp, and every hope he'd had shattered. He felt concussed, as if he had been under an artillery barrage. Anja was lost to him now, he knew. All summer, since he had ended it with Mila, he had been living the illusion that he and Anja might somehow repair the damage, get on with life. She seemed to be healing, seemed to have stopped blaming him for Sisi, seemed even as warm and affectionate as she had been before the Ischl tragedy. Had he misread her that badly? No, he realized. Mila had turned Anja by revealing their affair.

No matter that he'd broken with the Chetnik. He had, Fass admitted despondently, just lost his third war.

"Walter, I don't even want a wife's usual status in all this," he heard Anja saying crisply, all business. "The construction company, the other apartment building should be in your and Mila's names only. The company profits should be split between Mila and you only. All I want is this house. Mine, in my name. I'll give up the rents from the other three apartments here until the loan from Franz is paid off. Then I'll keep the rents to support Sophie and myself. Nothing from the business."

Now here was another surprise, Mila thought. In Anja's place, she would demand half of Walter's share of everything, as his legal wife. Ah, but Anja was wily. She knew Fass very, very well. He would give her everything, if it ever came to that, because of what she had just renounced. His conscience was his great weakness.

"Oh, God," Fass said.

"Stop it, Walter," Anja said, doing her best to imitate that command voice that Fass had used on her when she went down on the

Brenner. "You will put one foot in front of the other, then do it again, and again. This is your chance. You will go to Franz tomorrow. You will ask for a loan. You will do this. And then you and Mila will go to Petrocelli and buy his business on our terms."

"Not a problem," Mila said. "This Petrocelli, we wave cash in front of his face, right away in his mind he's sitting in the sun in Capri, fat old wife left here, his little whore bringing him cool drinks, no more worries. He's so happy he wants to kiss us."

Anja shifted her blank eyes to Mila's then. And Mila began to laugh. Anja joined her—in the way she had once laughed with Richter on certain occasions.

Yes, we can laugh together, fucking Chetnik scum, Anja thought in fury. Because we are both monsters, though you do not know it. Or do, and love it.

For a powerful intuition had suddenly come to her that Walter Fass truly wanted this woman out of his life, not more deeply entangled in it. She felt a tremendous urge to kill the scheme, to drive Mila from the house forever, to save Fass from what she realized might be the end of him.

Too late.

She could not do it.

She did not feel safe with Fass anymore. She did not feel she could count on him. She was on Krakow footing, and she must put Sophie and herself ahead of all else. Even if it meant chancing the sacrifice of a man who had once saved her, whom she had even come to love in her scarred, imperfect way.

She looked again at Mila, who was smiling at her with what the Chetnik no doubt considered affection—or more likely the pleasure one partner in crime takes at the sight of her accomplice. Anja was on the verge of getting all that she believed she needed to survive. But perhaps Mila had succeeded in outmaneuvering her. For

Anja now saw there could be a terrible cost she had not fully calculated before.

Never mind. You had to expect casualties in war. You had to accept losses. Anja made her face a mask. Her eyes went dead. The
Chetnik did not notice.

III

Walter Fass stood in thick black mud up to his calves, cursing like a sergeant. "Why in the hell didn't you tell me you'd hit a spring, Lucchese?" he shouted at his foreman. "Jesus Christ, we lay a foundation here, the whole thing subsides, the building collapses. You know that!"

"*Sì, Ingegnere.* But you told us we had to be finished by today. Who am I to stop the work? I sent someone to find you yesterday, to tell you. He don't find you."

"Goddammit. Goddammit." Fass knew he had not been found because he had spent the entire afternoon after lunch in Eppan with one of his concrete suppliers getting drunk, then weaving a dangerously erratic way home. "Get the backhoe over here and dig a side trench until you find the source of the spring. Then dig a runoff trench, pipe that goddamn spring away from here. Have this section of foundation torn down, too. We may have to sink piers, then lay a new foundation on top. But I won't know until you get this damn mud and water out of here. *Capito?*"

"*Sì, Ingegnere,*" the foreman said. He'd gone sullen, his feelings were hurt. Shit. A man he trusted and valued. A good man. Fass knew he was driving them all too hard, they were making mistakes they'd never have made before.

And so was he. It said "Dottor Ingegnere Walter Fass, Direttore, Gruppo Fass" on those business cards Mila had printed, on the company stationery, at the bottom of all the contracts they had signed, the contracts Mila won for them. And Fass directed nothing. Not his life, not even the building-site work, really. They had too many projects, he raced from one to another, gave a few orders, found the next day that they had been misunderstood or undone or done wrong. The foremen were good, they knew their jobs, but he was forcing them to act as engineers and that was beyond them. Mila said they could not afford to hire another engineer or two just yet. She said they had to clear their debt and improve their profit margin first. So not enough engineers, not enough heavy equipment. He was running twelve hours a day, six days a week and he could hardly keep up. Disappearing to get drunk on too many afternoons lately was certainly not helping matters.

Fass grabbed Lucchese's outstretched hand and hauled himself out of the muddy trench. He pulled out a pack of cigarettes, offered one to the foreman, who only looked at him, shook his head, and walked off to get the backhoe. Bad. Walter lit a cigarette and sucked hard on it, looking around the site. Lucchese kept it perfectly organized, he thought, observing the neat bundles of reinforcing rods, the regular piles of cinder blocks, the tidy array of steel I-beams, the stacks of corrugated roofing panels covered with heavy tarps. This was a simple project, a small single-story factory on a level site for a company based in Brescia that made electric motors for pumps. Even this spring they had hit was something easily solved. No call for him to blast Lucchese like that. He would have to apologize.

Fass watched the backhoe strain through the first scoop of heavy wet earth, then turned and looked across the valley toward the city. To his right, higher up, he could see where Wolfsgruben lay, though it and Franz's farm were hidden by the pine forest on the lower slopes of the Rittner Horn. At least he could face Franz, he thought with some relief. For, what, three years now since they had closed the deal with Petrocelli, Franz had been getting his money back on time, with interest. In fact, more than half had already been repaid, and the contracts they had now, plus the rents, were enough so that they could wipe out that entire debt early, within nine months or so. They probably could pay it off sooner, if Mila didn't insist on keeping a certain amount of capital in the bank. She sent Franz his money each month, and Petrocelli his share, out of the cash flow. And still they had more than enough to pay their suppliers promptly, and for themselves to live on. Hell, they had never lived so well, they bought a new Lancia and some new furniture and they dined out in good restaurants whenever they wanted to. And still Mila managed to add to their capital account each month. How she did this was a mystery to Fass. But things could not have worked out better, financially anyway.

And Fass knew Uncle Franz was very proud of his rotten nephew's success.

So he had to put in twelve-hour days? Was that reason enough to feel so miserable, so harried? Was that any excuse for being short-tempered and nasty and acting like a Wehrmacht captain to the men, most of whom had worked side by side with him since the day he'd started as a site foreman for Petrocelli, how many years ago now? Jesus, he had lost track. So much was only a blur now, the days and nights all run together so tightly it was almost impossible for Fass to focus on any single one, on any particular event. He could not even remember when Anja and Mila made the decision that Mila would give up her apartment to reduce expenses and move into the third bedroom of the Fass house. No, Anja's house.

The engineer flicked the butt of his cigarette into the mud, lit another with a chrome Zippo bearing the Gruppo Fass logo. Mila had had dozens of these made up, to give to clients and suppliers. No doubt she had got them from her American connections around Trieste, had them engraved by her Italian connections in Venice. Small tokens like that made a good impression, Mila said. Good impressions were important in business, she said. As soon as the contract with Petrocelli had been signed, as soon as she handed over the legal bank transfer from Franz's account to Petrocelli's that covered the stated purchase price, and her black money that made up the real amount, she had gone into action. She'd diverted a few men from one of the factory sites to clean up and stucco the shabby concrete office near the freightyard. She'd had the interior gutted, divided that one big room into four: an office for Walter, an office for her, a design and drafting room, and a lobby. All the battered wooden desks, creaky swivel chairs, the cardboard file boxes, the ancient typewriters—all the detritus of Petrocelli was tossed out. She bought the most modern desks and steel file cabinets she could find, installed the very latest lighting system, a couple of the best Olivetti typewriters, new telephones. She had the offices carpeted, a new stone floor laid in the lobby. There she'd placed a couple of very modern sofas, an Oriental carpet, a small, sleek receptionist's desk of chromed steel and blond wood. She commissioned a local photographer to take photos of the factories and bridges Walter had worked on, had them enlarged to poster size and framed in thin steel, and hung them on the walls. And she'd replaced the dented, scarred entry door with a magnificent sixteenth-century oak one, almost black with age and beautifully carved, that she had salvaged from one of the bombed-out buildings in the city. On it she'd placed a thick brass plate engraved with the Gruppo Fass logo.

Fass opposed it all. It was money they did not have, being

wasted, he protested. But he was out so much on the various construction sites, and so seldom at the office, that when Mila was finally finished and threw a cocktail party for clients, potential
clients, their suppliers of concrete and steel and electric cable and
plumbing fixtures and everything else, Walter was startled at the
effect. Gruppo Fass looked like a prosperous, well-established, reliable and high-quality enterprise, not a business that was shaky,
debt-ridden and of uncertain future. He watched the clients and
suppliers at the party, watched Mila move among them with a
charming grace, observed her skillful *chiacchiere*, and realized
that they, too, were impressed.

"The image, Walter. The right image we got now," Mila said
on their way home from the party. "With Herr Doktor Fass, engineer, director of Gruppo Fass, they will want to do business."

And business came. Mila not only searched out and won new
clients, she also proved herself a master at getting the lowest possible prices from Gruppo Fass's suppliers. She kept some of Petrocelli's old ones, but also struck deals with newer outfits, ones
willing to cut their margins a bit on orders of concrete and wiring
and roofing in hopes of establishing a long-term relationship with
Gruppo Fass.

"So easy, Walter," Mila explained. "They are seeing us as the
company of the future, the quality company. Not like those old-
fashioned cheats Petrocelli competed with. From them, we take
their lunch and their dinner, too."

God, had it really been three years? Fass tried to remember. He
scarely noticed the throaty grumbling of the backhoe straining behind him. Probably three years. It was only a week or so after Sophie's first birthday when Mila and Anja ambushed him in the
kitchen, cut off any line of advance or route of retreat, forced his
surrender. He slept not at all that night. His brain felt loose in his

skull, his mind dull with shock. Mila and Anja together in such a mad scheme. Anja knowing about his disaster with Mila, Anja forcing him to ask Franz for money. And dear Anja putting such distance between them, moving forever out of reach.

Mila's move into his household almost ruined him. The sight of that smirking Chetnik and Anja, sweet-faced and lovely Anja, every morning over coffee. The easy way she and Mila chatted while he sat there unable to meet their eyes, ashamed, humiliated. He got what he deserved, he supposed. They got what they wanted. He was a man to neither; he was only part of a deal between them, a pawn in their game. And, by God, he was still nothing more than their creature. They did with him exactly as they pleased.

In some twisted way, he must have welcomed it, Fass admitted to himself. He could have refused. But he saw in Anja's determination that the price of refusal would be Sophie. Her loss was the one punishment he was not willing to bear.

A peaceful household then, for them. Theirs, not his, and ever more prosperous. Despite the fact that Anja hated Mila to the heart. Fass was certain of this. Where in the world, he wondered, did that pale little Pole get her strength? And why had she used it in this way?

The engineer noticed that the backhoe had shut down. He saw men with shovels in the trench, other men bringing over lengths of pipe, Lucchese calling out directions. "We've got the damned thing, Signor Ingegnere," the foreman said. "We'll get the pipe in before the end of the day. I think maybe two or three more days though before we see about the foundation, whether we'll need the piers. It's got to dry out."

"Good," Walter said, beckoning the foreman away from the trench to where he was standing, out of earshot of the diggers.

"*Senti*, Gianni. I am sorry I spoke to you in the way I did before. I was wrong. So please, no more of this 'Signor Ingegnere.' I am 'Walter' to you. Remember, my friend?"

"I remember," Lucchese said. He grinned. "But listen, my friend, you are trying too much. It's no good for you, no good for the work. We need the engineer here more often than you can come. There are things I cannot do alone. This you know."

"*Certo*, you are correct, Gianni," Walter said. "I'm going to do something about it. Soon. Meanwhile, do as you've always done. Always you've done it well. Since that first bridge with Petrocelli, remember?"

"I remember some new son of a bitch claiming to be an engineer bending Petrocelli's ear, and the next thing we know we are tearing down the piers we've already built." Lucchese laughed.

Walter gripped the foreman's shoulder, smiled at him, and then turned to walk to his car. Inside, before he turned on the ignition, he drained the hip flask of Scotch—they could afford imported whiskey now—that he filled every morning from the bottles he kept behind some books on the shelves in his room. Only then did he begin to drive home. He was unaware that tears were streaming down his haggard cheeks.

IV

Anja, chopping vegetables in the kitchen, saw Sophie look up quickly from the black slate she'd been chalking as soon as a key clicked in front-door lock. "Pappa," the child piped, scrambling to her feet and dashing on unsteady little legs out of the kitchen and into the corridor. "Pappa! Pappa!"

"*Hallo, Spätzchen,*" Anja heard Fass say. Now he was picking her up and swinging her in a circle. Now she would squeal. And Sophie squealed.

"Early today, Herr Ingenieur." Anja smiled at Fass as he came into the kitchen, the little girl's arms circling his neck, her small voice chattering in his ear. "Damn, Walter, look at the mud you've tracked in! And look at your pants!"

"A little problem out at that electric-motor factory site. I lost my temper," Fass said.

"So the men threw you in a ditch?"

"They wanted to, after the way I yelled at them. But I jumped in myself, actually, to have a look. They'd hit a spring digging the foundation trench. We can fix it, but it's a pain in the ass."

"Don't move," Anja said, coming over and taking Sophie in her arms. She protested. "Pappa! Pappa!"

"Now take off your shoes and pants right here. Then carry them back to the garden shed. I'll clean them up later. You can mop up the corridor yourself. Or you can make dinner while I do it."

"I'll mop," Fass said, bending to pry off his shoes. "I'd forgotten completely about the mud. I think I'm overtired these days. Sorry."

"All these projects at once. Maybe it's as you say. We need to hire another engineer. Let's talk it over with Mila. But not tonight. She dropped by to say she's taking some shark out to dinner. He's apparently bought a lot down near Leifers, makes insulated wire or something, needs a building. She said she'd likely be late."

"Oh, Jesus, another one," Fass said, taking off his mud-caked trousers. At home, especially around Sophie, he did his best to mask the darkness he felt. But his best, more and more, wasn't so good. "Never thought there would be a time when I'd feel dismayed by the possibility of a new contract. God, I used to lose sleep thinking we wouldn't get any at all. I must be more exhausted than I realize. Do you know how lucky we've been, Anja?"

"Yes. But don't even think 'luckier than we deserve to be.' I do that enough for all three of us. It was hard work. You and Mila. It has all been earned. All of it."

"And we've paid, too, haven't we, Anja? We've lost too much. Lost what was best."

"You know I won't talk of that with you, Fass," she said brusquely.

Maybe it was only the Scotch doing a job on his brain, but Fass felt sure at certain moments that Anja endured some of the same grief he lived with, some of the same desolation.

"I cannot keep from thinking how it might have, could have all gone another way. A better way," he said.

"Stop whining. You could think that about our entire lives,

from the war on. What's the point in questioning any of it? You'd never get an answer. What happened, happened."

"*Klar*. Still, it is the universal question, isn't it? Men mortally wounded always wondered, why me? Men who escaped without a scratch always wondered, why me? Men who made it home and found their families alive and well wondered, why me? The same as men who didn't make it home, who lost everyone dear. Always, why? Why?"

"Stop it, Fass," Anja snapped. "I won't listen to this crap. It's no good. What happens is never personal. You imagine there is a God who's aware of each and every one of us and decides, hmmm, let's do this and this to Anja, and that to Walter, and this to Dizzi and that to Sisi and so on and so on until He's done every person in the world? Crazy idea. But unless you do believe that, 'why' means nothing. There is no why."

"I'll go put on some trousers."

"But Walter . . . why?" Anja laughed at him. "Do that, then come have a glass of wine and play with Sophie. She's been asking about you all day."

Christ, it was irritating when he started moaning like that, Anja thought as Fass left the room, Sophie trailing him. She stifled a groan. It was irritating only because he was right. They had lost the best, the small portion of goodness they'd possessed. But there had been no choice. He'd left her with no choice, no way back, no way at all except this damn way.

And no point to going over and over what might have been, either. She forced her mind onto another track. Better to be a happy idiot, without a thought in your head, no sense of past or future but only of now: what's for dinner, how good the wine tastes.

Or to be a child, Anja thought. How lovely the little girl was, how happy. Sophie did not remember yesterday and hadn't any idea of tomorrow. She only knew it felt nice to see her pappa, that she'd sit in his lap while she ate and that Mamma would give her a nice glass of milk, and Pappa would feed her some pasta, and then maybe Mamma would hold her and tickle her, or splash with her in the bath. And her *Kuschelbär* would snuggle her when she was tucked in bed. Her dreams would be happy ones.

And when she woke in the morning, it would be a fresh and clean and brand-new day. No sadness weighing on her mind, no apprehension, no regret, no uncertainty.

That was the best part of being a mother, Anja decided. You could be a child again with your child, if you tried. You could see each day through her eyes, feel each day as she felt it. At least a little. It was a lovely escape. Too bad it was so fleeting. Too bad you must always return, always begin again the labor of pretending contentment, of suppressing memories, denying dreams. If you could. If you could not, there was always drink. That helped sometimes.

Fass needed help every day. Fass drank far too much. It seemed the better things went, the more he needed to anesthetize himself. You could not risk that, you could not afford it when you were struggling, when you were trying to survive. You needed to be clear-minded, focused. Probably the necessary concentration kept most bad thoughts at bay. But when life became easier, you needed the alcohol to do that job.

Or some did, anyway. Mila never seemed to need to get drunk. She'd kept her mind under military discipline somehow. Anja never saw her broody, or melancholy, or mournful. Oh, yes, Mila sometimes displayed her scars, let some anguish flicker across her face. But that was something she did deliberately, Anja was sure, for show. That coldhearted bitch never really ever felt anything that would make her weep.

What a blessing, never to feel, Anja thought. No, a curse. Ah, shit, it was neither. Something inside Mila was just dead, had been for years and years. And, please God, may the cost of being oblivious to pain include being dead to any joy, any pleasure.

But Anja, even hurting the way she hurt, could feel joy. With Sophie almost always, except when she had troubled thoughts about the child's future, or about more present threats that might mean no future at all: whooping cough, scarlet fever, typhoid, polio, any sort of accident. Sometimes she felt joy with Franz, up at the farm. But only an empty shell of it with Fass and Mila, when the three of them were together and talking casually, laughing at something amusing, playacting a friendship. Drink was the essential prop, then. And ruthless, deliberate forgetfulness.

Finish chopping the carrots, Anja ordered herself. Steam the fucking green beans. Coat the cutlets with bread crumbs. And stop this nonsense! She had a child and a house and a comfortable life. She did not need to fear a knock on the door in the night, she did not need to feel any anxiety when she saw men in uniforms. She did not need to worry if there would be money to buy tomorrow's food or a warm winter coat for Sophie. And she especially did not need to brood on things she could not know.

Fass walked back into the kitchen then, holding Sophie upside down. Her skirt, fallen down around her face, muffled her screeches of delight. "Careful, Walter," Anja said. "God, you scare me when you do that. What if you should drop her?"

"She loves it," Fass said. "No chance I'll ever drop her."

The engineer righted the child and set her to scribbling on her slate. Then he came over to the stove and put the breaded cutlets into the heavy cast-iron frying pan, already oiled and hot. There was a snapping and a sizzling. Anja could smell the Scotch on him. "Spuds and onions, in motor oil, that's what we used to make at the front. In a pan just like this," he said. He poured himself a glass of white wine and drank it down all at once, then refilled his glass.

"No war stories," Anja said, sweeping the carrots off the cutting board into a bowl already full of garden greens.

"Spuds," Sophie said. "Spuds, Pappa."

Fass turned the cutlets. A few drops of the hot oil spurted out of the pan and burnt his hand. "Damn!"

"Damn, Pappa," Sophie said. The engineer laughed.

"Watch what you say, Walter," Anja said, spirits rising for just an instant, only to come crashing down as the illusion of a real family life vanished as quickly as it had come. She dribbled some olive oil and vinegar over the salad. "She's like a parrot these days."

"Now, Sophie, don't say that word," Fass said in his serious Father voice.

"Damn!" the little girl shouted. "Damn!"

※ ※ ※

Mila, satisfied, looked down at the young man she was straddling. She saw his short, curly hair black against the pillow, his face in profile with the lips slightly parted, his lean chest still heaving. She moved her hips in a very slow circle, and saw his lips tremble.

A fine boy. He knew nothing, did only what she instructed him to do. And that he did with eagerness, with concentration and intensity. A very useful boy.

She had found him in the *municipio* one morning a month or so ago. She had gone there to deal with a sticky building permit, the necessary lubricant—some reasonable thousands of lire—neatly folded in a small, plain envelope that she discreetly slid across the necessary official's desk just as he came to the problematic part of the document. The official slid the envelope off the edge of the desk and into his pocket without ever looking up from the permit. Very smooth, Mila thought. Lots of practice. The necessary signature and stamp were quickly applied to the document.

"*Grazie mille, Cavaliere*," she said, tossing her hair just enough to add a hint of suggestion to her smile.

"*Grazie a Lei, Signora*," the official replied, unable to keep his eyes from wandering over her as he smiled back.

Business done, she watched the boy intently studying a sheaf of papers at his desk in the official's outer office. She spoke to him. He was new, he said, a graduate of Bocconi University in Milan, intent on a career in the civil service.

From there to here had been easy. It was always so easy. The boy hadn't a thing in his head, he bored her immensely whenever he talked. But he was a useful boy. Good maybe for another month or two, maybe even three or four, if he did not lose his head. That ruined it, when they lost their heads. And sooner or later the useful boys always did. But it was of no importance. The world was very full of boys, there was no shortage, not even in a poky town like this one.

But not so poky anymore, she considered, at least in the way that counted. She'd had some fear that once the bombing damage had been taken care of, once the wrecked bridges and buildings had been repaired or rebuilt, the construction business would face very lean times. But the Italian government had decided to strengthen its hold on the Südtirol. There'd been agitation in Austria about getting the province back, great demonstrations in Innsbruck, diplomatic moves from Vienna. Italy's position, having been a wartime partner of the Third Reich, was not the strongest. So the Italians offered various incentives for businesses to establish new facilities around Bolzano, encouraged Italians from the poorer regions of the south to migrate north with the promise of jobs.

Just as the Duce had once done after the first war. Now again it happened.

Gruppo Fass was in exactly the right place at the right moment. Gruppo Fass was making more than she had calculated it ever might when she'd maneuvered the buyout of Petrocelli. Much more. Although the official books showed the firm was doing just a bit better than breaking even, she knew otherwise. And so did Petrocelli, who actually had left his wife and taken his little piece from Eppan to bask in the sun on Capri. But Fass and his little Pole? They knew only what she permitted them to know. It was more than enough, for them.

Mila looked at her wristwatch and slid off the boy, who moaned and begged her to stay. Stay in his wretched little room and listen to his boring talk? Mila laughed. Too bad, he was beginning to lose his head a little already. Soon he'd become very brave and demand that she stay. *Finito*, then.

"No, no, Paolo," she said gently to the boy as she dressed. "It is late. You are not happy with me tonight?"

"Oh, Mila, yes. It was beautiful," the boy said.

"Soon, *piccolino*. I come to you another night very soon," she said, leaving him still in the bed, propped up on his elbows watching her as she left his room.

The house at the edge of the *centro* was dark when she arrived, though it was only just past ten. She unlocked the front door, entered, locked it behind her and slipped off her shoes. Then she went down the corridor to her room, quiet as a cat. She stripped, hung her skirt and sweater in the armoire, tossed her brassiere and panties into a wicker hamper. Two or three times a week Anja collected all their things from the hampers in each room and did the laundry. It was as good as living in a hotel. Better, because it was more private. She put on a black silk slip and sat on the edge of her bed, smoking. She felt content as she gazed at the glowing red coal between puffs.

Mila stubbed out her cigarette, went over to her bureau. She reached behind the dark oak piece and retrieved a small key from the little niche she'd carved to hold it. She lifted a small steel box from the bottom drawer, unlocked it, and took out an agenda, an absurdly expensive thing of crocodile skin she'd purchased in Venice a few years before. She stroked the surprisingly smooth contours of the leather, then sat in a plush upholstered chair and opened it.

Inside the agenda, in Serb and coded in a way she based on Chetnik wartime code, was the record of Mila's fortune. She liked to start at the beginning, at the inception of Gruppo Fass, and go through the pages one by one, each page the accounts of a quarter-year, each fifth page the total of that year. The numbers were so small at first, though they had seemed quite something at the time. But how they grew larger, how many zeros attached themselves!

Mila saw the quarter when the number had become great enough to warrant a trip to Zurich, a numbered account. She saw when the numbers had seemed sufficient to risk some investments on the bourse in Milan, and when it seemed wise to change some dollars into Swiss francs. And where some selling on the bourse doubled part of her original investments, how those profits were hidden and sent to the numbered account.

God, she'd been good, Mila thought. If Gruppo Fass went bankrupt next year, she would still have enough to live on for the rest of her life. Where would she go? Rome, perhaps. Yes, Rome would be nice. Life could be very sweet in Rome. A little travel from time to time. Oh, say, Paris, even New York. Morocco for something exotic. Yes!

But not yet.

Mila returned the agenda to its secret place, then slid between the sheets, enjoying the softness of the down pillow beneath her head, stretching her long, lean legs, running her fingers through her thick hair. For a moment she called up the feeling she'd had with her little bureaucrat. Ah, it could be sweet, she thought. But it was only a need like any other. When she was hungry, she ate and that was sweet, too. Too many years of hunger. Never again would she go unsatisfied, in any way. No one, no one would ever keep her from whatever she wanted.

But Anja she could not understand. Had she no needs? All these years, living like a nun. Mila would go mad. Yet Anja was not mad. Very far from it. She seemed to desire almost nothing, and men not at all. Maybe one day she would take a lover. Perhaps not. Perhaps something had happened to her in Krakow, something very bad for a young girl. Perhaps she could not stand to be touched by a man. This was not so uncommon. This she had seen among girls in Yugoslavia who had had something very bad done to them—by Germans, by Partisans, by Ustaše swine, whoever. Perhaps all Anja needed was her child and her home, some bit of money.

How easy life would be, how simple and uncomplicated, Mila thought, to be content with so little. But perhaps very boring, *nicht wahr?*

V

S ophie Fass, age seven, loves navy blue. She loves the navy blue frocks and skirts and jumpers and pinafores Aunt Mila buys for her. She loves to wear these things with white ankle socks and black patent leather shoes. She is careful not to muss her pretty clothes and her shiny shoes when she plays with her classmates during recess. She loves to swing on the swings, adores the soaring feeling and the way her pale, heavy hair flies about her face. But nothing will persuade her to go into the sandbox.

Sophie loves it, too, when Aunt Mila takes her to Carlo's. Her hair is like cornsilk, just the same as Signora Anja's, thick and beautiful, he always says. Sophie loves that he cuts it exactly as he cuts Mamma's. When she comes home, she asks Mamma to stand in front of the mirror with her. Mamma always smiles when Sophie says, "We're twins!" Sophie knows all about twins. Sandra and Giordana Vicini are in her class. They have to wear name tags, because the teacher cannot tell who is Sandra and who is Giordana.

Sophie also loves to go up the mountain to visit Grandfather Franz. Sometimes she rides the bus with her mamma, and sometimes Pappa drives them there in his big black car, which has a smell she likes. Grandfather Franz helps her practice somersaults in the long grass of the orchard, or holds her up so she can pluck apples from the trees. She's a little afraid of the cows. She likes to watch them munching grass, she likes the sound of the big bells around their necks, but she backs away whenever they swing their huge, heavy heads around and stare at her. She likes to trace the carved letters of her name in the trunk of the big tree at the top of the pasture. Aunt Liese always gives her an extra cookie when Mamma isn't looking, when Mamma is outside walking arm in arm with Grandfather Franz, and Pappa is over at the wine vat with Uncle Sepp, drinking. Pappa gave her a sip once, but it was so sour. She prefers the milk Auntie Liese gives her with the cookies.

Sophie speaks German at home with Mamma and Pappa and Aunt Mila. Aunt Mila gets it all mixed up sometimes, it's so funny Sophie has to laugh. She speaks Italian at school with her teachers and her friends. Her mamma sometimes sings pretty songs to her while she is getting ready for bed in a language that sounds very strange. Her mamma says it is Polish. Sophie thinks she would like to learn this Polish someday, so that she could understand what the songs are saying to her.

Sophie almost never cries, except when she stumbles and skins her knees on the sidewalk, or when her pappa yells at her. She feels happy almost every day, even when it rains.

But Sophie Fass wonders sometimes why it is always so quiet in her house. People are chattering all the time in the houses of her friends, when she goes to play with them. She wonders why her pappa always seems to come home later than the fathers of her friends, why her pappa and mamma and Aunt Mila hardly ever say anything at dinner, why they all go to their rooms a long time before bedtime, why her pappa always has a sour smell when he kisses her goodnight. She wonders why they all laugh at certain things she says, and smile at her whenever they look at her, but seldom laugh or smile at each other. She wonders if they are cross with each other. She worries sometimes that it might be her fault.

Sophie Fass is very glad that she sleeps in a small bed next to the big bed where her mamma sleeps. She imagines she would be very frightened and lonely in a room all by herself. Every night after she has been tucked in and kissed, Sophie tries to stay awake as long as she can, watching her mamma read. So many books. Sophie has her own, too.

"Twins!" she thinks, watching her mamma.

⬚ ⬚ ⬚

When the engineer Dr. Walter Fass, director of Gruppo Fass, drives his new black Citroën around the valley from one construction site to the next, and sees the factories and apartment blocks and bridges he has built, he often imagines blowing them up.

He slows the car a little at each one, looks at each with an eye calculating exactly where he would place the charges, how many kilos of explosives would be required at each point. Then he remembers other explosions, explosions he knows he made somewhere a long time ago, so many that in his mind they all seem to have blended into one roar and blast. His memory is not what it used to be. He cannot recall anymore exactly how it felt before Mila came, when he shared a bed with Anja instead of sleeping alone, except that Anja was small and warm and always smelled so fresh, like wildflowers.

Other things have vanished, too. He cannot remember the sound of his friend Dizzi's voice, though once in a while something or other Dizzi said to him will enter his mind. He cannot call up the faces of his own father or mother, or his little sister and her baby, named after him. His years studying in Berlin are a complete blank. His time in the Wehrmacht is only a blur, his early years back in Bolzano cloudy, dim. He possesses only a faint impression of the day Sophie was born.

The engineer Walter Fass lives in a more or less constant state of pain. Like the victim of a slow-growing but surely fatal cancer, he imagines. Though his is of the soul, not the body. The daily sight of Anja, his pretty little Pole, wracks him with the agony of loss, of a possibility for happiness crushed by circumstance and his own stupidity. The daily sight of Mila, his predatory Chetnik, is a sort of silver surgeon's probe brushing the raw nerves of a wound that will not heal. Only his Sophie, with her innocent cries of joy at the sight of him and her delight when he lifts her and swings her, relieves him.

There is the alcohol for the rest, though now it does little more than erode what remains of his memory. But in his room at night, carelessly read newspapers and magazines scattered on the floor around his chair, a glass and a bottle of Scotch on the table beside it, Fass yet remembers one explosion in such clear and perfect detail that it feels as if he had made it only the day before yesterday. Totally absorbed, he does not notice the ash from the cigarette he's smoking falling on the fine wool of his suit pants.

The name of the village is Poljić, only a row of shabby, badly built houses and pathetic little shops on either side of a mud track on a small plateau in the mountains. Goats and sheep, a few dairy cows, some vegetable plots round about. A poor place, a place you'd be happier leaving than arriving in. We are only passing through, hurrying north that late winter of '45. We have no business here, no intention of stopping.

We're fifty meters past, our backs to Poljić, moving away.

The man beside me drops, blood welling from his eye socket, before I hear the shot. Then there's a lot of firing from the village, bullets cracking past, other men falling. One of our MG42s opens up, blasting through the windows of the houses, firing so rapidly it sounds like a huge zipper pulled closed fast. Then the deeper boom of eight-millimeter Mauser rifles, the higher crack of nine-millimeter MP40s. Stick grenades arc through the air, end over end, to explode in the village. Flames flare out of one or two of the houses after the grenades and the tracer rounds tear into them. Three Partisans stumble out, are stitched by a burst from an MG42, go sprawling in the track, their faces buried in mud and manure. At the far end of the village a couple of dozen other Partisans race off toward the forest. Several fall.

They are gone. It is silent again, except for the pop and roar of the burning houses. I see Zofia and her Chetniks form into squads and rush the village, hugging the walls of the houses, kicking down doors, lunging in with rifles and submachine guns ready. A shot or two in some of the houses, some screams. Then I see old women and old men and children and young mothers stumble out with their hands clasped over their heads, prodded into the middle of the track by the rifle butts and bayonets of the Chetniks. Squads of my unit are moving carefully behind the houses, searching sheds and small barns, scanning the forest edge. An MG42 team is prone near me, ready for covering fire.

Soon the track is teeming with villagers, ringed by Chetniks. Zofia goes from one to another, barking questions, backhanding one old man who can barely stand and splitting his lip, so that blood begins to drip from his chin. She tears a child of two or three from the arms of a girl and throws it down in the mud, where it wails. Zofia kicks the girl in the face when she bends to pick up the child, breaking her nose.

My machine-gunner looks at me hard. He spits.

These people have nothing. Their clothes are no better than rags. Their faces are sallow and pinched. Some of the little children have swollen bellies, legs and arms thin as sticks. They are starving. Zofia shouts something and the Chetniks begin to herd the villagers along the track and out of the village, toward the forest where the Partisans had fled. She strides back to me.

"Partisan rules," she says, cold-eyed. "There's a mine shaft three hundred meters past this pesthole. We'll need some explosives." Then she turns and follows her unit.

I stand there. The machine-gun team rises, shouldering their weapon and the belts of ammunition. I do not look at them. I do not look at the other three men who I order back to the Kübelwagen to fetch explosives and the detonator. I don't look back as they follow me following Zofia. We leave the village, the rest of my men converging behind me. I do not look back.

The mine shaft must be blocked a short distance in. The Chetniks have pushed and prodded and packed the two hundred or so villagers as tightly as they can, but still there are people close outside the entrance of the shaft. I stop a hundred meters from the mine. I order the three men to leave the exploder box with me and go place the charges around the entrance to the mine.

"Captain?" I hear one of them say.

"Do it," I shout. "Now!"

When they have placed the explosives and run the wires back to me, I unscrew the nuts on the two poles of the exploder. I cut a few centimeters of insulation off each wire and wrap the bright copper filaments on the poles, then screw down the nuts. The Chetniks are backing away from the mine. One village woman runs. Zofia shoots her. There is a great wailing from the mine. The Chetniks group up just in front and on either side of me. My men are behind me. The wailing from the mine is spine-chilling. A few of my men are cursing. I pull up the plunger to the ready position. There is more cursing behind me. Zofia comes close to me.

"Partisan rules," she hisses.

I am on my knees, my hand on the plunger. The wailing sweeps down over us. I stand up. I say "No."

Zofia barks something in Serb and suddenly every man and woman in her unit is pointing a rifle or submachine gun at me and my men. There are a hundred Chetniks. I have twenty-five men. I had thirty. Five are lying dead in the mud past the far end of the village, shot by the Partisans.

"Partisan rules, by God," Zofia hisses. "Blow 'em to hell, Kraut."

I stand there. I hear the clicks and rattles of equipment as the Chetniks fan out to get a clear field of fire on me and my men. I look at the mine shaft. The god-awful wailing rises. But none of the villagers moves. Not one bolts. They stand, packed body to body, transfixed.

I kneel down. I place my left hand on the plunger. I grip it tightly.

"Do it now, goddammit," Zofia growls. "Do it."

"Go to hell. Shoot me, Chetnik bitch," I hear. It is my voice.

Then Zofia slams her heavy, hobnailed boot down on my hand. I feel small bones crack under the blow even as the plunger descends. Instantly there is a roar and blast wave that makes the Chetniks hunch and crouch. I am knocked to the ground. In the great cloud of smoke rising from the mine shaft I see among the rocks and debris a single naked leg tumbling over and over, soaring above the smoke, slowing, then falling back into the billows.

Only the day before yesterday, the engineer Fass thinks, alone in his room in the pretty nineteenth-century house at the edge of Bolzano's old center. Always only the day before yesterday.

▧　▧　▧

Anja feels the enormous blue eyes of Sophie Fass on her. She looks up from her book and smiles. Sophie, tucked in up to her chin in her small bed, her head on the pillow, has a clear line of sight to her mother. She is holding a book of her own.

"You must sleep now, little sparrow," Anja says. Sophie dutifully closes her book, but continues to watch her mother.

"Close your eyes and sleep," Anja says.

"But I'm an owl," Sophie says. "I stay awake all night, watching."

"You are my little sparrow. Sparrows must sleep."

Sophie smiles, then turns on her side, clutching her *Kuschelbär*. Anja returns to her book. She reads a few dozen lines, pauses to let the verses cycle through her mind. She looks at Sophie; the child is still. She reads the next dozen lines. Then she looks at the empty half of the bed she once shared with Fass. Even now, Anja only sleeps on her half. Never sprawls, never moves across the invisible barrier into his space.

The rhythm of each verse she reads is an iteration of the one before.

Circles within circles within circles. Everything comes around again. There is nothing you can do about it. Everything comes around.

Must it? Is Sophie destined to be an iteration of me? What does the child think of as she drifts into sleep each night? In what language does she think? In what language does she dream?

For a long time I dreamt in German, but now always in Polish. Another circle. A large one. Now I think of Krakow without shuddering, now I have dreams of Krakow that are only dreams, not nightmares. Some of them are so pleasant I think I would like to see Krakow again. But I know I never will. There cannot be a circle big enough to take me back there.

In Krakow now, with autumn arrived, the lindens in the park will be changing from green to yellow, a delicate faded yellow, like the stucco on some of the old Austrian buildings. On crisp mornings a mass of fog will rise from the Vistula. But not very far! From the Wawel the river will seem to be a river of fog for a while, until the sun drives the mists away and you can see the gray waters again. The fallen leaves will stay damp with dew for a longer time, and when you walk on them you will smell a sweetish aroma, a scent of decay that nevertheless is pleasant, not repulsive at all.

But you smell that scent here in Bolzano, see the same early fogs on the river on chill mornings. It will be chillier in Krakow, but there are no mountain peaks already dusted with snow. There are no vast tracts around the city crammed with trees bearing bright red apples, or vines thick with bunches of grapes. They are harvesting beets and potatoes around Krakow.

Are there still books piled everywhere in my parents' apartment? Are any of my things still in my room, or have they stripped it bare, perhaps turned it into a small library? Do they sip coffee in the kitchen each morning, talking about everything under the sun? Do they ever speak of me at all? Do they remember their Anja, the first Wieniewski to be a scholar? To make the barest start at being a scholar, anyway. Three months. That was all the chance I got. Do they ever think of what might have been, of what I might have become?

Is there a photo of me displayed anywhere?

Sophie is soundly sleeping already. I know this just by the easy regularity of her breathing. Sophie is mine to know. Every word, every laugh, every passing expression on her face, every look in her changeable eyes, I understand.

No. Sophie is mine and she is not. I do not even know what language my daughter thinks and dreams in. So, later ... later she may change, become someone else entirely, someone unknowable even to her mother. I hope not. I pray Sophie will never have cause to become what I once was. What I am.

Anja absorbs the verse on the page before her:

Whoever has no house now, will never have one.
Whoever is alone will stay alone,
will sit, read, write long letters through the evening,
and wander on the boulevards, up and down,
restlessly, while the dry leaves are blowing.

Anja closes the book firmly on those desolate words. She imagines Fass, chin sunk to chest, brooding in his chair in the next room. Once, he would have been beside her, stroking her hair. Sometimes, even now, she can imagine tapping on his door and whispering, "Hey you. Fass?" But he would not hear in his stupor. He would not come. She imagines Mila making her solitary way late through a city silent but for the rustle of fallen leaves in her path. She turns off the lamp. She lies completely still, darkness her only companion.

She has her house. But whoever is alone will stay alone. And there is not a soul left in all the wide world, Anja knows as her heart hollows, to whom she could write a single line.

AUTHOR'S NOTE

The conditions prevailing during and after World War II in the areas of Europe where this novel is set are in general authentic and accurately described. Every year for more than a decade I spent some weeks or months in these regions, and talked extensively with many Austrian, Italian and Yugoslav men and women who lived there through the war years. Much of the detail comes from their remembrances.

For fictional purposes, however, some liberties have been taken with certain military and political facts.

Thomas Moran is the author of *The Man in the Box*, winner of the Book-of-the-Month Club's Stephen Crane Award for First Fiction; *The World I Made for Her*; *Water, Carry Me*, which earned an International IMPAC Dublin Award nomination and a Walter E. Dakin Fellowship; and *What Harry Saw*. His novels have been translated into seven languages.